# BY HARRY TURTLEDOVE

*The Guns of the South*

**THE WORLDWAR SAGA**
*Worldwar: In the Balance*
*Worldwar: Tilting the Balance*
*Worldwar: Upsetting the Balance*
*Worldwar: Striking the Balance*

*Homeward Bound*

**THE VIDESSOS CYCLE**
**VOLUME ONE:**
*The Misplaced Legion*
*An Emperor for the Legion*

**VOLUME TWO:**
*The Legion of Videssos*
*Swords of the Legion*

**THE TALE OF KRISPOS**
*Krispos Rising*
*Krispos of Videssos*
*Krispos the Emperor*

**THE TIME OF TROUBLES SERIES**
*The Stolen Throne*
*Hammer and Anvil*
*The Thousand Cities*
*Videssos Besieged*
*A World of Difference*
*Departures*
*How Few Remain*

**THE GREAT WAR**
*The Great War: American Front*
*The Great War: Walk in Hell*
*The Great War: Breakthroughs*

**AMERICAN EMPIRE**
*American Empire: Blood & Iron*
*American Empire: The Center Cannot Hold*
*American Empire: The Victorious Opposition*

**SETTLING ACCOUNTS**
*Settling Accounts: Return Engagement*
*Settling Accounts: Drive to the East*
*Settling Accounts: The Grapple*
*Settling Accounts: In at the Death*

*Every Inch a King*

*The Man with the Iron Heart*

**THE WAR THAT CAME EARLY**
*The War That Came Early: Hitler's War*
*The War That Came Early: West and East*
*The War That Came Early: The Big Switch*
*The War That Came Early: Coup d'Etat*
*The War That Came Early: Two Fronts*

# Two Fronts

THE WAR THAT CAME EARLY

# Two Fronts

## HARRY TURTLEDOVE

BALLANTINE BOOKS | NEW YORK

Published in the United States by Del Rey, an imprint of The Random House Publishing Group, a division of Random House, Inc., New York.

DEL REY is a registered trademark and the Del Rey colophon is a trademark of Random House, Inc.

Library of Congress Cataloging-in-Publication Data

Turtledove, Harry.
   Two fronts : the war that came early / Harry Turtledove.
      pages   cm
   ISBN 978-0-345-52468-3 (hardcover : alk. paper)—ISBN 978-0-345-52470-6 (ebook)
1. World War, 1939–1945—Fiction.   2. Alternative histories (Fiction)   I. Title.
   PS3570.U76T96 2013
   813'.54—dc23

                              2013010229

Printed in the United States of America on acid-free paper

www.delreybooks.com

10 9 8 7 6 5 4 3 2 1

First Edition

*Book Design by Mia Risberg*

# Two Fronts

# Chapter 1

Marine Sergeant Pete McGill lay in the *Ranger*'s sick bay. He had a cut from bomb shrapnel along one rib and another in the side of his neck. A couple of inches there and he would have been nothing but a snack for the shark that had circled him after he got blown off the *Boise*'s deck and into the tropical Pacific.

He knew he was lucky to be alive. A lot of good men hadn't made it off the light cruiser before she sank. The bomb from a Jap Val that flung him overboard broke her back, and she went down fast.

That blast also flung him clear of the fuel oil from her shattered bunkers. You swallowed some of that crap, you were history even if they did fish you out of the drink. And, even though his cuts must have been bleeding like billy-be-damned, the dorsal went away instead of slicing in for the kill. Maybe he was an off brand.

He'd managed to stay afloat, then, till the *Ranger* came over and started picking up survivors. That must have been a couple of hours. By the time he got rescued, he'd kicked off all his clothes so he could tread water better. And every square inch of him that had been above the surface for even a little while was sunburned to a fare-thee-well. The sunburn would have troubled him worse than his little wounds if they hadn't had to put about a dozen stitches in the one on his ribcage. They'd used novocaine when they sewed him up, but it had long since worn off.

The Japs had dive-bombed the *Ranger*, too, but the carrier, unlike the poor damned *Boise*, must have carried a rabbit's foot in her back pocket: all the bombs the Vals dropped missed, though none missed by much. She had some sprung seams, and blast and fragments had swept men from her flight deck. But she could still make full speed, and she still answered her helm. What more did you want—egg in your beer?

From what the other wounded men in the sick bay said, right this minute the *Ranger* was making full speed back toward Hawaii. The little task force of which she'd been the centerpiece had aimed to make life miserable for the Japs on some of the Pacific islands they held. What you aimed for and what you got, though, unfortunately weren't always the same critter.

A pharmacist's mate came through. Some of the guys in there were a lot worse off than Pete. Two or three of them, he feared, would go into the ocean shrouded in canvas, with a chunk of iron at their feet to make sure they didn't come up again.

"How you doing, uh, McGrill?" the pharmacist's mate asked.

"Hurts," Pete said matter-of-factly. He knew more about pain than he'd ever wanted to learn. On that scale, this wasn't so much of a much. But it *did* hurt. Without rancor, he added, "And it's McGill."

"Sorry." The Navy file sounded more harassed than sorry, and who could blame him? He went on, "I'll slather some more zinc oxide goop on where you cooked. You want a couple of codeine pills?"

"I'll take 'em." Pete knew they'd help a little, and also knew they'd help only a little. As he had experience with pain, so he also had experience with pain medicine. He wasn't bad enough off to need morphine: nowhere near. They'd want to save what they had for the poor, sorry bastards who really did need it.

"Here you go, then. Can you sit up some?"

Pete could, though moving made him hurt worse. He swallowed the pills, gulping all the water in the glass the pharmacist's mate handed him. He felt as if the salt water of the Pacific had sucked the moisture right out of him.

Whatever was in the ointment besides zinc oxide, it smelled medicinal and vaguely noxious. It soothed the skin on his cheeks and neck and shoulders and the top of his back. "I wish you could rub it in my hair, too," Pete said. That was, of course, cut leatherneck short, so he had himself a sunburned scalp.

"I will if you want me to," the pharmacist's mate said.

"Nah. It'd be too messy," Pete decided after a moment's thought. He asked, "Can your scalp peel?"

"Fuckin' A it can," the Navy man said. "I've seen some bald guys who toasted their domes. It ain't pretty, man. Like dandruff, only more so."

"Hot damn," Pete said resignedly. "So I've got something to look forward to, huh?"

"'Fraid so, McGrill." No, the pharmacist's mate hadn't been listening. And how big a surprise was that? He had bigger things to worry about than Pete's name. Off he went, briskly, to the guy in the next bed, who'd lost a sizable chunk of meat from one buttock, and who'd sleep on his stomach—if he slept at all—for the foreseeable future.

They got Pete out of the sick-bay bed a day later. Since he'd come aboard the *Ranger* with not even the clothes on his back, they had to give him everything from skivvies on out. Nothing fit real well, and his shirt chafed his tender hide. But clothes make the man. Once he had on even these hand-me-downs, he felt like a Marine again.

*Ranger*'s Marine detachment figured he was a leatherneck, too. They'd lost a few men to the Japs' near misses, and had several others worse off than Pete. He got to be low man on the five-inch-gun totem pole again, for the same reason as before: he was a new guy, and had no established place of his own. He didn't fret over it the way a more reflective man might have. It was useful duty, and duty he knew he could do.

His gun chief was a tobacco-chewing Okie sergeant named Bob Cullum. He had a narrow, ferrety face, cold blue eyes that seemed to look every which way at once, and hands with slim, almost unnaturally long fingers: a surgeon's fingers, or a fiddler's. He guided the dual-purpose gun with a delicacy and precision Joe Orsatti would have envied. Unless some other ship had plucked Joe out of the Pacific, he was dead. Pete hoped for the best there, but expected the worst.

Cullum's long, slim fingers had another talent, too. He could make a deck of cards sit up and beg. Since Pete came into the *Ranger* naked as the day he was born, that didn't matter much to him. Cullum said, "Hey, if you want to play I can front you. If you end up losing it, pay me back when we get in to Pearl."

"Thanks, but I'll pass," Pete said. "Never been much of a gambler, and I don't want to do it on borrowed money." That wasn't strictly true. He didn't add that Cullum seemed a little too eager, though. Anybody who could set the cards jitterbugging like that could probably make them behave in all kinds of interesting—and profitable—ways.

He must have sounded sincere, because the other sergeant didn't get mad. "Well, maybe you ain't as dumb as you look, then," he said. His drawl and Pete's adenoidal Bronx accent were halfway toward being foreign languages to each other.

"Up yours, too, Mac," Pete said. He didn't sound—and wasn't—especially pissed off. But if Cullum wanted to make something of it, he was ready. Sometimes you had to go through crap like that when you found yourself in a new place. He figured Bob Cullum was faster than he was, but he had two inches and at least twenty pounds on the other leatherneck. Things evened out.

Cullum thought it over. Pete must have said it the right way, because he seemed willing to let it alone. "And the horse you rode in on," he replied, also mildly. He eyed Pete. "You look kinda like a raggedy-ass scarecrow, you know?"

"Only things that fit are my shoes," Pete agreed. He spread his hands. "Shit, what can you do, though?"

"Let me work on it," Cullum said. "I've been on the *Ranger* since she was commissioned, and if I ain't the best scrounger aboard I dunno who the hell would be."

"Okay," Pete said, which committed him to nothing.

But Bob Cullum proved as good as his word. By the time the carrier did get to Hawaii, Pete had clothes that fit better than approximately. He had a wallet with five dollars in it. He had an obligation, too, and he knew it. When he and Cullum got some liberty, he'd be doing the buying.

He didn't mind. The other sergeant was plainly a guy with an eye for the main chance. If Cullum figured Pete might be connected to the main chance one way or another . . . *What am I supposed to do?* Pete thought. *Hope the son of a bitch is wrong?*

HANS-ULRICH RUDEL'S FLYING suit was made from fur and leather. No matter where you took off from, up above 5,000 meters the air was not only thin but far below freezing cold. In Russian winter, that flying suit came in handy when you were still down on *terra firma*. Rudel all but lived in it from first snowfall to spring's grudging arrival months later.

He sat in the cockpit of his Ju-87 at the end of a runway made by flattening out a long, narrow strip of wheatfield. The fall rains and the thick, gluey mud they brought were over. The ground under the Stuka's landing gear was frozen as hard as Stalin's heart.

He spoke into the voice tube: "Radio behaving, Albert?"

"Seems to be, sir," Sergeant Dieselhorst answered, voice brassy through the tube. Along with the radio, he was in charge of a rear-facing machine gun. Both he and Hans-Ulrich always hoped he didn't have to use it. The Stuka was a fine dive-bomber, but it had been in trouble against even the Czech biplane fighters it faced at the very beginning of the war. Fighters these days were a lot nastier—although the Ivans still threw biplanes at the *Luftwaffe*. The Ivans, from everything Hans-Ulrich had seen, threw whatever they could get their hands on at their foes. If not all of it was top quality, it could still do some damage before it went down in flames. That was how they seemed to think, anyhow.

A groundcrew man yanked at the starting crank in front of the port wing. The crank was hard to move; another mechanic joined the first fellow in coveralls. The Junkers Jumo engine roared to life. Smoke and flame belched from the exhaust pipes. The prop blurred into invisibility. The groundcrew men carefully stepped away from the plane. If you weren't careful around a spinning prop, it could cost you your head— literally. At least one groundcrew man had been shipped home from Russia in a coffin sealed tight because of a split second's inattention.

"Everything look good, *Herr Oberleutnant?*" Dieselhorst asked— shouted, really, because the racket was terrific even inside the soundproofed cockpit. Outside . . . Like artillerymen, a lot of the *Luftwaffe* troops in the groundcrew wore earplugs to try to save some of their hearing.

Hans-Ulrich checked the instrument panel. "All green, Albert," he answered, and gave the guys outside a thumbs-up to let them know the Stuka was ready to take off. They waved back.

The dive-bomber lumbered down the unpaved airstrip (as far as Rudel knew, there were no paved ones this side of Warsaw). When it reached takeoff speed, Hans-Ulrich hauled back on the stick, hard. The Stuka's nose came up. It sedately started to fly, rather like a fat old man doing a slow breaststroke across a public pool.

No Ju-87 ever made was or would be or could be a hot performer. All the same, Hans-Ulrich wished that particular comparison hadn't occurred to him. The weight and drag of the twin 37mm panzer-busting cannon under his wings only made his Stuka even more of a beast than it would have been anyhow. He'd used guns like this pair to blast enemy panzers here and, earlier, in France. He'd even knocked down a couple of fighters with them, more from desperation than tactical brilliance.

And he'd been shot down twice, once in France and once here in Russia. He and Sergeant Dieselhorst had both managed to bail out twice, and hadn't hurt themselves too badly either time. No enemy pilot had machine-gunned them while they hung helpless under their big silk canopies, either. The Frenchman who'd got Rudel's first Stuka must not have thought that was sporting. Victorious German pilots also didn't murder defenseless French flyers.

The Ivans . . . There were no guarantees with the Ivans, none at all. Hans-Ulrich knew how lucky they were not to have got perforated when the Russian pilot shot them down.

He spiraled slowly upwards. He wanted to gain altitude before he crossed the front and went hunting on the Soviet side. You couldn't die of old age waiting for your altimeter to unwind. It only seemed as if you could.

"Three thousand meters," he said at last to Dieselhorst. "Oxygen time."

"I'm doing it," the rear gunner/radioman answered. "Delicious."

"Well, that's one word," Hans-Ulrich said with a laugh. Sucked in through a rubber hose, the bottled oxygen always reminded him of gnawing on a tire tread.

He flew north and east, in the general direction of Smolensk. If everything had gone the way the *Führer* and the General Staff wanted, the city would have fallen to the *Wehrmacht* before the fall rains slowed everyone's operations to a crawl. (Of course, if everything had gone the way the *Führer* and the General Staff wanted, Paris would have fallen to German blitzkrieg before winter 1939 turned to spring. You had to deal with what you got, not with what you wanted.)

Other Stukas droned on in the same general direction. They spread across the sky too loosely to be in anything worth dignifying by the name of formation. They had no set target. If someone spotted something that seemed worth going after down on the snowy ground, he'd attack it. If not, he'd keep going.

If someone spotted something . . . The Russians had forgotten more about the art of camouflage than Germany knew. That was one of the reasons the hammer and sickle still flew above Smolensk: one of the reasons Smolensk still shielded Moscow from attack. The *Wehrmacht* had got more than its share of bloody noses on the way east from forces whose existence it hadn't suspected till it ran into them face-first.

"Hello!" Rudel exclaimed. "What's that?"

"What's what?" Sergeant Dieselhorst asked. Like Epimetheus in the myth, he could see only what already lay behind him.

"Train heading north," Hans-Ulrich said. "They've whitewashed the cars and the locomotive, but you can't whitewash the smoke plume coming up out of the stack." He spoke into the radio, too, alerting his squadron CO to what he'd found and where he thought it was.

"Go get it, Rudel," Colonel Steinbrenner answered. "Somebody may show up to give you a hand, too. Here's hoping it's a troop train full of French traitors on their way up to Murmansk or Arkhangelsk."

"Yes, sir. Here's hoping." Rudel switched off the radio and called into the speaking tube: "I'm going to shoot up the cars and then give the engine a couple of 37mm rounds through the boiler."

"That ought to do it, by God," Dieselhorst declared.

"It had better. And when I pull up, give the train a burst from your machine gun, too," Hans-Ulrich said.

"It'll be a pleasure," the rear gunner replied.

Hans-Ulrich didn't have to stand the Stuka on its nose to attack the train. He came in at a shallow angle, flying slowly, and shot it up from back to front and from only a few meters above the cars. Then, as he'd promised, he blasted the locomotive the way he was in the habit of shooting up enemy panzers through the thin engine decking that didn't do enough to protect them from attack from the air.

As he pulled back the stick to climb for another attack if he needed one, Dieselhorst did rake the train with a long burst from his MG-34. "That engine's blowing steam like a whale," the sergeant reported. "They won't be able to keep going like that for long. . . . *Ja*, the fucker's already slowing down."

"Good," Hans-Ulrich said. "I'll make another pass and chew up whatever's in the cars one more time. With luck, I'll start some fires."

What was in the cars were soldiers—Russian or French Rudel couldn't tell, since both wore khaki when not in winter white. They spilled out as he climbed for the new attack. By the time he dove again, muzzle flashes warned that they were shooting back.

Well, they could try if they wanted to. A Stuka was a tough target for a rifleman. Even if a bullet or two did hit, the Ju-87's cockpit and engine were armored against small-arms fire. Infantrymen, poor fools, weren't. Rudel's thumb came down on the firing button. His forward-facing machine guns chattered. The enemy soldiers ran every which way through the snow.

Sergeant Dieselhorst gave them a parting burst as the dive-bomber climbed away from the stricken train. "They're froggies, I think, *Herr Oberleutnant*," he said. "I'm pretty sure some of them were wearing the helmets with the crest."

"Good," Hans-Ulrich said savagely. "They need to know they can't play those games without paying the price."

"Damn straight, sir." But then Dieselhorst went on, "What kind of price will *we* have to pay when the war in the west starts cooking again?" Since Hans-Ulrich had no good answer for that, he pretended not to hear, but droned on back toward the airstrip west of Smolensk.

LIEUTENANT ARISTIDE DEMANGE had traveled in cattle cars before. In the last war, the French Army used them all the goddamn time: often enough to make stencils for painting the legend 8 HORSES OR 36 MEN on their sides. In the last war, the French Army'd used anything and everything it could find. Things hadn't changed much in the generation since, either. If it was there, you grabbed it. Legalities and other details would wait till later.

But the Red Army made Demange's countrymen look like a bunch of pikers. Fighting against the Russians, he'd seen they were in grim earnest. Now the French expeditionary force was in Soviet hands. The Ivans wanted them the hell out of their country. What they wanted, they got. And they didn't worry about legalities even a little bit. Legalities were whatever the commissars said they were. Anybody who didn't like it headed for Siberia or got a bullet in the back of the neck.

When Demange was a sergeant, he'd always tried to make his men more afraid of him than they were of the enemy. He'd done a damn good job of it, too. But, from everything he could see, all of Red Russia worked that way.

No doubt the generals and colonels who'd led this force in the biggest French invasion of Russia since Napoleon's day were riding north in the same kind of luxury high Soviet officers enjoyed when they weren't at the front, classless society or no classless society. No doubt. People who weren't generals or colonels headed north however the commissars wanted them to. And if the commissars felt like getting some of their own back . . . They might be godless Communists, but they were also human beings.

So Demange and too many men from his company were sardined into a cattle car the French Army would have been ashamed to use in the most desperate hours of funneling men forward into the Verdun charnel house. You could watch the sleepers go by through spaces between the floorboards as the train rattled up the tracks toward . . . wherever the hell it was going. Nobody'd bothered to tell Demange where that was.

Nobody'd bothered to muck out the car, either. As far as Demange could tell, nobody'd bothered to muck out the car since Tsar Nicholas was running things, or maybe Tsar Alexander before him. The Frenchman would never again doubt what bullshit smelled like.

Sanitary arrangements were a couple of honey buckets with covers. When somebody needed to crap, Demange told off a *poilu* to stand in front of his chosen bucket and hold up a greatcoat to give some rudimentary privacy. By what Demange had seen in the USSR, the covers on the buckets represented no small concession to French sensibilities from the Red Army.

His men were hardened to Russian conditions. They bitched about the stinks in the cattle car, but if you put a bunch of *poilus* fresh from the front in heaven they'd bellyache about that. Demange discounted it. Besides, some of the soldiers had vodka in their canteens instead of *pinard* or—God forbid!—water. They were the ones who pissed and moaned the loudest, and who fell asleep first. Hearing them snore, Demange wouldn't have minded a good slug of liquid lightning himself. He knew how to hold his booze. He wouldn't go out like a flashlight with a used-up battery.

Two French soldiers played piquet. Four more made what would have been a bridge table if only they'd had a table. One fellow leaned against the filthy boards of the cattle-car wall with a pocket New Testament a few centimeters in front of his nose. How anybody could go through more than five minutes of combat and still believe in God was beyond Demange, but Maxime was a long way from the worst man in his company. As long as that stayed true, the lieutenant didn't care how stupid he was every other way.

Demange stubbed out the tiny butt of one Gitane and lit another. While he was awake, he smoked. His cigarettes dangled from the corner of his thin-lipped mouth. Alert *poilus* gauged his mood by the angle of the dangle. Of course, the gamut of those moods ran from bad to worse. He wasn't about to waste his rare happiness on his men, the *cons*. He inhaled deeply. Gitanes were good and strong. The smoke helped him ignore the other foul odors in the cattle car.

He'd just blown out a long stream of gray when he cocked his head to one side. He was trying to hear better—which, in its own way, was pretty goddamn funny, considering how often he'd fired a rifle right next to his ear. If by some accident he lived through the war, he'd be deaf as a horseshoe five years later. And this train, clunking along over a railroad that needed way more maintenance than it ever got, didn't exactly make the ideal listening platform.

All the same, this new background noise didn't sound like anything that belonged with the train. It was getting louder, too, as if coming up from behind. It sounded like . . . "Fuck!" he said softly when he realized what it sounded like. He didn't get the chance to yell before machine-gun bullets tore through the cattle car's back wall and roof.

Something stung his cheek. Automatically, his hand went up to it. His fingers came away bloody. For a bad second or two, he wondered if he'd got half his face shot away and just didn't feel it yet. His hand rose again. No: he was still pretty much in one piece. Either a round had just grazed him or he'd got nicked by a flying splinter or something.

Not all of his men were so lucky. The iron tang of blood suddenly warred with the rest of the stinks. One of the bridge players was down. With most of the left side of his head blown off, he wouldn't get up again, either. The *poilu* beyond him clutched at his leg and howled like a wolf. The same bullet might have got them both.

Other wounded men added their shrieks to the din. At least one other poor bastard looked to be dead, too. And, to add insult to injury, a bullet had holed one of the honey buckets below the waterline. Only the goddamn thing didn't hold water.

The train slowed, then stopped. At first, Demange swore at the engineer. Why wasn't he going flat out, damn him? But that was a question with an obvious answer. If the German Stuka—Demange thought it was a Stuka, anyhow—had shot up the locomotive along with the cars behind it, the train wasn't going anywhere because it couldn't.

And if it couldn't . . . Demange knew what he would do if he were flying that ugly, ungainly bastard. "We've got to get out of here, dammit!" he yelled. "That cocksucker'll come around again for another pass now that he's got a target he can't miss." That he hated Germans didn't keep him from giving them the professional respect they were due.

There was a seal on the door. The Ivans didn't want their guests wandering around. They just wanted them out. He'd been told there would be hell to pay if that seal got broken. Well, too bad. There was already hell to pay, and his men were doing the paying. He broke the seal and slid the door open. He supposed he should have counted himself lucky that some subcommissar hadn't nailed it shut.

"Out!" he ordered. "Grab your rifles, too. Maybe we can fuck up the lousy Nazi's aim if we make him flinch or something."

Out went the French soldiers. The hale helped the wounded. Demange waited till everybody else had left the cattle car before he jumped down himself. He still carried a rifle. No officer's pantywaist pistol for him. If he spotted something half a kilometer away that needed killing, he by God wanted the proper tool for the job. He was damned nasty with the bayonet, too, and didn't flinch from using it: more than half the battle right there.

Here came the Stuka again, machine guns winking malevolently. It flew low enough and slow enough to let Demange see the pilot's face for a couple of seconds. He fired two shots, neither of which did any perceptible good. The plane's bullets kicked up puffs of snow. They thocked into the train. A couple hit with the soft, wet splat that meant they were striking flesh.

Some of the *poilus* fired at the Ju-87, too. It buzzed off toward the southwest. Demange looked around. Nothing to see but the shot-up train, snowy fields, and distant, snow-dappled pines. If he wasn't in the exact middle of nowhere, he sure as hell wasn't more than a few centimeters away.

And how long would the Russians need to figure out that this troop train was well and truly fucked? Would they get it before the French soldiers stranded here within a few centimeters of the middle of nowhere started freezing to death? All Demange could do was hope so. In the meantime, he lit a new Gitane and bent to bandage a man with a bullet through his forearm.

"MERRY CHRISTMAS, SERGEANT!" Wilf Preston said, and handed Alistair Walsh a tin of bully beef.

"Well, thank you very much, sir," the staff sergeant said, surprised and more touched than he'd dreamt he could be. The young subaltern was a decent enough sort. He might even make a good officer once he got some experience to go with all his Sandhurst theory.

Till he acquired that experience, he had Walsh as his platoon staff sergeant. Walsh had been in the Army since 1918, around the time Preston was born. The junior lieutenant had the rank, but men higher up the chain of command were more likely to hearken to Walsh. At a pinch, the British Army could do without subalterns, but never without sergeants. So it had been for generations. So, the admittedly biased Walsh suspected, it would be forevermore.

He hadn't thought to provide himself with a Christmas present for Preston. Truth to tell, he hadn't remembered it was Christmas. Well, there were ways around such difficulties. He took an unopened packet of Navy Cuts out of a breast pocket of his battledress tunic.

"Here you go, sir," he said. "A happy Christmas to you, too." He'd scare up more smokes somewhere. He could always cadge them from the men. They knew he didn't welsh on such small debts.

Even thinking the word made him swallow a snort. He *was* Welsh, as his last name suggested. He proved as much every time he opened his mouth; to English ears, his consonants buzzed and his vowels were strange. If he hadn't stayed in the service after the last war ended, he would have gone down into the mines instead. Chances were he'd been safer in uniform than he would have been had he taken it off with most of the Great War conscripts.

For all he knew, he was still safer here in North Africa than he would have been grubbing coal out of rock. As long as the Italians were England's only foes on this side of the Mediterranean, he'd reckoned his odds pretty good. Musso's boys made a feckless lunge into British-held Egypt, then retreated into Libya. Tobruk, their main base in the eastern part of the colony, had looked like falling soon.

But it hadn't fallen, and now it wouldn't—not in any kind of future Walsh could see, anyhow. The main reason Mussolini'd tried pushing forward was to punish England for backing out of its alliance with Germany against the Russians. With *il Duce* in trouble, Hitler had sent in planes and tanks and men to pull his chestnuts out of the fire. Who would have guessed that the *Führer*, always so ready to double-cross most of his neighbors, would prove loyal to this strong-jawed son of a bitch who didn't come close to deserving it?

At this season of the year, Libya wasn't so bad. Rain made the hillsides and even the desert green up a little. It wasn't blazing hot, the way it had been and the way it would be again before long. Even the flies and mosquitoes and gnats and midges were only annoying, not pestilential.

The Fritzes, now, the Fritzes were pestilential the year around. Walsh had fought them in France in two wars, and in Norway this time around as well. He didn't love them, but they knew their business in temperate climes and in the snow.

They knew it here in the desert, too. As always—and as dauntingly as always—they were very much in earnest. A lot of Italian units fired a few shots for honor's sake and then gave up, the men smiling in relief because they hadn't wanted to go to war to begin with. Not all the Eyeties were like that, but plenty were. Who could blame them? Fighting when you were short of aircraft and armor was suicidal, and they never had enough.

Tell a platoon of Germans to hold a hill no matter what and they damn well would, as long as flesh and blood allowed. And if the survivors did finally have to surrender, they'd spit in your eye when they came down from the hilltop, as if to say you'd only whipped them by fool luck. Bastards, sure as hell, but tough bastards.

Walsh wasn't the only soldier to feel the Royal Navy should have kept the Germans—and the Italians, for that matter—from reinforcing Tobruk. Say that any place where both sergeants and petty officers bought their pints, and you'd get yourself a punchup. *If we had Gibraltar, now* . . . the sailors would go.

They had a point—of sorts. Gibraltar had fallen to Marshal Sanjurjo's men way back in 1939. Without it, the Royal Navy had to run a formidable gauntlet to get into the western Mediterranean, and an even more formidable one to go farther east. These days, most naval support went all the way around Africa, through the Suez Canal, and over to Alexandria. Even there, the Italians had sunk a heavy cruiser with a limpet mine attached by a raider who rode a man-carrying torpedo (or maybe a one-man submarine; the stories wafting through the veil of secrecy varied).

With France back in the fight against Hitler and Mussolini, maybe things would get better. The Mediterranean was the froggies' natural naval province. They'd done a decent enough job in the narrow waters the last time around. Of course, Italy had been on their side the last time around.

Nowadays . . . Nowadays Musso was liable to grab Malta before England could take Tobruk away from him. That would hurt almost as much as losing Gibraltar had. *Well, I can't do a bloody thing about it,* Walsh thought. He might be able to help in some small way with the seizure of Tobruk—if Lieutenant Preston let him, anyhow.

A moment too late, he realized the subaltern had just said something more to him. Unfortunately, he hadn't the least idea what. "I'm sorry, sir. You caught me woolgathering there, I'm afraid," he confessed.

"I *said*"—Preston let his patience show—"that some doctors are telling us we'd be better off if we didn't smoke. As far as health goes, I mean."

"Bunch of ruddy killjoys, far as I'm concerned . . . sir." Walsh added the honorific in case Preston happened to believe the tripe he was spouting. "I might have better wind if I tossed out my Navy Cuts, but I'd be a hell of a lot grouchier, too. Can't get too many big pleasures at the front. Are they going to start begrudging us the little ones now? Wouldn't surprise me a bit." Doctors were natural-born wet blankets.

"I don't believe they're just speaking of wind," Preston replied. "If I understand this correctly, they say tobacco is bad for the health generally, and hard on the lungs in particular."

"Hmp," Walsh said: an eloquent bit of skepticism, even if unlikely to show up in the *Oxford English Dictionary*. "It'll be best bitter next, or I miss my guess." He eyed his young superior. "I don't notice *you* chucking your fags into the closest sand dune, either."

"Er . . . no." Preston had the grace to look shamefaced. "It's a funny thing. I never smoked much before I first went into combat. But in a tight spot a cigarette will steady your nerves better than almost anything, won't it?"

"Anything this side of a couple tots of stiff rum, any road." Walsh held up a hand before the subaltern could answer. "And yes, sir, I know what you're going to say. A smoke won't leave you stupid the way a tot or two will."

"Quite." Preston nodded. Then he chuckled wryly. "Doesn't seem to bother the Russians, by all accounts."

"No, it doesn't," Walsh agreed. By all accounts, the Russians drank like fish. "But then, by all accounts they're stupid to begin with."

German artillery, or maybe it was Italian, opened up just then. Walsh and Preston dove for holes in the sandy ground. As 105s burst around him, Walsh lit a cigarette. He would sooner have had the rum, but you took what you could get. And Preston was right—a smoke *did* steady your nerves.

# Chapter 2

I medal. Kisses on the cheek from a Spanish Republican brigadier who smelled of garlic. A three-day pass for Madrid, and a fat wad of pesetas to spend there. Vaclav Jezek couldn't have cared less about the first two. The medal was gilded, not gold; it clanked instead of clinking. The brigadier was just another Spaniard with a graying mustache.

The pass and the roll, though, those were worth having. The Czech sniper could hardly wait to go hunting for more Fascist generals. The Republic promised the sun, moon, and little stars for Marshal Sanjurjo, the *Caudillo* of the enemy's half of Spain. The payoff on General What's-his-name—Franco, that was it—wasn't half bad, either.

Vaclav didn't speak much Spanish. The only foreign language he did speak was German. Seeing as the Nazis backed the Spanish Fascists, in the Red Republic that was more likely to land him in trouble than to help him. But he could order drinks. He could get at least some food. And, eked out with gestures, he could let a whore know what he wanted her to do. The *putas* liked him fine: he didn't want anything fancy, and he had plenty of money to spend. As far as they were concerned, that made him the perfect customer.

Being a stolid, thrifty, solid man, he still had a little cash in his wallet when the leave, like all other good things, came to an end. A bus took him back up toward the stretch of front the soldiers of the Czechoslovakian government-in-exile held northwest of Madrid. Almost everything on the way was smashed by bombs, pocked with bullet holes, or both together. For a while, Sanjurjo's men had pushed into the capital's outskirts. Slowly and painfully, a few meters at a time, the Republicans had forced them back.

If France hadn't hopped into the sack with Hitler, the Czechs would have stayed there, making sure the Germans advanced only over their dead bodies. The cynical politicos in Paris thought they were generous to let the Czechs cross the Pyrenees instead of interning them. Maybe they were even right.

Now, though, Daladier and his cronies must have decided old Adolf made a lousy lay. They weren't in bed with him any more. That meant the on-and-off supply spigot between France and the Spanish Republic was on again. It also meant the Germans and Italians had trouble keeping *their* Spanish pals in toys for a while. If the Republican officials and officers didn't stow their brains up their asses, they'd try to take advantage of that.

The bus wheezed to a stop several kilometers short of the front. The driver said something in lisping Spanish. Since most of his passengers were Czechs or men from the International Brigades, his own language did him less good than it might have. Seeing as much, he solved the problem another way. He yanked the door open—whatever hydraulics it might have had once upon a time were long gone—and yelled, *"Raus!"*

Chances were it was the only word of German he knew. But it did the job here. Grumbling, the soldiers hopped out one by one. A hulking blond International said something in Polish. Jezek *almost* understood it. He cupped a hand behind one ear and said, "Try that again?" in Czech.

His words would have had the same annoying near-familiarity to the Pole as the other guy's did for him. The big, fair man repeated himself. Vaclav shrugged. He still didn't get it. *"Gawno,"* the Pole muttered. Vaclav followed that fine. Shit was shit in any Slavic tongue. Then the big guy did what a Pole and a Czech would often do instead of staying frustrated by each other's languages: he asked, "*Sprechen Sie Deutsch?*"

"*Ja,*" Vaclav answered resignedly. He'd gone through this before. He'd hoped to skip it this time, but no such luck.

"*Gut,*" the Pole said. "What I said was, we have had our holiday, and now we are going back to the factory." Like Vaclav, he spoke German slowly, hunting for words. As Poles would, he put the accent in every polysyllabic word on the next to last, whether it belonged there or not.

"To the factory, is it?" Jezek responded. "Well, here's hoping we stay away from industrial accidents."

"Here's hoping. *Ja*-fucking-*wohl.*" That wasn't exactly proper German, but Vaclav followed some improper German, too.

He and the Pole tramped along together for a while. They told each other the usual lies about the drinking and screwing they'd done in Madrid. A jackhammer couldn't have done all the pounding the Pole claimed. Vaclav pretended to believe him. Life was too short for some arguments.

They waved when they separated, and wished each other luck. The Internationals' trenches were north and east of the stretch the Czechs held. "Hey, look who's back!" Vaclav's countrymen shouted. One of them added, "You don't look as rumpled as you ought to, dammit!"

"Rumpled? I'll tell you about rumpled, by Jesus!" Vaclav retold some of the stories he'd fed the Pole. His buddies ate them up. He'd already thought them through once, and they sounded a hell of a lot better in Czech than they had in German. He hoped he gave good value.

Through all the stories, Lieutenant Benjamin Halévy listened with an ironically raised eyebrow. Everybody got promoted a grade on coming to Spain; that was why Vaclav was a sergeant now. Halévy had been a sergeant—a sergeant in the French Army. His parents were from Prague; he'd been born in Paris. Fluent in French and Czech (and several other languages), he'd served as liaison between French troops and the men who served the government-in-exile.

And he'd accompanied the Czechs to Spain. Like any other Jew, he couldn't stomach France's alliance with the Third *Reich*. French authorities hadn't much wanted him around, either. He could have gone back to civilian life with an honorable discharge. Instead, he'd kept on fighting Fascism.

He was a good soldier, clever and brave. Vaclav hadn't had much use for Jews till the war started. When it came to fighting the Nazis, though, they were in it to the end. A couple of Slovaks in Vaclav's squad at the beginning of things ran out the first chance they got. They were probably in Father Tiso's "independent" Slovakian army right now, fighting the Russians. Vaclav chuckled nastily. That'd serve the stupid shitheels right!

"Where's my toy?" he asked Halévy. He didn't bother with a *sir*; neither of them took the promotions they'd got from the Spaniards too seriously. The extra pay, in cash and in promises, did come in handy, though.

"Well, somebody saw an elephant out behind the Fascists' lines. He went hunting with your piece, and we haven't seen it or him since," Halévy answered blandly.

Vaclav snorted. "My ass! Is the beast still where I stashed it?"

"You bet it is," the Jew replied. "C'mon, man—get real. Who in his right mind would want the goddamn thing?"

"Well, I do," Vaclav said with such dignity as he could muster.

"I said, 'Who in his right mind?'" Halévy repeated patiently. Vaclav snorted again. Halévy led him to the bombproof where he'd left the antitank rifle before he went down to paint the town red (or, given its politics, redder). He'd taken it from a French soldier who was too dead to need it any more. It was a beast and a half: almost as long as a man was tall, and more than twice as heavy as an ordinary rifle. It fired rounds as thick as a thumb, and not much shorter.

Even with a muzzle brake and a padded stock, it almost broke your shoulder every time you pulled the trigger. But those fat bullets would pierce at least twenty-five millimeters of hardened steel, which made it death on armored cars and powerful enough to trouble any tank they'd had in 1938 (more modern marks shrugged off any rifle bullets).

It might not wreck a new tank. To the logical French, that made it obsolete and therefore useless. To Vaclav, it only meant he needed to use the monster for something else. The antitank rifle fired heavy rounds on a flat trajectory with a ridiculously high muzzle velocity. That made it a wonderful sniper's rifle, especially after he fitted it with a telescopic sight. He could kill a man two kilometers away.

He could, and he damn well had. General Franco hadn't been so far off—he'd been out around 1,500 meters. Franco, by all accounts, had been a careful and logical man, more methodical than brilliant. No doubt he would have agreed with the French about the obvious useless-ness of an outdated weapon. He would have, yes, till Vaclav plugged him. At the moment, he had no opinions about anything. And Vaclav planned on doing some more sniping tomorrow.


THE WINTER BEFORE, the *Wehrmacht* hadn't had proper clothes for fighting in Russia. The German greatcoat served tolerably well in West-ern Europe. Russian winds bit right through it. Willi Dernen had acquired—a polite way to say *had stolen*—a sheepskin jacket in a peas-ant village. German boots also sucked. The hobnails in their soles took cold right up to your feet, and they also fit too closely to be padded. Willi'd taken a pair of *valenki*—oversized felt boots—off a Russian corpse. He'd done much better after that.

Things were different this time around. German soldiers got cold-weather gear as good as anyone else's. Even the Ivans stole *Wehrmacht*-issue felt-and-leather boots when they could get them. Willi was relieved. Shivering and risking frostbite were bad enough. Having even your Polish allies laugh at you—or, sadder yet, pity you—because you were shivering and frostbitten was worse.

Willi came from Breslau. Just about everybody in the division was drawn from the *Wehrkreis*—the recruiting district—centered on that town. Poland bordered it on the east. Plenty of Poles lived in the district, and in Breslau. Like most Germans, Willi looked down his nose at them. Watching them look down their noses at him and his countrymen here was flat-out embarrassing.

The *Wehrmacht* first came east to help the Poles drive Stalin's hordes out of their country. The Germans had done that. Now they were in Russia up to their armpits, the boundary between Poland and the USSR hundreds of kilometers behind them, Moscow still hundreds of kilome-ters ahead.

Where, in all this Russian immensity, did victory lie? Anywhere? If it lay anywhere close by, Willi couldn't see it. He didn't think any of the other *Landsers* in his outfit could, either. He'd quit worrying about it. All he cared about were staying alive and coming home in one piece.

He peered out from the edge of some woods across the snow-covered fields to the east. His new winter coat was white on one side, *Feldgrau* on the other. He'd slapped whitewash on his *Stahlhelm*. With snow dappling the pines and birches that sheltered his section, any watching Red Army man wouldn't be able to see him from very far away.

Which proved less than he wished it would have. For all he knew, a Russian in a snowsuit was lying in that field not fifty meters away. The Germans didn't call their enemies Indians by accident. For one thing, Indians were red men. For another, Indians were supposed to be masters of concealment. They were supposed to be, and the Ivans damn well were.

If a Russian *was* lying in the field, he wouldn't give himself away by moving. He could lie there all day without doing that. He could lie there all day without freezing to death, too. German troops often wondered whether Russians were half animal. If they were, it was the wrong half, as far as Willi was concerned.

Boots crunched in the snow behind him. He turned his head. Nothing to get excited about: just one of his buddies. "Anything going on?" Adam Pfaff asked.

"Well, I don't *see* anything," Willi answered.

"Mpf," the other *Obergefreiter* said. Willi couldn't have put it better himself. Pfaff went on, "Maybe that means something, and maybe it doesn't."

"I was just thinking the same thing before you came up," Willi said. "If you want to look around for yourself, be my guest. I won't get pissed off if you spot Ivans I missed. I'll thank you kindly, on account of you'll be saving my ass, too."

"Sure, I'll look. I don't think I'm likely to spot anything you didn't, but even when it comes to cabbage two heads are better than one." Cradling his Mauser, Pfaff moved up alongside Willi. The woodwork on the rifle was painted a gray not far from *Feldgrau*. He'd carried that

Mauser since he joined the regiment as a replacement. Arno Baatz, the *Unteroffizier* who'd led this squad, tried to tell him to make the piece ordinary again. The company commander had said it was all right, though. That didn't make Pfaff and Baatz get along any better.

Then again, Awful Arno didn't get along with anybody. He and Willi had had run-ins aplenty. Right this minute, Baatz was recovering from an arm wound, and the squad belonged to Willi. He didn't care what Pfaff did with his rifle, as long as it fired when he pulled the trigger.

Willi's own weapon was a sniper's Mauser, with a telescopic sight and a special downturned bolt rather like an English Lee-Enfield's because the scope got in the way of an ordinary one. Awful Arno also hadn't liked him to carry that piece.

After scanning the landscape to the east, Pfaff said, "Looks a hell of a lot like Russia, y'know?"

"*Wunderbar*. And here I was expecting Hawaii," Willi said sourly. "Russia? I could do that well myself. Hell, I *did* do that well myself."

"Always glad to be of service." His buddy sketched a salute.

"You think we can advance across those fields?" Willi asked.

"Sure—as long as there aren't any Russians in the woods on the far side," Pfaff said. "But if they've got a couple of machine guns set up amongst the trees there, they'll screw us to the wall if we try it."

"Yeah, that's about how it looks to me, too. Not a pfennig's worth of cover along the way." Willi sighed out a young fogbank. "*Leutnant* Freigau, he kinda wants us to go forward, though."

The junior lieutenant commanded the company now for the same reason a senior private led the squad: the guy who should have had the slot was getting over a wound. Adam Pfaff sighed, too. "If he's so hot to go charging ahead like that, let him come here and scout it out. Christ, even ordinary riflemen'd give us a hard time. Like you said, they'd be shooting from cover, and we don't have any."

"Go tell him to come up and check for himself," Willi said. "If he sends us out anyway . . ." He shrugged. He would have made the effort, anyhow.

"I'll do it. Can't hurt. Maybe he'll have a rush of brains to the head." Pfaff's tone said that was likely to be too much to hope for. Even so, he bobbed his head at Willi and went back to the west.

Willi had time to duck behind a pine and smoke a cigarette before Pfaff came back with Rudi Freigau. The *Leutnant* was only a couple of years older than the two *Obergefreiters*. He wore a neat mustache that was blond almost to the point of invisibility. Instead of a rifle, he carried a Schmeisser. He greeted Willi with, "Pfaff says you're not too happy about moving up from here."

"See for yourself, sir," Willi replied. "If they're waiting for us in that next bunch of trees, we're sticking our heads in the sausage machine."

Lieutenant Freigau did look. He was as careful as Willi and Adam Pfaff had been. He'd seen his share of tight spots before; he didn't want to make things easy for a Russian sharpshooter. After eyeing the bare field and the woods on the far side, he said, "Everything looks quiet."

"Well, sure, sir. It would if they're trying to see whether we're dumb enough to go out there, too." As soon as he spoke, Willi realized he might have put that more tactfully.

"Or if they aren't there at all. Which is my judgment of the situation, Dernen." Freigau sounded irked. Willi supposed he would have, too, if he were an officer who'd just got the glove from somebody hardly even a noncom.

The lieutenant started across the snowy field. Yes, he wore winter white, but that didn't come close to making him invisible. Willi and Adam Pfaff exchanged stricken looks. "Sir, don't you want to come back? You've made your point," Willi called after him.

Freigau shook his head. "No need," he answered. "I'm not going to run away from shadows and ghosts and unicorns and other imaginary things. And every advance we make brings us that much closer to—"

A Russian machine gun barked to life. Willi and Adam Pfaff both flattened out. The gunner might not be aiming at them, but they were still close to his line of fire. Lieutenant Freigau went down, too, but not because he meant to. He writhed feebly and made horrible choking noises. He'd been hit at least twice: once in the belly and once in the neck. Blood darkened his snowsuit and pooled and steamed in the drift where he lay. After a couple of minutes, he quit gurgling and lay still.

"Well, you were right," Pfaff said to Willi.

"*Ja*. And a whole fat lot of good that does the lieutenant." Willi didn't even point toward Freigau's body, for fear of drawing the machine gunner's notice.

"Other thing is," Pfaff went on, "you'll be commanding the company pretty soon, the way the people above you keep stopping stuff."

"If I end up commanding the company, we're all in deep shit," Willi said. Adam Pfaff didn't try to tell him he was wrong. After all, what were friends for?


THE NATIONALISTS WERE spewing out the usual lies through their loudspeakers: "Come across to our lines and we'll fill you full of mutton stew! Lovely mutton stew! We eat it every day! We'll fill you so full, you won't walk any more—you'll waddle instead! *Lovely* mutton stew!"

Sometimes it was mutton stew. Sometimes it was chicken stew instead. The Nationalists' announcer sounded as smooth to Chaim Weinberg as any radio pitchman flogging Lucky Strikes back in the States.

Mike Carroll didn't take it so kindly. "I'm sick of that lying bullshit," the other Abe Lincoln growled. "I wish putting a bullet through his loudspeaker would make him shut up."

"As long as you know it's bullshit, it doesn't wear on you so much. And as long as you've got enough to eat yourself," Chaim added. "When times were tough, a big old bowl of stew sounded mighty fine."

"The Nationalists knew it was bullshit. They'd cross over to our lines, hoping we'd feed them," Mike said.

"Talk about optimists!" Chaim exclaimed.

"Yeah, well, sometimes they'd be skinnier than we were—and that wasn't easy."

"I remember. Those days on the Ebro . . . Everybody was hungry all the goddamn time. Hell, even I was on the way to being scrawny back then." Chaim was short and thickset; an unkind man would have called him squat. He looked and talked like the New York Jew he was. In Madrid, he'd got himself a different kind of handle: *el narigón loco*—the crazy kike. In bar brawls, he'd sail into guys half again his size. He'd flatten them, too, because there were times when he didn't give a rat's ass whether he lived or died and because he brought his front-line meanness with him when he went on leave.

Mike Carroll, by contrast, could have come off an SS recruiting poster. You'd lose teeth if you were stupid enough to tell him so, though. He was as good a Communist as Chaim or any other Abe Lincoln. He was probably a better Communist than Chaim, as a matter of fact. Chaim had a habit of asking pointed questions. Mike—Mike *believed*.

"Delicious mutton stew!" the Fascist announcer called again.

"What did you do to the sheep before you threw it in the pot?" Chaim yelled back. His Spanish was far from smooth, but he could make himself understood.

These days, Spaniards filled out the Abe Lincolns' ranks, and those of the rest of the International Brigades. They understood Chaim fine. Laughing, they started shouting "Sheep-fuckers!" toward the Nationalist trenches.

That pissed off Marshal Sanjurjo's heroes. It would have pissed Chaim off, too, and he didn't have the touchy Spanish sense of machismo. The Nationalists' machine guns started raking the Republican trenches. "Now look what you went and did," Mike said reproachfully as the Internationals returned fire.

"It's a war," Chaim explained. It wasn't the first firefight jeers at enemy propaganda had touched off, and chances were it wouldn't be the last.

But he stopped taking it lightly when the Fascists opened up with mortars and artillery. They were more than just pissed off, and they were taking it out on the Republicans. He dove into a bombproof dug into the front wall of the trench, hoping no shell would burst on top of it and bury him alive.

Then somebody banged on a big shell casing with an iron bar. "They're coming! The bastards are coming!" The shout rang out in English and Spanish.

Chaim scrambled out of the bombproof and took his place on a firing step. Sure as hell, the troops who followed Sanjurjo were rushing across no-man's-land. It wasn't like the doomed English plodding forward at the Somme. These fellows knew better. They stayed low. They kept in loose order. Every chance they got, they jumped into shell holes. Some of them fired while others scrambled forward.

That helped, but only so much. Many of them fell scrambling forward. Some lay still once they went down. Others writhed and thrashed and screamed. The noises ripped from the throats of wounded men sounded very much alike regardless of which side they fought on or which country they came from. Suffering was a more universal language than Esperanto ever would be.

One of his own cartridge cases bounced off Chaim's boot. He loaded and fired and loaded and fired, now and then ducking automatically when an enemy round cracked past his head. Sanjurjo's men got through the barbed wire with alarming ease. Had they sent out cutting parties the night before? If they had, this attack had been laid on all along; it wasn't mounted on the spur of the moment.

*I can worry about that later—if I'm still around to worry about it,* Chaim thought as he slapped a fresh magazine into his rifle. He started to fumble for his bayonet. Unless he was going trench-raiding himself, he used it for a knife and a tin-opener, not a weapon. But this might turn out to be one of the rare times he was glad to have it.

Then a Republican machine gun opened up on the Fascists. A moment later, so did another one. Now despair filled the shrieks from Sanjurjo's men. They'd braved rifle fire. Nobody, though, could hope to cross open ground in the face of the industrialized murder machine guns personified. Concentrated essence of infantry, someone had called them during the last war. That still seemed a plenty good label.

The Nationalists were recklessly brave (so were the Spaniards who fought on the Republican side). This time, their courage only cost them more casualties. They kept coming for a while after more pragmatic troops would have seen the thing was hopeless.

Some of them got close enough to the Republican trenches to fling grenades into them. A fragment ripped Chaim's baggy trousers. It didn't bite his leg, though, for which he thanked the God in Whom good Marxist-Leninists weren't supposed to believe. He didn't particularly fear dying in battle. Getting badly hurt . . . He didn't know anybody who wasn't scared of that.

At last, sullenly, the Nationalists pulled back. Some more of them got shot before they could reach the protection of their own trenches. Out in the space between the lines, the wounded groaned.

Some of the Abe Lincolns took pot shots at them, as much to shut them up as for any other reason. Part of Chaim thought that was cruel. Part of him hoped somebody would put him out of his misery if he lay there, helpless and suffering, out in no-man's-land.

Then one of the Abe Lincolns' officers said, "Let's bring in some prisoners and see what we can squeeze out of them. You, you, you, you, and you." Chaim was the second of those *yous*, Mike Carroll the third.

"Thanks a bunch," Chaim said. You could bitch about an order, but you couldn't disobey one.

Out he went, keeping his belly on the ground like a serpent. Finding Fascists to bring in wasn't the problem, not this time. Not getting killed bringing them in might be another matter. He'd worry about that when he came to it.

A Nationalist moaned in the next shell hole. Chaim scrambled down into it. "Aw, fuck," he said softly. His stomach did a slow lurch. The guy'd been blown almost in half. Why wasn't he dead? Human beings could be uncommonly hard to kill, yeah, but this was—what was the next step past ridiculous?

His eyes found Chaim's. *"Por favor, Señor Internacionál,"* he said clearly.

*Please, Mr. International.* He could even be polite about it. Chaim wanted to ask if he was sure, but, given the butchered ruin that he was, there couldn't be much doubt about that. "Fuck," Chaim repeated. But he would be doing the guy a favor—there couldn't be any doubt about that, either.

Chaim pulled out his bayonet and did what needed doing. Then he crawled off to find some other wounded Nationalist to haul back for questioning.

BACON AND EGGS and white toast with plenty of butter and marmalade. If that wasn't a breakfast to let you go out and spit in winter's eye, Peggy Druce had never heard of one. She said as much to her husband as she set the plate in front of him.

Herb nodded. "You betcha, babe. Of course, the hot coffee doesn't hurt, either." The plume that rose from his Chesterfield behind the morning's *Philadelphia Inquirer* might have been a smoke signal.

"Want another cup?" Peggy asked.

"Sure do." Herb murmured thanks when Peggy poured it for him. He tucked into his breakfast.

Peggy sat down and ate, too. "What we're putting away would feed a family in Germany for a week," she said. "I don't know when the last time was they saw white bread or eggs or real coffee."

"Breaks my heart." Herb stubbed out the cigarette and lit another one. "We ought to be at war with Hitler, too, same as we were against the Kaiser." He tapped the newspaper with a nicotine-stained forefinger. "What I want to know is, how'd it get to be 1942 already? Like a dope, I wrote '1941' on a check yesterday, and I had to void the darn thing."

"I've done it—not this year yet, but I have," Peggy said. "It's a pain in the keester, is what it is."

"What really frosts my pumpkin is, I'm supposed to be one of FDR's hot-shot efficiency experts, right?" Herb laughed at himself. "Here I can't even remember what year it is, for cryin' out loud. Some efficiency, huh?"

"If you don't tell the people you're dealing with, they'll never know," Peggy said reasonably. "And chances are they've all pulled the same rock one time or another."

"There you go." Herb lowered the *Inquirer* so he could grin at her across the table. "Which one of us is the lawyer? Remind me again."

"One of the girls in the dorm room next to mine at Penn State was from Alabama or Mississippi or somewhere like that. She always pronounced it *liar*."

"She knew what was what, all right." Herb put away the grub as if he were a doughboy shoveling food into his chowlock at a field kitchen in some ruined village in France. He paused to check his wristwatch. "I'm still good."

But even as he said that, he sent Peggy a pointed look, so she ate faster, too. "What time does your train head out? A quarter past nine?" she said.

"That's right." He nodded.

"You're fine, then," Peggy said. "Where are you going this time? Was it Kentucky?"

"Tennessee."

"Oh, yeah." She thumped her forehead with the heel of her hand, annoyed at herself for forgetting. "And who's mucking things up in Tennessee?" Herb had come back from other trips with amazing stories of waste and corruption and stupidity run amok. Anyone who listened to him for a while would be sure the United States couldn't possibly win the war—unless everybody else in the world was just as fouled up. Humanity being what it was, that made a pretty fair bet.

This morning, though, her husband's face closed down tight, as if he sat at a poker table or in a conference room with the other side's attorneys. "Sorry, babe, but I can't talk about that."

"What?" Peggy could hardly believe her ears. "I'm your wife, in case you hadn't noticed. What am I gonna do? Send Hitler a telegram?" She'd spoken to the *Führer* once, when she was marooned in Berlin. To say she had no desire to repeat the experience proved the power of understatement.

"I know, I know. But this is heap big secret—and even that's more than I ought to say about it."

"Some of the other stuff you've told me about was secret, too."

He sighed. "Peggy, I can't talk, not about this stuff. I can't even talk about why I can't talk about it. If they had any way to vacuum out my brains after I finish what I need to do there, they'd use it."

She wasn't going to get any more out of him. She could see as much, even if she couldn't see why. But if he couldn't talk about why he couldn't talk about why things were secret . . . "Would they hang me for a spy if I asked you for one of those cigarettes?"

"They'd have to hang me first." Herb shook the pack till a Chesterfield stuck out. Peggy took it. Herb flicked the wheel on his Zippo. As advertised, a flame shot up the first try.

Peggy leaned forward to get the cigarette going. She sighed out smoke. "That does go nice with food."

"Sure does." Herb smoked another one, too. Then he went upstairs, and came down with his suitcase. He shrugged into his topcoat. Peggy put on a coat, too. The dishes could wait till she got back from dropping him off. He said, "One thing about rationing gasoline—less traffic these days."

"You've got that right," Peggy agreed. Most people's "A" stickers limited them to four gallons a week. You couldn't go very far on that—to work and back every day, if you were lucky. The Druces' Packard got a good deal more fuel; because he was in what the government reckoned an essential occupation, he had one of the rare and coveted "C" stickers.

It was cold but clear. There wouldn't, or shouldn't, be any ice on the roads. Peggy got in on the driver's side. She'd have to bring the car back. As Herb slid in beside her, he said, "Lucky me. I've got myself the best-darn-looking chauffeur in town."

"You!" Peggy said fondly.

The Packard started right away. There went one more worry. Cold weather could do rude things to a battery. If Herb had had to wait till a taxi got here, he really might have missed his train.

She drove downtown, toward Broad Street Station. When she passed an Esso station, she saw a cop checking ration stickers. Herb noticed, too. "Some ways, it hardly seems like a free country any more, does it?" he remarked.

"Oh, it's not so bad. Trust me—it's not." Peggy had seen with her own eyes what things were like in a country that suddenly stopped being free. The grin on that German's face at Marianske Lazny after the Nazis invaded Czechoslovakia in the fall of 1938 . . . He'd been cutting off a Jew's beard with a big pair of shears. If he cut off some cheek or ear at the same time, well, hey, that only made the fun better. He thought so, anyhow, and he had enough rifles and machine guns and tanks on his side that the poor damned Jew had to stand there and take it unless he felt like dying on the spot. She still wondered sometimes what had happened to him.

"If you say so," Herb answered, which meant he didn't think it was worth an argument. He left no doubt where he stood, though: "I don't have to like it, and I darn well don't."

"Neither do I. Who does?" Peggy said. "But things are worse plenty of other places."

She pulled up in front of the station. Herb leaned toward her for a quick good-bye kiss. He got out, pulled his suitcase off the back seat, and lugged it inside. Peggy waited till he disappeared before heading back to the house.

A long sigh escaped her when she pulled into the driveway. It wasn't that she worried he'd go looking for some round-heeled waitress or hat-check girl as soon as he got to whatever super-duper-secret place he was inspecting in Tennessee. It *wasn't*, dammit. But they'd been apart for two years while she was stuck in Europe, and he'd had himself a little fling while she was gone. She'd had her own—*mishap* was probably the best word for it—over there, too.

When things came out, they'd forgiven each other. Peggy meant it when she did it. She was sure Herb was every bit as sincere. But forgiving wasn't quite the same as forgetting. Their marriage wasn't the same as it had been before she sailed for the Continent.

Peggy hadn't the least desire to go to Nevada and get a quickie divorce. Again, she was sure Herb didn't want to, either. It didn't seem like that to her. It was just one more thing the war had wounded. And it was also the reason she fixed herself a stiff highball as soon as she got into the house.

# Chapter 3

Winter on the Barents Sea. There was a handful of words to chill the heart, however you chose to take them. The wind had knives in it, and seemed to take a running start from the North Pole. Waves slapped the U-30, one after another. The submarine rolled, recovered, and rolled again, over and over.

All the same, Lieutenant Julius Lemp was happier to have chugged out of Narvik on patrol than he would have been to stay at the *Kriegsmarine*'s U-boat base in northern Norway any longer. To say his soldiers had worn out their welcome there was to belabor the obvious.

Port authorities thought his crew were a gang of hooligans. His men thought Narvik was as dull as embalming—about the worst thing a liberty port could be. As usual in such arguments, both sides had a point.

The southern sky glowed pink. In a little while, the sun would actually creep over the horizon for a little while. They were well past the solstice now, on the way toward the vernal equinox. Old Sol was heading north again. Darkness didn't reign supreme here all through the day, as it had a little while ago.

But it wouldn't stay light very long. England loved this season of the year. This was the time when convoys bound for Murmansk and Arkhangelsk had the best chance of sneaking past German patrol planes and U-boats from Norway. You couldn't sink or bomb what you couldn't find. Darkness was the freighter's friend.

Another wave, bigger than most, slammed into the U-30 portside. Frigid seawater splashed over the conning tower. Lemp and the ratings up there with him wore oilskins over their peacoats and wide-brimmed waterproof hats strapped under their chins to keep that raw north wind from stealing them. They got wet anyhow. When you got wet in these latitudes, you got cold. No—you got colder.

"*Scheisse!*" Lemp said, most sincerely.

One of the petty officers nodded. "We'll all end up with pneumonia," he predicted, his voice gloomy.

Lemp would have argued, if only he could. The one thing worse than getting splashed up here was going into the drink. You wouldn't last longer than a few minutes before the sea sucked all the warmth from your body and killed you. People said freezing to death was an easy way to go. Lemp didn't want to find out for himself if those people were right.

He tried to clean the salt water off the lenses of his Zeiss binoculars. How were you supposed to look into the distance when everything seemed blurry and smeared? Simple—you couldn't.

"In the summer," the rating said wistfully, "it's daylight all the time."

"And we can see them, and they can see us," Lemp replied. "Downsides to everything. No sneaking away from the destroyers under cover of night then."

Another big wave smacked the U-30. More icy water cascaded over the conning tower. More poured down the hatch, too. As if spawned by the law of equal and opposite reactions, hot language came out of the hatchway. Some of the water would get pumped out of the boat. Some, yes, but not all. Take any U-boat ever made, and she always had water in her bilges. And the water soaked up and redistributed all the manifold stinks that accumulated in a submarine.

Lemp sighed. Spillage from the heads? Puke? Rotting bits of sausage and tinned herring in mustard sauce? The thick animal fug of a boat full of poorly washed seamen? Diesel exhaust? Lubricating oil? They were all there, along with assorted other sordid but not so easily nameable stenches.

Pretty soon, the skipper's watch would end. He'd have to lay below. The air out here was bloody cold, but it was clean and fresh—none cleaner and fresher, in fact. People talked about air like wine. This wasn't wine: it was more like vodka straight out of the icebox, just as chilly, just as smooth, and just as potent.

And then he'd go down the hatch, back into the collection of reeks that put your average city rubbish tip to shame. They said you stopped noticing smells once you were stuck in them for a while. They said all kinds of things. Some of them were true. Some were crap. You might not smell the interior of a U-boat so much after a while, but you never had any doubts about where you were, even if you woke up with your eyes still shut.

Every time the boat came in from a patrol, it got cleaned up along with refueling and taking on fresh eels to shoot at enemy shipping and food both fresh and canned. Thanks to the bilgewater, though, getting rid of the stinks was and always would be a losing fight. The only way to do the trick would be to melt the submarine down to raw steel and start over. Even then, cleanliness would last only until the first clumsy sailor spilled something into the bilges.

In due course, Gerhart Beilharz emerged from the smelly steel tube. "I relieve you, Skipper," the engineering officer said. He smiled broadly as he inhaled. "My turn to breathe the good stuff for a while."

"Well, so it is. Enjoy it," Lemp said. "You get to take off your *Stahlhelm,* too."

Beilharz's grin got wider yet. "I sure do!" He was two meters tall. He didn't fit well into a U-boat's cramped confines. Men shorter than he was banged their noggins on overhead pipes and valves and spigots.

With a sigh, Julius Lemp descended. It was twilight outside, and twilight in the pressure hull as well. The bulbs in here were dim and orange, to help keep light from leaking out when the hatches were open at night. And the smell was . . . what it was. It didn't make Lemp's stomach want to turn over, the way it did with some men.

"Beast behaving, Paul?" he asked the helmsman.

"No worries, Skipper," the senior rating said.

"Good. That's what I want to hear," Lemp said. If Paul wasn't worried, there was nothing to worry about.

Lemp's tiny cabin held—barely—a desk, a steel chair, a cot, and the safe where he stashed codebooks and other secure publications. That made it far and away the roomiest accommodation on the boat. With the canvas curtain pulled shut, he had as much privacy as anyone here could: which is to say, not a great deal.

He filled his fountain pen and wrote in the log. His script was small, even cramped, and very precise. There wasn't a lot to record: course, speed, fuel consumed. No ships or airplanes sighted, either from his own side or the enemy. No disciplinary problems among his men, either, nor had there been since the patrol began. The crew weren't rowdies while on the job, and they weren't especially rowdy in any port even halfway equipped to show off-duty sailors a good time.

Would any of that matter to his superiors? The U-30's sailors had torn Narvik to pieces twice now. Things wouldn't go well for them if they tried it a third time. And they were liable to, as Lemp knew full well.

He could listen to what went on in the boat without drawing notice to himself: another advantage of the curtain. Even when he couldn't make out conversations, he could pick up tone. Everything sounded the way it should. If the men were plotting anything, they were doing it out of his earshot—and there weren't many places out of his earshot in the U-boat.

After Lieutenant Beilharz came off his watch, he paused outside the tiny cabin and said, "Talk to you for a minute or two, Skipper?"

"Sure. Come on in," Lemp answered.

Beilharz did, ducking under the curtain rod. He had the *Stahlhelm* on again. Lemp waved for him to sit down on the cot. Had something gone wrong with the *Schnorkel*? They were surfaced in the gloom, so they didn't need the gadget now. But when Beilharz spoke in a low voice, what he said had nothing to do with his specialty: "Sir, what do we do when the politics start boiling over again?"

That wasn't what Lemp wanted to hear, even if it was a damn good question. Plenty of high-ranking officers couldn't be happy to watch the *Reich* pulled into a full-scale war on two fronts. Some of them had already tried more than once to overthrow the *Führer*. The ones who had were mostly dead now, which might not stop their successors from taking another shot at it.

"Best thing we can do," Lemp said slowly, "is hope we're out on patrol when the boiling starts."

"*Ja*," Beilharz agreed. "But if we're not?"

Now Lemp spoke as firmly as he could: "I'm not going to borrow trouble. I'm going to do my job for the *Reich*. You do the same. Now get the hell out of here."

Gerhart Beilharz got. Lemp took a bottle of schnapps out of his desk and swallowed a good slug. He didn't think Beilharz was trying to trap him into saying anything disloyal about the *Reich*'s current leader. He didn't think so, no, but he couldn't be sure. After a moment, he tilted the bottle back again.

"LOOK OUT, YOU LUG. Here comes the Chimp." Several soldiers made dice and rubles disappear as if they'd never existed.

Ivan Kuchkov wasn't sure which one of them had used the nickname he hated so much. The sergeant hated it not least because it fit so well. He was short and squat and dark and hairy. Nobody would ever call him handsome. But he could break most men in half, and he wasn't shy about brawling. They must have figured he couldn't hear them.

He didn't want to tear into all of them at once. Well, part of him did, but he knew it wasn't a good idea. He wasn't worried about losing; that never crossed his mind. But he might get into trouble for leaving a fair part of his section unfit to fight the Fascists.

"Come on, you needle dicks," he growled. "We're supposed to go out and check what those Nazi cocksuckers are up to."

"All of us?" one of them yipped in dismay.

"Every fucking one," Kuchkov said. He raised his voice: "Sasha! Where are you hiding your clapped-out cunt?"

"I'm here, Comrade Sergeant." Sasha Davidov seemed to appear out of thin air. The skinny little Jew had a knack for that, as he did for most forms of self-preservation.

"Good. You take point. I'm leading these bitches out on patrol." His wave encompassed the dejected gamblers. He didn't have anything in particular against Davidov for being a Christ-killing kike. No—he really wanted him along, because Sasha was far and away the best point man in the company, probably in the regiment. With him out front, they all had a better chance to come back in one piece.

It was cold. The Ukraine didn't get as cold as Russia did (Kuchkov thought with a sort of masochistic patriotism), but it got plenty cold enough. Snow crunched under Kuchkov's *valenki*. He wore a snow smock over his greatcoat, and a whitewashed helmet. His mittens had slits through which he could fire his PPD-34 submachine gun at need. He held the slits closed when he didn't need them.

The Germans, of course, would be similarly swaddled. If his patrol ran into one of theirs, things could get interesting fast, depending on who first figured out the other bunch of sad, sorry, shivering assholes belonged to the wrong side. And, of course, there were the Ukrainians, who had trouble deciding whether they hated Stalin worse than Hitler or the other way round.

Artillery rumbled off to the west. Kuchkov cocked his head to one side, listening. Yes, those were Hitlerite 105s. The shells thudded down somewhere not close enough to worry about. A few minutes later, Red Army cannon answered. "Ha!" Kuchkov said. "Let the butchers blow the balls off each other." He hated big guns. What infantryman didn't? You hardly ever got the chance to shoot artillerymen, but they had all kinds of chances at you.

Kuchkov had started the war as a bombardier. He'd dropped plenty on the damned gunners' heads. The bastards had their revenge on him, though: they shot him down. He'd literally parachuted into the Red Army.

He tried to look every which way at once. You never could tell where the goddamn Germans would pop up. They weren't as good as Russians, or even Ukrainians, when it came to coping with winters in these parts, but they were getting better. The ones who couldn't learn got shallow graves marked by helmets hung on bayoneted rifles. Red Army men desecrated those graves whenever they ran the Fascists back a few kilometers.

"*Gruk! Gruk! Gruk!*" It was only a raven, flying along looking for dead soldiers who hadn't got buried yet. All the Soviet soldiers aimed their weapons at it, then sheepishly lowered them once more.

Sasha shook his head. "Anything moves, anything makes a noise, I want to kill it. If I live through the stinking war, I'll be ruined as a civilian. Any time somebody drops a plate, I'll dive under the table."

He must've had a wide streak of that before the war started. He wouldn't have made such a good point man if he hadn't. "You *don't* shoot any fucking thing that moves, you *don't* dive for cover when anybody farts, you won't need to worry about living through this cunt of a war," Kuchkov said. He was surprised he'd lasted as long as he had.

They tramped on. It started to snow, which cut visibility. Kuchkov hung on tight to his submachine gun. If they stumbled over the Nazis, he'd need to spray death around as fast as he could. The rest of the guys in the patrol, except for Davidov, carried rifles. A rifle could kill people out much farther than a PPD could. But so what, when you had to trip over the Hitlerites before you know they were there?

The wind blew harder. The noise it made would also mask approaching enemies. Ivan had to remind himself it would also mask his approach from the Germans.

Sasha Davidov suddenly stopped short. He waved one mittened hand behind him, so no one in the direction he was going could see the motion. Then he flattened out in the snow.

Kuchkov flopped down, too. He was on his belly before he had any notion how he'd got there. The other Red Army men went down, too. They might have been a fraction slower, but no more than a fraction. The really slow fools, the really stupid ones, died fast. Kuchkov had never heard of Charles Darwin, which didn't mean natural selection failed to operate on the battlefield.

For several breaths, Kuchkov saw nothing through the swirling snow. Was Sasha imagining shit again? Every so often, he did. It was the price you paid for having somebody out front who wouldn't miss any of the trouble that really was there.

But no. It wasn't imaginary this time. Out of the snow came a Nazi patrol. They were close enough that Kuchkov had no doubt who they were. Their helmets might be whitewashed, but no one would ever mistake one of those coal scuttles for a Red Army pot. The Fritzes even walked differently from Russians. Ivan couldn't have said how, but they did.

The wind blew their words his way. German was just ugly noise to him. The Russian word for Germans, *Nemtsi*, meant something like *babblers*. But their tone was the same as his would have been: halfway between resigned and nervous. They peered around, looking for Red Army men . . . but not spotting any.

Pilots always said the trick in aerial combat was getting close before you opened up. Then you couldn't miss, and the other bastard never had a prayer. It didn't always work like that on the ground. You had to respect machine guns. Try and close with them and you'd end up dinner for crows and foxes. Here, though . . .

Kuchkov's PPD already pointed in the right direction. He squeezed off a short burst, then another and another. The PPD pulled high and to the right if you just let it rip. The other Russian soldiers opened up, too.

Down went the Fritzes, tumbling like ninepins. Their dying shrieks rang through the stuttering thunder of gunfire. One of the Germans wasn't dead, though. He'd lain down in the snow and was shooting back. Finely machined Schmeissers didn't always like the cold. They'd freeze up when a German needed them most. Not this one, though. Maybe the guy used Russian gun oil.

Whatever he used, it didn't help him long. The Red Army soldiers spread out and went after him, staying as low as they could. He soon lay bleeding and lifeless like his buddies.

Sasha looked worriedly toward the west. Would the racket from the firefight draw more Nazis? Kuchkov was worried about that, too, but he also had other things on his mind. He bent down by a dead Fritz and fumbled through his belt pouches. "Fuck me!" he said in delight. The German had not one, not two, but three tinfoil tubes of liver paste—the best damn ration anybody's army issued. Kuchkov shoved them into a greatcoat pocket. The other Russians plundered the rest of the corpses. Then the patrol moved out again.

**ANASTAS MOURADIAN AND ISA MOGAMEDOV** eyed each other in what would have been loathing if they'd had the nerve to show it. "Well, well," Mouradian said in Russian. "Someone in the personnel office is having a little joke on us."

"Very likely, Comrade Pilot," his new copilot and bomb-aimer agreed in the same language. "Or else a sergeant with too much to do grabbed the first cards that came up . . . and here we are."

"Here we are, all right," Stas agreed dryly. Speaking Russian helped ease things a little. It was also the only language an Armenian and an Azeri were likely to have in common.

Armenians had lived in Armenia forever, or as near as made no difference. Azeris had lived next door to them—and occasionally (or sometimes not so occasionally) tried to overrun them—for the past 900 years or so. They used different tongues. They followed different faiths. Given a choice, Mouradian and Mogamedov would either have icily ignored each other or gone for each other's throats.

They got no choice. Brute Soviet force overrode their petty nationalisms, their different religions, their different tongues. They would work together—or the KGB would make them both sorrier than either could hope to make the other. That wasn't exactly the way Stalin's New Soviet Men were supposed to be forged, which wasn't to say it didn't work.

Of course, Stalin was a Georgian. Beria, who ran the KGB, was a Mingrelian. They both sprang from the Caucasus themselves. They understood the local feuds as no Russians—onlookers from outside—could ever hope to do. They understood the force required to supersede them. They understood . . . and they used it.

If a Red Air Force Pe-2 had an Armenian in one cockpit chair and an Azeri in the other, their superiors might indeed think it was funny, but wouldn't care past that—unless the two men in the cockpit showed they couldn't fight the Nazis. That, their superiors would care about. And Mouradian and Mogamedov would both regret making them care.

Business, then. In the air, they would have to try to keep each other (and their bombardier, a bad-tempered Russian sergeant named Fyodor Mechnikov) alive. On the ground . . . On the ground, Stas intended to have as little to do with his new crewman as he could.

"How much experience in the plane have you had?" he asked now.

"Fifteen missions," Mogamedov answered. "A 109 shot us down. I managed to get out. My pilot stopped a 20mm with his face."

"Something like that happened to me, too, when I was in an old SB-2," Mouradian said. "I'm surprised they didn't give you a plane of your own."

The other flyer shrugged. He was a little swarthier than Mouradian, his eyes a little narrower. To a Russian, all men from the Caucasus looked alike: in their charming way, the Russians labeled them black-asses. Men who were from the Caucasus knew better, not that Russians bothered to listen to them. "They put me in with you instead, Comrade Pilot," Mogamedov said, and not another word.

More words would have been wasted anyhow. Mouradian did waste a few: "We'll do our damnedest to give the Nazis grief, then." He wanted to sound loyal—and to be heard to sound loyal.

"*Da*," Mogamedov agreed. Mouradian needed a new copilot because his old one, Ivan Kulkaanen, had been rash enough to intimate that the USSR wasn't running the war so well as it might have. He'd tried to run when the Chekists came after him. He was a Karelian. He knew everything there was to know about snow. The secret police hunted him down anyway.

Right now, the new Caucasian cockpit crew wasn't going anywhere. Snow blanketed the airstrip. The clouds that dropped it weren't much higher than the treetops. Flying would have been suicidal. Such details didn't always stop the men with the fancy rank marks on their sleeves. Today, they sufficed.

Mouradian got a glass of tea and some bread and sausage in the officers' tent the next morning. When a bottle came along, he swigged before he passed it. He didn't drink like a Russian—he had but one liver to give for his country—but he drank. In weather like this, vodka made good antifreeze. It also helped you not notice the long, dull hours crawling by.

Lieutenant Mogamedov ducked into the tent not long after he did. The Azeri made a beeline for the samovar. As he gulped hot, sweet tea, he shivered theatrically. "Cold out there!"

Azeri and Armenian *could* agree on something. The Russian and

Ukrainian flyers who made up the majority only hooted at a southerner's discomfort. They started telling stories about really cold weather. Stas had flown against the Japanese in Siberia. He'd been through plenty worse than this himself. That didn't mean he enjoyed it.

Mogamedov tore at the coarse black bread with his teeth. He ignored the sausage. Stas realized after a minute that the cheap, fatty stuff was bound to be mostly pork. His new copilot didn't drink any of the free-flowing vodka, either.

That was interesting. Mogamedov might not be a pious Muslim— you couldn't very well be a pious anything and a New Soviet Man at the same time—but he didn't go out of the way to flout the tenets of his ancestral faith.

*If I want to, chances are I can use that against him,* Stas thought. All he had to do was whisper in an informer's ear, and Mogamedov would find Chekists crawling over him like lice. And all Stas had to do after that was look at himself in the mirror for the rest of his life.

One of his bristly eyebrows quirked. If only he didn't despise people who did such things. But he did. He knew exactly what he thought of people who sold out their friends and neighbors and acquaintances so they could move up themselves. No Russian, not even the filthiest *mat*, could describe the blackness of such treachery. For that, you needed Armenian.

Proof of how strongly he felt about it was that he wouldn't give an Azeri to the KGB. If Mogamedov did himself in by avoiding pork and alcohol, then he did. Stas wouldn't be especially sorry. But he wouldn't grease the skids—even with lard.

That thought, perhaps aided by the vodka he'd knocked back, made him chuckle to himself. Isa Mogamedov noticed. Unlike most of the men eating breakfast, he wasn't drinking part of it, so he noticed things they might have missed. "What's funny, Comrade Pilot?"

"I was just remembering a joke somebody told me," Mouradian answered—a lie, but a polite lie.

But the Russian sitting next to him gave him a nudge and said, "Well, tell it, then. I could use a laugh." By his slurred speech, he'd drunk more of his breakfast than Stas had.

Mouradian couldn't even shoot him a resentful look. Mogamedov might notice that, too. Instead, he really had to remember a joke, and he had to come out with it. He chose a long, complicated story about a pretty girl in Moscow who wanted to record a message for her grandmother in far-off Irkutsk but couldn't afford it, and about the lecherous fellow who ran the recording shop and saw a chance to take it out in trade. "So there she is, on her knees in front of him, holding it"—Stas illustrated with appropriate lewd gestures—"and he says, 'Well? Go ahead!' And she leans forward, and she says, 'Hello? Granny?'"

The Russian officer bellowed laughter. Tears leaked from the corners of his eyes. "That's good! *Bozhemoi,* that's good!" he spluttered, and laughed some more.

Mogamedov laughed, too, even if not quite so much. Everybody who'd listened laughed. You couldn't hear that joke without laughing— at least, Stas had never run into anybody who could.

Another vodka bottle came around. He swigged from it. No, vodka wasn't against his religion, even if he'd drunk wine more often before the Red Air Force pulled him out of Armenia. Wine tasted good, too. As far as he could see, vodka had only one purpose: knocking you on your ass. The stuff was damn good at it, too. He offered the bottle to the Russian who'd made him come up with the joke.

That worthy poured it down as if he never expected to see any more. He almost emptied the bottle. The guy beside him did kill it. Others were going round, though. Before long, one got to Isa Mogamedov. Polite as a cat, he passed it on. "More for the rest of us!" said the Russian he gave it to. That got almost as big a laugh as Stas' joke.


THEO HOSSBACH WAS a curiosity in the *Wehrmacht:* a panzer radioman who didn't like to talk. He doled out words as if somebody were charging him a half a Reichsmark for each and every one. The radioman in a Panzer III sat next to the driver, and also handled the bow machine gun. Theo'd liked his place in the old Panzer II better. He'd been in back of the turret, and most of the time nobody bothered him at all.

Only one problem there: the Panzer II was well on the way from obsolescent to obsolete. Its armor was useless against anything more than small-arms fire, while its 20mm main armament could pop away from now till doomsday without doing anything a KV-1 or a T-34 would notice. Panzer IIs soldiered on in the east. They still made decent reconnaissance vehicles—they could go places armored cars couldn't—but they weren't fighting panzers any more.

For that matter, a Panzer III's 37mm gun was only a door-knocker against a KV-1's or a T-34's front armor. It did have a chance of punching through their steel sides or into the engine. But German panzers were badly outgunned these days.

In weather like this, just getting German panzers to run was an adventure. The winter before, the *Panzertruppen* had often kept fires going through the night under their machines' engine compartments so they'd start up in the morning. The extra-strength antifreeze and winter lubricants were better this year. All the same, everybody who wore the black coveralls and death's-head panzer emblem envied the T-34's diesel motor. It seemed immune to cold and snow and ice.

Somewhere up ahead lay victory, if they could find it. Across the radio set from Theo, Adi Stoss grinned cynically. "Next stop Smolensk, right?" the driver said.

"Right," Theo said: fifty pfennigs expended. Adi's grin got wider, but no less cynical. The summer's campaign had been aimed at Smolensk, the great fortress on the road to Moscow. It wasn't summer any more. It wasn't 1941 any more, either. Smolensk was still in Russian hands.

The Panzer III clattered across the snowy landscape. *Ostketten*—wide tracks made for the mud and snow in these parts—helped it keep going. Even with *Ostketten*, it couldn't match a T-34's cross-country performance.

Other panzers advanced alongside Theo's. *Landsers* accompanied them on foot and in armored personnel carriers. Those were nice machines. They took infantry to where it needed to fight and kept it from getting killed on the way . . . unless, of course, something really nasty happened, which it always could. The personnel carriers also let infantry keep up with the panzers, always a problem. They would have done even better had the *Reich* had more of them.

Everything would have been better had the *Reich* had more of it. Sitting up here, Theo could see out. He missed his iron nest in the Panzer II. Seeing out, he was forcibly reminded how vast this country was.

It made even the *Wehrmacht* seem undersized and overstretched. You overran villages and towns. You shelled and machine-gunned the Ivans who tried to stop you. You went on. And what lay ahead? Always more villages and towns. Always more Ivans, too.

Somewhere up ahead here—probably not very far up ahead, either—more Russians waited. Theo cherished every moment of peace and relative quiet. He knew how precious such moments were.

Hermann Witt's voice came out of the speaking tube from the turret: "Panzer halt!"

"Halting," Adi said, and hit the brakes. "What's up?" he added. "I don't see anything."

Peering through his vision slits, Theo didn't see anything, either. It didn't prove much, not when he had little chance of seeing things while restricted by the slits. Like any good panzer commander, Sergeant Witt rode with head and shoulders out of the turret when bullets weren't flying, and sometimes even when they were. Somebody in the panzer needed a good view of the wider world.

"I'm not quite sure," Witt answered. "But take a look over about two o'clock. Something's not right there." As if to underscore the words, he traversed the turret, presumably toward two o'clock. Through the rumble of the idling engine, Theo heard him tell Lothar Eckhardt, "Give it a round of HE there."

Theo still didn't see anything funny. "One round of HE," the gunner agreed. The main armament bellowed. Inside the panzer, the noise wasn't too bad. The cartridge case clattered down onto the bottom of the fighting compartment. The harsh, familiar stink of smokeless powder made Theo cough.

The 37mm shell burst in what seemed no more than the middle of a snowdrift—till it came in. Then everything happened at once. How many Russians, how many panzers, had sheltered behind that tall, concealing drift? They all boiled out now, and they were spoiling for a fight.

"Get moving, Adi!" Hermann Witt yelled.

Adi was already gunning the Panzer III. He knew as well as Witt that you didn't want to be a sitting duck for a T-34. (Theo didn't want to be anywhere within a hundred kilometers of a T-34, but that was a different story.) The Soviet panzer's big drawback was that the commander also served as gunner—the French made the same mistake. That left the poor bastard as busy as a one-armed paper hanger with hives. Most Russians weren't good shots, either.

But T-34s carried 76mm cannon. If a round hit you, it was going to kill you. You didn't want to give those overworked, poorly trained sons of bitches a good shot at you.

A rifle bullet spanged off the panzer. The Russian infantry could shoot from now till doomsday without hurting it, but they were trouble for the *Landsers* with the German armor. Theo sprayed fire from his MG-34. He wasn't aiming at anyone in particular. As long as he made the Red Army men dive into the snow, he'd be happy. If he did let the air out of one or two of them, he'd be overjoyed.

"Panzer halt!" Witt ordered. Even as Adi Stoss braked, the panzer commander spoke to the loader: "Armor-piercing this time."

"AP. Right," Kurt Poske said, and slammed a shell with a black tip into the breech.

No more than a second and a half later, Eckhardt fired. Everybody in the Panzer III screamed "Hit!" at the same time. But the AP round glanced off the T-34's cleverly sloped armor. It didn't get through. And the enemy monster's Big Bertha of a gun swung toward them.

This time, Adi goosed the panzer without waiting for orders. Maybe that threw the Ivan's aim off just enough. Theo got to watch that big gun belch flame and smoke. He braced himself, as if bracing would do any good. He didn't know where the enemy round hit. He did know it didn't slam through the Panzer III's frontal armor—or through him. As long as he knew that, nothing else mattered.

"Panzer halt!" Hermann Witt ordered again. Adi swore, but obeyed. The 37mm roared twice in quick succession. The first round bounced off like the one before it. The second buried itself almost to the drive bands, but didn't get through. "Forward!" Witt yelled again.

Forward Adi went. When would Ivan take another shot at them? Yes, he had to do it all himself, but . . . An AP round from some other German panzer got through his side armor. His ammunition store went up, blowing an enormous, perfect smoke ring out the turret hatch.

Adi let out a war whoop. He sounded like an Indian himself, even if that was what German soldiers called their foes. Then he said, "It's nice to have friends."

"*Ja*," Theo agreed, and said not another word. A raised eyebrow and a small tilt of the head did his talking for him.

Even in the gloomy confines of the panzer, he could watch Adi redden. The driver would never have a lot of friends, and would of necessity trust the ones he did have with his life. Every panzer man did that to a degree, of course, but Adi's degree was bigger than most. "You know what I mean," he muttered.

Theo nodded. He didn't need to spend any speech on that. He peered through the machine gun's sight. It didn't look as if any of the Russian panzer crew had managed to bail out. He knew a moment's sympathy for the poor damned Ivans, though he would have done his best to cut them down had they escaped. He'd had to flee two wrecked panzers, and all he'd lost on account of it was half a finger off his left hand. That was luck, too, nothing else but.

# Chapter 4

Sarah Bruck was out shopping when the air-raid sirens in Münster began to wail. It was late afternoon, with clouds overhead and the light already leaking out of the sky. Jews couldn't go out any earlier. They had to wait till all the Aryans had picked over what little there was to buy.

All the same, she cocked her head to one side in surprise. Enemy bombers hadn't come over Münster by day before, even if this wasn't much in the way of daylight. She thought it was a drill till she heard the deep throb of airplane engines overhead. People around her started running.

She would have run, too, had she had anywhere to go. Behind her, someone yelled, "Head for the shelter, you *Dummkopf!*" in a loud, authoritative voice.

Her hair was a light brown, almost but not quite blond. She didn't look particularly Jewish. When she whirled, she saw a policeman pointing with his nightstick.

He opened his mouth to shout again. Then *he* saw the yellow six-pointed star on her shabby coat. "Oh," he said, and dashed for the nearest shelter himself.

"*Scheisse*," Sarah muttered. Jews weren't allowed in air-raid shelters. Those were reserved for citizens of the *Reich*, and Jews were at best grudgingly permitted residents. Here, she was like the dead atheist: all dressed up with nowhere to go.

She wasn't an atheist, though she wondered why not more and more with each miserable passing day. She wished she weren't so far from her husband's family's bakery. But the grocery store across the street from them had taken a bomb, so she had to go far afield for cabbage and beets to eat along with the bread the Brucks turned out.

Atheist or not, though, she was liable to end up dead. Bombs whistled down. She ran into the closest shop. It sold sewing accessories. Right this minute, it was empty but for her. The Aryans who ran it were down in a cellar somewhere. She couldn't join them. She lay down behind the counter, hoping it would give her a little shelter from bomb fragments. She didn't need to worry about flying glass. The plate glass in the window out front was gone, replaced by wood and cardboard. A thief could break in any time—not that there was much to steal inside.

Bombs started bursting. Münster lay close to the border with France. Sarah supposed French planes would have an easy time getting here now that their homeland was at war with Germany once more.

It was a strange business. Sarah had better reason to hate the *Reich* than she did with England or France. She wished something horrible would happen to Hitler, and she hardly cared what. But Hitler was safe— she presumed he was safe—in Berlin, and his enemies were liable to kill her here. It hardly seemed fair.

*Crump! Crump!* The ground shook. Antiaircraft guns hammered, though they had to be firing by ear, not by eye. The ground shook again, seriously this time, at an explosion bigger than any mere bomb. Maybe a Messerschmitt up there had shot down a bomber, and its whole load went up when it smashed to earth.

She couldn't root for some German fighter pilot. But she also couldn't cheer for flyers raining death and destruction on her city. Instead of rooting or cheering for anyone, she huddled there and hoped she'd stay alive.

Back at the bakery, Isidor and his father and mother would be doing the same thing. So would her mother, at the house where she and her brother had grown up. Her father—once a professor of classics and ancient history at the university, now a surprisingly proud member of a labor gang—would have scrambled for whatever shelter he could find, the same way she had. If he weren't a wounded veteran from the last war, he wouldn't have been even so fortunate as he was.

When this war started, Samuel Goldman had tried to rejoin the *Wehrmacht* even if he did limp, even if he was a Jew. So had young, athletic Saul, a footballer of professional quality—again, even if he was a Jew. The recruiters wouldn't take either of them; the law forbade it.

Saul wound up in the *Wehrmacht* anyhow. He'd somehow managed to get false papers while on the run after smashing in his sadistic labor-gang boss' head with a shovel. Sarah thought that was a fine joke on the Nazis. And even if Saul was fighting the Russians in the East, he had to be safer than he would be in the *Reich*.

The air raid didn't last long—no more than fifteen minutes. Sarah wouldn't have wanted to linger above a well-defended city during the day, either. The French or English bombers buzzed away to the west. Sarah climbed to her feet and dusted herself off.

She scurried out of the shop ahead of the all clear. To her relief, she got away before the owner emerged from a bomb shelter. Someone seeing a Jew coming out was all too likely to assume she'd gone in to steal while the place was deserted. People did that during air raids. A Jew, of course, would never get the benefit of the doubt.

No point going after groceries now. Along with the burbling wail of the all-clear signal, fire-engine bells clanged. Smoke rose in half a dozen places. Hearing the fire engines' motors—hearing any motors—seemed odd. Fire engines, an ambulance, doctors' cars: those were the only civilian vehicles still on the streets.

Sarah dithered for a moment. She was closer to the house where she'd grown up than she was to the bakery. Should she go make sure her mother was all right? She didn't see any smoke coming up from that direction. That made her decide to go back to her husband and his folks. She'd check on her own parents later.

An electric tram rattled past. Sarah kept walking, though it was going her way. In its wisdom and mercy, the *Reich* had declared public transport *verboten* to Jews.

The tram stopped short. A bomb had burst in the middle of the street. The Aryan passengers would have to hoof it just like her. The crater was five meters wide and at least two deep. Water from a burst main rapidly turned it into a pond. The blast had blown out the fronts of several shops. A gray-haired man in a leather apron stood on the battered sidewalk in front of his ruined place of business. What would he do now? By the way his head shook like a metronome, he hadn't the least idea.

On Sarah went. A fire crew sprayed water on a burning building. Perhaps thanks to the smashed main, they didn't have much water to spray. All they could do was try to keep the flames from spreading. They swore fierce, guttural oaths. Sarah admired the splendid profanity.

She'd thought of the ambulance a few minutes earlier. Its bell clanged on a note different from the fire engines'. A big splash of red against a wall said somebody hadn't made it to any kind of shelter before the bombs fell. Whoever he was, he was unlikely to need an ambulance now—or ever again. Except for the blood, there was no sign of whoever'd got in the way of that bomb.

No smoke rose from the bakery. All the same, Sarah stopped short when she rounded the last corner. There was another new pond in the street right in front of the place, with water slopping out and pouring down the uncratered pavement. And the building . . . The building had fallen in on itself.

"No," Sarah whispered, as if God could or would run the film of the world in reverse till this unhappened.

People were already attacking the wreckage with spades and with their bare hands. Not all of them were Jews, either. Germans could be decent. You just couldn't count on them to act like that. Sarah ran forward to do what she could.

A man with a white mustache gaped at her. "You're not in there," he said foolishly.

"I was shopping." Absurdly, Sarah felt guilty because she wasn't buried by bricks and beams.

"Lucky you." The man with the mustache lived half a block down.

Right this minute, she couldn't remember his name to save her life. She had bigger things to worry about. She dug through the wreckage like a badger.

"Here's one of them," another old man said. After a moment, with rough kindness, he added, "Well, he never would've known what hit him, anyway, poor bastard."

That had to be David Bruck. Except, as the rescuers pulled the body free of the rubble, it wasn't. It was Isidor. Someone draped a cloth over him, but not before Sarah saw how the left side of his head was all smashed in. The man who'd found him was right. That would have killed him right away.

Sarah made a half-choked noise, then started to cry. Within a couple of minutes, the would-be rescuers also found David and Deborah Bruck. They were dead, too. "It's a shame, girlie," the man with the white mustache said, offering Sarah a none-too-clean handkerchief so she could blow her nose. "They might've been Yids, but they were nice folks." A Jew in Germany was unlikely to win a better epitaph.

"What'll she do now?" a woman asked, and then aimed the question right at her: "What'll you do now, dearie?"

"I don't know." Sarah was just getting used to being a wife. Now, all of a sudden, she found herself a widow. "I don't have any idea. What *can* I do?" It was Hitler's war, and he wouldn't let Jews fight in it. It reached out and killed them just the same.


SERGEANT HIDEKI FUJITA swaggered through the streets of Myitkyina. He was in town on a pass, and drunk as a lord. There were things a member of Unit 113 wasn't allowed to talk about, no matter how drunk he got. That didn't worry Fujita. It hadn't worried him before he poured down a big skinful of the local rotgut, either. Germ warfare wasn't the kind of thing you wanted to sit down and gab about, not if you were in your right mind it wasn't.

Sooner or later, he'd queue up at an enlisted men's brothel and get the lead out of his pencil. That was an important reason to come into town, after all. But he wasn't ready yet. He had more drinking to do first.

He wasn't the only Japanese soldier wandering the Burmese town:

nowhere close. He kept an eye out for his countrymen. No matter how drunk he got, there was no excuse for not saluting an officer. No excuse. Ever. If you didn't show proper respect, you'd catch hell. In the Japanese Army, that was as much a law of nature as sunrise every morning.

He kept an eye on the Burmese, too. They looked like a pack of damned foreigners. They *were* a pack of damned foreigners. They were too skinny. They were browner than Japanese—not a lot, but enough to notice. Their features were softer than those of his countrymen. Their language sounded like barking dogs to him. It was even uglier than Chinese.

And he had other reasons for keeping an eye on them. Japan was running Burma at the moment because she'd chased out England, which had been running the place till the Japanese arrived. Some Burmese kissed their new overlords' feet, glad the white men were on the run. Others, though . . . Well, some slaves would always stay loyal to their old masters.

For the English still lingered in India, not far enough to the west. And they did their best to aid the Chinese bandits who went on struggling against the Japanese drive to shake some order into their miserable country.

That was why Unit 113 was in business. Cholera and the plague had broken out in Yunnan Province. Thousands, maybe tens of thousands, had died on account of the diseases. Let the English try to bring matériel into China from India. What good would it do them if the Chinese who were supposed to unload the guns and munitions were dead or sick or fled to escape pestilence? Not much.

A faded mug of beer on a sign outside a tavern made Fujita walk in. The place had started life as an imitation—no doubt a wretched imitation—of an English pub. It was dark and gloomy inside. The furniture was heavier than anything a Japanese would have made. There was a dartboard on the wall. Behind the bar hung a portrait of the Emperor of Japan in military uniform. Fujita would have bet everything he owned (not much at the moment, but even so) a picture of the King of England had hung there till Myitkyina suddenly changed ownership.

The bartender was Burmese. He'd learned enough of Japanese customs to bow to Fujita as the sergeant approached. Fujita nodded back, superior to inferior. "*Biru*," he said gruffly.

"*Hai.*" The man behind the bar bowed again. He set a bottle of beer and a pint mug—another survival of the vanished English—in front of Fujita. Then he pointed to a price list the noncom hadn't noticed. It was written in Japanese, and was bound to be as new as the photo of Hirohito.

Fujita pulled occupation money out of his pocket. He paid hardly any attention to how much he slapped down. Anna and rupees were fine for the Burmese. They meant nothing to him. Japan still did business in sen and yen.

As the bartender made the paper disappear, Fujita poured the pint full. He drank. It wasn't great beer, or even good beer. He hadn't expected anything different. Where would you get good beer in a third-rate colonial town in the middle of a war? This would keep him drunk and eventually make him drunker. He wasn't worried about much else.

He got to the bottom of the pint in three long pulls. "Fill me up again," he told the bartender.

"*Nan desu-ka?*" the Burmese said, sudden apprehension in his voice. "*Wakarimasen, gomen nasai.*" *What? I don't understand, excuse me.*

"Another. Give me another beer." Fujita spoke slowly and clearly. You had to make some allowance for stupid foreigners.

"Ah! *Hai!*" The barkeep bowed in relief. He got that, all right. Another beer appeared as if by magic. Fujita paid for it. He suspected he could have got away with just taking it after he'd scared the native. But it wasn't worth fussing about. If he'd been paying with real money instead of this meaningless stuff, it might have been. In occupation cash, though, even a miserably paid Japanese sergeant could play the rich man.

He sat down at an empty table. A couple of other sergeants were boozing at the one next to it. They owlishly eyed his collar tabs to see whether he was safe to associate with. They must have decided he was, because one of them nodded and said, "Come join us if you want to."

"*Arigato.*" Fujita got up and walked over. He gave his name. One of the other noncoms was called Suzuki; the second was named Ono. Fujita lifted his mug of beer. "*Kampai!*"

"*Kampai!*" They both echoed the toast and drank. Sergeant Suzuki was squat and looked strong. Sergeant Ono was thinner and quieter;

Fujita guessed he was clever, at least when he wasn't drinking. Right now, Ono and Suzuki had quite a start on him. He decided he needed to catch up.

After a while, Ono remarked, "Haven't seen you around here before, I don't think."

"Probably not," Fujita said. "My unit isn't based in Myitkyina. I just managed to snag some leave."

"Ah?" Sergeant Suzuki said. "Which unit is that? Where are you stationed?"

Fujita sat there and didn't answer. Unit 113 not only didn't advertise what it did, it didn't advertise its existence. He was already starting to feel his beer, but he knew better than to run his big mouth.

Suzuki scowled. "I asked you a question," he said, and started to get to his feet. *And I'll knock the crap out of you if you don't tell me,* that meant.

He was welcome to try. Fujita started to stand, too. He wasn't scrawny himself, and he figured he knew how to take care of himself. The pub might get knocked around, but that wasn't his worry.

But Sergeant Ono put a hand on his drinking buddy's arm. "Take it easy, Suzuki-*san*," he advised. "There are some units out there where the guys *can't* talk about what they do."

Suzuki grunted. Some people brawled for the fun of it. Fujita mostly didn't, but he wouldn't back down, either. Dying was better than losing face that way. Then the burly sergeant grunted again, on a different note this time. "Well, why didn't he say so?" he growled. He looked right at Fujita. "Why didn't you say so?"

"Because when you can't talk about something, you can't say you can't talk about it, because that makes people get snoopy about why you can't," Fujita answered reasonably.

He thought he was being reasonable, anyhow. Sergeant Suzuki scowled again. Fujita wouldn't have wanted to serve under him. Sure as sure, he'd be the kind who knocked privates around. "You calling me snoopy?" he rumbled ominously.

"You *were* snoopy." Fujita wasn't about to back down.

And Sergeant Ono nodded. "*Hai.* You were. Come on. We're here to relax, not to fight among ourselves."

"I'll take you both on." But Suzuki sat down again and waved to the man behind the bar for another drink. Fujita also waved for a fresh beer. Like Ono, he wasn't eager to fight, even if he was ready. Getting smashed hurt less—till the next day, anyhow.

MÜNSTER'S JEWISH CEMETERY was a sad place, and not just because the dead were lain to rest there. Brownshirt thugs had tipped over a lot of headstones and taken sledgehammers to others. Long, dead grass crunched under the soles of Sarah Bruck's shoes. The trees' bare branches reminded her of bones.

They'd been alive. Then, like that—she hoped it was *like that*—they were dead. And now, two days later, graves waited for them. Her husband and his father and mother lay shrouded in cloth inside coffins even a pauper's family would have been ashamed of before the war started. These days, the *Reich* felt Jews were lucky to get coffins at all. Of course, the *Reich* would have been happier if they all went into coffins, or at least into the ground.

Sarah huddled with her own parents near the caskets. A few of the Brucks' relatives stood with them. Everyone wore the same dazed, shocked expression. Death was never easy. Unexpected death from the air—death at the hands of Hitler's enemies—where was God, to let such things happen?

What did Elijah say about Baal? *Cry aloud: for he is a god; either he is talking, or he is retiring, or he is in a journey, or peradventure he sleepeth, and must be awaked.* But Sarah wasn't thinking about long-forgotten Baal. She aimed her cries at Elijah's God. And He seemed as silent as the old Canaanitish idol.

A rabbi with a yellow star intoned prayers. Would God be more or less inclined to hear them because he wore the Nazis' mark? Or was it all just a sham, much sound and fury signifying nothing? Shakespeare knew what he was talking about. Sarah wouldn't say the same about Elijah.

Into the holes in the ground went the coffins. Sarah and David Bruck's brother tossed earth onto them. The sound of the clods hitting the coffins' thin wooden lids seemed dreadfully final.

As the gravediggers got to work to finish covering over the bodies, the rabbi led the mourners in the Kaddish. Sarah had learned little Hebrew and less Aramaic, but she knew the prayer by rote: she'd been saying it since her last grandparent died not long before the Nazis took over. She often thought the old people were lucky because they hadn't lived to see what Hitler did to the Jews.

After the last *omayn*, people drifted away from the graveyard. The Brucks' kin went their way, Sarah and her parents theirs, and the rabbi, his head down, trudged off by himself. Sarah didn't even want to think about everything he must have put up with since the *Führer* came to power.

"I'm sorry, dear," Samuel Goldman said, not for the first time. "Isidor was a good fellow, and too young to be gone." He set a callused hand on her shoulder. "I know my being sorry doesn't make you feel any better, but I am anyhow. Your mother is, too."

"I am," Hanna Goldman agreed softly.

Father was right, as usual—it didn't make Sarah feel any better. With a sob that was at least half a hiccup, she shrugged his hand away. His mouth twisted, but he let his arm drop. He'd always believed reason and good sense would prevail against anything. The Nazis provided a horrible counterexample to that. Loss of a loved one gave another.

"What am I going to do?" Sarah said.

She knew what she'd do for the next little while: she'd stay with her parents, the way she had before navigating the shoals of Nazi bureaucracy to win permission to marry Isidor. All that work, all that *tsuris*—for what? For nothing. For a bomb howling down out of the sky and killing some Jews who hated Hitler but weren't allowed to use shelters along with the *Reich*'s Aryan citizens.

Father looked around. Seeing no one within earshot, he spoke in an even lower voice than Mother had used a moment before: "The Nazis are our misfortune."

No wonder he made sure nobody could overhear him! How many times had Hitler pounded his lectern and thundered *The Jews are our misfortune!*? More often than Sarah could count, anyhow. If someone heard one of those Jews mocking his slogan, what would happen to the scoffer? A beating? A trip to Dachau? A bullet in the back of the head? Something along those lines. Whatever it was, it wouldn't be good.

Mother clucked reproachfully. "Watch yourself, Samuel," she said.

"Oh, I do," he replied. "If I didn't, our misfortune would already have happened to me." The professor of classics and ancient history turned street repairman corrected himself with his usual precision: "More of our misfortune would have happened to me, I should say."

None of that answered Sarah's question, of course. Yes, it had been only two days since the air raid. As usual, Jews got their dead into the ground as fast as they could. Then something else occurred to her: "*Gevalt!* What will any of us do for bread now?"

"We'll probably do without, that's what," Samuel Goldman said, and he was much too likely to be right. The Brucks' bakery had been the only one in Münster from which Jews were allowed to buy any. Would the authorities let them visit an Aryan establishment because they had no other choice? Or would the brownshirts declare that it was their own fault the bakery got bombed?

"I can bake bread," Mother said, but with no great enthusiasm. And who could blame her for that? Baking every day from scratch was a devil of a lot of work. It wasn't as if she had lots of time on her hands, or as if she weren't worn out already.

"They'll probably set you to doing it without yeast, and tell me to make bricks without straw." One of Father's eyebrows quirked upward toward his graying hair. "My guess is, they would have done it a long time ago if they weren't so allergic to the Old Testament. I mean, those are tried and true things to make Jews do."

"God was the One Who made us bake without yeast. It wasn't Pharaoh," Mother pointed out.

"Well, what if it wasn't?" Father returned. "You don't think Hitler thinks he's God—and expects his good little Aryans to think so, too?"

A tram rattled past. It needed paint. One of the iron wheels clicked against the track as it went round and round. Repairs weren't coming any time soon, not with the war on. Sarah wasted no time worrying about that—or about getting on the tram. The motorman would have thrown her and her folks off the trolley had they tried. The yellow star made it easy for Aryans to follow laws against Jews to the letter.

In normal times, in sane times, Sarah would have had a claim on some of Isidor's estate. But facing Nazi bureaucrats again was too revolting for her even to think about, much less to do. If David Bruck's brother wanted to take them on, he was welcome to whatever he could pry out of them.

"All that time with Isidor—it might as well never have happened," she said in slow wonder. "He's—gone." She still wore her wedding ring. That and a little bit of dirt on her hand from where she'd tossed earth into the grave were almost the only signs she'd ever been married.

To her surprise, her mother shook her head. "You loved him, and that changed you, too," Hanna Goldman said. "Love is never wasted. You should always cherish it when you find it, because you never find it often enough."

"Listen to your mother." Samuel Goldman sounded serious to the point of solemnity. "More truth in that than in Plato and Aristotle and both Testaments all lumped together."

Was there? Sarah had no idea. Right now, she had no idea about anything. She didn't even know how much she'd truly loved Isidor. Not so much as she should have—she was pretty sure of that. He hadn't swept her off her feet: nowhere close. He'd never been a sweeping-off kind of guy. She'd liked him. She'd cared about him. She'd enjoyed the things he did when no one else was around, and she'd liked doing such things for him.

Did all that add up to love? One more thing she didn't have the faintest idea about. What she knew was, she wouldn't get the chance to find out now, not with Isidor she wouldn't. She wouldn't even have a child to remember him by—one more thing of which she was no longer in any doubt. When you got right down to the bottom of things, life was pretty rotten, wasn't it?

VERY LITTLE THAT Aristide Demange had seen in Russia impressed him. Very little that the veteran lieutenant had seen anywhere impressed him. He made a point of not being impressed. He'd done it for so long, it was second nature to him by now.

You couldn't help noticing Russia's vastness, though, even if you made your point of doing no more than noticing. You couldn't help noticing the fine tanks Russian factories turned out, either. Nor could you help noticing the frigid *con* of a winter Russia had. Well, hell, even Napoleon had noticed the Russian winter, though chances were he'd also done his goddamnedest not to let it impress him.

And you couldn't help noticing what a pack of thumb-fingered oafs the Ivans were. Half the time, they didn't know what to do with all those fancy tanks. Their tactics would have had to loosen up to seem rigid. They drank like swine. Of course, if Demange had had leaders like theirs, he would have drunk that way himself.

So here was Murmansk. Murmansk had but one *raison d'être*: to get men and things into and out of Russia the year around. Thanks to the last gasp of the Gulf Stream as it slid past the northern tip of Scandinavia, the local harbor never iced up. It was the only port in the USSR that could make such a boast.

But it was at best tenuously connected to the rest of the country. A single rickety rail line led down to Leningrad and ultimately to Moscow. Odds were no one knew how many men had died building that line during the last war, or how many perished every year keeping it usable. If anyone did know, he worked for the NKVD and didn't care. Demange had seen labor gangs of scrawny prisoners laying fresh ties under the watchful gaze of guards with submachine guns.

Murmansk itself was ugly as a toadstool. Wood huts housed the people who worked by the harbor. Wood smoke and coal smoke hovered over the town in a choking haze London would have envied. Except for fish pulled fresh from the Arctic Ocean, the food was bad and there wasn't enough of it.

He hadn't got away from the war, either. The Germans knew what Murmansk meant to the Ivans. Their bombers flew out of Norway through the long winter nights and pummeled the harbor and the rest of the city. Russian fighters buzzed overhead. Russian antiaircraft guns yammered away whenever the *Luftwaffe* came from the west. Russian papers claimed whole squadrons of He-111s and Ju-88s hacked out of the sky. French-speaking Russian officials delighted in translating those stories for any Frenchman who would sit still and listen.

Demange knew bullshit when he heard it. He also knew he was liable to end up floating in the cold, cold water if he gave forth with his opinions. He assumed anyone who knew French had to work for the

NKVD. He smiled and nodded in the right places. Hypocrisy lubricated human affairs here, as it did so often.

Getting into Murmansk had been an adventure punctuated by Stukas. Getting back to *la belle France* was liable to be an adventure punctuated by U-boats. A torpedo was the kind of thing that could ruin a troopship's whole day. And spring was in the calendar.

It wasn't in the air. The weather stayed colder than any Frenchman who hadn't been born in a deep freeze would have believed possible. Blizzards roared down from the North Pole one after another. Snow swirled through the air, thicker than tobacco smoke in an *estaminet*.

The French pissed and moaned about it. The stolid Russians clumped through it. Their *valenki* kept their feet from freezing. Their greatcoats, unlike Western European models, were made to withstand Arctic cold. They wore fur hats with flaps they could lower and tie to keep their ears from going solid and breaking off. And they figured large doses of vodka made the best antifreeze.

Not even their stolidity, though, could keep the sun from moving farther north in the sky every day. Daylight had been almost nonexistent when Demange got to Murmansk. He liked that fine. Darkness was the best time to get through the Barents Sea without being spotted by German submarines or bombers based in northern Norway.

But his regiment was somewhere down in the queue. The Russians were even more fanatical about queuing than the English were, and that said a mouthful. They were less efficient about it, though. And they didn't have enough freighters in Murmansk to deal with the influx of French soldiers.

For the life of him, Demange couldn't see why they didn't. They were good proletarians, so maybe their diplomats didn't wear pinstriped trousers the way French officials did. No matter what they wore, they must have spent a lot of time talking the French into climbing out of Hitler's bed and coming back to Stalin's. If they wanted French troops out of their country so badly, why in blazes didn't they have ships waiting to take them away?

Because they were Russians. That was the only answer Demange could see. They spewed propaganda about the dictatorship of the proletariat and about the glories of centralized planning. When the Germans made noises about planning, they meant them. The Ivans? They were like a chorus of whores singing the praises of virginity.

It would have been funny if it hadn't stood a decent chance of getting Demange killed. Once the equinox passed, days in these latitudes stretched like a politician's conscience. Murmansk went from having no daylight to speak of to having too bloody much in what seemed like nothing flat.

Demange shepherded his company aboard a rusty scow through more snow flurries. But it was going on nine o'clock at night when he did it, and he had no trouble seeing the falling snow. "Come on, my dears," he growled. "Out of the frying pan, into the fire."

"Don't you want to get home, Lieutenant?" one of his men asked as they stumped up the gangplank.

Demange still couldn't get used to being called *Lieutenant*. He'd spent too many happy years as a sergeant despising junior officers. Now he'd turned into what he'd scorned for so long.

To make matters worse, he'd run out of Gitanes. He was reduced to smoking Russian *papirosi:* a little bit of tobacco at the end of a long paper holder. Russian tobacco tasted funny, and the holder felt wrong in his mouth. All that left him even more short-tempered than usual. "Jules, I want to get home *alive*," he answered. "And we'd've had a hell of a lot better chance sailing out of here three weeks ago."

Jules opened his mouth. Then he closed it again. That was the smartest thing he could have done.

The freighter wallowed away from the pier. It took its place in a convoy. Royal Navy destroyers and corvettes served as escort vessels. Seeing them cheered Demange up—a little. On the water, the English had some idea of what they were doing. He certainly preferred them as escorts to ships from the Red Fleet. At least he could be pretty sure their skippers weren't blind drunk.

Out into the Barents the convoy went. It zigzagged till night finally fell. As soon as darkness descended, all the ships hightailed it west at the best speed of the slowest freighter. Demange would have been content to leave that sorry *con* behind to shift for itself . . . unless, of course, it happened to be the miserable tub that was carrying him.

In these latitudes and at this season, daybreak came all too soon. The ships stopped hightailing and started sedately zigzagging once more. Demange peered out at the gray-green water. He'd yell if he saw a periscope—which would probably help just enough to let him go down yelling.

He saw nothing but ocean and a few scudding seabirds. No Flying Pencils or broad-winged Heinkels droned overhead to bomb the convoy. No Stukas roared down on the ships with sirens screaming like the end of the world.

A few days later, he did see something he'd never seen before: a coastline that a sailor told him belonged to Scotland. He'd fought alongside Tommies in two wars, but that was his first glimpse of the British Isles. It made him think he likely would make it back to France. And the Germans, having missed this fine chance to kill him, would get more shots at it.

# Chapter 5

**H**ans-Ulrich Rudel lay beside Sofia in the narrow bed in her cramped little flat in Bialystok. "I don't know how often I'll be able to come back," he said sorrowfully, running his hand along the velvety skin of her flank. "Rumor is, they're going to send us to the West again."

If his half-Jewish mistress was spying for the Russians, he'd just handed her enough to get himself shot at sunrise. "That's a shame," she said, with an exquisite shrug. "I'll miss you—some." Like a scorpion, she always had a sting in her tail.

"I'll miss you a lot," Hans-Ulrich said. "I love you, you know."

"You think you do," Sofia answered. "But that's only because I let you get lucky. You'll get over it as soon as you find somebody else."

He shook his head and kissed his way down from under her chin to the tip of her left breast. She arched her back and purred. "It's not like that. You know it isn't," he insisted between kisses. "If things were different . . ."

"If things were different—if I lived in Byelorussia, say, instead of Poland—you would have dropped bombs on my head instead of trying to pick me up." As usual, Sofia reveled in being difficult. "And if you didn't blow me up for being a Communist, you would have shot me for being a Jew."

"I never shot anybody for being a Jew," Rudel said, which was technically true but made him out to be less of a good National Socialist than he was. "If things were different . . ."

She interrupted him again. This time, she didn't use any words, which didn't mean she was ineffective. As Hans-Ulrich had discovered before, the difference between being blown and blown up was altogether delightful. "My God!" he gasped when she finished. "I don't think I can see any more."

"Oh, no?" she retorted. "Then how come you were watching?"

"A blind man would watch when you did that," he said. "*Himmeldonnerwetter*, a dead man would."

"I've got a picture of that," Sofia said, mocking him the way she so often did.

"When we go—if you go—I'll miss you more than I know how to tell you," Hans-Ulrich said once more. "You're wonderful. I've never known anybody like you."

"You should have started fooling around with *Mischlings* sooner, then." No, Sofia couldn't quit jabbing, even when she was way ahead on points.

"I don't care what you are. I care who you are." While Rudel said it, it was true.

By the way Sofia's eyebrow quirked, she understood that better than he did. "Well, it's a story," she replied after a brief pause. Then she squeaked, but not in anger, because Hans-Ulrich was doing unto her as he'd been done by. She seemed to enjoy it quite as much as he had. When he finished, she nodded lazily and said, "I *will* miss you—some."

"I'm glad—I suppose," he answered, as gruffly as he could. But his expression must have given him away, because Sofia started to laugh. He went on, "I don't know for sure we'll be transferred. It just looks that way, with France sticking a knife in our back."

"Germany never did anything to anybody, of course," Sofia said.

"*Aber natürlich*," Hans-Ulrich agreed. She fired a sharp look at him, then caught herself and laughed some more.

He hated getting back on the train and heading into Russia. He also hated changing trains at what had been the border between Poland and the USSR. The wider Russian gauge was deliberately designed to keep Germany from using her own rolling stock and locomotives inside Soviet territory. All the way back in the days of the Tsars, the Russians had worried about invaders from the west. That worry hadn't gone away because the hammer and sickle replaced the old Russian tricolor.

When he got back to the airstrip, Colonel Steinbrenner greeted him with, "Have a good time on your furlough?"

"Yes, sir," Hans-Ulrich answered—that one was easy enough.

The squadron commander leered at him. "I hope you didn't do anything I wouldn't enjoy."

"Well, I don't know about that, Colonel," Hans-Ulrich said blandly. "I've never been in bed with you."

Whoops rose from the flyers and groundcrew men who heard that. Colonel Steinbrenner blinked. "You're right," he admitted. "There's something I probably wouldn't enjoy."

Getting back to business, Rudel asked, "What are our orders, sir? What's the latest news?"

"So far, all the talk about going back to the Siegfried Line is just that—talk," Steinbrenner answered. "But I wouldn't be surprised if it turns out to be real. The French *are* at war with us again."

"Treacherous pigdogs!" Hans-Ulrich said. "Anyone who counts on a Frenchman for anything is setting himself up to be sorry."

"And this surprises you because . . . ?" Steinbrenner said. "The only good thing about it is that, for the time being, anyhow, it's the same kind of war in the West it was while we went in and gave the Czechs what they had coming to them."

Rudel had no trouble figuring out what that meant: "The froggies don't have the nerve to go toe-to-toe with us."

"Count your blessings that they don't," Colonel Steinbrenner replied. "Two fronts going full blast would cause us problems."

He was old enough to remember the last war, when fighting on two fronts had proved more than Germany could manage. Hans-Ulrich wasn't, so he could say, "We were stabbed in the back at the end," and mean it.

"That's what they say," Steinbrenner—agreed? By *they*, he couldn't mean anyone but the officials of the current government. Was he criticizing National Socialism and the *Führer*? After the first attempted coup against Hitler, the SS had taken away the previous squadron commander, Colonel Greim. Greim hadn't been loyal enough to suit the powers that be. Colonel Steinbrenner, by contrast, didn't land in trouble with the authorities. He hadn't up till now, anyhow.

Not wanting to get into deeper political waters—not even wanting to get his political toes wet—Hans-Ulrich changed the subject in a hurry: "So we're still flying against the Russians, then?"

Steinbrenner nodded. "Till they tell us to do something else, that's what we're doing, all right." Some of the leer came back to his face. "Breaks your heart, doesn't it, staying someplace where you don't have any trouble getting back to dear old Bialystok?"

"I've heard ideas I liked less—I will say that." Rudel cocked his head to one side. Those were aircraft engines, off in the distance. A moment later, he realized they didn't belong to *Luftwaffe* planes. "The Russians are still flying against us, too!" he exclaimed, and ran for the closest zigzagging slit trench.

Steinbrenner and the rest of the men who'd greeted him on his return ran along with him. The flak guns around the airstrip started banging away even before he leaped down into the trench. He wished he wore a *Stahlhelm* instead of his officer's soft cap. Shrapnel falling from several thousand meters could smash in your skull as readily as a rifle bullet.

Russian bombs could punch your ticket for you, too. Down they whistled, and exploded with flat, harsh crumps. The Ivans' Pe-2s were good bombers. They carried as big a load as any German plane, and were faster even than Ju-88s, the newest and speediest medium bombers the *Luftwaffe* boasted. They could fly rings around Stukas, but all kinds of planes could do that. Speed wasn't what kept the Ju-87 in business. Being able to put bombs on top of a fifty-pfennig piece was.

The Pe-2s couldn't do that. They dropped theirs pretty much at random, then flew off to the east at full throttle before Bf-109s could tear into them. The raid couldn't have lasted more than fifteen minutes. Rudel stuck his head up over the lip of the trench. A Ju-87 burned inside its revetment, smoke rising high into the gray sky. A couple of big bombs, probably 500kg jobs, had cratered the runway. The flak didn't seem to have shot down any enemy planes.

Colonel Steinbrenner also surveyed the damage. He delivered his verdict: "Well, we fly against the Russians as soon as we fix things up around here."

"Yes, sir," Hans-Ulrich said. That was exactly how it looked to him, too.

PETE McGILL HADN'T known what they'd do with him once the *Ranger* got back to Hawaii. If they wanted him to stay aboard the carrier, he'd do that. Carriers took the fight to Japan. Or if they wanted him to splash up out of the Pacific and take some island away from Hirohito's slanty-eyed bastards, he wouldn't complain. The only thing that would have pissed him off was a training billet on the U.S. mainland. He wanted to go after the Japs himself, not teach other guys how to do it the right way.

He turned out not to need to worry about that. He stayed with the *Ranger*. Maybe Rob Cullum put in a good word for him. Maybe they just figured, okay, he was there, he had plenty of shipboard experience, and he knew how to jerk five-inch shells. Why complicate things?

*Because it's the Navy?* a sly voice in the back of his head suggested. To the peacetime Navy, Marines were an unmitigated nuisance. Once the guns started going off, leathernecks turned into a slightly mitigated nuisance. They were still a pain to have to cart around aboard ships, but they did have some minor uses: taking islands away from the nasty buggers who occupied them and who refused to get shelled or bombed into extinction, for instance.

Marines thought swabbies were boring. Sailors were convinced Marines stood in the muscle line twice and didn't bother waiting for brains. Marines figured they carried an extra couple of inches where an extra couple of inches mattered most. If you had to stand in line twice to get those, hey, what better cause was there?

Meanwhile, along with squabbling with each other (and with the Army, which both agreed was beneath contempt), the Navy and the Corps had to fight the Japs. Going toe-to-toe with them in the Pacific and knocking them flat hadn't worked out the way the admirals wanted.

Now the main idea was to keep Tojo's monkeys from landing in Hawaii. If the USA had to fight the war from the West Coast, all of a sudden it looked a lot harder to win.

Screened by destroyers and light cruisers, *Ranger* steamed back and forth west of the islands, her combat air patrol alert to anything the Imperial Navy might try to pull. Pete hoped like hell the flyboys were alert, anyhow. When the Japs got the drop on you, it could mess you up but good. He'd found that out in Manila, and several times since.

Little by little, his longing for lost Vera faded, as did the pain from the physical injuries he'd got when Chinese terrorists bombed that Shanghai movie theater. His shoulder and his leg would probably always tell him when rain was on the way. And his heart would always ache when he thought about his Russian sweetheart. But, in the homely, clichéd phrase, life did go on.

He felt less and less guilt when he visited the whores on Hotel Street in Honolulu. He couldn't bring Vera back. If he could have, he would have, and lived happily and faithfully ever after, too—he was sure of that. Being sure of it didn't make it true, of course—one more thing he didn't have to dwell on.

Vera was gone, though. He hadn't even seen her into the ground. He'd been too badly hurt himself. He had to do *something* with those extra couple of inches. And he did, as often as liberty and the state of his wallet would let him. He felt terrible the first few times. After that, he just felt good, which was, after all, the point of lying down with a woman in the first place.

Those were interludes, though. Most of his time passed aboard the *Ranger*. He'd never served on a carrier before. His duties stayed the same: the *Ranger*'s five-inch guns were no different from the ones the *Boise* had mounted. The ship itself? That was a different story.

*Boise*'s first order of business had been to steam and to shoot. *Ranger*'s was to get airplanes where they needed to go. They did the fighting for her. If her own guns went off, it was a sure sign something had hit the fan somewhere.

As Rob Cullum dryly put it, "You notice they gave 'em to us. They figured we'd get into some shit now and again."

"Think so, do you?" Pete answered, deadpan. The other sergeant grinned and thumped him on the back. It hurt, but Pete didn't care. It was a sign he was fitting in, and he wanted nothing more.

Being a portable airstrip made *Ranger* a special kind of seagoing beast. The vast, echoing space of the hangar deck under the flight deck amazed Pete. That it was usually echoing with the snarl of power tools and with Navy mechanics' inventive bad language as they worked on fighters, dive-bombers, and torpedo planes mattered little. The space was what got to him.

Carrying all those planes meant carrying thousands of gallons of the high-octane gasoline they burned along with the ship's own fuel oil. Fire at sea was any sailing man's worst nightmare. Fire at sea aboard an aircraft carrier . . . "We're nothing but a torch with a flight deck, are we?" Pete said when he got around to thinking about that.

"Oh, I wouldn't say so," Sergeant Cullum answered after a few seconds' consideration.

"No, huh? What would you call us, then?" Pete challenged.

"More like a furnace with a flight deck," the other Marine answered. "We'd burn a hell of a lot hotter than some lousy torch." It was Pete's turn to consider, but not for long. He nodded. Cullum was right.

No surprise, then, that the *Ranger* ran more firefighting drills than any other ship Pete had known. No surprise, either, that her sailors and Marines took them more seriously than he was used to. They did their share of goofing off and then some, but not about that.

And no surprise that they were cynical anyhow. "Basically, we better not catch on fire," Cullum said. "Once we go up, odds are we're fucked."

"That's about what I thought," Pete said. "I was hoping you'd tell me I was wrong."

"Oh, you're wrong about all kinds of shit," Cullum answered easily. "But not about that."

"Japs must know, huh? I mean, their carriers gotta work the same way." Having already been aboard one warship bombed and sunk from the air, imagining more dive-bombers and torpedo planes going after the *Ranger* made Pete feel as if a goose were walking over his grave—probably a goose with a radial engine and with meatballs on its wings.

The twist to Rob Cullum's mouth said he understood the touch of those heavy webbed feet—or were they tires slamming down on a flight deck? "They may suspect," he agreed. "Yeah, they just may. How many of our flattops did they sink when we slugged it out west of here?"

"Too many." Pete couldn't remember the exact number. All of them but *Ranger*, was what it amounted to. He did his damnedest to look on the bright side of things: "When the shipyards really get rolling, we'll build 'em faster'n the Japs can hope to sink 'em. What we've gotta do is stand the gaff in the meantime."

Cullum saluted him as if he'd sprouted stars on his shoulders. No, fat gold stripes on his sleeves, for the other sergeant said, "Thank you, Admiral King. Now that you've got all our troubles wrapped up with a pretty pink ribbon around 'em, you should write FDR a nice letter and let him know how he needs to be running the goddamn war."

"Ah, fuck off," Pete replied without heat. When guys didn't chin about women or gambling or sports or the crappy chow in the galley, strategy often reared its ugly head. "Tell me this, man. Suppose I was in charge."

"We'd be really screwed," Cullum said at once.

"Odds are," Pete admitted, which made his buddy blink. He went on, "But how could we be screwed any worse'n we already are?"

That did make Cullum stop and think. "Well," he said at last, "in the big fight the slanties might've sunk *Ranger*, too. Then we wouldn't have any carriers operating out of Pearl at all. Past that, though, it couldn't hardly be fubar'd any worse than it is right now."

"See?" Pete said triumphantly.

"Hey, a stopped clock is right twice a day. That puts it one up on you," Cullum said. Pete flipped him off. Slowly, without any fuss, they drifted back to work.

SPRING WAS IN THE AIR outside of Madrid. All things considered, Vaclav Jezek could have done without it. The bitter cold of winter in central Spain—a nasty surprise, that—kept down the stink of unburied and badly buried bodies, of which there were always far too many. It also fought the reek of latrine trenches, and of the waste that never got as far as the latrine trenches.

Pretty soon, flowers would bloom. They'd smell sweet, but not sweet enough to quell the stenches. Birds would sing, when you could hear them through the rumble of artillery and the machine guns' deadly chatter.

When Vaclav pissed and moaned about it, Benjamin Halévy eyed him with his usual air of detached amusement. "I didn't know we had a poet among us," the Jew said.

"Oh, fuck you!" Vaclav snarled.

Halévy tapped the little metal star that marked him as a second lieutenant. "That's 'Oh, fuck you, *sir!*'" he said.

Vaclav laughed. What were you going to do? In the line, you made your own fun. If you didn't, you sure as hell wouldn't have any. A few hundred meters away, the Fascist bastards on the Nationalist side were no doubt cracking the same kind of dumb jokes.

Then the Czech sniper stopped laughing. Homesickness and weariness hit him like a blackjack behind the ear. "Christ, I wish I were back in Prague!" he burst out. "I've been carrying a gun for three and a half years. I'm fucking sick of it."

"Here. Have a knock of this." Halévy offered his canteen. Vaclav took it. It was full of Spanish brandy—not good, but strong. He swigged, then wiped his mouth on his sleeve and handed back the canteen. The Jew went on, "Some of the people here started two years before you did, you know."

"That's right!" Vaclav said in surprise. Not many countries had got it before Czechoslovakia did, but Spain was one of them. He looked around. It was the landscape of war, all right: trenches, shell holes, barbed wire, ragged and muddy uniforms. How many times had this stretch of ground gone back and forth between Nationalists and Republicans? How many more would it change hands till somebody finally won, if anyone ever did? Better not to wonder about such things. Instead, Vaclav asked, "Got a cigarette?"

"That's also 'Got a cigarette, *sir?*'" the Jew observed, but he pulled out a pack and handed it to Vaclav. The smokes were Spanish: even harsher than the stove polish and barbed wire the French put in their cigarettes. Given a choice, Vaclav would have opted for a better brand. Given a choice, he never would have come to Spain to begin with. Beggars didn't get choices like that. He took a cigarette, scraped a match against the much-repaired sole of his boot, and hollowed his cheeks to draw in smoke.

He let it out again with a cough. "Jesus Christ! Is that phosgene, or what?"

Halévy also lit up. After a judicious puff of his own, he answered, "More like mustard gas, I'd say."

They both went right on smoking. You could complain about the tobacco as much as you pleased. Everybody did. You couldn't do without it, though. Almost everybody on both sides smoked like a factory chimney. Going without cigarettes while he hid himself somewhere in no-man's-land always gave Vaclav the jitters. He sometimes thought a smoke would be worth getting shot. He didn't yield to those temptations, but he had them.

As if to fuel them, Halévy said, "Marshal Sanjurjo's still out there somewhere."

"Yeah, yeah." Vaclav waved that away. "Like he's gonna come out and stand in the same place where I plugged what's-his-name—Franco. Nobody's that goddamn dumb, not even a Nationalist Spanish general."

"*Cojones*," Halévy murmured.

That was a Spanish word the Czech understood. There weren't many, but he'd picked up the dirty bits first, as he had with French. And maybe it *was* a question of balls. Would Sanjurjo say, in effect, *I'm not afraid to go where Franco got shot*? If he did, he was liable to be sorry— but not for long, not if he stopped a 13mm armor-piercing antitank round.

During the night, the Nationalists shelled the Czechs and the Internationals. They hit them harder than most Republican troops. Vaclav, huddling in what he devoutly hoped was a bombproof, could have done without the gesture of respect.

As soon as the shelling stopped, Jezek tumbled out and rushed to a firing step, ready to repel the enemy's infantry if they pressed the attack. But they didn't. The Nationalists just wanted to hurt their foes without much risk to themselves. Who wouldn't make war on the cheap if he could?

Republican guns gave back a belated response after sunup the next morning. Maybe the artillerists wanted to see what they were shooting at. Maybe they hadn't had any shells handy during the night. Maybe they'd been drinking sangria in a cantina back of the line, and catching crabs from the barmaids. Maybe . . . Who the hell knew, or cared?

Any which way, Vaclav got to scout no-man's-land while the Nationalists were keeping their heads down. The two barrages had torn up the landscape—again. He looked for new hiding places from which he might torment Sanjurjo's men. Then a short Republican round burst in front of the trench and showered him with dirt. He ducked as fragments whined not far enough overhead.

"Fucking assholes!" he shouted. "Whose side are they on?" He brushed at his uniform, for all the world as if it would do any good.

"They're artillerymen," Benjamin Halévy said. "If it's in front of them, it's a target—and it's all in front of them."

"Too right, it is," Vaclav said. Warily, he straightened and looked out toward the Nationalist trenches again. That new crater with the tall lip facing the enemy's line . . . That just might do. Republican shells kept coming down. With his luck, they'd flatten the hidey-hole before he ever got to use it.

But they didn't. He crawled out to it under cover of darkness. Yes, it was the kind of place he needed. He had foliage stuck to his helmet with a strip of inner tube. A muddy burlap cloak with branches thrust into it also helped break up his outline. And he camouflaged the anti-tank rifle's long barrel well before light could give him away.

Then he settled down to wait. He wanted a cigarette, but no, not enough to risk his life for one. He knew the urge would grow on him. He gnawed garlicky Spanish sausage instead. He'd taste that all day, too, but it wasn't the same thing, dammit.

He eyed the Nationalist lines through a magnified circle with crosshairs. Men in yellowish khaki did the kinds of things soldiers did. Out beyond ordinary rifle range of the Republican forward trench, they didn't take much cover. They didn't think they were in any great danger, and they were right. Jezek didn't feel like wasting his rounds on ordinary jerks. Those fat, fancy bullets were reserved for extraordinary jerks.

Maybe he'd lie here till darkness came again. He didn't fire every day. When he did pull the trigger, he wanted his shots to mean something. He also didn't want to get killed himself. He swung the heavy rifle a couple of centimeters to the right, then peered through the scope again.

A glimpse of a fabric long familiar but not seen for some time made his attention snap back to it. The Nationalists wore that diarrhea-colored khaki. Republican forces used khaki, too, khaki or denim or whatever civilian stuff they happened to own. No Spaniard, though, had a uniform of *Feldgrau*.

Sanjurjo and Hitler, of course, had been in bed together since the war in Spain started. The Germans had helped the Nationalists take Gibraltar away from England. German troops and flyers of the *Legion Kondor* let the Nazis field-test weapons and doctrines. But Germany'd paid Spain much less attention since the big European fight heated up.

So what was this Nazi officer doing here now? Whatever it was, he wouldn't keep doing it long. Neither he nor the Spaniard with him worried about snipers. They were more than a kilometer away from the front. Why should they?

Vaclav showed them why. The antitank rifle slammed against his shoulder. The German stood stock-still for a moment, then crumpled. No, he wouldn't report back to Berlin, or even back to Marshal Sanjurjo. They paid a sergeant pathetically little, but Vaclav knew damn well he'd earned his handful of pesetas today.

CHAIM WEINBERG HUDDLED in a hole scraped into the front side of his trench, waiting for the Nationalists to quit shelling the front. Sanjurjo's shitheads were ticked off about something, sure as hell. This was what they did when they got up in arms: used the big guns to make the Republicans sweat. Chaim was sweating, all right.

Latrine-trench rumor said the Czech sniper with the elephant gun had punched some *Wehrmacht* big shot's ticket for him. When you got punched with that piece of artillery, you stayed punched, too. *Gotta ask him the next time I see him*, Chaim thought as another round from a 105 crashed down. That Vaclav knew some German, and Chaim's Yiddish came close enough.

What really worried the International, though, was why a German officer had been looking over the Republican lines in the first place.

Ever since the balloon went up in Czechoslovakia, and especially since Gibraltar went under, they'd had Spain on the back burner.

His fertile imagination could conjure up plenty of reasons for them to bring it to the front of the stove again. If the Nationalists smashed the Republic, German planes in northeastern Spain could pay France back for rejoining the fight against Fascism by knocking the crap out of the southern part of the country. Maybe Sanjurjo could even mount some half-assed raid across the Pyrenees. That would set the froggies hopping like fleas on a hot griddle.

But the Republic wouldn't fall any time soon. It had been teetering in 1938. After Hitler jumped the Czechs, though, France and England threw enough supplies into Spain to level the war, and it had stayed pretty much level since. Chaim shook his head as he tried to make himself smaller. Christ, but 1938 was a long time ago now! A marriage ago. A child ago. A lifetime ago.

All at once, the shellfire let up. The first thing Chaim did was stick a cigarette in his mouth. His hands shook as he lit it. Shellfire always took a toll on you. Some guys couldn't get over it. There were beggars in Madrid who twitched all the time. Odds were they'd been reasonably good soldiers once. Modern war dished out more than a lot of human beings were made to take.

Chaim was still with it: at least well enough to make sure the Nationalists didn't try anything cute while they figured they still had the Abe Lincolns punchy. A couple of Republican machine guns sprayed murder out across the lunar ground between the lines to send Sanjurjo's men the same message. A Nationalist Maxim hammered back. Chaim ducked, though none of the bullets came close.

A few feet away, Mike Carroll hopped down off the firing step. He was a lot taller than Chaim, so more of him stuck up above the parapet unless he was careful. And he was: he'd been in Spain even longer than Chaim. You learned and you lived. You could learn and not live. Bad luck always lay around the corner somewhere. But you couldn't not learn and live. Stupidity was its own punishment.

"Wonder what the Fritzes are up to," Mike said. He'd also heard the scuttlebutt about Vaclav, then.

"Nothing good," Chaim said with doleful certainty.

"Tell me about it," Mike said. "Germans are nothing but bad news. Even the Fritzes in the Internationals are a bunch of Prussians. And if the Nazis are sniffing around again . . ."

"Less I see of 'em, better I like it." Chaim hadn't seen any Nazis here, not with his own eyes. But he believed Vaclav had shot one. The way the Nationalists were throwing hate around sure argued for it.

Mike changed the subject, asking, "How's your kid?"

"He's great," Chaim answered with a grin. "He's at that silly age, where his own toes are the funniest goddamn things in the world. He can laugh and roll over and kinda sit up. He says something that sounds like *dada*, but he doesn't know it's me."

"Sounds like a baby, all right." Mike might have heard more than he'd really wanted to know. Perhaps incautiously, he asked another question: "And how's his mother doing?"

Chaim's face went hard. "La Martellita is . . . going along," he said in a voice like a slammed door. She was not only going along, she was going out with a Red Army captain, one of Stalin's henchmen who'd stayed in Spain because they had no chance of getting back to the USSR. By everything Chaim had heard, the Russian was shorter and squatter and homelier than he was himself.

If he ever did see the guy, he figured he'd punch him in the nose. If La Martellita had given him the bum's rush for some tall, handsome Spanish grandee (a Spanish grandee with sense enough not to have joined the Nationalists; there were a few, though not many), he could have lived with that. But a Russian plug-ugly? Maybe she just liked apes.

It was, no doubt, a good thing Chaim had never set eyes on the Red Army captain. If he did give the son of a bitch a fat lip, he might end up in front of a firing squad. The Republic took its friendship with the Soviet Union *very* seriously.

Maybe La Martellita took up with him not because he was built like a hydrant but because he was a Russian Communist. Did it feel better because you were getting shtupped by somebody from Marxism-Leninism's holy land? If you expected it to, then it probably did. Women worked that way. Chaim thought it felt great all the goddamn time.

The Nationalists' loudspeakers came to life then. "You should all come over to our side. You're just helping the atheistical Russians!" The man at the microphone stumbled a little over *atheistical,* but he managed to bring it out.

He got nothing but laughs, though. The Nationalists were so wrapped up in the Catholic Church, they thought their enemies were, too. That screwed up their propaganda, especially when they aimed it at the Internationals. "Us, we're the atheistical Americans, by God!" Chaim said, and laughed harder than ever.

Then the Nationalist propaganda announcer said, "And half the filthy Bolsheviks—more than half—are Jews! Do you want to do what the disgusting Hebrews tell you to do? Of course you don't!"

Some of the Spaniards who filled out the Internationals' ranks these days might take that seriously. So few Jews lived in Spain—they couldn't do it legally till the Republic came along—that the locals believed a lot of the anti-Semitic bullshit the Fascists put out. They'd been hearing the same kind of nonsense their whole lives.

"No wonder the Republic shot so many priests," Mike Carroll said.

"No wonder at all," Chaim agreed. "Shame they couldn't have shot that braying jackass, too."

After the braying jackass finally shut up, one of the young Spaniards in the Abe Lincolns came up to Chaim and said, "You're the one they call *el narigón loco,* right?"

"The crazy kike, that's me." Chaim nodded, not without pride. He'd earned the nickname the hard way, with his go-to-hell, no-holds-barred style of cantina fighting. "What about it, Rodrigo?"

"Well . . ." Rodrigo, by contrast, sounded almost shy. "Are you a Marxist, then, or are you a Jew?"

"*Absolutamente,*" Chaim declared, clearly enunciating each of the six syllables.

For some reason, that didn't seem to help the Spanish Abe Lincoln. "But which?" Rodrigo asked.

"I sure am," Chaim replied. Rodrigo started to ask him another question, then plainly decided it was a losing fight. The kid mooched off, hands thrust into the pockets of his revolutionary coveralls.

Mike Carroll laughed, but softly, taking care that the proud Spaniard couldn't hear him do it. "That wasn't fair, man," he said.

"Hey, neither was the question. You can be a Jew and a Marxist at the same time. Look at all the Old Bolsheviks," Chaim said.

"Yeah, and look what happened to them, too," Mike said, which made Chaim wince. An awful lot of the Jews who'd helped bring off the Russian Revolution ended up starring in Stalin's show trials or going to the camps or to the wall without benefit of any trial, show or otherwise. The Soviet Union was a rugged place. As far as Chaim was concerned, it still beat the hell out of the *Reich*.

# Chapter 6

Alistair Walsh couldn't stand Germans. The war in North Africa had been going so well. No matter what Mussolini said, no matter how far he stuck out his breakwater of a chin, the Italians mostly didn't want to fight. The ones who did have some pluck didn't have the tanks or lorries or planes they needed to do anything with it.

But with the *Wehrmacht* and the *Luftwaffe* in the game, everything changed. Tobruk hadn't fallen. The road to western Libya hadn't opened. As a matter of fact, the English in Egypt were more worried about keeping the bloody Fritzes—and the Italians along for the ride—away from Alexandria, the Nile, and the Suez Canal.

*Lose the canal and we've gone a long way toward losing the war*, Walsh thought glumly. It hadn't come to that. It hadn't even come close to that—yet. But he watched the skies with a grim earnestness he hadn't needed till Hitler came down to give Musso a hand. He'd met Stukas in France and in Norway. He didn't much fancy them.

Hurricanes buzzed above the English army. Walsh approved. Hurricanes could give a good account of themselves even against 109s. And they were death on Stukas. Any planes that could hack dive-bombers out of the air seemed absolutely wizard to him.

He remembered again that he'd actually volunteered for this. *I could have stayed back in good old Blighty*, he reminded himself. *Spring would just be coming into the air.*

That was a good joke, or would have been if only it were funny. With no apparent effort, Egypt got hotter not long after the equinox than England did at the height of summer. Every time the wind stirred the desert, it was as if your eyes got sandpapered. He had goggles, but they didn't help much. And the flies, which were merely bad during the winter, turned horrific as the blast furnace heated up.

Tinned bully beef wouldn't have been inspiring in Norway in the middle of a snowstorm. Having choked it down in just those circumstances, Walsh could take oath on that. But it was worse when you always had to be shooing flies away from it, and when you couldn't shoo off all of them.

Like all his comrades in khaki, he ate some bugs along with his beef. They didn't improve the flavor. Anything that could make bully beef taste worse than it did to begin with went straight into Walsh's black book.

He blamed a case of the galloping shits on swallowed flies. A lot of the men in his company had the same complaint. About half of them blamed the flies for it, too. The rest pointed an accusing finger at the water. It was brackish and stagnant and sulfurous to begin with. Heroic doses of lime chloride only made it taste worse. They were supposed to kill the germs lurking in it, but Walsh wouldn't have bet on that. Some of those germs, land mines wouldn't have killed.

Another sergeant had an antidote in mind for the dicey water: "We need to drink best bitter all the bloody time. Or Guinness, by God! 'Guinness is good for you,' the adverts go."

"Got to be better than this fetid cow piss." Walsh was a great admirer of bitter. Guinness he could take or leave alone.

Sadly, no beer lorries rumbled west from Alexandria. More tanks did. They were newer models than the English armored fighting vehicles Walsh had seen in France. They seemed as nimble as their German counterparts; the others hadn't been able to go any faster than an infantryman could trot. And they mounted cannon rather than a machine gun or two.

Still and all . . . Walsh studied them with a certain air of discontent. German tanks, like German helmets, looked as if they meant business. He wasn't so sure about these. They were full of funny angles that might catch shells, and their armor plates were riveted together, not welded. He asked a corporal commanding one of the tanks about that: "What happens if you get hit? Don't the rivet heads break off and rattle about inside like shrapnel?"

"Well, myte, Oi 'ope not. 'Ope like 'ell not, in fact." The corporal was a scrawny Cockney with bad teeth: a nasty little terrier of a man, and one who'd take a deal of killing if Walsh was any judge. He added, "Fritz won't fancy stoppin' a two-pounder round, neither, not 'arf 'e won't."

He was bound to be right about that. Walsh did like the idea of fighting with as much armor on his side as the other buggers could throw at him. He hadn't done much of that, not against the Germans he hadn't.

He didn't need to wait long, either. The bright fellows with the red collar flashes laid on an attack "in the direction of Tobruk." By the way that read, they didn't expect to get there, and would be content with pushing the Germans back a bit.

Tanks and foot soldiers went forward together. Each helped protect the other. The Germans had figured that out straightaway. They'd used combined-arms operations even when they jumped Czechoslovakia. English generals had needed longer to work it out. They might never have got it if they hadn't watched the Fritzes in action.

Forward Walsh went. He carried a Sten gun, an English submachine gun. It was much uglier than a Schmeisser, and so cheaply made it was liable to fall to pieces if dropped. But it sprayed a lot of bullets around, and that was what he wanted.

Incoming German artillery whistled toward Walsh. "Down!" he yelled—he knew the sound of those damned 88s and 105s much better than he'd ever wanted to. The 88 was an antiaircraft gun by trade, and a fine one. But the Fritzes, being thoroughgoing buggers, also made armor-piercing and high-explosive rounds for it, so it could kill you in any of several different ways.

Fragments whined and snarled through the air. A couple of wounded men wailed. Either they hadn't started scraping the sand soon enough or their luck was just out. Walsh hoped they'd caught Blighties—wounds that would let them go back to England for a while, or at least to Alexandria, but that wouldn't kill them or ruin them for life. Stretcher-bearers with Red Cross armbands lugged the injured soldiers away from the fighting. Whether shell fragments or machine-gun bullets would respect those armbands was no doubt something the bearers tried not to think about.

Up ahead, the tanks were mixing it up with their German opposite numbers. Officers' whistles shrilled, ordering the foot soldiers forward to join them. Sods with Sten guns were what kept the Fritzes from chucking Molotov cocktails onto English tanks' engine compartments, or from lobbing potato-masher grenades through open hatches.

Walsh captured a German by literally catching him with his pants down. The luckless fellow was squatting behind a spiky thorn bush when Walsh trotted past it. "*Hände hoch!*" Walsh yelled, aiming the tin Tommy gun at the German's pale backside.

With a yip of fright, the German sprang in the air and yanked up his pants before raising his hands. He wore an officer's peaked cap and a first lieutenant's pips on his shoulder straps. Walsh relieved him of his pistol and of a map case. The Intelligence wallahs might eventually get some use from that. Then the sergeant gestured to the rear with the barrel of his Sten. Gratefully, the German went on his way, making sure he kept his hands up. So far here in North Africa, both sides seemed to be playing by the rules.

While Walsh was making his capture, the German tanks in the distance turned tail and rumbled back toward a ridgeline a couple of miles to the west. Like hounds after fleeing foxes, the English tanks raced in pursuit, their tracks kicking up clouds of abrasive dust.

"They're on the run!" Lieutenant Preston shouted exultantly. He blew his whistle with might and main, trying to get his men to keep up with the tanks.

For a few minutes, Walsh thought he was right: not a thought about the young subaltern he was used to having. Then the 88s on the ridge-line opened up on the approaching English tanks. Not even the fearsome Soviet KV-1 owned armor that would keep out an 88mm AP round. These machines didn't come close. One after another brewed up. Each rising plume of greasy black smoke, each burst of fireworks as ammunition cooked off, meant horrendous deaths for five men.

The English advance sputtered and stalled like a lorry with no air filter in the desert. Surviving English tanks turned and trundled out of range of the 88s as fast as they could go. The multipurpose guns knocked out several more before they could escape. Then the German armor nosed forward again. Now the Fritzes had the edge in numbers. An English advance turned into an English withdrawal.

*How many times have I seen that before?* Walsh wondered. More than he cared to recall: he was sure of that. Gloomily, he trudged back to the east. So did Lieutenant Preston. The enthusiastic youngster wouldn't meet his eye—and a good thing for him, too.

AS THEO HOSSBACH had discovered before, the spring mud time in Russia was even worse than the one in autumn. In spring, all the accumulated snow melted, seemingly all at once. Wheeled vehicles bogged to the axles—if they were lucky. Even Panzer IIIs with *Ostketten*, special wide tracks made for war in the east, had a devil of a time going anywhere when the mud was worst. Hell, even Soviet T-34s had trouble with it. Where a T-34 couldn't go, nothing could.

Well, nothing mechanized. Horse-drawn *panje* wagons brought things to the front for both the Ivans, who'd been building them since time out of mind, and the Germans, who commandeered as many as they could get their hands on. With their big wheels and almost boat-shaped bodies, *panje* wagons did better in snow and mud than anything with tracks.

A *panje* wagon brought a sack of mail to Theo's panzer company. Theo got a letter from his mother. Hermann Witt got several from relatives and friends. So did Lothar Eckhardt and Kurt Poske. Adi Stoss, as usual, got nothing from anybody.

None of his crewmates said a word. By now, they were used to his being the man the world had forgotten. When that thought went through Theo's mind today, he found himself shaking his head. It wasn't quite right. Chances were some of the world remembered Adi perfectly well. It just didn't want to get hold of him, for fear of endangering him or itself or both.

Oddly, that made Theo feel better. Thoroughgoing loner though he was, he'd pitied Adi's splendid isolation. Realizing a good reason lay behind it made it easier for him, and surely for the panzer driver, to take.

They were quartered in a Russian village that had gone back and forth several times between the Red Army and the *Wehrmacht*. Whatever Russian civilians had lived there in more peaceful times were long gone. Most of the houses had seen better decades, too. The panzer crewmen shifted for themselves as best they could.

Sleeping in one of the battered, thatch-roofed huts was asking for visits from bedbugs, lice, and fleas. That would have bothered the Germans more if they weren't already buggy. Sleeping under a roof, or even under the singed remains of one, seemed irresistibly tempting to men who were more used to rolling themselves in blankets and curling up under their panzer.

Curling up under a panzer wasn't such a good idea now for all kinds of reasons. The armored beasts settled even on dry ground. You were smart to do some digging underneath to make sure you didn't wake up squashed. With everything so squelchy during the *rasputitsa*—the Germans had borrowed the Russian word—waking up squashed got easier. So did waking up drowned.

Of course, you could wake up sliced to sausage meat in one of the village huts. Russian artillery, always the most professional part of the Red Army, seemed to know and to visit every place where the Germans were staying. Another crew in the company lost their driver—killed—and commander and loader—badly hurt—when a Soviet 105 blew the house in which they were billeted to smithereens.

"Could have been us," Sergeant Witt said unhappily after a *panje* wagon took the injured men back toward a field hospital. Everybody in the village hoped they would make it there alive. No guarantees, not the way a *panje* wagon moved; only hope. Witt went on, "Just fool luck."

"Always fool luck," Adi said. "Nothing but fool luck we haven't run into a T-34 in a nasty mood."

He spoke of the Soviet panzer as if it were a ferocious wild beast, as if gun and chassis and crew were all directed by one fierce will. Theo understood that. Lots of German soldiers thought of the T-34 the same way.

Hermann Witt nodded, so Adi's way of talking made sense to him, too. "War just isn't a healthy business," he said.

"Too right it isn't," Adi said with some feeling. But then he paused and qualified that: "Most of the time, anyhow."

"What do you mean, most of the time?" Lothar Eckhardt demanded.

Before Adi could say anything, Theo surprised his crewmates by breaking in with, "Sometimes you're dumb as an ox, Eckhardt, you know that?"

"Huh?" The gunner gaped, not so much because of Theo's response as because Theo had responded at all. "What'd I say?"

Having used up a good part of his daily word ration, Theo just looked at him. That was plenty to reduce Eckhardt to stutters. War was bound to be healthy for Adi Stoss. Driving a Panzer III, you risked your life only every so often: when you did run across a T-34 in a nasty mood, for instance. Absent his black coveralls, he would have been back in the *Reich*, in danger every minute of every day.

Lothar knew that, too—maybe not so well as Theo, but he did. But nobody would ever accuse him of being the shiniest bulb in the chandelier, so he didn't always understand what he knew.

"Don't worry about it, Lothar." Adi spoke in a soothing voice, as he might have to a child. He didn't want anyone, even the comrades who'd kept him alive again and again, thinking too much about who and what he was.

The next day, the *panje* wagon brought the village the regimental National Socialist Loyalty Officer along with a mail sack and two kilos of genuine ersatz coffee. The letters and the coffee were welcome. Theo didn't know about anyone else, but he could have done without Major Bruckwald. The major wasn't just in the war, which was a misfortune that could happen to anyone. Bruckwald *believed* in the war, the way a priest believed in the Holy Spirit. As far as Theo was concerned, that made him a dangerous lunatic.

Not only did Bruckwald believe in the German struggle, he was full of missionary zeal. His duty, as he saw it, was to make the ordinary soldiers believe in it, too. "This is a sacred crusade against Jewish Bolshevism!" he shouted, smacking one fist into his other palm. "We will drive the subhuman Slavs and their horrible Hebrew masters back beyond the Urals where they belong, and lay hold of the *Lebensraum* the *Reich* deserves. *Heil* Hitler!"

"*Heil* Hitler!" the listening panzer crewmen echoed, as they might have during church services. Adi Stoss was not behindhand. Theo would have been astonished if he were.

Major Bruckwald went right on fulminating. This was his closest approach to the front in some time. By the way he carried on, he was proud of his own bravery for coming so far forward, and expected the men listening to him to be at least as proud. And so they were—or they acted as if they were while he hung around.

"Remember, the *Führer* is always right!" he finished. "The Jews and Bolsheviks are trying to stab us in the back again, the way they did in 1918. See how the filthy Jew Léon Blum is back in the French government now that France has betrayed us again. See how the Jew-Bolsheviks here refuse to yield us the lands that are rightfully ours. The *Führer* smelled out this plot early on. Through his chosen instruments, the *Wehrmacht* and the *Waffen*-SS, he will make the enemies of our *Volk* pay. *Sieg heil!*"

"*Sieg heil!*" the men chorused. Seeming satisfied at last, Major Bruckwald went off to inflict himself on some other outfit.

"Well, that was fun," Sergeant Witt said, which was about what Theo was thinking. He added, "It sure is a good thing to know why we're fighting, isn't it?"

"Of course, we had no idea before," Kurt Poske said.

Adi made no snide political comments. He never did. Whatever he was thinking along those lines, he kept to himself. So did Theo, though for different reasons. But the panzer commander and the loader figured they could get away with speaking their minds. Theo wasn't sure they were right, but envied them the sense of freedom they felt.

As far as he was concerned, he was fighting for one thing: to stay alive and eventually to go home to Breslau. He'd do anything he could to bring that off. If it happened to help the *Reich* and the *Führer*, it did. If it didn't, he wouldn't lose any sleep over it.

You lost enough sleep in wartime because of things you couldn't help. Theo didn't want to lose any over stupid stuff like politics. But the morning might turn out to be a net gain. If playing Major Bruckfeld's inspiring words over and over on the phonograph of his mind didn't help him sleep better than chloroform would have, he couldn't imagine what would.

**"HEY, THE CORPORAL'S BACK!"**

The cry that rose in Willi Dernen's platoon was not one of unalloyed joy. He looked up from stripping his rifle, hoping against hope people were talking about some other *Unteroffizier*. But when hope and reality banged heads, hope lost, as it so often did. Sure as hell, there stood Arno Baatz, big as life and twice as ugly.

Awful Arno had a new wound badge on the front of his tunic and the same old gleam in his narrow, piggy eyes. Willi greeted him with, "Hey, hey, look at the hairball the cat yorked up."

"Fuck you, Dernen," Baatz replied, wasting no time in proving that a wound hadn't changed him. "I was wondering if they'd finally managed to kill you off."

By *wondering if*, he plainly meant *wishing*. No, he hadn't changed a bit. "Not me," Willi said. "And to tell you the truth, things around here have run a lot smoother since you stopped one." If he suggested that Awful Arno go stop another one, preferably with his face this time, he'd be insubordinate. If he let Baatz color in the picture for himself, on the other hand . . .

Awful Arno was plenty capable of doing that. "Smoother, huh?" he grunted, scowling. "You mean you've been screwing off more, is what you mean."

"We're farther forward than we were when you got hit," Willi said.

"And I'm sure it's all thanks to you and your asshole buddy, Pfaff." Awful Arno was full of snappy comebacks. Maybe they'd issued him some new ones at the hospital. He looked around the wrecked Russian village. "Where is Pfaff, anyway?"

"He's around somewhere," Willi said. "I think he went off to use the latrine trenches. He must have known you were coming."

"Nah, he's always been full of shit, just like you," Baatz retorted. He looked around again. "God, these Ivans live like swine."

The village no doubt hadn't been this bad before it got overrun a few times. Even so, Willi didn't think it was ever a place where he would have wanted to live. Finding he agreed with Awful Arno about anything annoyed him. Here came Adam Pfaff from the direction of the latrines. He carried his gray-painted Mauser. That was sensible. The Russians had the nasty habit of bushwhacking Germans they caught easing themselves—and of doing nasty things to their bodies, with luck after they were dead.

Willi waved to him. "Look at this!" he called. "Your old friend was just asking about you."

Pfaff controlled his enthusiasm at seeing Corporal Baatz. "Old friend?" he said, deadpan. "Where?"

"Ahh, your mother," Baatz said.

"Well, the voice is familiar," Pfaff allowed. "So is the charm."

Awful Arno told him where he could stick his charm. Then he noticed that Willi's rifle had a telescopic sight and the downturned bolt that went with it. "Still got that worthless sniping piece, do you?"

"It's not worthless," Willi said indignantly.

"In your hands, it is," Baatz said. "You can't aim well enough not to piss on your own boots."

"Bullshit." Willi pointed to the marksman's badge on his left tunic pocket.

"So you got lucky one day. Big deal," Baatz jeered.

*That's what they said to your old man, too.* Regretfully, Willi swallowed the crack instead of coming out with it. It might make Baatz swing at him, and then he'd have to try to knock Awful Arno's block off. He was pretty sure he could do it, but so what? If you brawled with a superior, you were the one who caught it every single time. It wasn't fair. Again, though, so what? Willi'd spent enough time in the service to know how little fair mattered.

Rather than making things worse, Adam Pfaff tried to defuse them: "What's the *Vaterland* like these days?" he asked Baatz. "None of us *Frontschweine*'ve seen it for a long time."

Some days, you just couldn't win. Awful Arno was as touchy as ever. "What? You telling me I'm no *Frontschwein*? Is that what you're saying?"

"No, Corporal. I'm not saying that. God forbid I should say that." Pfaff spread his hands in exaggerated patience. "What *is* the *Vaterland* like?"

"Chilly. Hungry. Not starving, but hungry. Pissed off at the froggies for changing sides again. Pretty much what you'd expect, in other words." Baatz hesitated, maybe wondering if he'd said too much. He made haste to add, "But everybody's behind the *Führer* one hundred percent, of course."

"*Aber natürlich*," Willi agreed. Pfaff nodded. Both men made sure they didn't sound sarcastic. Baatz was just the kind of pigdog who'd report you to a loyalty officer for defeatism if you opened your mouth too wide and let him see what you were really thinking—what any soldier with a gram of sense had to be thinking.

The really crazy thing was, what a *Frontschwein* thought about Hitler didn't matter a pfennig. The Ivans would slaughter you whether you thought the *Führer* was off his rocker or you went around shouting "*Sieg heil!*" all the goddamn time. You were up against the Red Army any which way. To the Russians, that was the only thing that counted. Which—*aber natürlich*—made it the only thing that counted to the guys in *Feldgrau*, too.

Cannon rumbled, off in the distance. Like Willi and Adam Pfaff, Awful Arno cocked his head to one side, listening. He delivered the verdict: "Ours."

"*Ja*." Willi nodded this time. "You remember that much, anyhow."

"Like I said before, Dernen, fuck you." With what he might have meant for an amiable nod, Baatz stumped away, boots squelching in the mud.

Willi sighed. His breath smoked. It wasn't snowing any more, but it wasn't what you'd call warm, either. "Why the hell did they have to give him back to us?" he said—quietly, because Awful Arno had ears keen as a wolf's.

"Most of the time, putting wounded guys back in the slots they held before they got hurt is a good idea. It helps morale, right?" Pfaff said.

"Right." Willi didn't sound like someone who believed it—and he wasn't. "Whoever wrote the rule book never ran into Arno Baatz."

"I'd like to run into him—driving a *Kübelwagen*," Pfaff said.

"A truck'd be better," Willi observed. They went on in that vein for some little while.

Baatz pissed and moaned about the barley-and-meat stew the field kitchen dished out. Nobody else complained. Willi was just glad the stew had meat in it. He didn't care about what the meat was. He suspected it had neighed while it was alive, but he would have eaten it even if he'd thought it barked. He'd spent too long in the field to be fussy. As long as there was plenty of it, he'd spoon it out of his mess tin. He'd go back for seconds, too. He would, and he did.

Afterwards, he did a good, thorough job of washing the tin and his utensils. No matter what Awful Arno said, he wasn't slack about anything important. Eat from a dirty mess tin and you were asking for the shits or the heaves. With what you got in Russia, you always took that chance. Making your odds worse was stupid, nothing else but.

Baatz also pissed and moaned about the pallet of musty straw where he was supposed to lay his head. "Poor baby," Willi said. "He's been sleeping on a mattress too long. He'll toss and turn all night."

"What a shame!" Adam Pfaff exclaimed.

They both laughed. They had straw pallets, too, and were damn glad to lie on them. Willi wondered how many nights he'd spent rolled in his blanket on hard ground or huddled in his greatcoat in the snow. To be fair, Awful Arno had also passed his share of nights like that, but he seemed to have forgotten about them.

Next morning, right at sunrise, the Russians launched a volley of Katyushas at the village. Most of the horrible, screaming rockets landed in the fields beyond it. All the same, Willi jumped into a muddy foxhole while they were still in the air.

Blast knocked Awful Arno off his feet, but he scrambled into a foxhole a few meters from Willi's. After the volley ended, he stuck up his head and said, "Jesus Christ, I forgot how much fun this is."

"Fun," Willi said. "*Ja.* Sure."

"You know what I mean," Baatz said.

"You bet I do—and don't I wish I didn't!" Willi agreed with deep feeling. He stuck up his head, too. As he lit a cigarette with shaking fingers, he looked east to make sure a million drunken Ivans weren't swarming forward shrieking *Urra!* Not this time, for which he thanked heaven. The Russians just wanted to harass the German positions. The bastards knew how to get what they wanted, too.

A SKINNY PEASANT with white whiskers stared suspiciously at Sergeant Ivan Kuchkov. He seemed to be the only male in the Ukrainian village except for an equally scrawny rooster. He was too old to have fought in the last war, and probably too old to have fought the Japanese. He looked old enough to have marched to war against the Ottoman Turks a generation before that.

Where were all the younger men who'd lived here? In the Red Army? Carrying rifles with some anti-Soviet guerrilla band? Kuchkov glowered at Comrade Whiskers. "We need bread," he growled.

"What?" The ancient cupped a hand behind his ear. "What's that you say?" He was trying to speak Russian, not Ukrainian, but making heavy going of it. He'd probably had it beaten into him in the Tsar's army, all right, and not used it much once they finally turned him loose.

"Bread!" Kuchkov yelled. "Food! Something to eat, you dumb, senile, cocksucking cunt."

"*Yob tvoyu mat*," the old man said, very clearly. *Fuck your mother.*

Ivan started to draw back a fist to knock the old fart's block off. Before he swung, though, he started to laugh. He laughed so hard, he had to hold his belly. "All right—you've got balls," he allowed. "But we still fucking well need to eat. So where's the bread?"

"What?" The old guy cupped a hand behind his ear again.

Chances were he heard well enough. He just didn't feel like coughing up whatever the village happened to have. These people had lived through Stalin's famine in the thirties, after all. They wouldn't be jumping up and down to help the Red Army.

Well, too bad for them. Kuchkov rounded on a stout *babushka* standing a couple of paces behind the man with the white beard. She was no spring chicken, either, but she didn't have as many kilometers on her as he did. "C'mon, Granny," Ivan said in what were meant for coaxing tones. "You can make it easy, or you can make it tough."

Granny looked death at him out of granite-gray eyes. Ivan didn't believe in witches, but that hate-filled stare tempted him to change his mind. The *babushka* gave forth with a stream of Ukrainian dialect nobody from more than a day's walk away from this miserable hole in the ground could possibly have understood.

"Talk Russian, you stinking bitch," Ivan snarled.

She did: she told him to fuck his mother, too. It wasn't so funny the second time around. He knocked her down. He could have done worse. Unslinging his machine pistol warned that he might. Slowly, she got to her feet. The other villagers' gaze swung from her to Kuchkov and back again.

"Last chance, assholes," Ivan said in his slowest, clearest Russian. "Cough up or we'll go through this shitty dump ourselves and clean you out good."

The villagers looked at the Red Army men at his back. Then they started producing loaves of black bread, small crocks of lard, and larger crocks of borscht and pickled cabbage. The whiskery man said, "If you are on our side, no wonder so many here like the Germans better." He was too old to bother hiding his bitterness.

But he only made Ivan laugh some more. "What I just gave you is a kiss next to what you'd get from the Nazis, you stupid, drippy prick," he said. "First they'd take everything you've got—and I mean every fucking thing. Then they'd burn every shanty in this pisspot place to the ground. And then they'd shoot everybody here, except the two cunts who aren't too goddamn ugly to fuck. And they'd shoot them, too, once they got the clap from them."

He wasn't kidding. He'd seen villages the Hitlerites had been through. It must have shown in his voice, because the old man's rheumy eyes blinked—slowly, like a lizard's. All he answered was, "You say this," but his own disbelief was less absolute than it might have been.

"Fucking straight I say it, Comrade," Ivan answered. "If you aren't so lucky, you'll find out for yourself."

He and his men settled down to eat. He didn't worry about what the villagers would think as they watched the soldiers go through the supplies they'd taken. If the peasants kicked up a fuss, he'd show them exactly what the Nazis did to a village. His superiors wouldn't give him any grief about it. They'd figure the locals had it coming—especially if he didn't leave any survivors to argue about how things happened.

Some of his men thought more than two girls in the village looked good enough to go after. Not surprisingly, the soldiers got what they wanted. Saying no was liable to be a—what did they call it?—a capital offense. And once the Red Army men's lust was slaked, they felt mellow enough to let the girls share some of what was really their food to begin with.

*From each according to his abilities—hers, too,* Kuchkov thought. *To each according to his need.* The Red Army men had needed pussy and chow. The villagers supplied both. Maybe Karl Marx wouldn't have approved of the shape the transaction took. Ivan didn't care, though he'd sooner have jumped on a grenade than let the *politruk* even suspect that. As far as he was concerned, Marx was just some kike from Germany.

He did make sure he set sentries all around the village before his section sacked out for the night. He made sure the rotation consisted of solid, reliable guys who wouldn't drink themselves blind. He wasn't worried about the Nazis. As far as he knew, the pricks in the coal-scuttle helmets weren't close.

If the villagers slithered out and went wailing to the Ukrainian nationalist bandits, though, that might not be such a whole bunch of fun. The Nazis clumped around, especially at night. They might beat you, but they probably wouldn't catch you by surprise.

Those nationalist bandits, though, knew the countryside better than Ivan and his buddies did. You didn't want to wake up and try breathing through a throat some funny-talking bastard had just slit. Forewarned was forestalled. Nobody sneaked out of the place, and nobody sneaked in to avenge the village girls' virtue, assuming they'd ever had any.

Things heated up the next morning. Off to the west, German and Soviet big guns started going at each other for all they were worth. Ivan cocked his head to one side, gauging the way the artillery duel was going. Except it wasn't going. It was coming this way.

"Dig, you cocksuckers!" he shouted to his men. "Dig like you're moles going after a kopek you dropped somewhere!"

His own entrenching tool made the Ukraine's black earth fly. Nothing would save you from a direct hit, but you could protect yourself against anything short of that pretty damn quick. His soldiers worked hard at their holes, too. The villagers gawped at them. They'd never seen anybody work so hard—so their eyes said.

Then the shellbursts started. At first the enemy rounds came down near the western edges of the fields, a couple of kilometers away. But they walked forward with Germanic precision and thoroughness. Some of the villagers jumped into their huts. Some tried to run off to the east.

Too late for either of those to do much good, though. Artillery scared ground-pounders worse than anything else. It caused more casualties than rifles and machine guns put together. And you couldn't hurt the sons of bitches who were slaughtering you. They sat there a few kilometers behind the line, eating sausage and swatting girls on the ass. Every so often, one of them would pull a lanyard and blow up some more guys who never did anything to them. That was how it seemed to infantrymen, anyhow.

The village was in flames by the time the shelling eased off. The old fart who hadn't wanted to feed the Russian soldiers lay dead in front of a wrecked shack, gutted like a mutton carcass. A *babushka* held him in her arms and wailed.

Only a couple of soldiers had got hurt. Neither wound looked serious. And Ivan was sure of one thing: no matter what Stalin had done to these people, now they understood Hitler was no bargain, either. The ones still alive did, anyhow. He wouldn't fret over the rest.

# Chapter 7

**S**tas Mouradian eased back on the stick, just a little, as the Pe-2's landing gear touched the ground. The bomber's nose came up by a corresponding fraction. That made the landing a bit smoother than it might have been otherwise. Beside him in the cockpit, Isa Mogamedov nodded. The copilot and bomb-aimer didn't like biting his tongue every time he came down any better than anyone else would have.

Riding the brakes hard, Stas steered the Pe-2 to a revetment and then killed the engines. As the props spun their way back into visibility and then stopped, he let out a long sigh. "Another one down," he said.

"*Da.*" Mogamedov nodded. "Not too bad this time around."

"We've been through worse," Mouradian agreed. But that wasn't the point, or he didn't think it was. He'd long since lost track of how many missions he'd flown. How many more would he have to tackle?

He didn't know the answer, not in numbers. Numbers weren't what counted. He'd keep it up till the war ended or he got killed, whichever came first. And he knew which was more likely to come first. He'd known for a long time. He was living on borrowed time. Well, who in the Soviet Union wasn't? The thing to remember was, the Germans were stealing sand from the hourglass, too.

He and Mogamedov scrambled out of the cockpit. Sergeant Mechni-kov opened the bomb-bay doors and dropped to the ground. That was so far against regulations, there weren't even any regulations against it. None of the fancy commissars had dreamt a lousy bombardier could imagine such a thing, much less do it. Well, it wasn't as if Stas hadn't noticed the commissars' failures of imagination before.

Noticing was one thing. Letting them notice you'd noticed . . . That put you into more danger than flying your Pe-2 into all the flak the *Wehrmacht* owned. You might escape the German guns. The NKVD would get you every goddamn time.

Groundcrew men in greasy coveralls trotted up to drape the bomber in camouflage netting. "How'd it go?" one of them called to Mouradian.

What were you supposed to say to something like that? Stas stayed strictly literal, which seemed safest: "We dropped our load. I think they came down about where we wanted them to. Then we turned around and got the devil out of there. As far as I know, the plane didn't take any damage."

"No Messerschmitts this time," Mogamedov agreed. "The ground fire could have been worse."

"Well, you like 'em easy once in a while, don't you?" the groundcrew man said. "We'll tend to the engines and the guns and the tires, and the armorers will bomb you up for the next run."

"*Khorosho.*" Stas left it right there. What could you say but *fine*? Nothing, not unless you wanted the Chekists to get their hooks into you.

All the same, he and his copilot and his bombardier exchanged a quick glance the groundcrew men wouldn't see—and wouldn't understand if they did happen to see it. Easy? Everything was easy after the fact. Going in, your mouth was always dry. You had to clench your asshole tight by main force—same with the sphincter that kept you from pissing yourself.

Because you didn't, you couldn't, know ahead of time how things would go. The 109 you imagined was even scarier than any actual Nazi airshark. The flak burst that shook your plane for real went off right in the cockpit in your fears, and those were your guts it splattered over the instruments.

It wasn't cowardice. It was nothing like cowardice. You went ahead and did your job. But you had to have had your soul surgically removed not to think of all the things the enemy or simple mechanical failure could do to you. A few stolid pilots did seem to have undergone that depsyching. Even among Russians, though, not many men were so nerveless. And, of the ones who were, not many flew.

"I want my hundred grams," Fyodor Mechnikov declared, in tones that warned somebody would get hurt if the sergeant didn't get his vodka ration right away.

Most of the time, the way Russians drank appalled Stas. Most of the time, but not always. Right after he came back from a mission, alcoholic oblivion often looked good—better than those imaginary Messerschmitts and the flak burst that could have butchered him, anyhow.

More Pe-2s landed at the airstrip. One by one, they sheltered in revetments and were hidden from above. On a dirt road north of the runway, tanks rumbled west. So did big, square-shouldered American trucks full of big, square-shouldered Red Army men.

Every one of them would get his hundred grams. And then, maybe, they'd link arms, grab their submachine guns, and swarm toward German entrenchments yelling "*Urra!*" at the top of their lungs. A few lucky ones might get to sober up and try to carry out their superiors' next brilliant orders.

From everything Stas had seen and heard, the Red Army's approach to putting out a fire was smothering it with bodies. The trucks kicking up dust on the road argued that they still had plenty of bodies to throw. Whether they could develop a better approach . . . They were Russians, after all.

He stumped over to the officers' tent. Sweat sprang out all over him as he walked. In winter, the furs and leather in which he flew also kept him warm on the ground. It wasn't winter any more. He didn't quite want to run around naked, but changing into a more comfortable outfit was definitely on the list.

So was vodka. For now, loosening snaps and zippers and shedding his jacket would do. He ducked inside. He wasn't the first flyer inside, or the first drinker. There were gherkins and slices of sausage to eat with the vodka. Pelmeni—meat-stuffed dumplings—were even better when you were setting out to tie one on, but they also took work to make. Pickles and sausage didn't.

"To blowing the cocks off the Fascist hyenas!" another pilot said. He raised his glass, then knocked back the shot.

Stas and his comrades followed suit. The vodka snarled down his throat. He felt as if he'd swallowed a lighted spirit lamp, then had a grenade go off in his stomach. "*Bozhemoi*, that's good!" the other pilot said. Stas wondered if they were drinking the same stuff. They were.

Isa Mogamedov stuck to tea. He drank sometimes, but not often. He was always sorry afterwards, and not just because vodka seemed to hurt him badly. Maybe he got more from his sins because he regretted them more.

Mouradian ate some sausage. It was the cheap stuff you got in wartime: more fat than meat, and about as much filler as fat. Most of the time, he would have sneered at it. Not today, not when he was going to do some serious drinking. The fat would grease his stomach lining the way oil greased the cylinders in his bomber's engines. With luck, it would slow down the alcohol soaking into his system. It wouldn't stop the stuff, but all you could do was all you could do.

*Click!* Someone turned on the radio, which was hooked up to a truck battery. The set was a standard Soviet receiver, which meant it only brought in frequencies on which the state broadcast. You couldn't get anyone else's views even if you were rash and unpatriotic enough to want them. When it came to preserving their own authority, the USSR's rulers were ruthlessly efficient.

After the set warmed up, syrupy music blared out of it. Stas wasn't the only flyer who pulled a face. You *could* get in trouble for showing you didn't fancy what came out of the radio, but most of the time you wouldn't. And it was just a few minutes before the top of the hour. The news would start then. The news, of course, came with heavy doses of propaganda, but what could you do? One of the things you could do was gain facility at reading between the lines. That Stas had done.

"Moscow speaking," the newsreader said, as if any Soviet citizen could wonder where his news came from. "French and English tanks have begun to probe Hitlerite defenses in Belgium. The Fascist monsters claim that many of our allies' armored fighting vehicles were destroyed, but, like any of Dr. Goebbels' claims, that one is bound to be a lie."

Flyers drunk and sober nodded, Stas among them. Goebbels *did* lie. Then again, so did his own lords and masters. And France and England were suddenly allies again, not jackals scavenging scraps from the German hyenas. In other words, France and England didn't have expeditionary forces on Soviet soil any more.

He wondered whether his comrades—even the relatively sober ones—noticed the change. He couldn't very well ask them. Asking would be showing that *he* noticed. It would also be asking for a one-way ticket to the gulags. Even fighting the Nazis was a better bet than that.

WEARING RUBBER GLOVES and a gauze mask like the ones surgeons used in the operating room, Hideki Fujita helped manhandle a wheeled cart along a dirt airstrip toward a waiting Army bomber. The other soldiers pulling and pushing the cart along also came from Unit 113, and also had on masks and gloves.

He wondered how much the protective garb helped. All he knew was, he hadn't come down sick yet. No. He knew one thing more: he didn't want to, either, not with the diseases the unit was generously donating to the Chinese farther north.

*Thump!* One of the cart's wheels went into a pothole. A couple of the porcelain bomb casings on the cart clattered against each other. One of them made as if to fall off. If it did . . . If that casing broke . . . Fujita wasn't the only khaki-clad man frantically shoving the germ bomb back where it belonged. The soldiers wanted to give their enemies in China this present. Get it themselves? Oh, no!

"*Eee!* Careful there!" said the armorer in charge of the cart. "Treat these babies like they've got real explosives in them."

He had a Tokyo accent that sounded as modern as next week. He was only a sergeant like Fujita, but it was the kind of accent the noncom from the country associated with officers and orders. And the fellow spoke plain good sense. If anything, the porcelain casings were worse than explosives. If a real bomb hit you, it was probably *sayonara* in a hurry. From what these bastards carried, you'd have time to hurt . . . and to regret.

The Kawasaki Ki-48 to which the men from Unit 113 lugged the germ-warfare bomb reminded Fujita of a Russian SB-2. He'd been on the receiving end of visits from those beasts in Mongolia and Siberia, and had seen several on the ground, knocked down by Japanese fighters or antiaircraft guns. Somebody'd told him that the SB-2's design had inspired the Ki-48. He didn't know whether that was true. He did know the Russian bombers had caused a lot of trouble. However his own side got planes like them, he was glad to see the Rising Sun on this machine's wings and fuselage.

A bombardier stuck his head out of the open bomb-bay doors. "So you've got my packages for me, *neh*?" the man said. "Why didn't you do them up with ribbons and fancy bows?"

"Funny. Funny like a truss," the armorer said. He and the bombardier grinned impudently at each other. The armorer turned back to his work crew. "Come on, boys. Let's get 'em into the plane. And be careful, remember! Don't act any dumber than you can help."

They loaded the porcelain casings into the bomb bay. The space was cramped, and grew more so as one porcelain casing after another went into place. The bombardier gave directions. That impudent grin came back to his face—he liked telling people what to do. He'd have to take orders, not give them, while he was flying. The men up in the cockpit were bound to be officers. He'd seem no more than a beast of burden in a uniform to them.

"You should wear a mask, too," Fujita told him. "What's in these eggs isn't anything you'd want for yourself."

"Eggs, huh? That's pretty funny." But the bombardier shook his head. "I have too many other things to worry about to bother with a mask. Those Chinese rat bastards, they shoot at you when you're over their cities, y'know. And they send up fighter planes, too, the assholes. You earn what they pay you when you go up in one of these crates. It's not like it is for you guys, where you've got nothing to do but eat and sleep and screw comfort women."

The unfairness of that almost took Fujita's breath away. It wasn't just that he'd put in his time and then some fighting the Russians. But he would much rather have faced antiaircraft fires and fighters' machine guns than the bacteria Unit 113 turned into weapons.

"You don't know what you're talking about," he said hotly. "Some of the things I could tell you—" He broke off. If he did tell anybody about those things, even bacteria would be the least of his worries. The *Kempeitai*—the Japanese secret military police—would take him apart a millimeter at a time.

"Yeah?" By the way the bombardier spoke, he didn't believe a word of it.

"*Hai. Honto,*" Fujita insisted. And it *was* true, as he knew full well. No matter how true it was, though, he couldn't talk about it. And when he didn't, the bombardier laughed at him.

He and his comrades hauled the cart away from the Ki-48. "Nothing you could do, Sergeant," a soldier said sympathetically. "If that guy wants to take a chance on coming down sick, he's too big a jerk to worry about any which way."

"*Hai. Honto,*" Fujita repeated, in the same tone of voice he'd used with the bombardier. The other men chuckled.

They sprawled on the grass by the edge of the airstrip. Before long, the pilot and copilot climbed into the bomber's cockpit. As Fujita lit a cigarette, the plane's engines growled to life. Flame and gray smoke belched from the exhaust pipes. The bomber taxied down the strip and climbed into the air. The landing gear folded up into the wings. One after another, more Ki-48s loaded with germ bombs took off. They formed up into a neat V and flew north.

"Let me have a smoke, will you?" the armorer said. As Fujita handed him the pack, the fellow went on, "Well, the Chinamen'll catch it now. Just what they deserve, too." He lit a cigarette and gave back the pack. His stubbly cheeks—he was heavily bearded for a Japanese—hollowed when he sucked in smoke. He blew it out again. "If they'd just see they need us to knock their heads together and turn their stupid country into a place that really works . . ."

"If they had that kind of sense, they wouldn't be Chinamen to begin with," Fujita said. "Even in the places where we run the show, you can't turn your back on 'em for a minute."

"These Burmese, now, they know what's what," the armorer said. The coal on the end of the cigarette glowed red as he took another deep drag. "They had the Englishmen telling 'em what to do before we cleared out those big-nosed fellows. They've got to figure we're a better bargain."

"No honor to white men," Fujita said. "They fight well enough. You could even say they're brave—as long as the fighting goes on. But if they lose, they just give up."

All the Japanese soldiers shook their heads in wonder and scorn. If you lost, better to kill yourself and get everything over with at once. You forfeited your humanity—certainly your manhood—when you surrendered. Your captors could do anything they pleased with you. Here in Burma, English prisoners were building a railroad through the jungle. Up in Manchuria, Unit 730 tested its germs on Russian, English, and American captives—and on the luckless Chinese they got in large numbers.

After a while, Fujita said, "We ought to get back to the unit," but his voice held no conviction. The armorer was attached to the airstrip. He also stayed put instead of getting up and going back to whatever his duties were. If somebody needed him, he'd hear about it. In the meantime, why not grab the chance to sit around and do nothing?

*Yeah, why not?* Fujita thought. He couldn't find any reason—not that he looked very hard.

Strange birds made strange noises in the bushes. Fujita wished he knew what they were. They had calls unlike any he'd heard in Japan or China or Siberia. Many of them, even the ones shaped like sparrows, were gaudy beyond belief. If their like had lived in the Home Islands, they would have been prized cage birds. The Burmese took them utterly for granted. Most of the time, they ignored them the way Fujita would have ignored a white-eye. Sometimes they caught them and killed them and ate them.

One of the privates fell asleep. A few minutes later, Fujita did, too. He woke up when engines announced the bombers' return. One by one, the planes bounced to a stop on the rutted grass airstrip. Fujita counted them. They'd all come back. One had a chunk bitten out of its tail, but the groundcrew men could fix that. Before long, they'd go out again—and, pretty soon, more Chinese would sicken and die.

"ALL ABOARD!" THE conductor shouted.

"See you in a week!" Herb Druce said on the platform at the Broad Street station. He hugged Peggy like a sailor going off on a cruise that would last for months. He kissed her like a sailor going to sea, too. Then, agile as a man half his age, he hopped up into the car that would take him—well, wherever he was heading. He'd always been conscientious, and he took security seriously. What Peggy didn't know, she couldn't blab if Japanese spies stuck burning slivers of bamboo under her fingernails.

That there probably weren't any Japanese spies within a thousand miles of Philadelphia, and that they were unlikely to grab Peggy and start torturing her to learn what he was up to even if they were around, bothered him not a bit. It was the principle of the thing, dammit.

He reappeared a moment later at a window seat. Peggy waved. He waved back. The train started to roll. It was bound for Dallas. Where he would get off, whether he would get back onto another train after he did . . . All that was stuff he knew and she didn't need to.

She kept waving till she couldn't see his car any more. She wasn't the only woman on the platform doing that—nowhere near. A few men waved, too, but only a few. Not far from her, two boys in short pants, one maybe six, his little brother a couple of years younger, were crying as if their hearts would break. Their daddy was going off to do something far away, and they didn't like it for beans.

Well, Peggy wasn't thrilled when Herb went off and did whatever he did for the government, either. She walked out of the train station and caught a northbound bus. The Packard mostly sat these days. The gas ration was too small to let you go anywhere you didn't really need to.

Things could have been worse, though. She knew that. In Hitler's Germany, doctors were the only civilians who could get any gas at all. Most private cars had had their batteries and tires confiscated for the war effort. The Nazis weren't melting them down to turn them into tanks and U-boats, but that was probably just a matter of time. From all she'd heard, things weren't much better in France and England. She wondered what they were like in Japan. How many cars had the Japs had to begin with? It wasn't as if they built them for themselves, the way the European countries and America did.

The very idea of Japanese-made autos set her to laughing softly as she got off the bus. What were Japanese factories good for except cheap tin knockoffs of better goods made somewhere else? If you saw something with MADE IN JAPAN stamped on it, you knew it would fall apart if you looked at it sideways.

But the laughter stopped as she headed home. American fighting men had assumed the Japs' planes and warships were made of tinfoil and scrap metal and rubber bands, too. That turned out not to be quite right. The Jap Navy ruled the Pacific everywhere west of Hawaii, and it seemed only dumb luck that the Rising Sun didn't fly over Honolulu, too.

She hadn't bothered locking the front door when she and Herb headed for the station. She knew there were burglars, but she didn't worry that anyone would break into the house the minute the people who lived there left for a little while. People who did worry about silly stuff like that were also people who snapped their fingers all the time to keep the elephants away.

Sure enough, no one had absconded with the silver and the fine china by the time she got back. No masked thug waited in the foyer to knock her over the head and beat it out the door with her handbag. It was just the good old familiar house, empty but for her. She turned on the stove and waited for the coffee to start perking again.

Coffee, now, coffee was a blessing she appreciated. Considering the horrible stuff that degraded its name and reputation on the Continent, she didn't think she'd ever take the real McCoy for granted again.

She turned on the radio. A chorus of singers was celebrating the virtues of Ivory soap. Another chorus, this one masculine, sang the praises of Old Gold cigarettes. A happy couple made it plain they wouldn't have been happy if not for Spam. A local shoe store told the world—or as much of it as this station's signals reached—that it was having a sale. Eventually, music that wasn't trying to sell you something came on.

That didn't mean it was good music. Peggy turned the dial. The next station over boasted—if that was the word—a fast-talking comic going through ways of beating the very mild American rationing system. His routine lacked the essential quality of humor known as being funny.

Peggy thought so, anyhow, and changed the station again. Maybe somebody who hadn't seen what real shortages were like would have thought the comedian was a riot. But all the commercials she'd listened to before made it plain how much the United States still had, and how much of that abundance remained available to civilians. If you complained about it, what were you but a spoiled little brat?

Or maybe you were just an American who'd never been abroad and had no standards of comparison. By all the signs, that made you the world's equivalent of a spoiled little brat. People here hadn't the faintest idea of how lucky and how well off they were.

On the next station Peggy found, a woman was talking seriously about wives and girlfriends who feared their menfolk would be unfaithful to them after being in the service for a while, or who were afraid they might decide to look for new companions themselves once they got lonely enough. That was a genuine problem, all right, here and in every other country at war. Even so, Peggy twisted the tuning dial again, and twisted it hard. She knew too well what a problem it was, and didn't want to have to think about it now.

She finally found some news. The world report was over, though. A train derailment in South Dakota had killed four people. The longshoremen's union on the West Coast was threatening a strike if working conditions didn't improve—and local authorities were threatening to jail all the union leaders if the longshoremen did presume to strike. The mayor of Kansas City was under arrest on corruption charges, some of which went all the way back to before the last war. "Another machine politician bites the dust," the newsman intoned piously.

"Business as usual," Peggy said, and turned the dial again. This time she discovered, to her surprise, a baseball game. The Athletics had scheduled their matchup with the Browns for ten in the morning: "To give the people who work the later shifts the chance to see it," their broadcaster explained. Since the A's and the Browns had both sunk like a rock in the standings ever since Opening Day, odds were not too many fans would have gone to Shibe Park no matter when the game started. Peggy did admire Connie Mack. He'd managed the A's since the start of the American League, back when she was a little girl. The Tall Tactician, people called him. He wore a suit and a hat, even in the dugout. He'd had some great teams—but not lately.

The Browns, by contrast, had never had any great teams. They were the only American League franchise without a pennant to their name. When you played in the same town as the powerhouse Cardinals, drawing crowds was tough. The Phillies, at least, were as wretched as the A's, and historically even more so.

Peggy listened to the game till the bottom of the hour. The A's botched a rundown. The Browns' left fielder dropped not one but two fly balls. Both clubs were in midseason form. At half past, she switched stations again (not without regret, for the ballgame was funnier than the comic making wisecracks about rationing) and found some more news.

She got the international reports, but they mostly consisted of both sides' lies about what was going on in Russia. Whoever finally came out on top in the war, truth had been one of the first casualties. She wondered if anything could bring it back to life. She doubted that. After Dr. Goebbels' ministrations and those of his Soviet counterparts, it would need Jesus' touch even more than Lazarus had.

Then the newsman talked about skirmishes on the Franco-German frontier. Peggy smiled. With a two-front war on his hands, the *Führer* wouldn't be doing the same.

SOMETIMES YOU HAD to take the long way around to get where you wanted to go. Julius Lemp and the U-30 certainly had. Setting out from Wilhelmshaven after a refit more thorough than the U-boat could have got in Namsos, he'd taken it all the way around the British Isles to reach the western end of the Channel. Minefields and nets kept German warships from making direct attacks.

He had to be careful in these waters. The Royal Navy and the RAF knew that U-boats might come calling. The welcome they laid on was warm but less than friendly. Along with the enemy patrols, there were also nets and minefields on this side of the Channel. That forty-kilometer-wide stretch of water was vital for getting soldiers and supplies from the island to the Continent.

If a U-boat could slide past the barriers, it might hurt the enemy badly. Plenty of U-boat skippers curled up in their cramped cots each night dreaming of sending a fat troopship to the bottom or of blowing a freighter loaded with munitions halfway to the moon.

Dreams like that came with a price, as Lemp had better reason to know than most. Even if you did sink an important vessel in the English Channel's narrow waters, you might not come home again to celebrate. The Royal Navy viciously hunted submarines, and had all the advantage in these parts.

Or you could make a mistake. Lemp's mistake, back when the war was new, was the reason he remained a lowly lieutenant more than three years later. Sinking a troopship or a big, fast freighter was splendid. Sinking a liner with Americans aboard when you thought it was a troopship or a big, fast freighter . . .

Well, they hadn't beached him. And if he could get into the Channel, anything he found there would be a legitimate target.

He ascended to the top of the conning tower. It was night now, with a fat moon, nearly full, in the sky. He wouldn't want to venture into the Channel surfaced in daylight hours. Going in submerged would be too slow—so he told himself, at any rate. He'd sneak in under cover of darkness, pick his spot, and go down to periscope depth. Then he'd see what came by and what the U-30 could do about it.

Even though it was dark, ratings with field glasses scanned sea and sky. You never wanted to get taken by surprise, and seven times never in waters like these. The U-boat would be hard to spot, and an enemy ship or plane might take it for one of their own rather than a German vessel, but . . . you never wanted to be taken by surprise.

No sooner had that thought crossed his mind than he heard what could only be airplane engines approaching rapidly from the north. The plane didn't sound very high. "Go below, boys," Lemp told the ratings. He shouted down the hatch: "Dive!"

Half a minute was all the U-30 needed to submerge. A good thing, too, because not long after the U-boat went under a bomb burst in the ocean not nearly far enough away. It shook the submarine. A couple of light bulbs popped. A wrench fell off a rack and hit the deck with a clang of iron on iron.

"Good thing we got under in a hurry," Gerhart Beilharz said.

"*Ja.*" Lemp nodded, not very happily. "That was a damned good night attack, damned good. He really rattled our teeth there."

"The moon *is* bright," the engineering officer said.

"*Ja,*" Lemp repeated, even less happily than before. "As bright as that, though? I don't think so."

"Luck." Beilharz was always inclined to look on the bright side of things: a useful attitude for a man who nursed along the sometimes-temperamental *Schnorkel.*

"Well, I hope so," the skipper said.

"What else could it be?"

"I know for a fact the English have radar, the same as we do," Lemp answered. "If they've found a way to make a set small enough to stuff it inside an airplane . . ."

Beilharz looked horrified. "That would be awful!"

"It would make our lives harder, that's for sure," Lemp said.

"How can we find out?" Beilharz asked.

"Carefully." Julius Lemp's voice was dry. The thought of surfacing and seeing whether they got attacked again had crossed his mind. No sooner had it done so, though, than he torpedoed it. Things were dangerous enough in these waters. Inviting an attack when you didn't have it might add injury to insult.

"You want to make our approach at *Schnorkel* depth, then?" Of course the engineer would plump for his favorite toy.

Lemp nodded, though. "Yes, I think we'd better. We won't get where we're going as fast as I'd like, but we have a better chance of getting there in one piece. And the Channel seems calm enough. We probably won't have waves tripping the safety valve and making the snort suck all the air out of the boat." He made a popeyed face, miming what happened to the submariners when the *Schnorkel* did just that.

"It doesn't happen very often . . . sir." When Beilharz used military formality, he wanted Lemp to know he was affronted.

"Once is plenty," Lemp said. "but the beast does have its uses. I can't imagine a radar set that could spot a *Schnorkel* tube." The engineering officer beamed when he added that. Lemp smiled to himself. You had to know what made your crew tick, all right.

It was as if the war were new. Ships carried England's soldiers and everything they needed to fight with over to France. Get into a likely sea lane and you could make them sorry. It *would* take longer chugging along with only the *Schnorkel* and periscope surfaced, but once they did it . . .

He heard occasional distant pings from enemy ships' echo-locating systems, but no vessel fired on the U-30 and started an attack run. Overhead, day slowly vanquished night. Lemp could see much farther with the periscope. He could be seen more readily, too. He had to remember that.

There! That was what he wanted: several freighters waddling across the water, escorted by a sleek destroyer that chivvied them along like a sheep dog guiding a flock of animals too stupid to remember where they were going unless they got some help.

He stayed on the *Schnorkel* as long as he could. The diesels gave him that unexpected extra submerged speed. Then, when he feared some alert sailor might spot the tube, he ordered it lowered and proceeded on battery power.

He fired three eels, one after another. He kept the last one in a forward tube in case he had to use it against the destroyer. The U-30's bow tried to break the surface as it got lighter after the torpedoes zoomed away. One missed, but the other two struck home: the explosions and the breaking-up noises from the stricken ships came clearly through the hull. The men raised a cheer.

"Now comes the interesting part," Lemp said to no one in particular. He turned the boat away from the stricken convoy. Looking back over his shoulder, so to speak, with the periscope, he saw what he knew he'd see: the Royal Navy destroyer rushing up to pay him back. Its pings sounded furious. Maybe that was his imagination, but he didn't think so.

The destroyer would expect him to dive deep and sneak away at the pitiful pace the batteries gave. It would rain ash cans down on his head and hope to sink him. But he didn't feel like enduring another depth charging. "Raise the *Schnorkel* again," he ordered. "We'll get out of here twice as fast as he thinks we can."

He caught the ratings glancing at one another as they obeyed. If this worked, he was a genius. If it didn't, if the Royal Navy ship's echo-locater located them . . .

*We can dive deep then*, he thought hopefully. In the meantime, that destroyer would be pinging in the wrong place. He was betting his life, and his crewmen's lives, that it would, anyhow.

He won the bet. Other Royal Navy ships pinged away, too, but all of them well to the east of U-30. The crewmen wrestled fresh eels into those bow tubes. The "lords"—the most junior sailors—would have more room to sleep tonight, because they bunked in the compartment where reloads were stored. And then the U-boat would go hunting again.

# Chapter 8

"What the hell have you got there?" Mike Carroll asked, staring at the fat book Chaim Weinberg was reading.

"New Hemingway." Chaim held it up so Mike could see the spine—the cover was long gone. "It's called *For Whom the Bell Tolls*, and it's about the war here before the fighting started all over everywhere."

"How is it?" Mike asked.

"Pretty damn good. I wish I could get a pretty girl to hop in my sleeping bag as easy as this guy Jordan does, though."

"I was up on the Ebro when he was in Madrid," Mike said. "Hemingway, I mean, not the guy in the book."

"I understood you. So was I," Chaim said. "I know some guys who knew him while he was here, though."

"Oh, sure. Me, too." Carroll nodded. The sun glared down on the trenches. Spring in Spain didn't last long. It quickly rolled into summer, and summer in central Spain, like summer in central California, was nothing to joke about. Mike went on, "Didn't Hemingway have that lady war correspondent hopping all over him then? What the hell was her name?"

"Gellhorn. Martha Gellhorn." To show how he knew, Chaim flipped back to the very beginning of the book. "It's dedicated to her. They're married now, I think."

"Yeah, I think you're right." Mike nodded again. "Married and living in Cuba or some such place. That's the nice thing about covering a war when you're a reporter. You can leave once you've got your story, and then write a book while you're pouring down rum and Coke thousands of miles away."

"You got that right. He wrote a good book, though—I will give him that much," Chaim said. "The stuff about what the Republicans and the Fascists did to each other when the war was breaking out . . . I've talked to enough Spaniards to have a notion of how it was, and what's in here feels real."

"Okay. Give it to me when you're done with it, then," Carroll said.

"Will do. Just so you know, it's not one of your cheerful-type books. No matter how much screwing this Jordan guy does, no way in hell he's gonna live to the end of it," Chaim warned.

"I'm a big boy, Mommy." Mike grinned to take away the sting.

Chaim grinned, too. "Fuck you, big boy." They both laughed. Chaim wiggled his back so the forward wall of the trench didn't dig into it in so many places—or at least so the trench wall dug into it in some different places—and went back to plowing through *For Whom the Bell Tolls*.

He was about fifty pages from the end when Nationalist howitzers opened up on the stretch of line the Internationals held. *The nerve of the bastards!* he thought as he huddled in the almost-bombproof he'd scraped in that forward wall. Couldn't they even let a guy finish his book? He didn't remember the Czech sniper's monster rifle going off, so Sanjurjo's men weren't taking revenge for some newly fallen alleged hero.

Or he didn't think they were. Hemingway had sucked him in deeply enough that he might not have noticed the Czech firing the antitank rifle. The damn thing was hard to ignore, though. Chances were the Nationalists were just being their usual asshole selves.

More 105s came down. How crazy would it be if an American International in Spain who was reading about an American International in Spain who was going to get killed by the goddamn Nationalists got killed by the goddamn Nationalists while he was reading? Well, not at the exact moment he was reading, but close enough to satisfy even the most dedicated coincidence-sniffer.

Chaim didn't want to get killed. Well, Robert Jordan didn't want to get killed, either, but that wouldn't do him any good. The god named Hemingway was one merciless son of a bitch. Jordan could screw till the earth moved for him and Maria; his movie wouldn't have a happy ending even so.

The earth was moving for Chaim, too, but he couldn't enjoy it the way Jordan did in the book. The damn shell bursts were making it shake. If one of those shells came down too close, Chaim's story wouldn't have a happy ending, either.

*Hey*, he thought, *I did some fancy fucking in Spain, too. I even have a kid to prove it.* La Martellita was nothing like Maria. She was as tough as Pilar, if you could imagine Pilar beautiful. And if you could imagine Pilar beautiful, you could imagine just about anything.

After forty-five minutes or so, the shelling let up. No, the Nationalists didn't mean anything in particular by it. They were throwing some hate around—that was all. Chaim had heard an English International give artillery fire that name. God knew it fit. Whenever Chaim said it himself, the people he was talking to always got it.

Stretcher-bearers carried a moaning wounded man back toward the doctors. Chaim hoped it was one of the Spaniards who filled out the Abe Lincolns' ranks these days. Not many Americans were left any more. He didn't want to lose a friend—or even a jerk who spoke English.

*For Whom the Bell Tolls* had got dirty and a little crumpled when he dove for cover. He figured Hemingway would approve. From things he'd heard, the writer was a blowhard and drank like a fish, but the man could sure as hell put words on paper.

Back behind the line, Republican guns came to life. They started repaying the Nationalists for their bad manners. If only they could take out Sanjurjo's artillery . . . But they didn't seem interested in trying. They inflicted the same kind of misery on the enemy's forward trenches as the Fascists had sent this way.

Chaim hated artillerymen. He didn't know a foot soldier who didn't. He suspected the Roman legionaries had hated the bastards who served the Parthian catapults—and their own as well. How could you not hate someone who could hurt you at a range where you couldn't hurt him back? There the son of a bitch was, drinking coffee and smoking a cigar, maybe with some cute dancer on his lap, and all he had to do was yank that rope to blow you into the middle of next week. It wasn't even close to fair. No matter where you were in the world, it had to look the same way.

When storming parties went forward, enemy machine-gun teams had a tough time surrendering. They dished out too much woe to atone for it by throwing up their hands. Artillerymen were the same way, only doubled and redoubled. The trouble was, storming parties rarely got far enough into the rear to give them what they deserved. That took more artillery, dammit.

After a while, the Republican gunners decided they'd done what they could for their benighted brethren in the trenches. Their cannon fell silent. Chaim waited to see if the Nationalist 105s would open up again. They didn't. Maybe they were short on shells, maybe on outrage.

Either way, he settled down not far from where he'd sat before and went back to the novel. When things were quiet, you savored the moment. Looking back, he'd done more sitting around and waiting than fighting. That might be true, but when he did look back he knew he would remember the moments of terror and the even rarer moments of exaltation far better than he recalled the longer boring stretches.

When he looked back. If he looked back. If he lived to look back. He'd been in the war a long time, and he hadn't once got badly hurt. That made him even luckier than a guy who broke the bank at Monte Carlo. The gambler only won money and all the fine cars and champagne and loose, beautiful women it could buy. Chaim won the precious chance to be that guy.

If he stayed long enough, he'd catch it as surely as Robert Jordan was going to in the story. A shell would come down in the wrong place or he'd make the unwanted acquaintance of a machine-gun bullet or some Fascist would smash in his skull with an entrenching tool in a raid. In the long run, the house always won.

They'd been on the point of demobilizing the Internationals when the big European war blew up. That would have been his chance to leave with his honor still in one piece. But it hadn't happened. He was still here—and still reading.

Robert Jordan blew the bridge. The Republic fucked up the attack he was supposed to blow the bridge for. Sure as hell, he got it. And so did the one halfway decent Nationalist Hemingway stuck in the book. War sucked, all right. Hemingway might be a drunken blowhard, but he sure as hell knew that.

COLONEL STEINBRENNER STOOD under the broad Russian sky, looking at the assembled pilots and radiomen and groundcrew personnel in their black coveralls. He'd climbed up onto a ration crate so they could all see him, too: not much of a podium, but it was what he had.

Hans-Ulrich had elbowed his way up toward the front of the squadron. He wanted to hear what the CO had to say. The cynical part of him that had sprung up during the war wondered why. He'd get the same orders no matter what Steinbrenner said now. But, cynical part or not, here he stood. Like Luther, he could do nothing else.

Steinbrenner raised both hands, almost like a minister offering benediction. The *Luftwaffe* men in front of him quieted down. A couple of guys who didn't quiet down fast enough to suit their comrades got elbows in the ribs to encourage them

"Well, boys, it's finally gone and happened," Steinbrenner said. "We *are* being recalled to the West."

A buzz ran through the flyers and groundcrew men. Rage and disappointment warred within Hans-Ulrich: rage that betrayal from England and France was forcing the *Reich* to shift the squadron away from the vital war against Bolshevism, disappointment that his affair with Sofia was being forcibly ended.

"When they told me they were transferring us, they warned me, 'You'd best be careful in the West—you'll be going up against the hottest new RAF Spitfires and French Dewoitines,'" Steinbrenner went on. He raised one eyebrow till it almost disappeared under the patent-leather brim of his officer's cap. "And I looked at them, and I said, *'Ja? Und so?'*"

The squadron exploded into laughter. Hans-Ulrich barked as loud as anyone else. Yes, modern RAF and *Armée de l'Air* fighters could hack

Stukas out of the sky with the greatest of ease. But so could the biplane Po-153s the Red Air Force was still flying. The Ju-87 was not made to dogfight, or even to run away. You had to be an optimist to use it where you didn't have unchallenged air superiority.

Which meant somebody in the *Luftwaffe* high command probably *was* an optimist. There wouldn't be unchallenged air superiority in the West. The comment Colonel Steinbrenner had got from his superiors made that only too plain. Hans-Ulrich had been shot down once in the West and once here in the East. He and Sergeant Dieselhorst had managed to bail out both times. He supposed they might stay lucky once or twice more.

He also had the feeling they would need to. If they went hunting panzers in France, the gun pods would make their plane even less airworthy than it was without them. Maybe he could surprise enemy fighters with the 37mm guns. Any cannon that would do for a panzer would do for a Spitfire . . . if you could hit it. He'd knocked down a couple of enemy planes with the big guns. Again, he supposed he might stay lucky.

Or he might not. And if he didn't, his story wouldn't have the kind of ending a cinema audience liked.

"We fly west day after tomorrow," Steinbrenner said. "Our new base will be in Belgium, not far from the French border. Groundcrew men will come by rail—we won't mount you on the wings and drop you over the new airstrip."

He got another laugh, this one mostly from the men in the black coveralls. Hans-Ulrich envied his ease up there in front of everybody. The pilot wished he could match it himself. He knew he had a long way to go.

When he and Albert Dieselhorst climbed into their Stuka for the journey into the wild, exotic, and almost forgotten West, Dieselhorst said, "Well, I won't be sorry to get the hell out of Russia, and you can take that to the bank."

"Neither will I," Hans-Ulrich agreed. The next German he met who admitted being sorry to leave Russia would be the first. But he couldn't help adding, "The *Reich* isn't leaving. We've still got a lot of men here on the ground."

"Some of them will head west, too," Dieselhorst said. "If the froggies and the Tommies are serious, we sure don't have enough troops there now to do more than annoy them."

"Two-front war," Rudel said gloomily. "*Damn* the Englishmen! It's their fault."

"It sure is." Sergeant Dieselhorst chuckled, almost too low for Rudel to hear him. Hans-Ulrich didn't swear very often. Maybe that meant he got more mileage out of the cussing he did use. Maybe it just meant he was a prig.

Bf-109s flew top cover as the Stukas buzzed back toward Byelorussia. If the Ivans had somehow heard the squadron was pulling back, it would be just like them to try to ambush it. But the planes escaped without harm, and came down somewhere not far outside of Minsk.

The Germans were putting their mark on occupied Byelorussia. White signs with black letters from an alphabet a man could read marked the airstrip and the roads around it. Opel trucks—gasoline tankers—rattled up to refuel the dive-bombers. Then the Stukas flew off again, their next stop not far from Bialystok.

Hans-Ulrich thought about asking for a little leave to give Sofia a proper good-bye. If she weren't a *Mischling*, he thought he would have done it. After all, the worst Colonel Steinbrenner could tell him was no. But in this time of trouble for Germany, he didn't want even the tolerant colonel noting how attached he'd got to a half-Jew. Sometimes the best thing you could do was keep your big yap shut.

Before the flight crews climbed back into their Ju-87s for the journey across the rest of Poland and back into the *Vaterland*, Sergeant Dieselhorst set a hand on Hans-Ulrich's shoulder for a moment. "Every so often, life can be a real bastard, you know?" he said, rough sympathy in his voice.

"*Ja*," Hans-Ulrich replied, and not another word. Whether or not Colonel Steinbrenner knew how he felt, his rear gunner sure did. Well, Dieselhorst wouldn't blab. Hans-Ulrich was sure of that.

Their next stop was in Breslau, not far from where Hans-Ulrich had grown up. Signs at the airport were in German. Some smiling young women from a relief agency brought the *Luftwaffe* men sweets and something they called tea. What leaves or roots they'd brewed it from, Hans-Ulrich had no idea. It tasted like something halfway between licorice and cough medicine. But it was hot, and they were pleasant, and they had accents like his. He didn't have to stop and puzzle out what they were saying, the way he'd so often needed to with Sofia.

After a little while, though, he realized how much he missed her clever tartness. He had no trouble understanding these girls, no, but what difference did it make if they had nothing interesting to say? And, after her sharp, angular features, the German girls seemed doughy.

When they went off to minister to another crew, he said as much to Dieselhorst. The older man's smile was bittersweet. "Ah, sonny, you really did have it bad, didn't you?" he said.

"No." Hans-Ulrich shook his head. "I had it good. I didn't know how good I had it."

Dieselhorst patted him on the back. "That's what I said." Hans-Ulrich only frowned.

They flew across the *Reich*. As they got farther west, they flew over towns the RAF had bombed. The devastation in the *Vaterland* shocked Rudel. He'd visited the same kind of devastation on Czechoslovakia, the Low Countries, France, and Russia, but that wasn't the same, not to him it wasn't. Those were foreign countries, enemy lands. They weren't *Germany*.

The squadron's new home in Belgium was outside of Philippeville, a small town south of Charleroi, which had been the scene of a thunderous battle in the last war's opening round. The people spoke French. The black-on-white signs in German seemed almost as alien here as they had in the Soviet Union.

No smiling, friendly girls greeted the *Luftwaffe* men. The snouts of 88mm flak guns pointed skyward to shoot at enemy raiders. Barbed wire held saboteurs at bay—people hoped.

Surveying the scene, Dieselhorst said, "Are you sure we left Russia?"

"Pretty sure," Hans-Ulrich answered. "If we get shot down on this front, odds are they won't stab us with pitchforks or start carving on us. We're back in the land of the Geneva Convention."

"Boy, sir, you sure know how to ease my mind," Sergeant Dieselhorst observed, and Rudel found himself with no reply to that.

THERE WERE TIMES when Sarah wondered whether she'd ever been married at all. Officially, her last name was Bruck now, not Goldman, but how often did you need to worry about your last name, or even remember you had one? She was living with her parents again, in her old room, almost as if the months with Isidor had never been.

Almost. Her clothes had gone to the Brucks' flat above their bakery—and had gone up in flames when the bombs hit the place. She was left with no more than she'd had on her back the night of the RAF raid. Even Aryans in the *Reich* got scanty clothing rations; those for Jews were smaller still. Replacing what she'd lost would take, well, forever, or twenty minutes longer.

Mother shared what she had. But that was already shabby, and would only get shabbier faster from being worn by two people rather than one. Then, out of the blue, the rabbi who'd intoned prayers at Isidor's small, sorry funeral showed up with a bundle.

"Not much," he said, "and I know not stylish for a pretty young girl, but with luck better than nothing."

The dresses and blouses must have come from little old Jewish women who'd died in Münster. Some of them hadn't been stylish since the days when the Kaiser still ruled Germany. Not everything looked as if it even came close to fitting.

None of which mattered a pfennig's worth to Sarah. What she couldn't alter, her mother could. "Thank you so much!" she exclaimed, moved almost to tears. She'd never had much to do with the synagogue. Like her parents, she'd been secular, assimilated . . . and much good it did her once the Nazis started screaming about how the Jews—any Jews at all—were their misfortune.

"We try," the rabbi answered. "We don't always do as well as we wish we could, but we try."

"Thank you," Sarah said again. "Thank you for thinking of me." *Even if I never thought of you* went unsaid but, no doubt, not uncomprehended.

No, not uncomprehended. "We are all in the same boat," the rabbi said. "It may be the *Titanic*, but we are all in it together whatever it is. *Alevai* one day it *will* come to a safe harbor."

"*Alevai omayn!*" Sarah agreed. The rabbi touched the brim of his hat and said his good-byes. His black suit was shiny in the seat and down the sleeves; his trousers showed a deftly mended rip. The six-pointed yellow star labeled *Jude* on his left lapel was noticeably newer and fresher than the coat it defaced.

Sarah and her mother sorted the clothes. "Well, we've got some work in front of us before you'll want to go out in any of this," Hanna Goldman said, as diplomatically as she could.

"Oh, sure." Sarah nodded. "But it's cloth!" She might have been one of the Children of Israel, talking about manna from heaven. She *was* one of the Children of Israel, she felt she *was* talking about manna, and the Third *Reich* was a desert beside which wandering through Sinai would have seemed a holiday by comparison.

She and her mother were still excited when her father came back from his shift on the labor gang. Benjamin Goldman's mouth twisted when he saw the clothes. "Very nice," he managed at last.

"I know they're old," Sarah said. "We can do things with them, though. We really can, honest."

"She's right," Mother agreed.

"Oh, I believe you." Believe her or not, Father sounded uncommonly bleak. "But those people shame me. We paid them no attention for so long, but they remember us. How can I *not* be ashamed?"

"The rabbi said we were all in the *Titanic* together," Sarah said. The rabbi, actually, had said it better than that. He'd said it in a way Father might have, but Sarah couldn't quite remember how. She had the gist, though: "How can we not help each other at a time like this?"

Her father's mouth turned down on one side once more. "I never had the least trouble ignoring the *frum*." He used the Yiddish word for *observant* as if it were from a foreign tongue. For an assimilated German Jew, it was. "I'm embarrassed, dammit. If we could find charity anywhere else . . ."

"Beggars can't be choosers," Mother said, her voice sharper than usual. "And we are beggars right now, whether it embarrasses you or not."

Samuel Goldman sighed. "I wish I could tell you you're wrong. Instead, I have to tell you you're right, and you have no idea how much more that hurts." In spite of everything, he still kept his touchy pride.

For a couple of days, playing with the old clothes and trying to turn them into something wearable kept Sarah too busy to worry about what *she* kept: a boatload of *tsuris*. Isidor had no brothers or sister. Sarah and Isidor's uncle were the family heirs.

In a civilized society, it would have been a serious, even a solemn, business. In the *Reich*, it carried more than a few elements of farce. For one thing, quite a bit of her late husband's family property had gone up in fire and smoke. For another, Münster's Nazi hierarchy seemed bound and determined to steal what was left in the Brucks' bank account.

Scowling at yet another threateningly official letter, Sarah put down her pinking shears for a moment. "The *gonifs*! It's so unfair!" she burst out.

"And this surprises you because . . . ?" Hanna Goldman had lived with Samuel for a lot of years now. She could do an excellent contralto impression of him. The voice might be too high, but the sardonic tone was perfect.

It teased a snort out of Sarah, but she quickly soured again. "They have everything!" she said. "Everything! And they want to take away some nothing that's supposed to belong to a couple of Jews." As far as she was concerned, Isidor's uncle would have been welcome to whatever the Brucks had. She'd been part of the family only a little while. An inheritance like that would have made her hands feel slimy with blood if she were trying to take it from him.

But the Nazi hooligans were another story. Why had the Brucks died, anyhow? Because Hitler started his stupid war, that was why. If he hadn't tried to rob the Czechs and Slovaks of whatever small store of happiness they possessed, her in-laws and husband would still be baking bread today.

And she couldn't even scream *Why didn't the RAF bomb the stupid Führer instead?* Her mother would understand. Understand, nothing—her mother would agree with her. She still didn't know for sure whether the house was bugged, though. The whole family would head straight for Dachau if the SS heard something like that from her.

Hitler had started the war, and the Nazis were intent on making—on stealing—a profit from it. What could one Jew do against a Juggernaut's car? Try not to get crushed under the enormous wheels: that was all she could see. Long odds against managing even so little.

In lieu of her scream, she said, "Something needs to happen. Something good, I mean. We've had too much of the other stuff."

"I know," Mother said. "But what can you do?"

"Nothing." Sarah let even more bitterness out. "Nothing is all they'll let you do. They're going to take away whatever the Brucks had, and they're going to find some stupid reason to pretend it's legal."

She imagined herself writing an indignant letter to the *Führer*. She imagined her clever words persuading him that his henchmen were overstepping. She imagined him being so impressed, he decided he'd been foolish to hate Jews all these years.

Then she imagined the attendants at the asylum strapping her into a straitjacket so she couldn't hurt herself or anyone else. Hitler wouldn't listen to her. Hitler never listened to anybody. That was part, and not such a small part, of what made him Hitler. No, he didn't listen to anybody. He made everyone else listen to him instead. And if you didn't, if you wouldn't . . . Well, that was what places like Dachau were for.

They *were* going to steal the Brucks' estate, or confiscate it, or whatever other label they'd slap on it to make it seem good to them. She *wouldn't* be able to do anything about it. Except hate them. And she was already awfully good at that.

**SUMMER IN EGYPT.** Alistair Walsh swore at himself for volunteering for . . . this. He'd been swearing at himself ever since the Germans pulled Musso's fat out of the fire at Tobruk. Now the question was whether Fritz would spread his fire all the way to Alexandria and beyond to the Suez Canal.

Fritz, damn him, had a dashing panzer general, and the dashing panzer general had the bit between his teeth. Walsh had seen photos of him. He didn't look like anything special: kind of pudgy, more like a Bavarian tavernkeeper than a fifth-generation Junker trying out the General Staff's latest bit of trickery.

But, no matter what Walther Model looked like, he knew his trade as well as any starchy Prussian with a poker up his arse. German tanks kept driving deep into the desert and coming back into view anywhere the hard-pressed English commanders didn't expect them.

No one would have accused the English officers defending Egypt of much in the way of dash. They weren't the Donkeys who'd led the King's Army during the last war—Walsh didn't suppose they were, anyhow—but they weren't a great deal better.

Every time Model drove deep into the desert like a dolphin after tunny in the sea and then came up for air in their rear, it took them by surprise. Every time they got taken by surprise, they retreated. They'd be back in Alexandria pretty soon. And wouldn't that make a pretty kettle of tunny, by God?

Of course, General Model wouldn't be able to go around them and flank them out of Alexandria, the way he had so often farther west. Alistair Walsh didn't suppose he would, anyhow. Wouldn't the Nile get in the way? You couldn't cross that on little rubber rafts the way the *Wehrmacht* had paddled over so many smaller streams in France.

Could you?

That Walsh had to wonder didn't speak well for his confidence in his country's officer corps. *If I were in charge . . .* he thought, but then, *If I were in charge, what?* The officers weren't doing any too well, true. But it wasn't as if he had any better ideas himself.

He didn't even have the better 'ole Bruce Bairnsfather's Tommies had sheltered in during the last dust-up. He rode in the back of a lorry whose engine hacked and wheezed with too much inhaled sand. All the lorries were alleged to have desert-strength air filters. So were all the tanks. Lorries and tanks nevertheless went down for the count with depressing regularity.

The soldiers jammed in there with him shared cigarettes and food. One of them squeezed liver paste from a tinfoil tube onto a cracker. As far as Walsh was concerned, that paste was the best ration in anybody's army. Pointing at the tube, he said, "Took that off a dead Fritz, did you, Algie?"

"No, Sergeant. Off a prisoner," Algie answered. He was half Walsh's age, and red and peeling from sunburn. Gingery whiskers sprouted on his cheeks and chin and upper lip. He hadn't found a chance to shave any time lately, and wouldn't have cared to any which way: the sun would have left his skin as tender and sensitive as a baby's. He stuffed the cracker into his mouth. With it still full, he added, "Not half bad."

"That's a tasty one, all right," Walsh agreed.

He didn't sound wistful or expectant. He made a point of not sounding that way. He was nonetheless a staff sergeant: perhaps not God Incarnate to a private soldier, but certainly no lower than His vicegerent on earth. Algie held out the tube to him. "Want some for yourself?"

"Obliged," Walsh said, and he meant it. He'd have to find some way to pay back the youngster before too long. In the meantime . . . In the meantime, he'd eat. You grabbed food and sleep whenever you could. You never could tell how long you'd have to do without them.

As far as Walsh was concerned, the only ration that even came close to the German liver paste was tinned steak-and-kidney pie. It wasn't *as* good, but it was plenty good enough—and you didn't have to kill or capture somebody to get your hands on it. As long as he had the real prize, he'd enjoy it. He tried to remember not to make too much of a pig of himself as he squeezed the tube onto a cracker of his own.

His belly growled when food first hit it, then grew quiet and contented. He pulled out a packet of Navy Cuts, lit one, and passed the packet first to Algie. One fag wasn't enough to give for a squeeze from that tube, but it made a start.

The lorry rumbled along. The road, such as it was, was bad. Along with the wheezy rumble, the lorry gave forth with an irregular series of thuds and bangs. And so Walsh and his comrades didn't hear the German fighters till the 109s were right on top of their column.

His head had just come up in alarm when machine-gun bullets stitched through the rear compartment of the lorry. Blood splattered. Men tried to topple, wounded or dead. The driver let out a hideous shriek. The machine slewed sideways and went into the sand. The driver's foot must have come off the pedal, because it quickly slowed to a stop.

"Out!" Walsh yelled. "Out and take cover!"

Some of the men were already moving when he shouted. They got the wounded out of the lorry as gently as they could. One man they left behind: a 7.92mm round had gone in one side of his head and blown off most of the other. No medic would help him—nor would anything else this side of Judgment Day.

Walsh ran around the lorry to get the driver out if he could. "It hurts!" the man moaned. "It hurts!" There was blood all over that compartment, too.

But he was lucky, even if he didn't think so. He'd got shot through the right nether cheek—no wonder his foot came off the accelerator! "Come on, dammit!" Walsh said, hauling him out from behind the wheel by main force. "That's a Blighty wound, or it is if you don't get hit again."

"Hurts!" was all the driver said.

He was liable to get hit again. Walsh was liable to get hit, too. The Bf-109s still buzzed above the stricken convoy like wasps above a jam jar.

Sure as hell, here came another one, seemingly straight at Walsh. Its machine guns winked malevolently. He fired his Lee-Enfield at it. He had a better chance of knocking it down than he did of flapping his arms and flying to the moon, but not a *much* better chance. He knew as much. He fired anyway. What did he have to lose?

Bullets stitched through the sand all around him, kicking up spurts that got in his eyes and spoiled his aim—if a rifleman on the ground shooting at a fighter going upwards of 300 miles an hour could be said to enjoy anything so refined as aim.

Then the Lee-Enfield fell from Walsh's hands. All at once, they were both clutching his left calf. He didn't know how they'd got there, but the damn thing hurt like blazes. Bright red blood seeped out between his fingers. That bubbling, obscenity-filled shriek came from his wide-open mouth.

"Catch one, Sergeant?" a soldier asked.

"Too bloody right I did," Walsh answered, now through clenched teeth—he'd bitten down hard on that shriek.

He took a hand away from the hole in his leg and fumbled for one of the wound dressings on his belt. He'd got scrapes and cuts and nicks in this go-round, but he hadn't really got shot since 1918. He'd forgotten how very much fun it wasn't.

He unsheathed his bayonet and used it to cut away his trouser leg. The wound was through-and-through, but it didn't look too bad. If it stayed clean, if it didn't get infected . . . Like the driver, he'd got himself a Blighty one. It wouldn't kill him, but he couldn't possibly fight for some little while.

Now that the first shock had passed, his fingers knew what to do. Gauze pads slowed the bleeding. More gauze and tape held the pads in place. If he had to, he might be able to stump along for a little ways, using his rifle as a stick.

He didn't have to. Stretcher-bearers lugged him and the driver with the wounded arse to an aid station. A doctor poured alcohol on Walsh's leg, which almost made him rise off the canvas cot like Lazarus. "Sorry, old man," the medico said, "but we do need to clean it out, what?"

"Fucking hell . . . sir," Walsh wheezed—doctors were officers by courtesy, and had to be treated as such. Tears ran down the veteran's grimy, unshaven cheeks. "That hurts worse than getting hit to begin with." The sawbones only shrugged. It wasn't *his* leg.

# Chapter 9

illi Dernen trudged across Russia. He'd worn out a lot of boots here, and that despite the cobblers' best efforts to make each pair last as long as it could. A German artillery barrage had torn up the ground. A few dead Russians lay in shattered foxholes. There was more military junk: a shattered helmet, a Mosin-Nagant rifle with a long bayonet, a puttee untidily unrolled and spread across the dirt.

He walked past everything. Sometimes military junk came in handy. Sometimes, especially in Russia, it was booby-trapped. It wasn't as if he'd never taken a chance. This morning, though, he didn't feel like it.

A hooded crow on the wing came out of the thin mist on his left, flew past him only a few meters away, and vanished into the mist on his right. Its harsh call faded in the distance.

"Damn bird wants to stop for lunch, and we're interrupting," Adam Pfaff said.

"Tough," Willi answered. Except for being gray-and-black instead of solid, glossy black, hooded crows were just like the carrion crows they had farther west. That included their eating habits. Dead dog? Dead cow? Dead horse? Dead Ivan? Dead *Landser*? It was all the same—and all delicious—to them. "Ought to be a bounty on the stinking things."

His eye fell on Arno Baatz. The corporal was as awful now as he had been before he got wounded. Willi'd hoped a stay in the hospital would mellow him (actually, Willi'd hoped Awful Arno would get inflicted upon some other unit altogether, but no such luck). He wouldn't be altogether unhappy to watch a hooded crow gorging on Baatz's mortal remains. But if Baatz caught one, he was much too likely to stop something himself.

Up ahead, a machine gun fired off a long burst. It wasn't *that* close, but Willi clutched his Mauser more tightly all the same. Unless you were a raw, raw rookie, you needed only a moment to recognize the difference between an MG-34 and an old-fashioned, water-cooled Russian Maxim. The Maxim's report was duller, and it couldn't shoot nearly so fast. With its cooling jacket and heavy wheeled mount, it also weighed a tonne.

None of which meant it couldn't kill you or maim you. Once it got set up, it made a perfectly respectable murder mill. Other German soldiers' heads also swung toward the gun, gauging distance and likely danger. Like Willi, his buddies decided the Ivans' gunners weren't aiming at them right now.

Even Awful Arno didn't need to read the tea leaves to figure that out. "Come on! Keep moving!" he bawled, his voice as nasty and raspy as a buzz saw biting into a nail.

"Who appointed him *Generalfeldmarschall*?" Pfaff wondered out loud. "I don't see the red collar tabs with the oak leaves or the baton."

Willi offered an opinion about where Baatz could stow his baton. Marching would have been uncomfortable had he put it there, but Willi wasn't inclined to quibble about such details. By Adam Pfaff's giggles, neither was he.

"What's so funny, you clowns?" Baatz growled. He couldn't have heard what they were talking about, but he hated jokes on general principles— and because he suspected they were commonly aimed at him. He was commonly right, too.

"A field marshal's baton, *Herr Unteroffizier*." Willi gave back the exact and literal truth.

"A baton? Be a cold day in hell before you ever get your filthy mitts on one," Awful Arno said, which was also true. To show what he thought of things, he added, "If you make field marshal—Christ on a crutch, if you make sergeant—the *Reich* is really and truly fucked." He turned his glower on Pfaff. "And what the devil makes a baton worth laughing at, anyway?"

By the look on Pfaff's face, he was thinking about telling the corporal precisely what made it worth laughing at. That wouldn't have done him any good, even if he might have enjoyed it for a little while. You had to understand when giving in to your impulses wasn't such a good plan.

Or sometimes you got saved by the bell. Willi's head swung to the left, toward the north. If the noise had come from the other side, he might not have heard it. He'd squeezed off a lot of Mauser rounds by his right ear. It wasn't much for catching small noises any more. It wasn't so very much for catching large noises any more.

These small noises got bigger too damn fast: the clanking rattle of panzer tracks and the belching rumble of diesel engines. Since they were diesels, those tracks had to be attached to Russian panzers—German machines all used gasoline motors. And those dinosaur shapes looming through the mist had sloping sides and turrets; they weren't all straight slabs and right angles like German panzers.

"They're T-34s!" Willi shouted: the worst thing he could think of, basically.

Awful Arno whirled away from Adam Pfaff. His Mauser leaped to his shoulder with commendable haste. He fired at one of the enormous Russian panzers. Nothing wrong with Baatz's balls. His common sense left a bit to be desired, though—not that Willi had already seen as much time and again.

Willi's own balls wanted to crawl up into his belly. He feared even that wouldn't save them. No German panzers were within kilometers, not so far as he knew. Panzer IIIs and IVs didn't stand a great chance against T-34s themselves. Infantry, now . . . Awful Arno's shot might make the Ivans notice him. It couldn't possibly hurt the steel monsters.

They said necessity was the mother of invention. As usual, what they said was a crock. Pure, raw panic sparked Willi's invention. Fumbling at his belt, he shouted, "Shoot your flare pistols at them! Maybe in the fog they'll think they're seeing antipanzer-gun tracers!"

He suited action to word. A red flare hissed toward the nearest T-34. And damned if the glowing flare *didn't* look something like a tracer from an antipanzer cannon. The mist helped, too. It concealed Willi, and it extended the glowing trail the flare left behind in the air.

Seeing how well the first one worked, Willi frantically fired off another flare. Pfaff sent his own red ball of fire at the oncoming enemy panzers, and then one more after it. Even Awful Arno got the idea. So did several other *Landsers*. If all those red fireballs really were antipanzer tracers, the T-34s were rushing headlong into deadly danger.

You never could tell with Russians. Sometimes they would stolidly take poundings that would make Germans fly for their lives, and would ambush you after you thought they had to be knocked to pieces. But sometimes, if you took them by surprise, they'd run from their own shadows. Not always—not even close. But sometimes.

This time. The Ivans didn't expect foot soldiers to try to scare them off with flares. If they saw red fireballs flying their way, they expected guns that could smash even a T-34's formidable armor. And, believing that what they saw was what they expected to see, they turned as fast as they could and roared away toward what they hoped was safety.

"Well, fuck me!" Willi said, amazement and relief warring in his voice. "It worked. It really worked!"

"Damned if it didn't," Pfaff agreed. "I'd kiss you if you weren't so ugly and if you didn't need a shave so bad."

"So would I," Arno Baatz said. "That was quick thinking, Dernen." By the way he said them, the words tasted bad in his mouth, but say them he did.

"Yeah, well . . ." Willi scuffed the toe of his boot in the dirt like a schoolboy embarrassed on the playground. It wasn't as if he *wanted* praise from Awful Arno. After a moment, he went on, "You see T-34s coming down on you, you'd damn well better come up with something in a hurry."

"They should put you up for a medal." Pfaff looked pointedly at Corporal Baatz. Awful Arno pretended not to see him.

Willi cared not a sausage casing for medals. He already wore the ribbon for the Iron Cross Second Class. He couldn't imagine *not* winning that one, not when he'd been a *Frontschwein* since the war started. If they pinned the Iron Cross First Class on him, he didn't see how his life would change. And his stunt wouldn't have rated the Knight's Cross even if he were an officer rather than a lousy *Obergefreiter*. "Hey, we're still here," he said. "Who cares about anything else?"

FRANCE DISGUSTED ARISTIDE Demange. Well, when you got right down to it, damn near everything disgusted Demange. He supposed that meant he ought to feel at home again. He didn't, though.

French civilians had always disgusted him. He'd been all for bashing the Nazis in the teeth as soon as they showed they were growing some. If the French army had moved when the *Boche*'s troops marched into the Rhineland . . .

It didn't happen. France huddled behind the Maginot Line. Plenty of civilians—mostly rich ones, but not all—wanted to hop into bed with Hitler. Others wanted to roll on their backs and show the Germans their bellies. Hardly anyone wanted to take them on, dammit. Not even the French officer corps wanted another war with Germany. The officers didn't trust England to help them out, and knew they had no prayer without her.

Well, here it was heading toward four years after France found herself in the war whether she much wanted to be or not. The civilians still hated it. From everything Demange could tell, most of them would rather have kept on fighting Stalin.

"No way in hell the Ivans would ever come this far," said a gray-haired fellow drinking up his paycheck in an *estaminet* not far from the border with Belgium. "But the damned *Boches*, the *Boches* are right here." In Demange's ears, his northern accent made him sound halfway toward being a *Boche* himself.

The lieutenant felt like smashing in his stupid face. He knew that would get him talked about. Now that he was an officer, it wouldn't do much more. At worst, he'd get busted down to sergeant again. If he did, he'd be happier than he was now.

But military discipline was a formidable thing. Instead of kicking the gray-haired *con* in the belly and then in the chops as he folded up like a concertina, Demange stubbed out one Gitane, lit another, and merely blew smoke at the bastard. "They won't be so close once we push 'em back," he growled.

"Once we do *what*?" By the way the local gaped, Demange might have suddenly started spouting Hausa or Cambodian. When the man spoke again, it was with exaggerated reason, as if to an obvious lunatic: "Come on, *Monsieur le Lieutenant*. What are the odds of that?"

He could read Demange's rank badges. Well, not many Frenchmen of his age wouldn't be able to. He'd probably done his time during the last war as a typist somewhere a hundred kilometers behind the line, pinching the cute secretaries on the ass every chance he got and worrying more about a dose of the clap than about gas or shell fragments.

"We can do it." Demange tried his own version of reason: "Honest to God, man, we can. The Germans are up to their chins in Russia. They couldn't do two fronts last time, and they can't now, either."

"They can bomb the crap out of us, though. They already have," the other guy said.

"As close as you ever got to them, I bet," Demange retorted. So much for reason.

"I did my bit last time," the local said. Demange had already figured that out. The local's tone disgusted him, too: full of a righteousness he'd already heard too goddamn often.

"Yeah, you did your bit, and then you forgot about your *patrie* and hoped like hell the old *patrie* would keep on forgetting about you. Your kind makes me sick," Demange snarled.

"What do you want to do about it?" The gray-haired man reached for the bottle of *pinard* on the zinc-topped bar in front of him, so he wasn't altogether a virgin at these games.

But he'd never brawled with anybody like Demange, either. Pasting on as broad and friendly a smile as his ferretlike face would hold, the veteran set a soft hand on the other man's shoulder. At the same time, he spoke mildly: "Well, pal, it's like this—"

Distracted by touch and voice, the local never saw the sharp, short left that buried itself in his soft midsection. "Oof!" the other fellow said, and doubled over. Demange didn't kick him while he was down, but he sure did kick him on the way down. The local would need some expensive dentistry real soon, but Demange's boots were thick enough that he didn't care—the kick didn't hurt him one bit.

The bartender yelled and reached under the bar for whatever kind of peacemaker he kept there. Demange was too busy to worry about the fine details. One of the gray-haired man's buddies grabbed him and spun him around. That was a mistake—the guy should have hit him from behind. Demange butted him with the top of his head. That did hurt some, but his skull was harder than the other clown's nose. He felt it flatten out. This *con* hadn't been pretty to begin with, but he'd be uglier now. Demange slugged him for good measure.

Somebody did tackle him from behind then. A split second later, another soldier hauled the local off him and treated the bastard like a rugby ball. The technique of the *savate* left something to be desired, but never its sincerity.

A split second after that, the whole crowded *estaminet* went berserk. There were more local tradesmen and farmers than soldiers in the joint, but the soldiers were mostly younger, in better shape, and more practiced at helping one another. They held their own and then some.

Demange didn't enjoy bar brawls. He didn't shy away from them, but he would rather have drunk quietly and then picked up a barmaid or gone to the local *maison de tolérance*. One thing you had to give officers' brothels: the girls were fresher and prettier than they were at enlisted men's houses. Less jaded? Well, you couldn't have everything.

Just because he didn't enjoy bar brawls didn't mean he wasn't sudden incapacitation on two legs when he found himself in one. As far as he was concerned, the Marquis of Queensbury was nothing but some English fairy. The only rule he recognized was to do unto others before they could do unto him.

Furious whistles squealed outside the *estaminet*. "The *flics*!" someone yelled needlessly. The cops waded into the fray, which then became that rare and ugly thing, a three-cornered fracas. The *flics* had truncheons. They were—presumably—sober. But there weren't enough of them for those advantages to help as much as they'd no doubt hoped.

In short order, some of the soldiers and some of the locals had truncheons, while some of the *flics* didn't. A policeman went out through the front window. Since it was covered over with plywood, he probably didn't much fancy that. Demange didn't think *he* would have.

He rabbit-punched somebody on his way to the door. The evening had turned more strenuous than he really cared for. Once he pushed his way out past the blackout curtain, he paused and lit a Gitane. If German night bombers could spot the flare of a match from 6,000 meters, they deserved to score a hit. After he blew out the match, even the cigarette's coal seemed bright.

He got called on the carpet a couple of days later. He'd expected he would. "That was quite a scrum in the *estaminet*," remarked the mustachioed colonel who commanded the regiment.

"Yes, sir," Demange said woodenly, and not another word.

"The civilians are hopping mad," the colonel observed. Demange stood mute, at stiff attention. The colonel's right eyebrow quirked. "You were there, *n'est-ce pas?*"

"Yes, sir," Demange repeated, with, again, no more.

"Have any idea what touched off the riot? That's what it was, or near enough."

"No, sir."

"I've heard—just heard, mind you—you might have had something to do with it."

After a few seconds, Demange decided merely standing mute wouldn't do. He grudged the regimental CO a shrug.

The colonel snorted. "All right. Get the hell out of here. And stay out of trouble for a while, you hear me? If you'd kicked that one bugger any harder, you might have broken his neck, and then I'd have a tougher time sweeping all this *merde* under the rug."

With mechanical precision, Demange saluted. He did a smart about-turn and walked out of the colonel's tent. He didn't crack a smile till he got outside. It had all gone about the way he'd figured. They wouldn't do anything to an officer who hadn't committed murder, not in wartime they wouldn't. Chuckling, Demange lit a fresh Gitane.

ANASTAS MOURADIAN EYED with undisguised admiration the planes that shared the airstrip with his squadron of Pe-2s. He whistled and silently clapped his hands. "Now those babies," he said, trying to sound slangy in Russian, "those babies mean business."

"The *Stormoviks*?" another pilot said. "Bet your dick they do." Only Russians could bring out *mat* as if born to it, because they damn well were.

What the Il-2 ground-attack planes really reminded Stas of were Stukas. They weren't just the same. They didn't have that vulture-like kink in the wing. They did boast retractable landing gear. They lacked the Stukas' dive brakes, which let the German aircraft put their bombs right where they wanted them to go. Instead, the *Stormoviks* carried a cannon and lots of forward-facing machine guns, plus one that the rear gunner used, Stuka-style, to fire at enemies coming up from behind.

Like the Stuka (and like the Pe-2, come to that), the Il-2 looked as if it meant business. Maybe that was the long in-line engine *Stormoviks* and the German dive-bombers both used. Those gave both airplanes a sharklike profile. But the Ilyushins weren't purpose-built dive-bombers, though they could carry bombs. Their main mission was to roar along at just above treetop height and shoot anything that moved.

"They did something sneaky with them." The Russian flyer waved toward the closest *Stormovik*.

"Ah? Tell me more," Stas said. The other fellow obviously wanted to do just that.

"You see the rear-firing machine gun?" the other pilot asked.

"*Da.*" Mouradian nodded.

"Well, what I hear is, when they first started flying against the Fritzes, when the rear gunner got it, he'd slump down onto the breech of the gun, and his weight would make the barrel point straight up. The fucking Germans aren't dumb, damn them to hell. When they saw that, they knew they could attack from behind without worrying about getting shot at. Cost some of our pilots their necks. Now there's a gearing mechanism in the gun mount so it won't tell everybody in sight when the poor asshole in the back seat stops one."

"How about that?" Stas said, which was a safe thing to come out with almost any old time. The gearing system was clever: coldbloodedly clever. It struck him as a very Russian—or perhaps very Soviet—way to solve the problem. Protect the rear gunner better? That would add weight and degrade performance. But if a Nazi in a Messerschmitt couldn't be sure the guy was wounded or dead, he might not bore in and shoot down the Il-2.

Yes, clever. Clever in a way that made Mouradian want to shiver. However much he wanted to, he didn't. The Russian pilot wasn't a man he knew well. He had no way to be sure the fellow didn't report to the NKVD. (For that matter, you had no way to be sure your best friend, the guy who'd had your back since you were both four years old, didn't report to the NKVD. The gulags were full of people whose best friends had sold them down the river. And some of those best friends had ended up in camps themselves. What went around came around, all right.)

"*Pilot's* got good armor, though," the Russian said.

Stas nodded again. The rear gunner might be expendable. the pilot wasn't. He could bring back a *Stormovik* with a dead rear gunner . . . as long as the Fritzes didn't realize the rear gunner'd bought his plot. Armor for the pilot. A gear mechanism for the gunner. Priorities. Russian priorities. Soviet priorities.

He figured the Il-2 pilots would have high morale. Why not? Their planes were made to chew up Germans, and looked as if they could do what they were made for very well.

How about the rear gunners? How enthusiastic would they be about flying into places where the *Luftwaffe* was strong? Mouradian snorted softly. If they didn't like it, some Chekist would give them a bullet in the back of the neck and then go to supper without a backwards glance. You had a chance in a plane, which was more than you could say if you wound up in the infantry and got told to charge that machine-gun emplacement over there.

The Russian figured angles as if he were playing pool: "With these cocks flying low and us up high, Fritz'll have to split his planes in half. That gives us a better chance to come home again, y'know? Anything that does that, I'm all for it."

"Me, too." Mouradian nodded one more time. Even in the Soviet Union, you were allowed to want to live. You weren't always actually allowed to live: if the Germans didn't do for you, the regime very well might. But it didn't begrudge your wanting to. Such generosity! A lesser country would be incapable of it.

Thus encouraged, Stas listened to Lieutenant Colonel Tomashevsky's next mission briefing with more than a little detachment. Tomashevsky was anything but detached. "The strategic situation is starting to look up," he declared. "The war in the West is on again. It's not boiling yet, but it's on. The Fascist hyenas have to split their forces. They can't concentrate on us the way they could before. But we can concentrate on them. We can, and we will. We'll show them what they get for messing with the workers and peasants of the Soviet Union!"

When the other pilots whooped and cheered, Stas did the same. His heart might not have been in it, but informers couldn't read his heart. They had to content themselves with his actions. So long as he was seen to be conspicuously loyal, he couldn't get in too much trouble . . . unless, of course, he did. Sometimes, like unexpected bad weather, bad things just happened.

The squadron would be supporting an armored column that was counterattacking against the latest German push toward Smolensk. That the Red Army could counterattack during the summer rather than merely defending showed how *Stavka* was learning its trade in the harsh school of war. As Tomashevsky had said, it also showed how the Nazis were fighting a two-front war again.

Stalin was not a lovable man or a reliable ruler. Stas knew that, and knew where he'd wind up if he were ever foolish enough to show what he knew. All of Western Europe's bourgeoisie and upper classes hated and feared Communism. Yet Hitler hadn't been able to keep England and France on his side against the USSR. They'd looked at Stalin, they'd looked at him—and, despite going over to him for a while, they hadn't been able to stomach him in the end. Stalin seemed better to them.

And if that wasn't a suitable measure of Hitler's damnation, Mouradian couldn't imagine what would be.

People who hadn't flown talked about looking down on the chessboard of war. As usual, people who hadn't done something but talked about it anyway didn't know what they were talking about. The whole point to chess was being able to know all the rules and see everything on the board.

This wasn't like that. The opposing sides didn't take turns. They didn't follow any real rules, either. They hid whatever they could wherever they could hide it. They bushwhacked. And they made mistakes that would have been impossible on the gameboard. A white pawn couldn't take a white knight. But it would be all too easy for the Pe-2s to drop their bombs on their own tanks instead of on German machines. Stas hoped he'd never done anything like that. He hoped he hadn't, but he wasn't sure.

Football had its own goals. And everything on the pitch happened at once. So that came closer. But your foes in a football match weren't trying to kill you. Somebody'd told Stas that the Japanese played a variant of chess where you could use captured pieces against the fellow who'd once owned them. That fit reality all too well.

He ordered Isa Mogamedov to drop the plane's bombs when the squadron commander declared that they were over the Fritzes' lines. He had to believe Tomashevsky knew what he was talking about. All those explosives coming down on the Germans' heads would make them very unhappy—which was the point of the exercise, if it had any point at all.

The other point was going back and landing without getting shot down or crashing. Along with bombing your friends, you could kill yourself playing the game of war. Several men Stas had known had done just that. Then the game ground on without you. It didn't care. You'd better.

A RUSSIAN BOMB went off much too close to Theo Hossbach's Panzer III. The ugly steel machine shuddered. Fragments of bomb casing clattered off the armored sides. A direct hit from a 250kg bomb, or whatever that bastard had been, and you were dead. The Krupp works didn't make enough armor to withstand the force of a direct hit.

On the far side of Theo's radio set, Adi Stoss grinned toothily. "Boy, that was fun!" he said, for all the world as if he meant it.

Theo couldn't let that go unchallenged, even if rising to it meant spending a couple of words. "Well," he said, "no."

Adi's grin only got wider. He'd made Theo talk. Making him talk, or trying to, was sport for all his crewmates. Adi put his mouth to the speaking tube that led back to the turret. "Two!" he announced, triumph in his voice.

"Lucky," Hermann Witt came back. "Hell, we're all lucky that one didn't land right on top of us."

That meshed too well with what Theo'd thought right after the bomb burst. But the Panzer III was a tough beast. What didn't kill it might not make it stronger—Nietzsche's famous ideal—but usually wouldn't harm it much. The Ivans were fighting back harder than usual, but summer was Germany's time in the East.

So Theo thought, anyhow, till the panzer closest to his blew up. That wasn't a bomb hit—it was a round from a T-34 or a KV-1. The murdered machine was one of the new Panzer III Specials, too. It had a long-barreled 50mm gun that gave it at least a chance of piercing a T-34's frontal armor. But nobody had a chance if the other guy's first shot hit.

Theo peered out through his vision slit. Was that T-34 drawing a bead on *his* panzer now? "Jink, Adi!" Sergeant Witt yelled.

Jink the driver did. He threw the Panzer III this way and that as if he were racing a Bugatti at Monte Carlo. Theo grabbed on to anything he could to keep from getting pitched out of his seat. The inside of the panzer was full of sharp, hard steel edges and projecting pieces of iron-mongery. Whoever'd designed it must have assumed the crew would have a smooth, easy ride all the time. He'd been a cockeyed optimist, in other words.

Witt fired the main armament: once, twice. Firing on the move was a mug's game. You had about as much chance of hitting your target as you did if you spat at it. The 37mm gun wasn't stabilized. Your rounds might go anywhere, and probably would—not where you wanted them to go, though. Witt was a thoroughly capable, highly experienced panzer commander. So what the hell was he doing?

"Jink right, Adi, and then halt!" he ordered now.

The panzer swung in the direction he wanted. As soon as it had halted, Theo saw a T-34 not nearly far enough away. Its turret traversed toward the Panzer III. The gun on that turret looked big as death—which, for all practical purposes, it was.

But Hermann Witt already had his gun pointing the way he wanted it to. Two armor-piercing rounds slammed into the T-34, one right after the other. Had they hit the thick, cleverly sloped frontal plate, they would have bounced off like rubber balls—Theo'd seen that only too often. Instead, they slammed into the side plate, just above the road wheels. The armor there was thinner and more nearly vertical. Both rounds holed it.

Smoke and flame burst from the T-34's hatches. Everyone in the Panzer III—Theo very much included—whooped like a scalping party of Red Indians. The T-34's turret hatch flew open. Out scrambled the panzer commander, his coveralls on fire.

Before he could drop down and use his machine's wrecked carcass as cover against the Panzer III, Theo picked him off with a burst from the hull machine gun. One of the Ivan's arms jerked despairingly. Then he slumped back into the inferno from which he'd almost escaped.

"You might have done him a favor there," Adi said seriously.

"Maybe." Theo grudged another word. The same thought had crossed his mind. If you were burning, you might want somebody to end your agony. But that wasn't why Theo had punched his ticket for him. The Soviet panzer commander had been good enough to murder at least one Panzer III. Leave him alive and he'd get himself another T-34 and cause more trouble. *Next time, it might be me* wasn't what you'd call a charitable thought, but if you didn't look out for yourself who would do it for you?

"The Ivans are as busy in the turret as a one-armed paperhanger with the hives any which way," Adi said. "The guy who commands the panzer handles the gun, too. That prick had to know his business if he could kill one of our machines single-handed."

Theo nodded. The driver's thought closely paralleled his own. That Russian—or Armenian, or Azeri, or Kazakh, or Karelian, or whatever the hell he was—needed killing exactly because he knew his business. And because he would have smashed this panzer like a cockroach if it hadn't got him first.

"Good job, everybody," Witt said. "Panzers are just like fucking, y'know? You don't have to have the biggest one around. Knowing what to do with what you've got counts for more."

That was good for several minutes' worth of filthy banter. The panzer commander must have known it would be. And letting it out relieved the tension of nearly stopping one of the T-34's big rounds—and big they were.

After the chatter died away, Adi turned to Theo and said, "Catharsis." Theo nodded again. He must have raised an eyebrow, too; that wasn't a word you heard every day, no matter how well it fit here. Looking slightly shamefaced, Adi said, "My old man taught ancient history and classics for a while."

As far as Theo could remember, that was the first time Adi'd ever said anything at all about his family. As far as Theo'd known, the driver might have been born, or possibly manufactured, in a replacement depot. Some kind of response seemed called for. "Is that a fact?" Theo ventured.

"Too right, it is," Adi answered ruefully. "He wanted me to follow in his footsteps, too, the way a father will." Acid tinged his laugh. "Tell me, man—do I look cut out to do ancient Greek?"

He looked cut out to be a blacksmith or a professional footballer or a soldier. He wasn't stupid—nowhere close. But he had instinctive excellence with his body, not with his head. Things must have worked the other way for his father. Carefully, Theo asked, "What does he think of you being here?"

"He was at the front last time." Now Adi sounded proud. "Wounded, too. Walked with a limp as long as I can remember. Sometimes this is the best place to be."

"Could be," Theo allowed. Considering some of the other places where Adi might have been, he was bound to have that one right. Theo did something unusual then—he asked another question: "What's he doing these days?"

"Street labor." Adi made a face, as if regretting he'd opened up as much as he had. He pointed a blunt, grimy forefinger with dirt and grease under the nail (a finger a lot like Theo's, in other words) at his crewmate. "That's for you to know, understand? Not for blabbing. Too goddamn much blabbing in this outfit." He looked very fierce.

"I don't blab," Theo said, which was such an obvious truth that Adi not only nodded but even chuckled. As long as Theo was running his mouth, he decided to run it a little more: "If there was too much blabbing here, you'd've been gone a long time ago."

"Huh." Perhaps to give himself a chance to think, Adi lit a cigarette. He offered Theo the pack. Theo took one with a grunt of thanks, then leaned across the radio so the driver could give him a light. Adi blew a long stream of smoke out through his hatch. "Keep your mouth shut about that one anyway, you hear? It makes things kind of obvious."

Theo nodded. There was only one likely reason for a scholar of classics and ancient history to end up in a labor gang. Oh, Adi's father might have been a Communist. He might have been a queer—but, since he had a strapping son, he damn well wasn't. No, what he was was . . . probably lucky to be alive at all. *Well, so is Adi, and so am I,* Theo thought, and tapped ash off the end of his coffin nail.

# Chapter 10

The *politruk* was haranguing the company. Ivan Kuchkov wished he could turn off his ears. He didn't need political indoctrination to understand that he was supposed to kill as many Germans as he could. The fuckers would sure do for him if he didn't kill them. Or, if he tried to bug out, the Chekists would take care of the job instead.

You couldn't win. Sooner or later, somebody's fragment or bullet would have your name on it. (Kuchkov could neither read nor write, but he understood what people were talking about when they said things like that.)

"Now is the time to press on to victory!" Lieutenant Maxim Zabelin shouted. "Even the degenerate bourgeois capitalists of the West have finally realized that the Fascist jackals are beyond the pale. The Hitlerites will be pressed from both directions, smashed like bugs between two boards!"

*Even if you're right, so what?* Ivan thought. One thing he'd found out over the years was that being right mattered a lot less than most people thought it did. The Nazis were still here, deep in the Ukraine, only a long piss away from Kiev. They could still shoot your dick off—and they damn well would, if you gave them half a chance. Or maybe even if you didn't.

"Attack! Attack fiercely! Never a step away from the enemy! Never even a single step of retreat!" the *politruk* said. "Do you understand me, bold soldiers of the Red Army?"

"*Da!*" the men chorused. Kuchkov joined in. Somebody would be watching. You didn't want to get tagged as a shirker, even if you were. Especially if you were, and he was, every chance he got.

"Questions?" Zabelin asked.

Now Kuchkov kept his big mouth shut. You didn't have to ask questions. You took a chance every time you did. They didn't care what you knew. They didn't want you to know anything but what they told you. And if you let them know you wanted to find out more than that, or you already knew more or knew better, they wouldn't pat you on the back and tell you what a clever fellow you were. Oh, no. They'd figure they couldn't trust you, and they'd give you one in the neck first chance they got.

Kuchkov knew such things instinctively, the way he knew he breathed air and drank water (or vodka, whenever he could get it). He never failed to be amazed that men better educated than he was, men by all accounts smarter than he was, didn't get it. Almost every time the *politruk* asked for questions, he found some suckers who came out with them.

Sure as hell, a soldier raised his hand now. "Comrade Political Officer, are the English and the French still class enemies of the Soviet state now that they're fighting the Hitlerites again?"

"What a *clever* question, Sergei!" Maxim Zabelin beamed at the soldier, the way a village butcher would beam at a fat sheep. "Yes, of course they are. The revolution of the workers and peasants will find a home in those lands, too. This shows the inevitability of the historical dialectic."

The company commander ambled over. First Lieutenant Obolensky puffed on a *papiros* while he listened to the *politruk*'s blather. He outranked the other man, which meant exactly nothing. The *politruk* had the Party behind him. He could countermand the company commander's orders whenever he felt like it. If he said Obolensky was ideologically unsound, his alleged superior would find himself in the gulag or a penal battalion, and would no doubt spend the short rest of his life wondering what the devil he'd done to deserve that.

A couple of other fools asked questions, too. The *politruk* handled them with the effortless ease of a circus performer going through an act for the thousandth time. He was also bound to be noticing who they were and what they wanted to know. If he didn't fancy the questions, or the questioners, the dumb dickheads would wind up unhappy pretty damn quick.

As usual, the *politruk*'s meeting closed with a shout of "We serve the Soviet Union!" When the men went off to do what they should have been doing instead of listening to him, the political officer aimed a sloppy salute at the company CO and said, "All yours, Comrade Lieutenant."

"Thank you so much, Comrade Political Officer," Obolensky replied dryly. Kuchkov's head went up as if he were a wolf taking a scent. Sarcasm was what educated people used instead of *mat*. No wonder Kuchkov had an inborn sensitivity to it. The *politruk* never noticed. No surprise there: he was so full of himself, such things flew right over his head.

Off to the west, German artillery growled itself awake. Kuchkov's head came up again. Artillery was serious business—it could slaughter you without giving you a chance at the bare-chested cunts serving the big guns. But this barrage would come down on some other sorry bastards' heads. Kuchkov relaxed.

He wondered whether the Nazis were saddled with *politruks*. He would have bet against it. If they had those fuckers looking over their commanders' shoulders, too, how could they have pushed this far into the *Rodina*?

In spite of the *politruk*'s bold words, the whole regiment fell back the next day. There were rumors the Germans had tanks in the neighborhood. Kuchkov knew damn well the Red Army didn't. The Red Army was so worried about Smolensk—and about Moscow, which Smolensk shielded—that that part of the front had first call on men and matériel.

When rumors failed to turn into slab-sided German panzers painted dark gray, the retreat stopped. The men dug in amongst the brush and scrubby trees on the east bank of a stream that might slow down an arthritic goat but that wouldn't keep anyone serious from crossing.

Lieutenant Obolensky came up to Kuchkov. "You've been around the block a time or two, eh, Comrade Sergeant?"

"Oh, fuck, yeah." Kuchkov remembered formality at the last instant: "Uh, sir."

One corner of the lieutenant's mouth twisted upward. "What do you think of our dispositions?"

That was a word Kuchkov had learned in the military. It still sounded faggy to him, but he got what it meant. Shrugging, he answered, "We've got some cover. We've got fucking mortars. We've got our machine guns. If the cocksuckers in *Feldgrau*'re dumb enough to stick their dicks into the sausage grinder, we can chop 'em up pretty good—for a while, anyways."

"Yes. For a while." This time, Obolensky's smile lifted both sides of his mouth, but it never touched his eyes. He peered west, as if expecting to see a whole *Wehrmacht* division bearing down on the company. He did see the same thing Ivan saw: nothing. With a sigh, he said, "Well, all we can do is all we can do." Was he trying to reassure Kuchkov or himself?

The Germans showed up late in the afternoon, when the sun setting behind them made them harder to spot. It might have been chance. It might have been, but Kuchkov didn't figure it was. The Nazis still in business in Russia were pros, damn them. The dumb ones were mostly dead by now.

Scouts in Nazi gray filtered forward across the fields. The Red Army men in khaki sat tight, waiting for bigger, tastier targets. With the sun going down, they probably wouldn't get them till morning. They'd have some then, though. The Germans had got better at concealing themselves, but they still weren't up to Soviet standards.

And it all turned out not to matter. The Hitlerites slipped across the stream a few kilometers south of the company. They didn't have tanks, but they did have armored cars and armored personnel carriers, which were almost as deadly. The Red Army fell back again.

Falling back meant watching out for Ukrainian nationalist bandits as well as the Nazis. By now, Ivan was used to it. He also watched out for vodka to liberate over and above the daily hundred grams, and for peasant girls who didn't bother with bourgeois affectations like morals. Even when he didn't find those, he watched out for his men. They'd be fighting the Hitlerites again, and probably soon.

WHEN THE U-30 put in at Wilhelmshaven, technicians swarmed over the boat the way they always did. But something about the way they went about it put Julius Lemp's wind up. He went back to the engine room to talk with a diesel technician he'd known for a long time.

"What's cooking, Gustav?" he asked quietly. "Something's going on, sure as hell."

Gustav was checking a valve's clearance with a butterfly gauge. After a satisfied grunt, he went on to the next one. "Don't know what you're talking about," he replied, his voice elaborately casual. To judge by his broad Bavarian dialect, he might never have set eyes on the sea. It only proved you never could tell.

Lemp's snort filled his nostrils with the heavy stink of diesel oil. It was even stronger back here than it was in the rest of the boat. That really said something—nothing good, but something all the same. "*Quatsch!*" Lemp said, more quietly than he was in the habit of using the word.

If Gustav would understand one word from how Berliners talked—so different from his own way of speech that it might almost have been a different language—it would be their pungent slang for *rubbish*. He chuckled. Then he looked around to see if any of the other men working on the engines were paying him any special attention. So did Lemp. Nobody seemed to be. What was more natural than a U-boat skipper hashing things out with somebody from the maintenance crew?

"Nothing for someone who spends most of his time at sea to worry his head about," Gustav answered after due consideration. "Politics starting to bubble again, that's all."

Lemp wanted to clap a hand to his forehead. That was the stuff of bad movies most of the time, not a U-boat's crowded confines. Every so often, though, life wanted to imitate art, even bad art. "Politics is never 'that's all,'" Lemp said with great conviction that he hoped would re-place the extravagant gesture. "Who's gone and pissed in the stewpot now?"

"Huh." Gustav said nothing more for a little while: not till after he'd made sure the next valve was still working as designed. He checked his comrades again, as carefully as he'd checked the valve. Then, not quite whispering, he continued, "Well, you won't be too surprised to hear some folks aren't jumping up and down now that we've got our two-front war back."

"*Ach, so,*" Lemp said, and pointed at the valve Gustav had just exam-ined. The mechanic's thin smile said he appreciated the artistic touch. While eyeing the valve, the U-boat skipper went on, "Haven't we gone through that nonsense already?" He knew too well they had; machine-gun fire that confined the crew to barracks during the last failed *Putsch* wasn't how he'd wanted to spend precious time ashore.

"As long as things are going good, politics looks like nonsense, *ja,*" Gustav said. "When they aren't . . ." He didn't go on, or need to.

Now Julius Lemp felt like banging his head against one of the engine's sharp, greasy projections. "The more we squabble amongst ourselves, the more the Ivans and the Tommies and the froggies laugh."

"Well, there you are," Gustav replied, which might have meant any-thing or nothing. "But folks are as jumpy as a pail of toads."

He wouldn't say anything more than that. He'd told Lemp what the U-boat skipper absolutely had to know. Who was doing what to whom . . . Lemp would have to piece that together for himself.

The officers' club would have been a good place to check, if only anyone were saying anything. But it was uncommonly quiet there. Peo-ple drank with a grim intensity Lemp had seen before. Even when they'd taken on enough torpedo fuel to sink them deeper than the *Titanic,* though, they didn't open up. They just put head on hands and fell asleep.

All the schnapps was rotgut. Lemp drank anyway. If you couldn't talk about the monster under the bed, at least you could blur its out-lines. He didn't seem to be the only one with that attitude. Oh, no. No-where close.

"This place is like a morgue," he said to the petty officer behind the bar. The man was older than he was, and might have mixed drinks here for the Kaiser's bewhiskered officers during the last war.

"Yes, sir. Sure is," the rating agreed. "Wish we could pep things up a bit."

Before Lemp answered, he asked himself the necessary question: *to whom does this man report?* The bartender was bound to report to somebody. If it was only the base commandant, that was one thing. If it was the *Gestapo* or one of the *Reich*'s many other security agencies, that was something else again. You went into one of those interrogations as beefsteak, but you came out as ground round—and maybe burnt ground round, at that.

With such gloomy reflections on his mind, Lemp answered, "Sometimes peace and quiet is the best thing you can hope for," after what he hoped was an imperceptible pause.

"Well, I don't expect anyone could argue about that." The petty officer pointed to Lemp's empty glass. "You need to take some more ballast on board, sir?"

"Oh, you bet I do," Lemp said.

He woke up with cats yowling the next morning. Timbermen, the Danes called a hangover: little guys felling trees inside your sorry skull. By the way he ached, they were using power saws. He dry-swallowed three aspirins. They helped some. The coffee he poured down would have done better had it held more of the real bean and less chicory or whatever other ersatz they used to stretch it. The military got the best the country could give. If this *was* the best, no wonder the political pot had started bubbling some more.

Lemp had better sense than to say that out loud. He got called on the commandant's carpet even so. Rear Admiral Markus Apfelbaum looked as if he'd been left out in the North Sea brine too long. He stared at Lemp with eyes of Baltic gray. "You have been asking questions." By the way he said it, that might have been a capital crime. And indeed, if the *Reich* was in ferment, it might prove to be one.

"Sir, it's always a good idea to find out which way the wind's blowing," Lemp said stolidly. "How else do you judge how to trim your sails?"

"You trim them by loyalty to the *Reich*," Apfelbaum ground out. "First, last, and always. You can do nothing else."

"I don't want to do anything else. If anyone doesn't think I'm loyal to the *Vaterland*, he should go talk to the English and Russian skippers I've sent to the bottom."

But that wasn't good enough. Lemp might have known it wouldn't be. As a matter of fact, he had known, but he'd hoped against hope he was wrong. "You are loyal to the *Vaterland*, you say." Apfelbaum sounded implacable as fate. "But are you loyal to the *Führer* and the National Socialist *Grossdeutsches Reich*? They are not necessarily one and the same, I must remind you."

When some families lost a son in the war, the death notice said *died for* Führer *and* Vaterland. Other notices simply said *died for the* Vaterland. It was one of the few ways people had to show what they thought of the current regime.

"I am loyal to the *Führer*," Lemp replied, as he had to—and as was true. He hadn't said anything to the petty officer behind the bar that would have made Markus Apfelbaum summon him. What he'd said to Gustav the diesel mechanic, though . . . *Well, now I know to whom* he *reports, anyhow*, Lemp thought.

Admiral Apfelbaum went on studying him. "People who are loyal don't need to go snooping around." The senior man might have been Moses delivering the Tablets of the Law—except Moses was a damn Jew, while Apfelbaum was anything but.

What the admiral said admitted of only one possible response. Lemp gave it: he came to stiff attention, saluted, clicked his heels, and said, "*Zu Befehl!*"

"All right. Get out of here. You've wasted enough of my time," Apfelbaum said.

Lemp saluted again, and got. He half wondered if a couple of blackshirts would be waiting for him outside the commandant's office. But no. He let out a discreet sigh of relief. The enemy, you could fight. Your own side? That often seemed a hell of a lot harder.

ELECTIONS WERE IN the air. It was a midterm campaign, of course, with only Congressional seats up for grabs, not the White House—the big prize. All the same, the Democrats were doing their best to hang on to as many seats as they could. The GOP tagged the fight against Japan FDR's war, and said he wanted to mix it up with Germany, too.

Peggy Druce would have liked nothing better than giving Hitler one right in that stupid little toothbrush mustache. Charlie Chaplin had worn one like that for comic effect. The damn thing wasn't so funny on the *Führer*'s upper lip, though.

She'd seen photos of Hitler from before he got famous, from the days when he was just another soldier in the trenches during the last war. He'd had a mustache then, too, but an ordinary one. She wondered what had made him change it to such an unbecoming style.

But that was neither here nor there. The Republicans were screaming at the top of their elephant lungs that FDR was such a donkey, he wanted to drag the country into a war with the Nazis while it was already fighting the Japs. Peggy only wished the President *would* take the USA into a fight against Germany. But Roosevelt moved with public opinion. He didn't—he couldn't safely—get too far out in front of it.

All the same, that put him well ahead of the GOP. She was convinced it did, anyhow. And she was willing—hell, she was eager—to say so in front of anyone who would listen.

"I don't know why the Republicans use the elephant for their mascot," she told a big crowd at a Masonic lodge in Scranton. "They ought to use the ostrich instead, because all they want to do is stick their heads in the sand!"

People laughed and clapped. She knew she wasn't being fair. Wendell Willkie hated and distrusted Hitler at least as much as Roosevelt did, which was saying something. But more isolationists lived in his party than in the President's. And politics wasn't about being fair. Politics was about winning elections. If you did that, you got to do what you thought needed doing. If you didn't, the yahoos on the other side grabbed the chance to pull off their stupid stunts instead.

"The Republicans think—when the Republicans think; if the Republicans think—the Republicans think, I was saying, *Well, we've got oceans on both sides of us, so nothing can get us even if we do stick our heads in the sand*. But I'm here to tell you, oceans don't always mean you're safe any more. I was in Berlin when British bombers flew hundreds and hundreds of miles and bombed it.

"And look at all the trouble Hawaii is having from bombers flying off the islands the Japs grabbed right after they jumped us. If they'd got lucky and grabbed Hawaii, too, they might be doing that to the West Coast right now."

"Little yellow monkeys!" somebody in the crowd yelled. That drew more cheers and applause. The Japs were easy to hate, especially in a place like Pennsylvania, where hardly any of them lived. They looked odd. They spoke a language nobody could understand. The nerve of them: Orientals who thought their country deserved to be a great power!

Getting worked up about the Germans was a lot harder in this part of the country. So many people here had parents or grandparents or great-grandparents who came from Germany. Even people who didn't knew or were married to people who did. Germans looked like anybody else, too. It made a difference. Maybe it shouldn't have, but it did.

"They're the measles," Peggy said firmly. "The Germans . . . The Germans are smallpox." Shudders ran through the crowd. Plenty of people there, like Peggy herself, were old enough to remember when the horrible disease hadn't been rare. Warming to her theme, she went on, "And the Republicans are a social disease."

She smiled suggestively. People whooped and hollered. A couple of wolf whistles rang through the hall. "They are," Peggy insisted. "They want to get rid of Social Security. They still want to do all the things they did that gave us the Depression. Want another dose?" She leered again. "Then vote for the grand old GOP!"

They gave her a big hand as she stepped away from the mike. She waved—she knew she'd earned it. The local politico who came up to introduce the next speaker wore an electric-green jacket with a big purple windowpane check. The hand-painted hula dancer on his scarlet tie was either voluptuous or built like a brick shithouse, depending on your attitude toward the language.

"It's my great pleasure to present to you, ladies and gentlemen," he boomed, as if announcing at a prize fight, "di-rect from Hollywood, California, that fine actor and good guy, Mis-ter George Raft!"

Raft didn't especially look like a good guy. He looked more like the small-time hood he was supposed to have been before he got into acting. His shiny black silk shirt and knife-sharp lapels did nothing to lessen the impression.

He grinned out at the gathering. "I was gonna say I didn't want to go on after Mrs. Druce, on account of she did such a great job there," he began, and led a fresh round of applause for Peggy. Not surprisingly, she found herself liking him even if he did look like a hoodlum. When the clapping died down, Raft continued: "But I *really* don't want to go on after Eddie Gryboski's necktie. Ain't that a beaut?"

Peggy laughed so hard, she almost wet her pants. She wasn't the only one, and wondered how long it had been since the Masonic hall rocked with mirth like that. Gryboski stood up to show off the hula dancer again. The crowd cheered him. They cheered again when he sat down.

George Raft had a performer's sense of timing, all right. He sensed just when to start his own speech. The audience was still happy after giving Eddie Gryboski a hand, but they were also ready to listen to whatever the marquee name had to say.

And Raft had plenty. Herb would have said that he tore the GOP a new one. He wouldn't say what the new one was, not where Peggy could hear him, not unless he was extremely provoked and probably not then, either. It wasn't that he thought she didn't know or couldn't figure it out. But he'd been taught not to cuss in front of women, a lesson no doubt driven home by a clout in the ear when he goofed.

The crowd ate it up. Well, no surprise there. They wouldn't have come to this hall if they were America Firsters or other people with views like that. When Raft finished, he got a roar of applause. A big hand, yeah, but Peggy didn't think it was much bigger than the one she'd earned for herself.

As things were breaking up, the actor came over to her and said, "I really meant what I said when I was working the crowd. You were great. You've done this a time or two before, I betcha."

"Now that you mention it," Peggy said, "yes." They smiled at each other.

"Me, I haven't done a whole lot of politicking. Never saw much point to it, not till the fighting started," Raft said. "Maybe you could give me some pointers, like."

Peggy blinked. "You're kidding!" she blurted.

"Not me." Raft shook his head and raised his right hand as if swearing an oath. "Nope, not me. How's about you come up to my hotel room? We can talk about stuff there. I'll call room service for a bottle of champagne on ice or somethin'. Help us relax while we talk, y'know?"

She laughed out loud. "Oh, I know all right, you wolf." When he said *talk*, he meant *screw*. She spread the fingers of her left hand so the rock in her wedding ring flashed. "Thanks for asking, but no thanks." How many women did he casually proposition? Quite a few, by his practiced ease. How many came across? Also quite a few, unless Peggy was all wet.

He laughed, too, also unabashed. "Can't shoot a guy for trying."

"Sure," Peggy said. He'd been a gentleman about it, or as close to a gentleman as a guy who'd started out as a small-time hood could come. Getting asked never bothered Peggy. What bothered her were guys who didn't understand when no meant no. George Raft plainly did. As he turned away—looking for someone else to try to charm—part of Peggy went *Too bad*.

MAIL CAME TO the Republican lines north and west of Madrid when it felt like coming. The Spaniards called that kind of thing *mañana*. Vaclav Jezek looked down his blunt nose at such inefficiency. The Czech hated and feared his country's German neighbors, but they'd rubbed off on him more than he realized.

Not that he ever got mail, anyway. The only people in the world who cared about him and weren't in the Czech government-in-exile's army lived in Nazi-occupied Prague. He hadn't heard from family or friends since the war started. He had to hope they were all right.

The Spaniard who carried the burlap mail sack made a horrible hash of Benjamin Halévy's name. But the Jew was used to Spaniards botching it. "*Sí, Señor. Estoy aquí*," he said. He'd learned a lot more Spanish than Vaclav had. Oh, he was a cunning linguist, all right.

"Here." The Spaniard handed him an envelope with his name typed on it, and with a printed return address Vaclav couldn't read upside down.

It wasn't upside down for Halévy, of course. He whistled several tuneless notes. "Well, well. Isn't that interesting?" he said. "I wonder what the Ministry of War wants with me."

"The *French* Ministry of War?" Jezek asked in disbelief.

"No, of course not. The Paraguayan Ministry of War," Benjamin Halévy answered tartly. Vaclav's ears heated. Halévy pulled his bayonet off his belt and opened the letter with it. Letter opener, tin opener, candlestick . . . Those were all more common uses for the bayonet than sticking enemy soldiers. The Jew took out an official-looking—which is to say, typed on letterhead—letter.

"What's it say?" Vaclav asked. If it was from the French military, it would be in French. Even if it weren't upside down for him, he wouldn't have been able to make much of it. German he could speak and read. He could swear in French, and order booze and food—and come on to the barmaid, too, if he was so inclined. But the written language was a closed book to him even if the book chanced to be open.

Instead of answering, or perhaps by way of answering, Halévy threw back his head and laughed as if he'd just heard the best dirty joke in the world. He laughed till tears cut clean tracks down his grimy cheeks. Speechless still, he held out the letter to Vaclav.

Vaclav pushed it back at him. "Just an asswipe to me," he said impatiently. "You know I can't make heads or tails of French."

"Sorry. Oh, *mon Dieu!*" Halévy wiped his eyes with his sleeve. He started laughing again. Only half kidding, Vaclav made as if to slug him. Halévy took a deep breath, hiccuped, and made himself calm down by what seemed main force of will. He held out the letter once more. This time, though, he explained it, too: "The Ministry of War, in its infinite wisdom, desires to recall me for service in the Army of my *patrie*, the Republic of France."

"You're shitting me!"

"Could I make up such a thing?" Halévy shook his head, answering his own question. After a moment, Vaclav did the same thing. He didn't believe it, either. The Jew went on, "I have a good imagination, sure, but not that good. It takes a government ministry to have an imagination that good."

"But they waved bye-bye when you left," Vaclav said. "They didn't want you around after they cozied up to Hitler. You didn't want to stick around after that, either."

"You bet I didn't," Benjamin Halévy agreed. "But now I am recalled 'to fight the Fascist foes of France.'" He waved the letter around. "That's what it says here, anyway."

"What are you going to do about it?" Jezek asked. Halévy might be a Jew with parents from Prague, but he thought of himself as a Frenchman. He'd been proud to think of himself as a Frenchman till his government hopped into the sack with the Nazis.

That, though, must have been the last straw, because he answered, "What am I going to do? This." He crumpled the letter into a ball. "And this." He flipped it up and over the earthen parapet in front of the trench.

A split second later, a rifle shot rang out from the Nationalist lines. A bullet thudded into the dirt in front of them. "Hel-lo!" Vaclav said. "They've got a sniper over there keeping an eye on us, to hell with me if they don't." Sometimes you'd fire at any motion you saw and worry later about what it might be.

Halévy didn't care about that. He knew better than to stick his head up where anybody on the other side might see it. And he managed to strike a silent-movie pose without putting himself in danger. "Here you see me, a man without a country!" he said in melodramatic tones.

"Big fucking deal." Altogether undramatic, Vaclav fumbled in his tunic pocket for his cigarettes. As he lit one, he went on, "About a division's worth of men without a country within mortar range of where we're at."

By some standards, he and the other Czechs in the line here were men without a country themselves. The Germans sat on two-thirds of what had been Czechoslovakia. Father Tiso ruled the Slovaks in the remaining third as a Fascist dictator—and as a Fascist puppet. The Czechoslovakian government-in-exile insisted that would all be put right one day. Jezek had to hope it was right. The Germans and Poles and Magyars and suchlike in the International Brigades had even less reason for optimism, and less of a chance of ever seeing their homelands again.

"I know, I know." Halévy pointed to the pack. "Give me one of those?"

Vaclav did. "You're a scrounge without a country, is what you are," he said. "Plenty of those within mortar range of here, too." It wasn't as if he hadn't bummed plenty of butts off the Jew.

After lighting up, Halévy said, "All of us guys without a country, we should get together and make our own new one. Hell, we could conquer a province somewhere—a lot of us carry guns, right?"

"Sounds great," Vaclav said. "We could fight some big old wars against our neighbors, whoever our neighbors turn out to be. And if that ever gets boring, we can have civil wars about which language we should speak or whether we should raise taxes or not."

"I like it." Halévy clapped his hands together. "We're not even a country yet, and already we've got big-time things to fight about."

"Oh, hell, yes. Nothing but first class for us." Vaclav sent him a sly look. "Good thing we'll have some Jews to kick around."

"Jews are the original people without a country," Halévy said seriously. "Hard to be a number-one country without 'em. I mean, look at Germany. How much fun could the Nazis have if they just went and persecuted Gypsies and queers and Czechs and no-account folks like that?"

"Oh, I expect they'd manage." Vaclav sounded as dry as his cosmopolitan comrade usually did.

Halévy grunted. "Mm, you've got something there. The Nazis are a cancer on humanity. They'll eat up whatever they're next to. Unless surgery works, they'll eat up the whole world."

Cancer. Surgery. Vaclav had heard a lot of nasty talk about the Nazis, but none that made more sense to him. "You've got a way with words, you know that?" he said, genuine admiration in his voice.

"Oh, sweetheart, I didn't think you cared," Halévy lisped, and blew him a kiss. The Jew was as grimy and bestubbled and smelly as any other soldier who'd stayed in the front line too goddamn long. When he swished that way, he caught Vaclav by surprise and reduced him to helpless laughter.

"You *son* of a bitch!" the Czech wheezed when he could talk at all.

"Well, at least you smiled when you said it," Halévy replied. The other Czechs were gaping at them as if they were both nuts. *I guess we are*, Vaclav thought, not without pride.

# Chapter 11

Hideki Fujita rolled off the comfort woman, stood by the side of the bed, and pulled up his trousers. The rules at military brothels didn't let him take them off, or even his boots. All that dressing and undressing wasted time. The comfort women wouldn't have been able to service so many horny soldiers.

As he fastened his belt, he said, "*Arigato.*"

The comfort woman just stared at him. She stared through him, really: her eyes were a million kilometers away. She was Burmese—a couple of shades darker than a Japanese would have been, with less angular features. She looked as different to him as an Italian would have to an Englishman. That he looked as different to her as an Englishman would have to an Italian never crossed his mind.

Somebody banged on the door to the humid little room. "Hurry up in there!" the man outside yelled in Japanese.

Out went Fujita. As he'd hoped, the man standing in the hallway was only a corporal. "What was that?" he growled.

"Please excuse my bad manners, Sergeant-*san.*" The lower-ranking noncom quailed, as he had to. Fujita could have mashed him like a yam without getting into trouble. Superiors could always do what they wanted to inferiors—that was how the Japanese system worked.

Sated, though, Fujita didn't feel like fighting now. He walked down the hall to the stairs. Behind him, the Burmese girl's door slammed shut. The corporal would get his sloppy seconds, just as he'd got someone else's a few minutes before. When you thought of things like that, wasn't it something close to a miracle that the whole Japanese Army hadn't come down with one venereal disease or another—or with one venereal disease *and* another?

Locals and Japanese soldiers led oxen up and down Myitkyina's streets. Some of the oxen had sacks of grain strapped to their backs. Some pulled two-wheeled carts or four-wheeled wagons. None of them moved very fast. Trucks were few and far between in Burma. Nothing seemed urgent here, the way it had on the border between Manchukuo and Mongolia, in Siberia, and in Unit 731 south of Harbin.

One of the fighting fronts was off in the west, by the border between Burma and India. The other was up north, in southern China. Myitkyina was a long way from either of them. If not for the bacteriological-warfare unit outside of town, this would have been a complete backwater.

Once upon a time, when he was younger and more eager, the way things went here would have bothered Fujita. No, it would have done worse than that—it would have driven him crazy. Not any more. Rushing toward an attack—what did that really mean? It meant rushing toward a chance to get killed: nothing else. Living was better, if they gave you even half a chance. You could do better than laying these resigned Burmese women, but you could also do an awful lot worse.

Not far from the brothel was the hotel the English Army had used for a headquarters till the Japanese chased out the white men and took over the place for themselves. It was the best Myitkyina boasted, which wasn't saying much. A third-rate colonial copy of a third-rate English provincial hotel . . . Fujita didn't know the details. All he knew was, the place was a dump.

But it was a dump with a bar, so he walked in anyhow. Ceiling fans spun lazily in the battered lobby. They stirred the air without doing much to cool it. The bar was all dark wood and brass. The kind of place it was modeled on might have felt cozy and inviting back in England. Here in Burma, the bar seemed out of place, to say nothing of bewildered.

They had beer. Fujita had never been in a bar anywhere that didn't have beer. They had sake—a bad local imitation of what the Japanese made. And, no doubt because they'd started life as a bad copy of an English hotel, they had what they called whiskey. That was a worse local imitation of what the English made. It smelled and tasted like kerosene, and felt like burning kerosene on the way down. Once, Fujita had asked the native behind the bar what it was distilled from. The man had seemed fluent enough in Japanese, but he suddenly lost his ability to understand the language.

This was a different bartender now. "Beer," Fujita said, and set some occupation money on the bar. The native scooped up the bill and made it disappear. He filled a mug and handed it to the sergeant.

It wasn't good beer, either. It was thin and sour. But beer was harder to screw up than sake or whiskey, even if the bar did serve it at room temperature. The barmen swore up and down that the English wanted it that way and complained if it was cold. Fujita had never known a barman who wouldn't lie, but he couldn't see why the Burmese would come up with such unlikely nonsense. Maybe they meant it—you never could tell. He hadn't figured Englishmen were so stupid, though.

He carried the mug over to an empty table (he didn't lack for choices) and sat down in one of the massive wooden chairs that were another holdover from England. In Japan, a chair like that would have marked a *daimyo*, a great lord. Ordinary people sat on mats or made do with stools. The English had different ideas about what was comfortable. Maybe they had more wood, too. They must have, if this paneled barroom gave any clues.

After he drank the first beer, he had another, and then a couple of more to weight down the earlier ones. By then, his head was buzzing nicely. It might not have been the best beer in the history of brewing, but it packed a punch, all right. He shambled over to the barman again. "Where do I piss?" he asked.

The Burmese jerked a thumb at a door he hadn't noticed amidst all the fancy woodwork. As soon as he opened the door, the smell told him the water didn't run any more. He got rid of his beer and escaped as fast as he could.

"Another, Sergeant-*san*?" the bartender asked.

"No, thanks." Fujita walked out. He thought about going back to the brothel, but he wasn't sure he could manage another round. Having a girl look through him was one thing. Having a girl sneer if he couldn't keep it up was something else again, something much worse. Even if she had too much sense to show she was sneering, she would anyhow. He knew that.

Which left . . . what? He didn't want to go back to his unit so soon. What was leave for but getting away from the people whose ugly faces you saw every day? Well, down the block stood the movie house. He could sit in the dark there and not think about anything. If the film turned out to be a stinker, he could fall asleep. Nobody'd care.

The movie house took only Japanese money. He paid his fifty sen and went inside. As in the hotel lobby, ceiling fans spun without accomplishing much. A newsreel showed Japanese tanks roaring forward in China, Japanese bombers dropping their loads on Hawaii, and a POW camp in the Philippines full of skinny, dirty Americans bearded like animals. He wondered whether they'd get shipped to Unit 731, or whether the Japanese Army would set up a germ-warfare center near the camp.

Then the feature came on. It was set in China, and featured espionage, intrigue, and a gorgeous heroine. The people playing Chinese probably were: they spoke very bad Japanese. The hero foiled their plot to bomb a general's residence and got the girl. It was as good a way to kill a couple of hours as any Fujita could have found.

He paused at a newsstand next to the movie house. A Japanese magazine showed a greenish-skinned Roosevelt on the cover. The American President's teeth were sharp and pointed like a vampire's. He looked like something that would sleep in a coffin and come out at night to suck blood, all right. Creatures like that weren't native to Japanese legend, but Fujita was one of the many, many people who'd shivered through *Dracula* when it came to the Home Islands.

He bought a girlie magazine instead. You could always think about pretty girls and what you wanted to do with them. Vampires were a sometime thing.

And then he did head out into the countryside again. His unit, no matter how much he might want to get away from it, was as close to home as he had. *Too bad*, he thought. *It's true, but too bad all the same.*


AIR-RAID SIRENS HOWLED, both on the *Ranger* and ashore. Pete McGill tumbled out of his bunk and dashed for his antiaircraft gun. "Battle stations!" the PA system howled unnecessarily. "All men to battle stations!"

Searchlights were already stabbing up into the warm tropical night. Here and there, they picked out the silver sausages of barrage balloons that had sprouted above Pearl Harbor and Honolulu to make life difficult for Japanese bombers. They didn't stab any of the bombers themselves. The Japs flew high above the barrage balloons and sensibly painted their planes' bellies matte black.

Guns ashore and aboard the ships at Pearl were already going off. Tracers added to the Fourth of July atmosphere the powerful searchlights created. Pete had no idea whether the guns were radar-guided or just putting lots of shells in the air in hopes of hitting something.

Something was up there, all right. Through the guns' thunder, Pete caught the drone of the bombers' unsynchronized engines. To him, Bettys sounded like flying washing machines. Their motors didn't have the rich, masculine growl that American planes' did.

They also caught fire at any little hit. Americans often called them Zippos—they lit the first time, every time. They'd got slaughtered when they came over Oahu by daylight. Hitting them at night was a whole different story, though. They did have their virtues. They were fast for bombers. And they had a hell of a long range: the flip side of the lack of protection that made them such lightweights. These bastards had flown all the way from Midway.

Here and there, bomb bursts outshouted the antiaircraft guns. Pete's gun started shooting at—well, something. He passed shells one after another. Sweat soaked him.

Off in the distance, a Betty cometed down into the Pacific, trailing smoke and flame. Somebody'd got lucky, anyhow. As the English, the French, and the Germans had found out before them, the Americans were discovering that stifling nighttime air raids was anything but easy. By the engine noises up in the sky, some night fighters had got airborne. They also needed to be lucky to find the enemy, though.

They needed to be lucky not to get shot down by the flak the guns on the ground and on the ships were throwing up, too. Anybody down below who saw or imagined he saw anything up above would do his goddamnedest to knock it down. If it happened to be on the same side as he was, well, that was its hard luck.

What saved most of the night fighters was the same thing that saved most of the Bettys: when you were shooting four miles straight up into the darkness, chances were you'd miss. Even as he grabbed another heavy brass shell, Pete understood that.

Shrapnel pattered down. He put on a helmet—one of the new pots that were replacing the English-style steel derbies U.S. soldiers and Marines had used since the last war. If you got hit in the head by sharp fragments of steel and brass coming down from four miles up, you'd be sorry, but not for long.

The all-clear sounded after twenty minutes or so. Some of the gunners were so keyed up, they kept firing for a while even after they had no more targets. Not the ones on the *Ranger*, though—this was a ship with discipline.

"Raid's over," Sergeant Cullum said, and lit a Camel. After a deep drag, he went on, "Now we can all hit the sack again, right?"

Most of the answers he got were inventively profane. Leathernecks who'd been jerked out of bunks and hammocks and straight into combat were running on nerve ends. Their hearts would be pounding too hard to let them sleep as quickly as they'd wakened.

Or maybe not. Pete was ready to give it a try. He'd been in the Corps long enough to understand that you grabbed Z's whenever you could, because you were bound to get screwed out of a lot of them.

Sure as hell, he slept till 0600. It was getting light out by then. A couple of smoke plumes rose into the air. The Japs must have hit something worthwhile, or those fires would have been out by now.

He got coffee and scrambled eggs and toast in the galley. The eggs were fresh, a shoreside luxury. He could eat the powdered ones—you'd starve if you couldn't stomach them at all—but they weren't the same.

A petty officer sitting across the table from him said, "We've got to find some kind of way to take back fuckin' Midway. This air-raid shit gets old fast, y'know?" He punctuated his opinion with a yawn, then headed back to the Silex for more java.

When he came back, Pete said, "Sounds good. But how d'you aim to pull it off?"

"Can't be *that* tough," the Navy man said. "C'mon, man. How many carriers you figure the Japs keep in these waters?"

"Enough," Pete answered. Since the *Ranger* was still the only American flattop in the Pacific, that didn't have to be any enormous number.

He waited to see if he'd get an argument. He more than half expected one. Navy files reflexively disagreed with Marines. When that happened in a Honolulu bar, it usually led to a fight. Aboard ship, it had better not. He didn't feel like wasting time in the brig on bread and water—piss and punk, in the pungent language swabbies and leather-necks used among themselves.

But the petty officer's broad shoulders slumped as he sighed. "Yeah, I guess you're right," he said. Pete wanted to dig a finger into his ear to make sure he'd heard that right. The man in warm-weather whites went on, "We fucked this war six ways from Sunday, didn't we?"

"Well, I'll tell you," Pete said. "I was in Peking. Then I was in Shanghai, on account of Peking's way inland and they decided they couldn't get us out if the balloon went up. Then I got blown up in Shanghai"—he scowled, remembering poor, dead Vera—"and they shipped me to a military hospital in Manila, 'cause they didn't figure they could get us out of Shanghai, either."

"They were right, too," the petty officer said tactlessly.

"Yeah, I know." Pete didn't want to think about the buddies he'd had to leave behind in Shanghai. They'd be dead now, or prisoners of the Japs. From things that leaked out of China, it wasn't obvious which fate was worse. Scowling some more, he went on, "I got out of Manila on the *Boise*, one jump ahead of the invasion. I'll tell you, man, I'm goddamn sick of going east."

The petty officer nodded. "I hear you. Oh, boy, do I ever! But when we went west against the Japs, a lot of good guys went west for good, if you know what I mean."

"You bet I do. I was almost one of those guys myself," Pete said. "When the *Boise* went down, you guys fished me out of the drink. Otherwise I'd be nothing but sharkshit by now."

"Sharkshit." The Navy man considered that. A slow smile delivered his verdict. "Way to go. I didn't think anybody could come out with a dirty word I never heard before, but you just went and did it."

Pete had never heard it before, either. It just came out of his mouth. He hadn't thought about it before it did. He didn't have much time to think about it now. He got to his feet and gave his tray and dishes to a Samoan steward in what looked like a skirt—only the guy was about six feet four and almost as wide as he was tall, so ribbing him about it wasn't the smartest thing you could do.

They'd put out one of the fires by the time he got topside. The others went on burning. The Honolulu papers were sure to have rude things to say about that. Civilians here didn't like getting bombed any more than civilians anywhere else in the world. Come to that, Pete hadn't met a whole lot of men in uniform who enjoyed explosives dropping on their heads.

He didn't see how Japan could hope to conquer the USA. But Japan didn't have to. As long as she hung on to her conquests in China and the Pacific, she won. And Pete had no more brilliant plans to keep her from doing that than the petty officer did.

VACLAV JEZEK DIDN'T know what a wrecked and rusty Citroën was doing out between the lines the Republicans and the Nationalists held. More than the rust said it had sat here for quite a while. Scavengers had stripped it of tires and inner tubes. Rubber was precious for both sides. They'd taken the battery from under the hood, too. The poor dead son of a bitch who'd been driving the car still lolled behind the wheel. He was dried out, half mummified, and hardly stank at all any more: another proof how long the Citroën had been there.

That the dead man didn't stink much made the wreck all the better for Jezek's purposes. He spent one night digging a hidey-hole under the car. He made sure to keep the dirt he dug out behind the chassis. He didn't want the Nationalists to see anything had changed.

He slithered in under the Citroën. The day dawned gray and gloomy. Pretty soon, it might rain. He did some more digging. Rain would soften the ground and might make the car settle. If it settled on him, it would also settle his hash.

Once he was satisfied he didn't need to worry about that any more, he scanned Marshal Sanjurjo's positions with binoculars he'd taken from a German International who'd never need them again. The field glasses were from Zeiss, which made them as good as any in the world.

Men in yellowish khaki, some with field caps, others wearing almost-German helmets, went about their business. As long as they were out of rifle range of the Republicans, they didn't bother concealing themselves. He could have potted one of them as easily as he pleased, but he didn't put down the binoculars and set his shoulder against the antitank rifle's stock. When he killed somebody, he wanted it to mean something.

A skylark sang sweetly overhead. The bird knew nothing of war, save the war it made on mosquitoes and butterflies and crickets. Vaclav wished he could say the same.

He traversed the Zeiss glasses as if they were a machine gun. Suddenly, they stopped and snapped back, almost as if they had a will of their own. What the devil was that? A moment later, he had his answer. *That* was a German in *Feldgrau*, no doubt a survivor from the *Legion Kondor*. And damned if the son of a bitch wasn't carrying the long asbestos hose of a flamethrower, with the fuel tanks strapped on his back.

Vaclav hadn't killed many Germans since he came to Spain. He would have gone after anybody who carried a flamethrower, no matter who the bastard was. He couldn't imagine a filthier weapon. Cooking a man like a pot roast . . . He shook his head in disgust. He'd never yet heard of anyone who lugged one of those horrible things being able to surrender, and no surprise, either.

He shook his head again, this time to drive the hate and revulsion out of it. He needed to be steady to do his job. He needed to be, and he would be. He aimed his elephant gun at the German. The sight, of course, had crosshairs. He put them right where he wanted them. The

German wasn't going anywhere fast. He stood there talking with a Spaniard, and paused for a moment to get his pipe going.

The antitank rifle smashed against Vaclav's shoulder. A split second later, the 13mm bullet smashed through the flamethrower's fuel tanks. They weren't armored; that would have added weight. The jellied gasoline caught. Then it exploded, covering the German—and, as a bonus, his Spanish friend—in unquenchable fire.

"There you go, cocksucker!" Vaclav muttered as he chambered another round. "See how you like getting it instead of giving it."

Flame and smoke soared skyward from the enemies' pyre. The Nationalists close by ran every which way, as if a small boy had brought his foot down hard on an anthill. But what could they do? The flamethrower man and his chum were nothing but charred meat now. Even if somebody managed to extinguish them before they died, the kindest thing to do would be to shoot them and take them out of their agony.

Some ants—the red ones—had stings. Vaclav waited to find out if anyone over there had spotted his muzzle flash. No machine guns snarled at the dead Citroën. No mortar bombs walked toward it. He decided the excitement created behind the enemy line made the Spaniards forget about everything else.

Marshal Sanjurjo's men didn't even start shelling the Republican trenches to avenge the fallen flamethrower specialist. They almost always did that after Vaclav killed somebody. From their quiet, he concluded that they were as uneasy about their late German friend and his little toy as soldiers from the other side would have been.

It was funny. There wasn't likely to be much difference between any one man on Vaclav's side and his opposite number on the other. Both guys worried about staying alive, about not getting maimed, about their rations, and about making themselves as comfortable as they could while they fought this stupid war. Taken in a mass, though, the guys on his side were his friends, while the guys who followed Marshal Sanjurjo were nothing but Fascist swine.

Of course, they'd call his buddies a bunch of Reds and swear on a stack of Bibles they had God on their side. But what the hell did they know?

The sun eventually burned through the morning clouds. It crawled across the sky. When it went down, Vaclav wriggled out from under the dead Citroën and crawled back to the Czech positions. When he scrambled down into the trench, he found his usually stolid countrymen more excited than he could remember seeing them for a long time.

"What's going on?" he asked after he fired up a cigarette—first things first.

"We can go back to France and shoot Nazis again if we want to!" one of the men answered. "The French government asked our government-in-exile to send us up there again."

When the Third Republic jumped into bed with the Third *Reich*, the soldiers who still fought under Czechoslovakia's red, white, and blue tricolor turned into an embarrassment. Vaclav supposed they were lucky to have been allowed to go to Spain instead of getting interned or turned over to the Nazis. Now, though, Daladier had decided Hitler wasn't the lover of his dreams after all. And so the Czechs turned useful again. When it came to cynicism, Frenchmen were hard to beat.

"What's the government-in-exile got to say?" Vaclav asked. If it tried to give orders, he didn't know if he'd be any happier following them than Benjamin Halévy had been with his from France.

"So far, it hasn't said anything," the other Czech answered. The Czechoslovakian government-in-exile had abandoned Paris the last time the French switched sides—no, the next to last time now—and was currently ensconced in Barcelona. Marshal Sanjurjo's bombers visited Barcelona every so often. Otherwise, from what little Vaclav had seen of it, it was a nice place. It was a lot nicer than these trenches; the sniper was sure of that.

"Can't say I'm surprised," he observed. "They've probably caught *mañana* from the Spaniards." Most of the people in Barcelona thought of themselves as Catalans. Hearing themselves called Spaniards would have pissed them off, the way Slovaks got pissed off if you mistook them for Czechs. Vaclav didn't worry about that. Catalans had *mañana* fever, too.

"My bet is, if they tell us to go, they don't know whether we will or not," the other soldier said. "They don't know whether the Republic will let us go, either."

Vaclav grunted. France was clogged with soldiers. The Spanish Republic starved for them. On the other hand, the Republic was only fighting the equally half-assed Spanish Fascists. France was up against the Germans. Anybody up against Germans had his hands full by the nature of things, as Vaclav had too much reason to know.

"Me, I'd go to hell to kill Nazis," he said. "I guess I'd go to France, too."

"Yeah, that's the way it looks to me," his countryman agreed. "Christ only knows what the government-in-exile will decide, though. Christ only knows what the Frenchies'll end up doing, too. Maybe they'll flip over one more time. How are you supposed to know?"

"Good question." Vaclav found another good question: "What's in the stewpot? After sausage and hard bread all day, I'll eat damn near anything."


ALISTAIR WALSH REMEMBERED telling another English soldier he was lucky to have caught a Blighty wound. That was just before he'd caught one himself. You didn't think it was such ruddy wonderful luck when something laid open *your* leg.

He didn't know whether they'd taken the other wounded man back to England. He did know he hadn't said boo when they decided to ship him home instead of letting him recover in Egypt and go back to war against General Model's *Afrika Korps*.

Had someone behind the scenes quietly pulled wires for him? He hadn't tried to get anybody to do that. He'd pulled wires to get to Egypt. He wasn't about to do the same thing to get away.

And even if someone had, he didn't know whether that someone was necessarily doing him a favor. For the second time in this war, England had troops on the European mainland. One Staff Sergeant Alistair Walsh, who'd done a tour in France the last time around and another much more recently, might make a prime candidate to go back yet again.

He might once he recovered, anyhow. He'd gone back to Blighty the long, slow way: through the Suez Canal and around Africa. That was what losing Gibraltar did to you. By the time his hospital ship reached London, he was limping on the deck with a stick.

He was limping through London now, still a convalescent. The leg hadn't festered—not badly, anyhow—but it wasn't up to the demands going into the field would put on it. The people at the hospital had made noises about turning him into a behind-the-lines type: a military bureaucrat, in other words. The look he gave them put paid to that. He had the front-line soldier's essential quality—he wanted to go out there and do for the buggers on the other side. He just didn't want them to have too good a chance to do for him instead. At least the doctors and such had the sense to see that.

And maybe, again, he had people pulling wires for him. How many career NCOs got visits in hospital from sitting MPs? Ronald Cartland and Bobbity Cranford both called on him. "Heard you stopped a packet in the desert," Cartland remarked. "Hard luck, that."

"Yes, sir. Afraid so, sir," Walsh replied. Along with being a Tory MP, Cartland was also a decorated captain. He'd seen France, too: this time around, since he was too young to have served in the last war's trenches.

"Well, we do muddle along here in spite of everything," he said.

"A good thing we do," Walsh said. Cartland and Cranford and some of the other aristos had played a bigger part than Walsh in overthrowing the reactionary government that cozied up to Hitler, but the part Walsh had played left those aristos still interested in him. Speaking carefully, he went on, "How *are* things here in Blighty these days?"

"Interesting times, old man. Definitely, interesting times." One of Cartland's elegant eyebrows rose toward his hairline.

They weren't alone in the sitting room. A glance from Walsh didn't show anyone else overtly snooping, but he knew perfectly well how to listen in without seeming to do anything of the kind. He had to assume other people could aspire to the same low talent. Since he did, he contented himself with saying, "Like that, is it?"

"Very much like that. Almost too much like that, in fact." The slight smile on Captain Cartland's face said he understood perfectly.

Later, Cartland and Cranford filled in more details at a pub where the only customers were likely to be friends. "It's on tenterhooks, really," Bobbity Cranford said, slugging back a whiskey with the air of a man who badly needed one. "If we can make a go of knocking Hitler for a loop, I daresay we'll be forgiven our constitutional trespasses—Lord knows the other side also has a deal that wants forgiving. But if it looks like bogging down into a long, bloody slog like the one you cut your teeth in, Sergeant, we may have ourselves a bit of a problem."

"Yes, just a bit," Cartland agreed, deadpan.

Walsh wasn't used to hearing *bloody* as anything but an obscenity, and needed a moment to realize the MP meant it literally. A bloody slog the Western Front in the last war had indeed been. Walsh knew he'd been lucky to come out of it with only a wound himself. Well, now he had himself a matched set: one from each war. He would gladly have forgone the honor.

"Have we still got . . . those blokes safe and sound in prison?" he asked. Even in a safe place, he didn't want to allude too openly to the men who'd taken the country down the path of working with the Nazis.

"Oh, no. That would be illegal and immoral. But we've taken a worse vengeance yet," Ronald Cartland answered, straight-faced. "One of them is his Majesty's ambassador to Liberia, another to Peru. Yet another heads up the consulate in . . . where was it, Bobbity?"

"Guatemala City, if I remember rightly," Cranford said. "Or possibly one of the towns in Cuba. I forget which."

"You get the idea," Cartland said to Walsh, who nodded—he did indeed. Cartland continued, "And the former head of Scotland Yard now employs his gift for wiretapping and interrogation as chief of police in Jerusalem. If the Arabs don't put paid to him, likely the Zionists will. And if by some mischance he survives them both, he may even do the Empire some good."

"More than he'd ever manage here," Walsh said savagely.

"Quite." Cartland nodded. "But that particular lot won't come back to that particular mischief any time soon. Their letters and cables are quite closely monitored, I assure you."

"Well, good," Walsh said. That was hoisting the collaborators with their own petard, all right. Even so, he found another question: "So much for the leaders, then. But what about the spear-carriers, the blokes who went and did what the big men told them to?"

Cartland and Cranford looked at each other. "That's rather harder to deal with, you know," Cranford said slowly. "There are a good many more of them, and their guilt is less blatant."

"But they're the ones who'll make you trouble—make us trouble," Walsh predicted. "Some of them will just have done what their bosses told them to do. That kind's safe enough. They'll do whatever anyone tells them to, and not a farthing's worth more. The others, though, the others will still believe in what they were about. Those are the buggers you've got to watch out for."

The two MPs eyed each other again. Slowly once more, Bobbity Cranford said, "How is it that you're not a brigadier, Sergeant?"

Walsh snorted laughter. "The likes of me? If I weren't in the Army, I'd be grubbing coal out of a seam back home in Wales. More likely, I'd be on the dole wishing I were grubbing coal. A brigadier?" He laughed some more.

"You have the mother wit for it. You've proved that time and again," Cranford said. "Should you be denied the right to rise to the extent of your ability because you come from a coal town, and had the misfortune not to be to the manor born?"

Walsh didn't know how to answer that. He took the class system very much for granted, as a career soldier was bound to do. At last, he managed, "I have more say with a mark on my sleeve than plenty of toffs with shoulders straps do."

That made Captain Cartland laugh, but he quickly sobered. "You're right, Sergeant—I've seen as much—but you're also wrong. You have plenty of say about the little things, but none whatever about the big ones. Bobbity's right, too. It shouldn't work that way."

"Are you sure you don't belong with Labour?" Walsh wanted to make a joke of it. Politics gave him the willies, and all the more so since he'd found himself in them up to his eyebrows.

"Labour knows one thing," Cartland said. "Labour knows it better than plenty who call themselves Tories, too: Labour understands who our true enemy is." All three men nodded and solemnly drank together.

# Chapter 12

Ⅱll kinds of interesting things were coming off the *Reich*'s assembly line. Along with his crewmates, Theo Hossbach gaped at the Panzer IV that chugged past their stopped III. "What the devil?" Hermann Witt said, eyes almost bugging out of his head.

"Damn thing's got a hard-on—a big one, too," Adi Stoss opined.

The rest of the panzer crew fell out laughing, Theo among them. Up till now, Panzer IVs had been infantry-support vehicles. They carried a stubby, low-velocity 75mm gun, good for firing HE and scattering enemy foot soldiers, but not worth much against armor.

Not this baby. Theo thought its gun was also a 75mm, but it was a long one with a muzzle brake to lessen the recoil. That beast could fire a big AP round with muzzle velocity to match. Any Soviet panzer—or any French or English one, come to that—in the way would soon be very unhappy.

No sooner had that thought crossed Theo's mind than Kurt Poske said, "Now we've got something that'll make a T-34 roll over and play dead."

Everybody nodded. The other men in black coveralls wore fierce grins on their faces. Theo couldn't see his own, but he would have bet he did, too. An ordinary Panzer III's 37mm rounds either bounced off a T-34's glacis plate and turret or stuck in them without penetrating. Even a Panzer III Special with a 50mm main armament failed more often than not. This new Panzer IV sure looked as if it could do the job, though.

Adi said, "You know what we really ought to do?"

"Tell us, *Herr Generalfeldmarschall*." Sergeant Witt clicked his heels and saluted the *Gefreiter* who drove his panzer.

"Ah, stuff it, Sergeant," Adi said—in the right tone of voice to keep from getting his tits in a wringer for showing disrespect. Then he went ahead and told them: "We ought to stick an 88 in a panzer—that's what."

Theo whistled softly. The 88 was designed as a flak gun. But, with Germanic thoroughness, the powers that be manufactured AP ammo for it, too. It was often the only piece in the *Wehrmacht*'s arsenal that could knock out rampaging T-34s or the even more thickly armored KV-1s. As a towed gun, though, too often it wasn't where it needed to be. Stuck in a turret, with an engine and tracks, it could make a world-beater.

It could. If . . .

Hermann Witt came out with the obvious objection: "That thing is fucking enormous. How big a panzer would you need to haul it around?"

"A big one." Adi admitted what he couldn't very well deny. "But God knows we need something like that. The only reason the Ivans aren't kicking our asses around the block is that we're three times the panzer-men they'll ever be."

The crewmen nodded again. It wasn't as if he were wrong. All the same, Witt said, "Make sure the National Socialist Loyalty Officer doesn't hear you talking like that. Make good and sure."

"*Zu Befehl!*" Adi said. He'd better obey that order if he knew what was good for him. With the fight in the West starting to pick up again, the authorities jumped on anyone they imagined to be disloyal or defeatist with both feet. And they had lively imaginations. Oh, did they ever!

Just then, a *Kettenrad*—a half-tracked motorcycle—fetched the ammo the panzer crew was waiting for. They didn't know the driver or the fellow riding shotgun (actually, he carried a captured Russian machine pistol). Since they didn't, they were immediately on their best behavior. After they bombed up the Panzer III, they fired it up and rattled forward again.

"I want one of those IVs with the big *Schwanz*," Adi said to Theo, who sat across the radio set from him. "I mean, I want one bad." He laughed harshly. "Remember when we felt that way about this critter?"

"*Ja*." Theo expended a word.

He needed only one; Adi was in a talkative mood: "Some poor, sorry bastards are *still* in Panzer IIs, for crying out loud! Lord, some poor bastards are still in Panzer Is. How'd you like to take on a T-34 in one of those?"

"No, thanks," Theo said. A Panzer I mounted a pair of machine guns. Anything heavier than machine-gun bullets would hole its thin armor. But they and the slightly tougher IIs soldiered on because they were better than nothing. The only thing either could do against a T-34 was run like hell.

When the company bivouacked, they were only a few hundred meters from a platoon of the long-snouted Panzer IVs. Naturally, they ambled over to get a closer look at the machines they'd just glimpsed before. As naturally, they carried Schmeissers when they crossed the Russian steppe. Never could tell if a few Ivans hadn't got cleared out the way they should have.

No trouble like that this time. Ravens and hooded crows rose skrawking from a corpse in khaki, but he *was* a corpse, not a live Russian with a PPD shamming. The panzer men from the IVs seemed glad enough to talk about their fancy new toys.

"I'd say we're pretty close to even with the T-34 now," said a sergeant commanding one of them. "We're uparmored, too, even if theirs is still thicker. But this is a better gun—higher velocity, way better fire control. You'll know about *that*, anyhow." Damn him, he sounded sorry for them.

"Oh, yes," Witt said. German sights beat the snot out of what the Ivans used. And a German panzer commander didn't have to be his own gunner, which made shooting much more efficient. But when all you had was a Panzer III's popgun, you were too likely to end up efficiently killed.

"Performance is decent, too," the other sergeant went on. He wore an Iron Cross First Class, the ribbon for the Iron Cross Second Class, and a wound badge, so he'd had enough fun to know what he was talking about. "With the wide *Ostketten* they'll issue when the rain starts, we should take mud, mm, almost as well as the Russians do."

That struck Theo as reasonable. The Red Army designed machinery with these conditions in mind. The *Wehrmacht* was learning on the fly. It was doing a pretty good job—which was why the Germans were holding on and even still advancing in places even though the war was on two fronts again. Would pretty good prove good enough? Only one way to find out. Theo hoped it wouldn't be the hard way.

Along those lines, Adi said, "We shouldn't just be as good as the Reds. We need to be better, 'cause they'll always have more of whatever they make."

The Panzer IV commander rubbed his chin. He needed a shave; whiskers rasped under his fingers. "I hear that's coming. It isn't here yet, but it's on the way." He rubbed his chin again. "You're Stoss, you said?"

"That's right," Adi answered. Theo wondered if he should have. He'd just disapproved of something the *Reich* did. If this guy wanted to get pissy about it, he could.

But all the sergeant said was, "I've heard of you. You're the footballer, right? I'd like to see you on the pitch."

"I'm the footballer," Adi said tightly. He was too good a footballer. People remembered him and noticed him and talked about him, which was the last thing he wanted or needed. He went on, "Haven't had much chance to play lately, though. Who knows when I'll get out there again?"

"If you're as good as people say you are, you could probably get on one of those teams that go around putting on exhibitions." The Panzer IV commander sounded plenty shrewd. "You'd sure have a better chance of coming out of this in one piece if you did."

"Fuck it. I signed up to be a soldier, not to run around in short pants," Adi said.

"All right. All right. Take an even strain, pal. I wasn't out to piss you off," the sergeant said. "I mean, I'm halfway decent playing football, but I'm only halfway decent, y'know? I've paid my dues up here and then some. If they let me put on shows for the troops instead of getting smashed to blood sausage, I'd do it in a red-hot minute."

"I kind of like it at the front. I didn't expect to, but damned if I don't." Adi raised an eyebrow. "They say the *Führer* did, too, don't they?"

"Yeah, I've heard he—" The Panzer IV commander broke off. For the life of him, he couldn't see why these guys were losing it right in front of him. They didn't explain, either.

ONE MORE APPALLINGLY official, eagle-and-swastika-bedizened letter in the mail. To make matters worse—at least as far as Sarah Bruck was concerned—the stamp stuck to this one bore Adolf Hitler's petulant face. A double dose of Nazism, all to tell her . . .

She opened the envelope, taking a certain malicious pleasure in tearing the *Führer*'s face in half. That was the last pleasure she got. When she unfolded the letter, it was just what she thought it would be.

"*Scheisse!*" she said loudly.

"What is it, dear?" her mother asked from the kitchen.

"They *are* taking everything the Brucks had—'in the interest of the welfare of the state,' they say." Sarah knew she sounded disgusted. She was. "It doesn't mean anything but 'because we can.'"

Hanna Goldman sighed. "Well, you're right. I don't know what we can do about it, though. Do you want to sue them?"

"Of course I do!" Sarah answered. Her mother let out a yip of alarm. Quickly, she went on, "But I know I can't." Making the Nazis notice her was the fastest way she could think of to end up in Dachau or Mauthausen or Theriesenstadt or some other place where she didn't want to be.

Mother let out a heartfelt sigh of relief. "Oh, good! You do have some sense left after all," she said. "For a second there, I wondered."

"Yes, I do," Sarah agreed, "and I wish to heaven I didn't. I *want* to take them on. Of course, the mice wanted to bell the cat, too, and look how much good that did them."

The mice in the fable would have stood a better chance against the cat than Germany's Jews did against the government. If a mouse with a bell came up to a cat, the cat would have a snack, wash its face and paws, and curl up somewhere to go to sleep afterwards. But the Nazis wouldn't content themselves with eliminating the one uppity Jew. They'd make every Jew in the *Reich* sorry. Chosen People? The Nazis would choose them, all right! Wouldn't they just?

"What I'm really worried about is getting bread now that the bakery's gone," Mother said.

"You bake as well as the Brucks did." Sarah meant it. She knew more about baking now than she'd ever dreamt she would. Her mother's loaves were at least as good as any commercial product.

But Mother made an exasperated noise. "I don't want to do it every couple of days. It's a lot of work, and it takes a lot of fuel. Our coal ration isn't very big, and it's full of shale anyway. They have bakeries so most people don't need to bake all the time. Only Jews in Münster *don't* have a bakery any more."

Sarah imagined some Nazi functionaries sitting in the *Rathaus*, hands comfortably cradling their bellies, laughing like brown-shirted hyenas at the Jews' predicament. She hoped the next time the RAF came over, bombs would rain down on the bureaucrats' houses. That would give them . . . some of what they deserved, anyhow.

As if reading her mind, Mother said, "Nights are getting longer now. We may see the bombers more often. Places in the east that haven't got it for a while may see them, too."

Father came back that evening with a joke making the rounds among the Aryans. As usual, he told it with a somber relish all his own: "When you see a friend after an air raid, if you say 'Good morning,' that means you've got some sleep. If you say 'Good night,' that means you haven't. And if you say '*Heil* Hitler!'—well, that means you've always been asleep."

Sarah and her mother both giggled in delicious horror. "People say those things?" Sarah exclaimed. "Aren't they afraid the blackshirts will haul them away and start hitting them with hoses?"

Samuel Goldman's mouth twisted in amusement—wry amusement, but amusement nevertheless. "If the *Gestapo* grabbed everybody who told jokes like that, the *Reich* wouldn't be able to make bobby pins any more, let alone rifles and planes and panzers. People aren't happy. Everybody keeps wondering how long the war can go on."

"We did that the last time around, too," Mother said. "We thought it had to end pretty soon. But it just dragged on and on."

"Tell me about it," Father said. "In the trenches, we used to look forward to raiding the Tommies' lines even if we were liable to get killed doing it. If we lived, we'd eat their bully beef and smoke their tobacco. They had so much more than we did, especially toward the end . . ." As if reminded, he rolled a cigarette from newspaper and dog-ends scrounged in the gutter. That was how Jews got their cigarettes these days; their ration had been cut off a long time ago. He smoked the nasty stuff with as much enjoyment as if it were a blend of the best Virginia and Turkish.

"I wonder if it's that bad this time around," Sarah said.

"Probably not quite," Father answered judiciously. "We're still living off what we've taken from places like Holland and Denmark. And most of what we've got goes to the soldiers. If they can't fight, everything falls apart." He grimaced. "Everything may fall apart no matter how well they fight."

"No Americans this time around," Hanna Goldman observed.

"That's true." Now Father spoke in musing tones. "I don't think I ever came up against them—I was farther north. But people I know who did say they took a lot of needless casualties. They didn't quite know what they were doing, not like our old sweats. They were brave, though. Everybody says that. And there were more and more of them, and we knew there'd be more still the longer we kept fighting. Ludendorff saw when to make terms, all right."

"No 'stab in the back'?" Sarah sounded more malicious than curious.

"No, of course not." Her father waved the idea away. "We were whipped no matter what Hitler says. One *Landser* was worth more than one Tommy or one *poilu* or one doughboy, but so what? We weren't worth two enemy soldiers apiece, or three, or five. If we'd kept going, they'd have steamrollered us in 1919—and don't forget, the Austrians and the Turks had already given up and started falling apart. Stab in the back!" He snorted.

"Can we fight to a draw if the Americans stay out of Europe?" Mother asked.

Samuel Goldman rolled his eyes. "What am I? A prophet out of the Old Testament? I don't know, but I don't see Russia going out of the fight this time. The Tsar didn't really believe his people would rise up against him if he gave them half a chance. Stalin's like Hitler—he doesn't trust anybody. Anyone who tries to overthrow him will have his work cut out. So the two-front war *will* go on. What comes of that . . ."

Sarah had a different question: "Will anything be left of us by the time the war finally ends, if it ever does?"

By *us* she meant *us Jews*. She would have explained that at need, but Father understood right away. He rolled his eyes again. "You really want me to play the prophet, don't you? I think we'd all be dead if Poland were on Stalin's side. Poland's full of Jews. If they're with the enemy, that would only make the Nazis go after us even harder than they already do."

"Like stealing the Brucks' estate." Sarah didn't bother hiding her bitterness.

"It could be worse," Father said. "Most of the time, they have to think we did something before they throw us in a camp. They aren't doing it just for the fun of it or throwing everybody in no matter what. Not yet they aren't, anyway. And, *alevai*, they won't start."

"*Alevai omayn*," Sarah echoed. The Yiddish reminded her what she was. Could things really get worse? She supposed they could—and maybe that was the scariest thought of all.

THEY'D STUCK ARISTIDE DEMANGE up at the front again, the worthless *cons* with the fancy embroidery on their kepis. He would have been more disgusted were he less surprised. He was a damn nuisance. Worse, he was proud of being a damn nuisance. Of course his superiors wanted him dead. They lacked the balls to take care of it themselves. That being so, they had to hope the *Boches* would do the job for them.

The *Boches* hadn't managed to tend to it in the last war, or in this one, either. The Reds also hadn't done it this time through, when the rich guys decided they were even more trouble than the Nazis. So now

Hitler's boys got another crack at him. *Happy fucking day,* Demange thought.

"Lieutenant?" One of the *poilus* in his company broke into his gloomy reflections.

"Waddaya want, François?" Demange had no trouble learning his soldiers' names. Sounding as if he gave a damn about them came harder, especially since he didn't.

"Lieutenant, shouldn't we attack the Nazis?" François must have found some raw meat somewhere.

"Go ahead." Demange pointed northeast, toward the Franco-Belgian border. "They've spent the last year digging in, but don't let that stop you. Be my guest, in fact. Then I won't have to put up with your bullshit any more."

François turned red. He was a new recruit. He hadn't gone to Russia; he had no idea what combat was like. He'd find out pretty soon any which way. Then Demange—and he himself—would see what he was worth, and whether he was worth anything. In the meantime, he complained: "No, Lieutenant, I mean the whole army!"

"Oh, you can't kill all of them by yourself?" Demange sounded amazed. "Listen to me, you . . . you bedbug, you. When we get orders, we move. Till we get orders, we sit tight. That will keep you alive for a while, probably longer than you deserve. Got me?"

"Got you," François answered. Demange's Gitane sent up angry smoke signals. Hastily, François changed his tune: "I understand, Lieutenant!"

"Good. Marvelous. *Wunderbar.*" Demange used the German word with an irony so savage, it almost turned unironic. And he was altogether serious when he jerked a thumb toward the tents where François' comrades were huddling. "Now fuck off."

François stayed out of his hair after that. Only an idiot would have gone on messing with a lieutenant who still behaved like the bad-tempered top sergeant he had been. While François—to Demange, at least—was definitely a moron, he wasn't (quite) an idiot.

A couple of *poilus* in the company damn well were. Jean and Marcel were both Communists, which—to Demange, again—merely gave a name to the kind of idiot they were. Like François, they were hot to storm after the Nazis right away. Unlike François, they didn't want to take no for an answer.

One of them was tall and skinny, one short and kind of plump. They looked like a bad comedy team, in other words. Demange didn't bother remembering which was which. He did hope one of them would stick a finger in the other one's eye. That was always good for a laugh.

"We must slay the Fascist hyenas!" the tall one gabbled. "The safety of the world proletariat depends on it."

Demange's Gitane twitched. "Oh, yeah?" he replied. "Says who?"

The Reds looked at each other. He'd seen before that Communists were as bad for that as fairies. After a pregnant pause, the short one said, "It is a well-known fact, Lieutenant."

"Well known to who?" Demange didn't bother with grammar.

"Why, to those who know such things, of course," the soldier spluttered.

"Yeah, well, you can kiss my balls with your well-known facts, and so can they," Demange snarled. "I'll give you some well-known facts of my own. When the war started, you fucking Reds didn't want to fight at all. Then when Hitler started jumping on Stalin's corns, all of a sudden you couldn't fight hard enough. And then, after France decided Hitler made a better bet than Stalin, all of a sudden you were yellow again, not Red. Now it's rush the German trenches one more time!" He spat out the tiny butt and lit another cigarette. "You worthless pukes make me sick."

"Come the revolution, you will be remembered," the tall Communist said somberly.

"Good," Demange growled, which made them both stare at him. He condescended to explain: "No one will ever remember you two dingleberries for anything. I've shot Russians and Germans who were worth ten times both of you put together. God only knows why France doesn't use punishment battalions. That's where you belong."

They licked their lips. They knew what those were, all right. If you screwed up in the Red Army—and, these days, in the *Wehrmacht*, too—they handed you a submachine gun and sent you where the fighting was hottest to redeem your honor. Odds against your living through it were long, but you got blown up knowing you were doing your precious country some good.

Assuming that made you happier while you were trying to shove your guts back into your belly where they belonged.

Demange had long been sure he had an easier time coping with the enemy than with people who loudly declared they were on the same side. The *cons* in the fancy kepis were a case in point. François, Jean, and Marcel were another. And the peasants of northeastern France made one more.

Well, actually they didn't declare they were on Demange's side. By the way they acted, he wouldn't have bet on it, either. They were most of them big, fair fellows who looked more like Belgians—or Germans—than proper Frenchmen. He understood only about half of their clotted dialect: less than that when they larded it with Flemish words to make it harder. What he did understand, he commonly didn't like.

For their part, they didn't like the French Army. They'd been occupied by the *Boches* during the last war and the first part of this one. That gave them plenty of practice at hiding anything an occupier might want. These days, they figured their own country's armed forces were doing the occupying.

To say they were reluctant to cough up supplies for the *poilus* beggared the power of language. You wouldn't see a sack of grain or a chicken or even a turnip anywhere near their farmhouses. They would spread their hands and go "*Rien.*" Looking around, you'd be tempted to believe they had nothing.

But their bellies hung over their belts. Their wives had double chins. Demange knew what hungry people looked like. He'd seen enough of them in Russia, and in Germany right after the end of the last war. The peasants hereabouts weren't hungry. They just wanted to hang on to what they had.

They weren't shy about letting you know what they thought of you, either. After Demange and some of his men requisitioned three fat geese, the farmer from whom they took them growled, "You people are as bad as the *Boches.*" He could speak perfectly plain French when he felt like it.

"Ah, your mother," Demange replied. The thought of goose fat on his tongue helped mellow him as much as anything ever did. "If we were *Boches,* we'd be banging on you with our rifle butts right now."

"*Merde.*" The farmer spat. "The *Boches* were here, remember. Not that you *cons* did anything to keep them out. And they were correct enough. They paid for what they took, in fact."

"Oh, it's pay you want?" Demange flipped him a franc. "Here. And I'm giving you something else to go with it, too."

"What's that?" The farmer stared at the gold-colored (but only gold-colored—it was really aluminum-bronze) coin in disgust.

"Your fucking big mouth, with all its teeth still in it. And believe me, pal, you don't know how lucky you are." Demange gestured to his men. Off they went with the geese, leaving the farmer staring after them, his fists clenched uselessly by his sides.

THE AIRSTRIP BY Philippeville was every bit as grim as the barbed wire surrounding it had made Hans-Ulrich Rudel fear it would be. The locals were surly. The food was worse than it had been in Russia. That didn't just dismay Hans-Ulrich; it horrified him.

Sergeant Dieselhorst complained about it, too. He was a noncom, after all. Pissing and moaning were second nature to him. But, unlike Rudel, he knew the ropes. Hans-Ulrich often suspected the older man had been born knowing the ropes. "Rules are different here," he said after Hans-Ulrich made rude noises about the stew the mess cooks had ladled out.

"Rules? There weren't any rules in Russia." Hans-Ulrich didn't want to think about the fat that had flavored those potatoes. If it wasn't motor oil, it had no business tasting so much like it.

"That's the point . . . sir," Sergeant Dieselhorst said patiently. "In Russia, we went and grabbed whatever we wanted. We didn't care whether the goddamn Ivans liked us or not. It's different here. We don't want the Belgians to hate our guts and go playing games with the froggies. So we can't take as much from them as we did in the East."

"So we get stuck with that hog-swill ourselves." Rudel belched. The last stew didn't improve when it came up instead of going down. "Sure makes me want to jump into the Stuka and kill things—I'll tell you that."

"There you go." Albert Dieselhorst grinned wryly. "You see? It boosts morale."

Hans-Ulrich said something he was ashamed of as soon as it came out of his mouth. He didn't talk like that most of the time. He was a minister's son, after all. And his father's hard hand, applied to the seat of his pants or the side of his head, had done its best to make sure he never talked that way. Every once in a while, though . . .

Sergeant Dieselhorst laughed so hard, Hans-Ulrich wondered if he would have a heart attack. "Oh, shut up," the pilot muttered.

*"Jawohl, mein Herr! Zu Befehl!"* Dieselhorst came to attention, clicked his heels, and shot out his arm in a Party salute all the more sarcastic for being so full of vigor. Then he dissolved in mirth again.

"It wasn't *that* funny," Rudel said. Sergeant Dieselhorst wordlessly called him a liar. In something close to desperation, Rudel added, "Shut up or I'll pop you one."

He got his crewmate's attention, anyhow. Dieselhorst favored him with a mild and curious gaze. "Well, sir, you can try, anyhow," he said.

Hans-Ulrich was larger and younger and stronger. He neither smoked nor drank, so he was bound to be in better shape, too. Sergeant Dieselhorst just stood there, waiting to see what happened next. He wouldn't start anything, not when he was squaring off against an officer. Something about the way he stood suggested that he expected to finish whatever Rudel did start, though. How many dirty tricks had he learned, in the *Luftwaffe* or in one barroom brawl or another?

More than Hans-Ulrich really wanted to find out about. With dignity, the pilot said, "There. That's better. You aren't braying like a jackass any more."

Sergeant Dieselhorst's expression might have said it took one to know one. It might have, but Hans-Ulrich didn't try to find out. Sometimes—pretty often, in fact—you were better off not knowing things officially.

RAF bombers droned overhead on nights when the English thought the time was ripe to drop some *Schrechlichkeit* on German cities. They didn't bomb Belgium very often, though. Nor did the *Luftwaffe* pound the French positions just over the border, though German bombers hit Paris and London under cover of darkness.

Sitting there outside of Philippeville not doing anything much finally irritated Hans-Ulrich enough to make him complain to the squadron commander. "We should have stayed in Russia, sir! At least there we'd be flying and blowing up Ivans."

Colonel Steinbrenner smiled and raised an eyebrow. Hans-Ulrich wondered whether Steinbrenner would point out that, had they stayed in the East, he might still be able to get leave in Bialystok and disport himself with Sofia. But the colonel didn't. All he said was, "Both sides here have their reasons for not pushing things as hard as they might."

"Sir?" Rudel's one-word reply politely declared he didn't believe it for a minute.

Colonel Steinbrenner's sigh said he understood as much, and that he thought he was dealing with a classic specimen of boy idiot. "We're at war with France and England, yes," he said, coming as close as he could to explaining things in words of one syllable. "But that's not the war we want, and it's not a war they want very much. If we don't push it, maybe, just maybe, the boys with the top hats and striped trousers can make it go away. Then we *will* see the Ivans again—count on that."

"Ah." Hans-Ulrich was an indifferent chess player. Someone else's clever move often made sense to him—once a man who knew the game better explained it. He never would have seen it or made it himself. He found himself with the same feeling now.

"So that's what's happening—I mean, what isn't happening," Steinbrenner said. "For the time being, we have to stay ready, that's all. If the diplomats bugger it up, we'll get all the flying we want and then some. Or if England and France decide they do mean it after all . . ." He made a sour face. "Here's hoping they don't. Life is complicated enough as is."

As he'd needed to more than once before, Rudel reminded himself that Steinbrenner had taken over the squadron after the *Sicherheitsdienst* hauled away the previous CO because he wasn't loyal enough to satisfy them. So the colonel was politically reliable. And if a man who was politically reliable could go so far . . .

In that case, life really was complicated enough—and then some.

"*Heil* Hitler!" Steinbrenner said, which meant he'd had as much of Hans-Ulrich as he aimed to take.

"*Heil* Hitler!" Hans-Ulrich echoed. His arm shot out in the Party salute. So did Colonel Steinbrenner's. The junior officer beat it.

Before long, though, not flying started to drive him crazy (or, depending on how you looked at things, crazier). The Stukas remained grounded. He talked himself onto a Fieseler *Storch* reconnaissance plane for a look-see above the French lines.

It was like piloting a dragonfly when you were used to flying a crow. Sergeant Dieselhorst came along for the ride. Like the Stuka, the *Storch* carried a rear-facing machine gun. It was almost the only resemblance between the two planes. "I forgot how much fun flying could be," Dieselhorst said as they buzzed along not far off the ground.

"I know what you mean," Hans-Ulrich answered. The *Storch* took off in nothing flat and could land in even less. You could make it hover like a kestrel in any kind of headwind. "What will you use that gun for?"

"Shooting ducks," Dieselhorst said. "If we can keep up with them, I mean." He wasn't kidding, or not very much. The *Storch* cruised along at 150 kilometers an hour. A Stuka going that slow would have been hacked from the sky in nothing flat. But the Fieseler was so nimble, and could go so much slower than its cruising speed, that enemy planes were almost bound to overshoot it.

Here and there, *poilus* down below took pot shots at the *Storch*. When a French machine gun opened up on Hans-Ulrich, he decided it was time to head for home. As he banked out of trouble, Sergeant Dieselhorst fired a defiant burst at the machine gunners on the ground.

"That's telling 'em," Rudel said.

"Bet your ass," Dieselhorst replied. "If they forget we're a warplane, hell, we're liable to do the same thing."

Hans-Ulrich didn't think that was likely. But the trip in the *Storch* reminded him there were plenty more ways to fight the war than he was used to.

# Chapter 13

At sea. Julius Lemp had forgotten how beautiful those words could be. Yes, the U-30 was still a claustrophobe's worse nightmare. Yes, it smelled like a rubbish tip crossed with an outhouse. But nobody on the U-boat gave him a hard time on account of his politics.

He made a sour face. He stood on the conning tower, hands raised to hold binoculars to his eyes, so chances were no one noticed. Somebody aboard the boat was bound to report to the people who worried about what snoops aboard submarines said.

His own view was that those people would serve the *Reich* better if they picked up Mausers and killed Russians till the Russians got lucky and killed them instead. He understood the worst thing he could do was to announce his view. People like that wouldn't know what to do if they had to fight. Suggesting that they should would only scare them. And if you scared those people, they'd kill you. You couldn't count on many things in this old world, but you could count on that.

The U-boat rolled. Of course it did. A U-boat would roll in a bathtub, and the North Sea made about the most unruly bathtub there ever was. A faint stink of puke rose from the hatch that led below. But up here, Lemp had some of the freshest, purest air in the world blowing into his face. It was cold, but warmer than it would be in a couple of months—or up in the Barents Sea. Probably warmer than it would be in the Baltic this time of year, too. Which, when you got right down to it, wasn't saying one hell of a lot.

He wouldn't have to worry about the Baltic or the Barents this time around. The U-30 was ordered out into the North Atlantic. He looked forward to that the way he looked forward to getting a tooth pulled by a drunken pharmacist's mate. The Atlantic's broad, tall swells made the North Sea seem like a wading pool, if not quite a bathtub, by comparison.

Somebody had to sink the ships from America that gave England the food and supplies she needed to keep fighting, though. This time, the *Kriegsmarine* handed him the job. He'd do it, too, or die trying. Too many officers he'd known at the start of the war had already died trying.

He wished he hadn't thought of it like that. You felt the footsteps of a goose walking over your grave often enough as things were. When you might as well have invited the damn goose into the churchyard . . .

"*Scheisse!*" said one of the ratings up on the tower with him. A moment later, he amplified that with, "Plane—heading our way!" He pointed.

Lemp saw it even without his binoculars—not a good sign. He said "*Scheisse!*" too, most sincerely. "Go below!" he added, and shouted down the hatch: "Dive! Dive! Crash dive!"

Klaxons hooted inside the steel cigar as the sailors on the conning tower hurtled themselves down the ladder. Air hissed and bubbled from the U-boat's tanks as she started down. She could submerge in less than half a minute. How much less? Enough to save them from the flying marauder? Well, they'd know pretty soon.

It was a Swordfish, a biplane that should have been obsolete—and was, except for flying off Royal Navy carriers and raising havoc in other people's navies. The conning tower was already three-quarters of the way underwater when Lemp went below. He slammed the hatch and dogged it shut after him.

Being years out of date, the damned Stringbag couldn't come on very fast. Not much in the way of good news, but Lemp cherished what he had. "Hard right rudder!" he ordered. "All ahead full!" Eight knots submerged would drain the batteries in an hour, but he didn't intend to go on anywhere near that long. He guessed the Swordfish would drop its depth charge along his previous course, and wanted to get as far away from that as he could.

"Hard right rudder," Paul the helmsman answered, sounding calmer than he probably was. "Down past twenty-five meters, now thirty . . ."

*Wham!* The first depth charge staggered Lemp. Light bulbs blew out with pops that sounded too much like gunshots. The U-boat shuddered as if it had just taken a body blow from Max Schmeling. Sailors swore when the explosion flung them into some of the boat's many sharp projections.

*Wham!* There was another one—farther away than the first, and not quite so horrific. The U-Boat lost a few more bulbs, but only a few. Lemp dared breathe again. He'd guessed right. And he didn't *think* a Swordfish carried more than two depth charges.

Now, would the pilot loiter to see if he could machine-gun a surfacing submarine? To say Lemp didn't want the pressure hull colandered proved the power of understatement.

"Bring us down to all ahead one-quarter," he told Paul, who relayed the order back to the engine room. "And take us up to periscope depth. I want to see what's going on upstairs before we come up for air."

He swept the periscope around in a complete circle. At the very edge of visibility, he spotted the Stringbag flying away. It had done what it could do. The crew wouldn't know whether they'd damaged the U-boat or not. They would know they had to get back to their carrier to rearm before they went out on another patrol.

That thought sparked another one in Lemp as the plane vanished over his short horizon. He noted its course. "Raise the *Schnorkel*," he ordered. "I want eight knots at *Schnorkel* depth. Paul, turn us to course 320." That was more or less northwest, and the direction in which the Swordfish had flown away. "Maybe they'll lead us back to where they came from."

"That'd be nice, eh, Skipper?" Paul swung the U-30 to the heading Lemp wanted. They exchanged sly grins. A U-boat couldn't ask for a more important target than an aircraft carrier.

*Sinking one just might get me promoted at last, or at least win me the Knight's Cross,* Lemp thought as the diesels roared to life and the familiar vibrations rose up through the soles of his shoes to fill him again. With the *Athenia* to blot his escutcheon, even sinking a carrier might not haul him up to lieutenant commander.

He knew he'd have to be lucky to get to launch a spread of eels. The carrier would have to be somewhere close by. And he'd have to find it in the vastness of the sea. Well, all he could do was try.

A rating brought him something from the galley: sliced tinned meat on sliced tinned bread. It was the body's diesel oil. He fueled mechanically. The less he thought about what he was swallowing, the better.

He turned the periscope back and forth, back and forth, sweeping as wide an arc as he could. He didn't expect to see anything for quite a while. (He didn't really *expect* to see anything at all, but you had to go through the motions as if you did. They would have been in the soup for sure if that rating hadn't spotted the Swordfish.) Patience paid. Patience always paid, even if it didn't always get its reward.

No way to know what course the carrier was steaming. No way to know how far off it was. Darkness came early in these latitudes at this season. If it put paid to his search . . . *I'll go out into the Atlantic and hunt freighters. What else can I do?*

Back and forth. Back and— Lemp stopped swinging the periscope. *Something* stuck up on the horizon. "I will be damned," he whispered. Then he spoke aloud: "Change course to 295, Paul. And I want eleven knots from the engines."

The engines weren't the problem. When the U-boat made much over eight knots at *Schnorkel* depth, though, it shook as if it were coming to pieces. But if that was the carrier, and if he was going to have any chance at all to hit it . . . Things started rattling as speed picked up.

It was the carrier. It loomed out of the water like an enormous cliff. A pair of destroyers shepherded their charge. Both sent out pings from their dangerous new fancy hydrophones. Neither was close, though, and neither changed course as if catching an echo from the U-30.

Lemp wanted to sneak within a thousand meters of the carrier before firing his torpedoes. What you wanted and what you got turned out differently too damn often in this world. He had to shoot the eels from a kilometer and a half. Aiming got harder. The target was smaller. Travel time stretched. If the limeys were alert, they might be able to turn away.

They started to. One torpedo missed, but two struck home: one at the bow, the other back toward the stern. The carrier began listing and settling in the water right away. Lemp could see she wouldn't stay afloat.

He didn't need to see that the destroyers would do their best to pay him back for shooting their big friend. Their pinging picked up. They might have the torpedo wakes to guide them toward him. He dove deep and steered near the sinking carrier. Let all the noise coming from that shattered ship confuse their detecting gear.

It must have worked. The destroyers dropped depth charges, but none near him. When the U-30 surfaced after sundown, it was in the middle of a broad, empty ocean. Lemp ordered a bottle of beer for every crewman from the crates the boat carried for celebrations. The first depth charge had smashed some of the bottles, but there were still plenty left. And how the ratings cheered him!


PEGGY DRUCE DELICATELY turned the radio dial. All of a sudden, she heard Edward R. Murrow's voice, and there was London, right in her living room. The wonders of living in modern times! A set that could get shortwave transmissions brought the whole world to your door.

"The British Admiralty has confirmed the loss of the *Ark Royal* northeast of Scotland," Murrow said mournfully. "German naval authorities claimed the sinking yesterday, but the Germans, during this war, have claimed a good many things that later proved not to be true."

That was slightly unfair. The *Luftwaffe*, from what Peggy had seen while she was in Europe, lied whenever its lips started moving. German land forces told lots of what they'd called stretchers in the old days, but you could usually tell what was in fact going on from what they said. And the *Kriegsmarine*, most of the time, stuck close to the facts.

"Loss of life on the torpedoed aircraft carrier is believed to be heavy," Murrow went on. "Some sailors were killed while struggling in the water when the destroyers escorting the stricken carrier depth-charged the

U-boat that had attacked it. There is no evidence the submarine was damaged."

"Well, shit," Peggy said. Alone in the big house, she could come out with whatever she pleased. For that matter, she could have come out with the same thing if Herb were home. The most he would have done was cluck. More likely, he would have laughed.

Static hisses and pops rode the shortwave signal. As long as Peggy could make out what Edward R. Murrow was saying, she didn't mind. In fact, she liked the noise. It reminded her how far away the American broadcaster was.

"England eyes the American Congressional elections with more worry than usual," Murrow said. "Gains by the isolationist wings of the two parties could make the USA concentrate on the war in the Pacific and slow efforts to keep Europe's democracies supplied with the arms they need to boost the fight against the totalitarian powers.

"And that supply is vitally necessary if England and France are to continue the struggle. Many here and more across the Channel were happier with their stitched-up peace with Germany than they are at the moment."

"Shit," Peggy repeated, more sharply this time. She was worried about the elections, too. Who in her right mind wouldn't be? Anybody who'd seen Hitler's Germany with her own eyes knew the only thing you could do with it was squash it with the biggest rock you could find.

But most people in Arkansas and Nebraska and Wyoming—and Philadelphia—hadn't seen the Third *Reich* with their own eyes. That was the trouble. It didn't seem real to them. They couldn't believe anyone would really do the kinds of things the Nazis did every day without even thinking about them. And so they didn't care whether the English and French kept fighting. It wasn't their worry.

Only it was. If somebody didn't take care of Hitler now, before too very long he'd decide he could take care of the United States. The really scary thing was, he might turn out to be right.

It was rainy on election day. Peggy's polling place was at a fire station a couple of blocks from her house. She squelched over in galoshes and under an umbrella. A bored-looking cop with a bigger bumbershoot stood watch. Every once in a while, a wardheeler would follow a voter toward the polling place.

"No electioneering within a hundred feet," the cop would growl.

Of course the wardheelers bellyached. They were out there in the rain to snag votes any way they could. The cop ignored their complaints. He had the law on his side, and he knew it.

Peggy voted. She'd done more for FDR and his foreign policy than any of the Democratic wardheelers. She was as sure of it as the cop was about the electioneering statutes.

The fire station was warm. It smelled of tobacco smoke and something Peggy finally decided was brass polish. She didn't want to go back out into the wet. At last, with a martyred sigh, she did.

Rain drummed down on her umbrella. The cop was going, "Louie, if you don't knock it off, swear to God I'm gonna run you in."

Louie, by then, had dogged a man almost to the fire-station door. "Have a heart, Walt," he whined. Yes, he was enough of a wardheeler to know the cop by his first name. But he also must have known Walt wasn't kidding, because he skittered away.

Tipping his fedora to Peggy as they passed, the man he'd been trailing remarked, "Those guys are harder to get rid of than the ringworm."

"They've got a job to do, too." Peggy did the same job, if at a different level. It gave her more sympathy for the wardheelers than most people felt. The man rolled his eyes and walked inside, closing his dripping umbrella as he did.

Peggy went home. The house still felt too big and too empty and too quiet. She still liked having Herb around, and she missed him when he rolled out of town on one of his hush-hush trips for good old Uncle Samuel.

To make some noise, she turned on the radio again. She sat there, not really listening, and read an Agatha Christie. She didn't pay that much attention to the mystery, either. It was something that kept her eyes moving back and forth so she didn't have to think about the miserable state of the world or the almost equally miserable state of her marriage.

Cigarettes were good for not thinking, too. She methodically went through them, almost the way Herb would have. At least smoking in the

States was a pleasure. It had been a duty while she was stuck in Europe. You got the jitters and the jimjams if you quit. But Jesus God, the tobacco over there was awful! When it was tobacco, anyway. Maybe it was horseshit after all. Some of it sure tasted as if it was.

Bread crumbs. An egg. Chopped scallions. Salt. Pepper. A can of salmon. Some lard in the pan. A few minutes later, croquettes. Canned string beans heated in a little pot. Supper. A stiff bourbon-and-water kept her from noticing whatever deficiencies it had. After supper, she sent the bottle a longing look. A little to her own surprise, she put it back on the high shelf without opening it again.

When she turned on the radio this time, election returns were starting to come in. Her own Congresscritter got reelected handily. He was a Republican; no, her neighbors hadn't seen the joys of the *Reich* for themselves, either, so they still thought of FDR as That Man In The White House. But she'd known he would win. The only way he could blow the election was by molesting a nun in the middle of the street at rush hour. Even that might not do it.

Before midnight, though, the prognosticators on NBC, CBS, and the Mutual Network agreed that the makeup of the next Congress wouldn't be too different from this last one. "President Roosevelt does seem to have lost some ground," Lowell Thomas intoned gravely. "Incumbents usually do in offyear elections. But it seems unlikely that the new Congress will upset his foreign-policy apple cart. In any case, the general working rule for the USA is that partisanship stops at the frontier."

Peggy nodded to herself. She'd heard that rule before. It did seem true more often than not, no matter how little the isolationists liked it. And hearing a veteran reporter talk about it that way reassured her. Nobody was going to go and do anything stupid, anyhow.

She made a small, unhappy noise. Nobody was going to go do anything stupid? Was that the most you could hope for from government? She made the same noise again, louder now. More often than not, it was. And, a lot of the time, you couldn't even get that much.

RAIN CAME DOWN on the trenches northwest of Madrid. Chaim Weinberg swore as he stumped along one. "My goddamn boots are gonna rot right off my feet," he groused. "You think anybody'll care? Not fuckin' likely!"

Mike Carroll was properly sympathetic: "They'll care, all right. The way your feet smell now, they'll get you new boots in a minute if the stink leaks out through holes in the old ones."

"Funny, man. Fun-ny. Har-de-har-har. See? I'm laughing my ass off." Chaim laid on the sarcasm with an entrenching tool. "Funny like stepping on a land mine, you ask me. That'll ventilate your boots, too. Better to venti late than never, right?"

"Right." Mike's tone suggested he meant anything but what he said. He went on, "We've been here long enough. We damn well oughta be used to living out in the rain when winter comes by now."

"There is that," Chaim admitted. "Man, when I got here I never figured I'd stay so long. Fight for a while, then go home and try and set things right in the States . . ." He shook his head. "But the Spaniards really meant it. You're ashamed to show you don't. And they're in the fight till there's two left on one side and one on the other. And when the two kill off the one, waddaya wanna bet they start fighting each other 'cause that's all they know how to do any more?"

Carroll sent him a disapproving look. "No wonder you keep getting in trouble with the Party."

"No wonder at all," Chaim agreed cheerfully. "Hey, but they haven't gone and purged me yet. Long as I've got a rifle in my hands, I'm more dangerous to the fuckin' Fascists than I am to my own side."

This time, Mike looked around to make sure none of the seriously ideological Abe Lincolns could hear him through the rain's plashing before he answered, "That's what the anarchists and the Trotskyists thought, too."

There still were anarchist outfits up in the Catalan and Basque country. People who didn't much want to be part of Spain to begin with . . . Well, no surprise that they wanted damn all to do with any government whatever. The Republic quietly used those regiments for cannon fodder and gave them the oldest, most beat-up equipment it had. If you didn't approve of government, you couldn't very well expect government to approve of you, either.

Chaim was neither Trotskyist nor anarchist. He followed Moscow's line . . . in his own way, when he felt like it. He might be sure he was more dangerous to Sanjurjo's men than to the progressive forces in Spain. But Mike had a point, too. The longer the war dragged on—and it had already passed its second birthday and grown into a big, healthy boy when the main European brawl erupted—the less patience people here had with what they called deviationists.

He managed a ragged grin. "Hey, if La Martellita didn't purge me, I'm good for a while longer, right?"

"If you hadn't knocked her up, she would've," Mike responded.

There, Chaim thought his buddy was wrong. La Martellita was never one to let sentiment get in the way of doctrine. And, no matter how much he missed her (missed sleeping with her, anyhow), she'd never felt much in the way of sentiment toward him to begin with. Which, when you got down to it, was a goddamn shame.

He was going to expound on that theme. Soldiers since the days of Hammurabi had wasted time when they weren't fighting (most of the time, in other words) talking about women. But instead his head came up sharply. "Incoming!" he yelled, and dove for a muddy hole in the front wall of the trench.

Mike Carroll dove for the same hole at the same time. It wasn't quite big enough for two people. That didn't stop either one of them. They were pressed together at least as tight as Chaim had ever been with La Martellita when the Nationalists' shells started bursting on their line.

Getting shelled wasn't nearly so much fun as getting laid. Chaim suspected he might not be the first one to have made that particular discovery. Sanjurjo's bastards hadn't thrown this much hate at the Republicans for a while. He wondered where they'd come up with the ammo. Wherever it was, they sure didn't worry about using it up.

Mike jerked and almost kneed him in the nuts. "Watch it!" Chaim said indignantly, trying to twist away.

"Fuck yourself." Carroll hissed the words out through clenched teeth. "I'm hit, dammit."

"Ah, shit." Chaim tried to wiggle out of the hole to do what he could for his friend. That was harder than getting into it had been. Shells were still coming down when he finally slithered out into the trench. He ignored them—this was important.

A fragment had ripped up Mike Carroll's calf. His trouser leg was dark with blood. Chaim yanked the wound bandage off his own belt and did what he could to stanch the bleeding. He yelled for stretcher-bearers at the top of his lungs.

Naturally, they didn't show up as fast as he wanted them to. A bad time for *mañana*, but what could you do? Before they did, Carroll asked, "How bad d'you think it is?"

"Not too," Chaim answered, telling more truth than not. He didn't think it would kill Mike—as long as it didn't go septic, anyhow. He also didn't think the docs would have to amputate the leg, though he was less sure about that. But he was a hundred percent positive he wouldn't have wanted his own leg furrowed like that. He yelled for the bearers again.

"About fucking time," Mike said when the Spaniards finally showed up. One of them jabbed him with a syringe. Chaim was glad they had morphine. *Have to get my hands on some of that shit myself,* he thought. *Would have been good if I had a syringe, or if Mike did.* The drug hit hard and fast. The bearers almost poured Mike onto the stretcher and slowly lugged him down the muddy track toward a zigzagging communications trench that led back to the rear and to the aid stations there.

Meanwhile, the shells kept coming in. Chaim jumped into the hole again. He couldn't believe he and Mike had both fit into it. It felt crowded with him in there by his lonesome. Well, it hadn't quite fit all of poor Mike, had it?

He popped out again as soon as the bombardment stopped. Maybe the enemy was just being obnoxious, but maybe this was a real push, too. They'd fired off a lot of ammo. They wouldn't do that for the fun of it, would they?

No. Here they came: men in yellowish khaki running and crawling and scrambling toward the wire. A couple of tanks were coming, too. They were little old German jobs, obsolete in the rest of Europe but plenty good if the guys on the other side had even less in the way of armor.

Concrete emplacements protected the Internationals' machine guns. They started spitting death at Sanjurjo's men. Spaniards of any stripe were recklessly brave. The Nationalists came on where more sensible soldiers would have gone to ground or run away. They fell, writhing or ominously still. Chaim finally drew a bead on one of the writhers. He fired. The Nationalist lay ominously still thereafter.

One of the concrete emplacements proved to protect an antitank gun, not a mere Maxim. An enemy tank spurted fire and smoke. Crewmen bailed out. Chaim didn't think they got far. The other tank seemed to decide it had an urgent appointment somewhere else. It turned around inside its own length and got the hell out of there.

Without armor support, the attack bogged down, metaphorically and literally. No matter how brave you were, you couldn't storm machine-gun nests with foot soldiers alone. The rest of Europe had bloodily learned that lesson a generation earlier. The Spaniards understood it by now.

Nationalist stretcher-bearers came out for their wounded. Remembering Mike and hoping he'd be okay, Chaim didn't fire at them. Some of the other Internationals were less particular. Watching a bearer go down and the poor bastard he'd been helping to haul spill into the mud, Chaim reflected that it was a tough old war. Well, that was nothing he didn't already know.

WILLI DERNEN AND Adam Pfaff squatted in the ruins of what had been a Russian peasant family's hut to get out of the chilly rain. It was better than being out in the open, but not a lot. One wall was mostly a memory, while what was left of the thatch on the roof hadn't been tended to for a long time. It was almost as wet in there as it would have been in the street.

Pfaff was brewing ersatz coffee on his little aluminum stove. The fuel pellet didn't boil water very fast, but it also didn't show smoke or flame.

"How many times d'you suppose this village has changed hands?" he asked.

"Shit, I dunno. Two, three, maybe four," Willi answered. Pfaff looked like hell. He hadn't shaved for several days. His dirty, stubbly face showed nothing but exhaustion. His eyes . . . You didn't want to look into his eyes. Willi would have said something about it, only he was sure he looked the same way himself.

Instead, he held out the tin cup from his mess kit. Pfaff took the pot off the stove and poured some of the coffee into the cup. Willi sugared it and drank it while it was still hot. The warmth was its main virtue. It bore about the same relationship to the real bean as dealcoholized beer did to the genuine article.

Pfaff also poured down some of the near-coffee. "Smolensk," he said, in the way a knight-errant might speak of the Holy Grail. You could go after it, sure, but you didn't really expect to find it shining in front of you.

"Smolensk," Willi echoed. By contrast, he sounded bitter. He put the best face on things he could: "We aren't any farther from it than we were this past spring." After lighting a cigarette for himself and giving one to Pfaff, he added, "Of course, we aren't much closer, either."

"Too right we aren't," his friend said. His cheeks, already hollow, pulled in tighter yet on his bones as he sucked in smoke. "No wonder this lousy place keeps going back and forth between us and the Ivans."

"No wonder at all." Willi yawned till his jaw hinge cracked like a knuckle. "Christ, I could sleep for a year."

"Tell me about it. We all could, every goddamn one of us," Pfaff said. "Only if we all did, we'd wake up with our throats cut."

"I know," Willi said. What German in Russia didn't know that? Ivan could be anywhere. You didn't want to close your eyes unless a *Kamerad* close by kept his open. Sometimes you had to, but you didn't want to.

Arno Baatz stuck his head into the hut through one of the big holes in the wall. His piggy eyes narrowed. "Oh, you two rotten bums," he said, distaste clogging his voice. "Sitting around with your thumbs up your assholes. Why am I not surprised? Tell me why."

"Take an even strain, Corporal," Willi said. You couldn't tell a superior to whip it out and play with it, no matter how much you wanted to. A guy like Awful Arno would make you pay.

"What's to do, anyway?" Pfaff was more inclined to try to reason with Baatz. "We're here. The Reds aren't, not right this minute. We don't have sentry duty. Why not relax while we've got the chance?"

"Lazy fuckoffs, that's what you are. Both of you." But Awful Arno went away to inflict himself on someone else.

Once Willi was sure the underofficer had got out of earshot, he said, "Why couldn't the Russians have shot him in the head, not the arm?"

"Bullet would've ricocheted," Pfaff answered. Willi laughed till he almost pissed himself, a telling measure of how tired he was.

A field kitchen—a goulash cannon, in the *Landsers'* slang—made it into the village. The unit was horse-drawn, and not much different from the ones that had served the men who'd fathered this crop of soldiers. A motorized oven probably would have got stuck in the mud fifty kilometers back.

It wasn't goulash in the big pot. There were Hungarians in the fight against the Ivans. Willi wondered whether their field kitchens really did dish it out, all red and spicy with peppers. What he got was kasha and onions and meat, all boiled together till they turned into something halfway between stew and library paste.

He'd had worse. He'd had nothing, too, and nothing was much worse. "Do I want to know what the meat is?" Adam Pfaff asked the potbellied, gray-mustached *Feldwebel* dishing out the stuff. It was a standard soldier question.

It didn't get a standard soldier answer. "Why? Is your sister missing, or something?" the noncom returned.

He didn't faze Pfaff. Not much did, from what Willi'd seen. All Adam said was, "I think Ilse would cook up greasier than this."

One corner of the cook's mouth twitched. Then he chuckled. He made a face, as if he was mad at himself, but he couldn't help it. "All right. You're a funny guy," he said gruffly. He might have accused Adam of carrying a social disease.

"He's funny like a truss," Arno Baatz declared.

The *Feld* just looked at him—no, looked through him. Unlike the men in Awful Arno's section, he didn't have to put up with the *Unteroffizier's* guff. He outranked Baatz, too, so nothing held him back from speaking his mind, which he did with more than a little relish: "I want to know what you think, sonny boy, I'll blow my nose and check the boogers on my snotrag."

A slow flush mounted from Baatz's thick neck all the way to his hairline. The *Feldwebel* couldn't have cared less. He'd seen real action in his career. He wore a wound badge of his own, the ribbon for an Iron Cross Second Class so faded that he might well have won it in the last war, and, on his left breast pocket, an Iron Cross First Class.

Behind Awful Arno, somebody said, "Let's give three cheers for Booger Baatz!"

The *Unteroffizier* jumped straight into the air, as if someone had jabbed him in the ass with a hat pin. He whirled around before he came down. Had anyone else done it, Willi might have admired the performance. As things were . . . Admiring Awful Arno—no, Booger Baatz— was more trouble than it was worth.

"Who said that?" Baatz shouted furiously. "Who said that? Out with it, you gutless son of a bitch!"

Naturally, no one said a word. All the *Landsers* spooning up their stew might have been little angels. Willi knew Awful Arno would have blamed him had he been standing over there. He only wished he would have been clever enough to stick Baatz with the new handle.

"You bastards! You miserable, stinking turds!" Awful Arno was really working himself up into a first-class snit. "You—"

"Shut up." The middle-aged cook's quiet voice cut through his bluster like a hot knife slicing lard. "They don't hang names like that on guys who haven't earned 'em."

Baatz's jaw dropped. The last thing he'd looked for was a surprise attack from a fellow noncom. The private who served the goulash cannon with the *Feldwebel* snickered. He could afford to; he wasn't under Baatz's orders.

"I've run across pukes like you before," the *Feld* with the gray mustache went on. "You're just lucky nobody's shot you in the back yet. You keep on the way you're going, you'll find out."

Willi looked down at the muddy ground. It wasn't as if plugging Baatz hadn't crossed his mind. He didn't want that to show on his face, though. Next to him, Adam Pfaff was eyeing his scuffed boots, too. Odds were half the men in the section were doing the same thing for the same reason. And odds were, after the field kitchen rolled away to feed the next German detachment, Awful Arno would make more soldiers want to murder him.

# Chapter 14

Pete McGill was always happy when the *Ranger* steamed out of Pearl and headed west. They were going out to give the Japs hell. Giving the Japs hell was what he wanted more than anything else on earth.

Some of the other Marines who served with him were less enthusiastic. "Man, those assholes, they can sink us, too," a corporal named Barney Klinsmann said at breakfast the morning after they headed out on patrol. He shoveled corned-beef hash into his face as if he thought they'd outlaw the stuff tomorrow. Some guys needed to get their sea legs under them before they started stuffing themselves like that. Not him.

"Fuck 'em," Pete said flatly. "You don't think we'll lick 'em, fuck you, too. In the heart."

Klinsmann surged to his feet. Pete was big and as solid as he could be after his injuries—he'd worked hard putting muscle back on. The other guy had a couple of inches and twenty pounds on him even so. He didn't care. He stood, too. "Nobody talks to me that way, you bastard," Klinsmann growled.

Other leathernecks grabbed them and kept them from going at each other. "Take an even strain, the both of youse," Sergeant Cullum said. "We're supposed to be fighting the slanties, remember?"

"I remember," Pete said. "This bum, he wants to hide under his bunk instead." He tried to point at Klinsmann, but the Marines holding his arms wouldn't let go.

"Bullshit," the bigger man said. "I just said we gotta watch ourselves. And we do, on account of this here is the only carrier in the Pacific what still floats. The only American carrier, I mean. The Japs, they got a shit-pot full."

"Enough, dammit." Cullum let his impatience show. "Am I gonna hafta talk to an officer or somethin'?"

That subdued both Pete and Barney Klinsmann, as he must have known it would. Squabbles between noncoms weren't worth getting ex-cited about—till an officer noticed them or had them brought to his attention. Officers could throw the book at you. Pete often thought the book was the only reason officers existed.

He quit struggling against the men who held him. So did Klins-mann. Cautiously, their fellow Marines turned them loose. They both settled down to their interrupted breakfasts. Sergeant Cullum beamed beatifically at one and all.

As they walked out of the galley, Pete spoke in a low voice: "You know that little compartment aft of the portside heads, the one where they stow the mops and brushes and shit like that?"

"Oh, fuck, yes," Klinsmann answered, also quietly. "What time you wanna be there?"

"How about 0200 tomorrow?" Pete said. "Not like we need a bunch of busybodies around."

"You got that right," the other man said. "See you then."

When Pete officially slid out of his bunk at 0530, one eye was almost swollen shut. He had a cut lip and a broken bottom eyetooth. His ribs felt as if someone had been kicking them. Well, someone had. They didn't seem broken, though, so that was okay. He dry-swallowed a couple of Bayer's finest, not that they'd help one hell of a lot. He didn't feel a day over ninety-seven.

Sergeant Cullum raised a quizzical eyebrow. "You go and trip over the deck rivets again?" he inquired.

"That's right." Pete moved his mouth as little as he could. Talking hurt. So did breathing, come to that.

"What happened to Barney?" Cullum asked.

"Barney who?" Pete answered, deadpan. "You givin' the deck rivets names now? That's a little Asiatic, you want to know what I think."

"I don't want to know what you think. I don't even want to know *if* you think," the senior noncom said. "C'mon. Let's go get some chow. And some joe. I run on joe like it's gasoline."

So did Pete. So did half—more than half—the other leathernecks and swabbies on the *Ranger*. The stuff they served in the galley wasn't always good, but it was always strong. It was always hot, too. Aspirins or no aspirins, drinking it made Pete's lips and the less visible injuries inside his mouth hurt like hell. The salt he sprinkled on his scrambled eggs and the salt already in his slice of ham were no fun, either. He ate stolidly just the same, keeping his eyes down on his own tray.

Other Marines kept looking at him. Well, his battered puss invited looks. The leathernecks kept looking around for Barney Klinsmann, too. Klinsmann was nowhere to be seen.

Very softly, Sergeant Cullum asked, "You didn't go and kill him, didja?"

"Kill who?" Pete said. "That deck rivet you gave a name to?" But he gingerly shook his head. That hurt, too. Everything today hurt. He hoped the Japs would leave them alone till tomorrow, or even the day after. Right this minute, he wasn't worth the paper he was printed on.

But, as people and countries often found reason to say, you shoulda seen the other guy.

Eventually—after loading up on ham and eggs of his own—Cullum called down to sick bay. "You got a leatherneck name of Klinsmann down there?" he asked the pharmacist's mate on the other end of the line.

"What's he say?" Three or four Marines asked the same thing at the same time.

He waved them to silence, listening to what the pharmacist's mate was telling him. When he hung up, he said, "Barney's in there, awright. He says he tripped and fell down a stairway on his face. He's busted up enough, the sick-bay guys almost believe him. He musta hit every tread with his nose, though, or his teeth, or one eye or the other."

"Isn't that interesting?" Pete said when Cullum finished. A long time ago, somebody—damned if he could remember who now, but it must've been somebody with brains—had told him that phrase was one of the handful of things you could come out with damn near anywhere and be okay. *How about that?* was another one, he'd said. There weren't many, but knowing one or two came in handy all kinds of weird ways. Whoever the guy was, he'd known what he was talking about, sure as hell he had.

"Interesting," Sergeant Cullum echoed. "Yeah. Right. Doesn't sound like you'll be taking any more shit from Klinsmann for a while."

Pete shrugged, which also hurt. "Wasn't that big a deal."

"Huh." Cullum's grunt was redolent of skepticism. "Way the guy down in sick bay was going on, Barney's fucking lucky nobody had to send a radiogram to his next of klins, man."

"Ouch!" Pete said when the pun got home. Several of the other leathernecks groaned. McGill went on, "I didn't know you went in for shit like that." By the way he said it, he might have accused the other noncom of wearing frilly scanties under his uniform.

"Too goddamn bad," Cullum answered. "I didn't know you went in for ruining guys. It really does sound like Barney almost woke up dead this morning."

"I don't know what the hell you're talking about," Pete said.

"Uh-huh. And rain makes applesauce. I don't gotta be Sherlock Holmes to see what's going on when you're beat up and Klinsmann's like he got run over by a tank."

"I got nothin' special against Klinsmann," Pete said.

"Good thing you don't! If you did, some shark'd be hunting for a toothpick right now, I bet."

"Honest to God, all I wanna do is kill Japs," Pete insisted. "Kill Japs an' kill Japs an' kill more Japs."

Nobody argued with him. The other Marines didn't seem even a little bit interested in saying anything that might provoke him. Barney Klinsmann hadn't worried about it, and Barney was damn near pushing up a lily right this minute. Barney was a big, tough guy, too. And a hell of a lot of good that had done him. Pete went up onto the *Ranger*'s flight deck to look for more Japs to kill.

THE FALL *RASPUTITSA* meant Stas Mouradian's Pe-2 wasn't going any-where for a while—unless, of course, it vanished into the bottomless mud. After rain turned to snow and mud froze hard, the air war would pick up again. And, for the first time since the war was new, Stas didn't worry too much about going back into action.

He'd been fighting the Fascists from the very beginning. When Hitler invaded Czechoslovakia—four years ago now!—Mouradian had served as copilot and bomb-aimer on an SB-2 helping the Czechs from an airstrip in Slovakia. They'd called the SB-2 a fast bomber because it had proved able to outrun the biplane fighters it met in Spain. Stas had thought it would be able to do the same thing against whatever the Nazis threw at it.

Then he'd met the Bf-109. Unlike a lot of Soviet flyers who made the Messerschmitt's acquaintance, he'd survived the first encounter. But that imaginary sound, as of breaking glass, stood for the shattering of his illusions.

Even in a Pe-2, a plane much more modern and much speedier than the old allegedly fast bomber, he still feared the 109. Bombers were made for dropping bombs. Fighters were made for shooting down other planes. If you asked a bomber to try to do a fighter's job, you'd be sorry—although probably not for long.

When the air war did pick up again in a few weeks, chances were the *Luftwaffe* wouldn't have enough 109s (or their fearsome new friends, the blunt-nosed, deadly FW-190s) to go after all the bombers the Red Air Force would throw at it. The Fritzes had to split their planes be-tween this front and the revived one in the West.

Stas approved of that. The Germans would still throw up monstrous fireworks displays of flak, of course. Flak could kill you, too, but he didn't worry about it the way he worried about 109s and 190s. Flak was impersonal, like the weather. If you weren't lucky, some would hit your plane. But flak didn't come hunting you in particular, the way fighter pilots did.

A lot of Russian flyers drank their way through the *rasputitsa*. To an Armenian's way of looking at things, Russians drank at any excuse or none. And they didn't drink for the taste of it. They drank till they got drunk or, at least as often, till they fell over.

Maybe that was because, when they drank, they drank vodka. Oh, they had beer, too, but they scorned it. What Russians mostly didn't have was wine. Every valley in the Caucasus had its own vintage. Few of them made France look to her laurels, but a good many weren't bad. A glass or two with a meal—that was civilized. Cultured, a Russian would say.

What was cultured about swilling vodka till you passed out? What was cultured about swilling it till you puked, or till you choked on your own puke? What was cultured about swilling it till you fell out a window, or fell through one you thought was open? Russians killed themselves like that all the time, and killed one another in drunken brawls.

You couldn't talk about it with them, either. They wouldn't listen, even if they happened to be sober at the time. The most they would ever say was *This is how we are. This is how we've been forever. We aren't about to change, not for you and not for anybody.*

Change? It was to laugh. Russians reveled in the way they were. And, like any imperial nation, they tried to remake in their own image the peoples they ruled. Which other army in all the world gave its soldiers a daily ration of a hundred grams of high-octane vodka?

Oh, sure, soldiers all over the world drank. Considering what went into the soldier's trade, how could you blame them? But, outside the Red Army, they drank unofficially. Inside the Red Army . . . Tanks ran on diesel fuel. Trucks ran on gasoline. Soldiers ran on vodka. That was how *Stavka* looked at things.

Full of such pointless reflections (and they were—that the Tsar had tried to impose prohibition during the last war was one of the reasons, and perhaps not the least of them, Tsars ruled Russia no longer), Stas slogged through the mud to the tent where flyers ate and drank (and drank, and drank) and listened to Radio Moscow.

To make sure flyers and other Soviet citizens listened only to Radio Moscow, to make sure no unauthorized opinions corrupted them, radio sets manufactured in the USSR received just the frequencies on which Radio Moscow and other Soviet stations broadcast. Somewhere (somewhere unauthorized, as a matter of fact), Stas had heard that

Hitler admired the system when he learned about it, and wished Germany had one like it.

A samovar bubbled on a rickety table in one corner of the big tent. To give them their due, Russians always had tea handy. Sweet tea soothed a hangover if anything did. Tobacco smoke was thick enough to make Stas' eyes water. Hard rolls, pork sausage, a pot of borscht, a pot of *shchi* if you felt like cabbage soup instead of beet soup . . . It wasn't exciting, especially if you were an Armenian who expected more in the way of spices than dill and caraway seeds. But you could fill your belly.

Vodka bottles were making the rounds, too. No surprise there. They always did. No one could even think of complaining, not when the *rasputitsa* grounded the squadron. Stas passed one along without drinking when it came his way.

"More for me," said the Russian to whom he handed it. The man's larynx worked before he sent it along.

Stas cut thin coins of sausage and dropped them into a tin bowl of *shchi*. No, it wasn't what he would have eaten back home. But Armenia was a little land. When you went out into the wider Soviet world, you found that Russians were an imperial nation even in such matters as what their non-Russian comrades ate.

A glass of tea in front of him might deflect the peripatetic vodka bottles. Or it might not. But he wanted the tea any which way. The thick soup was salty. So was the sausage. Tea helped dilute things.

He'd almost got to the bottom of the bowl when two more officers strode into the mess tent. Like most of the men already inside, he casually glanced up to see if the newcomers were people he wanted to talk to.

They weren't. They were strangers. But he didn't go right back to eating, any more than the other flyers in the squadron did. The strangers' cap bands and collar tabs were bright blue: the color of the NKVD.

They carried identical PPD machine pistols. They had identical Tokarev pistols on their belts. But their arm-of-service color was much more frightening than their weapons. One of them glanced at a scrap of paper in his free hand. "Pyotr Konstantinovich Filimonov!" he barked.

Had Stas been the luckless Pyotr Konstantinovich, he would have run—or else he would have opened fire. It almost surely wouldn't have helped—he knew that—but he thought he would have done it anyhow. How could they treat you any worse afterwards than they were going to anyhow?

The genuine Filimonov sprang to his feet and came to attention so stiffly, he might have been embalmed—and if he wasn't, chances were he would be pretty soon. Well, buried, anyhow; they might not bother to embalm him in the Lubyanka or at a camp. "I serve the Soviet Union!" he said, as if the Chekists were about to pin an Order of Lenin on his chest.

They had other things in mind. He must have known as much, even if he didn't show it. The NKVD man who'd read his name tossed away the bit of paper and ground it under the heel of his boot. Both Chekists looked relieved he wouldn't cause any trouble. They gestured with their PPDs. "Come along, then," one of them said, and Filimonov came.

A vast silence filled the mess tent. *Well, it wasn't me—this time*, Stas thought. He would have bet anything he owned that his comrades-in-arms were thinking exactly the same thing. And when another vodka bottle came his way, he grabbed it and drank like a Russian.

IVAN KUCHKOV SHORED up the sides of his foxhole with planks from a wrecked hut a few meters away. That helped, up to a point. The muddy walls probably wouldn't cave in and squish him now. But he was still hunkered down in a muddy foxhole that got muddier by the minute as the autumn rain went on plashing down.

"Fuck me!" he muttered. "This is pure shit!" That was his opinion of most of Red Army life. Before that, the sergeant had had an even lower opinion of Red Air Force life. Flying personnel in the Red Air Force didn't get a vodka ration when they went on missions, which accounted for the difference.

He glanced back over his shoulder, wondering whether he'd be more comfortable in what was left of that peasant hut. He didn't think so, which only proved not much of it was left. And, even in the rain, he was liable to get shot if he came out of the foxhole. The Germans had their lines out in the middle of the unharvested fields, and some of them were much too handy with their Mausers and machine guns.

"Stinking cunts," Ivan said. Most of the time, he'd made a good thing out of his service to the Soviet state. He'd done better for himself as a soldier than he would have as a laborer on a collective farm or a small-time hooligan—he was sure of that.

Most of the time. But squatting in a boggy foxhole wasn't his notion of fun. Even a real fight would have been better than dicking around here and waiting to come down with trench foot.

So he thought, anyhow, till Lieutenant Novikov, the latest zit-faced officer to command the company, squelched and slithered over to him and spoke in a low voice: "I have a job for you, Kuchkov."

"What's up, Comrade Lieutenant?" Ivan didn't even add *Besides your dick*, the way he would have most of the time. Unlike a lot of punk officers, Novikov seemed to try hard. He didn't get the vapors when the Hitlerites shot at him, either. So why not give the kid the benefit of the doubt?

He found out why not immediately afterwards: "Division HQ wants to interrogate some German prisoners. Take a few men—take a squad if you think you'll need to—and go get 'em for us."

"Fuck me!" Kuchkov said again, this time sorrowfully. He could think of a million good reasons why someone else should lead the raid, or why it shouldn't go on in the first place. He kept his mouth shut. None of those reasons mattered a fart's worth when weighed against *Division HQ wants*. What Division HQ wanted, Division HQ got.

Novikov tried to butter him up. "You're the best man we've got for it. Nobody else comes close."

"Happy cocksucking day." Ivan knew the rest of the pricks in the company pretty well. The lieutenant was right. That didn't make him any happier—just the opposite, in fact.

The first guy he snagged for the raiding party was Sasha Davidov. The scrawny Jew let out a sigh the Nazis could probably hear back in Berlin. "What did I do to deserve this, Comrade Sergeant?" he asked resignedly.

"You fucking well stayed alive walking point," Kuchkov answered. "I ain't gonna choose one of the dead pussies, y'know? They don't move any too fuckin' swift."

He got the ghost of a chuckle out of Davidov. "Maybe I'll stay lucky one more time," he said. "Stranger things must have happened some-where." The *Zhid* didn't sound as if he believed it.

Speaking of luck, Kuchkov had figured it would quit raining before he went prisoner-hunting. If anything made him more likely to get plugged, that would be it. But the rain came down harder than ever.

He waited till the wee small hours just the same. He gulped tea to stay awake, and gulped vodka to feel brave. He didn't get toasted to the point where he started falling over his own feet, and he didn't let his fellow raiders get that drunk, either.

To his surprise, Davidov didn't drink at all. He just smoked *papiros* after *papiros*, cupping them in his hands to keep the rain from dousing them. The Jew didn't play teetotaler all the time, so Kuchkov asked him, "What's up with you?"

"I don't want to miss anything, that's all," Davidov answered. "Maybe I wouldn't with the vodka in me, but maybe I would, too. I'll drink plenty after we get back—you can bet your dick on that."

Hearing *mat* from him made Ivan laugh. "We're all betting our dicks," he said, and then, "When we grab the fucking Fritzes, you can palaver with 'em, right? I mean, you're a *Zhid*, so you know Yiddish, don't you?"

"Yes, Comrade Sergeant," the point man said patiently. "It's not the same as German, but it's not as different as Ukrainian is from Russian. If they don't kill me, they'll understand me well enough."

"Bugger shit-eating Ukrainian," said Kuchkov, who'd heard more of it down here than he'd ever wanted to listen to. He didn't notice Davidov's irony till they were sneaking out toward the German lines. Too late to do anything about it then.

He couldn't see more than a few meters. He couldn't hear more than a few meters, either; the rain took care of that. If Mauser rounds cracked past, or if one of the nasty machine guns the Russians called Hitler's saws started spitting bullets twice as fast as a Maxim gun could, he fig-ured he'd notice that.

Through the rain, Davidov called, "Wire here! Hold up while I cut it." He pitched his voice perfectly to reach his Red Army comrades and go no farther. Ivan hoped like hell he did, anyway. After a minute (and,

TWO FRONTS

presumably, after some snipping Ivan couldn't hear), the Jew said, "All good now. This way—toward my voice."

Kuchkov sliced the back of his hand on a barb from the cut wire. He cussed furiously under his breath. "Maybe you'll get lockjaw, Comrade Sergeant," one of the Russians said. "What would you do then?" The other raiders all laughed—quietly, but they did. Ivan couldn't even think about revenge till later. The Red Army men crawled on.

"Hold up!" Davidov hissed urgently from out in front. "I can hear Germans talking." Kuchkov cocked his head to one side. He still heard no Fritzes. Maybe the point man had stayed alive as long as he had not least because his ears were better than other people's.

Kuchkov crawled forward. "Where are the dicks?" he asked. The Jew pointed. Ivan could barely make out his arm in the rainy gloom. He knew what he had to do now, though. He held his PPD a little tighter. Odds were it had got muddy. Well, it would work even so. German Schmeissers were much better made, but mud and grit in the works and they turned up their toes.

The Red Army men slithered closer. Now Ivan could hear the Fritzes, too. He couldn't understand them, but they didn't sound worried. They had no idea enemy soldiers were in the neighborhood. "Grenades!" he called to his men. "Grenades, and then we rush. Don't shoot too fucking much. Remember, we gotta bring a couple of these bitches back alive."

They would remember as long as remembering didn't put their asses on the line. He was sure of that. He felt the same way. No German ever born—not even a blonde with big tits and legs up to there—was worth getting killed for.

"On three," he said. "One . . . Two . . . *Three!*" Grenades flew. They burst all around the Germans (not busty blondes, he was sure—too bad!) the Russians wanted to grab. "*Urra!*" the Red Army men yelled as they dashed forward and jumped down into the Nazis' fieldworks.

"*Hände hoch!*" Davidov screamed. Ivan was disappointed. He could *sprechen* that much *Deutsch* himself. But he couldn't have followed the terrified babble that came back. The point man could, and did: "They surrender. They just want us not to kill them."

"Tell 'em we won't. Let's get the fuck out of here," Kuchkov said.

217

What the NKVD interrogators would do to the Fritzes once they had them . . . wasn't his worry. No, that would be for the *Feldgrau* boys to sweat.

The other Germans came back to life in a hurry. They were pros, all right, damn them. Machine-gun tracers hissed through the wet air. But the Hitlerites fired just a little high. When you were down as flat as your buttons would let you get, a few centimeters mattered. And the captured Germans did their best impressions of squashed snakes, too. They didn't want their own friends punching their tickets for them by mistake.

Then Ivan had to worry about *his* friends punching his ticket for him. He knew too well the Russians were capable of it. Yes, they knew he'd gone raiding. Yes, they expected (or at least hoped) he'd come back. They might open up anyway.

But they didn't. After some soldiers hauled the miserable Fritzes away, Lieutenant Novikov pounded Ivan on the back. "I'll get you a medal for this," he said happily—his behind would have been in a sling had the raid failed.

"If it's all the same to you, Comrade Lieutenant, I'd rather have a blowjob," Ivan answered. "Or at least some extra vodka."

Novikov let out a startled yip of laughter. "The vodka I can arrange. You're on your own for getting your dick sucked." Kuchkov nodded. That was how things worked, all right. The really good stuff, you had to grab for yourself.

**HIDEKI FUJITA STOOD** at stiff attention before Captain Ikejiri. Anything less than stiff attention would have doomed him before he started. Even by Japanese Army standards—some of the highest in the world—Masanori Ikejiri was a stickler for discipline. "Yes, Sergeant?" he said now. "You wish . . . ?" By his tone, *he* wished Fujita would dry up and blow away.

But Ikejiri acted as if he wished every enlisted man ever hatched would dry up and blow away. So Fujita didn't let that worry him—too much. He saluted with mechanical precision. "Please, Captain-*san*, I would like to be placed in a position where I see more action," he said.

He'd thought about calling Ikejiri Captain-*sama*—Lord Captain—but decided that would be laying it on too thick even for the self-important officer.

"Oh, you would, would you?" Now Ikejiri sounded as if he had trouble believing his ears.

"*Hai*, Captain-*san!*" Fujita saluted again, then resumed his posture of respect.

Captain Ikejiri rubbed his chin. "Well, I don't hear that one every day," he allowed. "Most of the time, people come in here to ask me to put them in slots where they *don't* go into harm's way."

"Sir, I serve the Emperor. I *want* to serve the Emperor, may he live ten thousand years. I want to serve him the best way I can." All of which was true. Fujita didn't say he was bored green in Myitkyina, although that was just as true if it wasn't even more so.

"Well, your attitude does you credit." From Ikejiri, that was no small praise. He glanced down at some papers on the little table that did him duty as a desk. *My service record*, Fujita realized. The captain continued, "No one can complain about your performance since you came to Burma."

That was why Fujita was a sergeant again. His performance in China, on the other hand, had got him demoted and made the powers that be approve his request for a transfer as soon as he handed it in. If you fouled up, you would pay for it. And he had, and he'd come to this miserable place to atone for fouling up. Now he'd managed that, too. Having managed it, he wanted more, as people have a way of doing.

"You realize, if you see more action, the Chinese will shoot at you?" Captain Ikejiri said.

"Sir, you will know I fought the Russians on the Mongolian border and in Siberia." Fujita couldn't sound affronted before an officer, but he wanted to. "After them, I hope I'm not going to hide under the bed on account of the *Chankoro*." He brought out the scornful Japanese slang for *Chinks* without even noticing he did it. Japan had been taking what she wanted and needed in China ever since the end of the nineteenth century. The Chinese almost always gave way before Japan's might. When they didn't, they almost always lost. No wonder Japanese soldiers scorned them and their fighting skills.

"Yes, yes." Ikejiri's patience showed, which meant it would fray soon. "But you would be up in an airplane, and they would be shooting at you from the ground. You wouldn't be able to shoot back. That may not be the kind of action you crave."

"Oh, I'd shoot back at them, all right, Captain-*san*," Fujita replied. "Only I'd use a different kind of bullet, *neh*?" Security at bacteriological-warfare units ran deep. Fujita didn't call a Chinese a Chinese, and, just as much without thinking, he didn't call a germ a germ.

The way he did say things made Masanori Ikejiri smile for the first time. "So you would," the captain agreed. "Since you put it that way, Sergeant, I think we can give you what you asked for. Sure enough, your attitude is commendable—I will say that much for you."

"*Domo arigato*, Captain-*san*!" Fujita exclaimed, saluting yet again.

Ikejiri kept smiling, but in a less pleasant way. "Don't thank me until after you've flown a few missions. You may not be so happy about it then."

Fujita thought that was nonsense—till he went on his first mission. He'd wheeled plenty of porcelain biological-warfare bomb casings across the airstrip outside of Myitkyina and loaded them into the bomb bays of the Japanese Army planes that would fly them up to Yunnan Province and drop them on the heads of the obstreperous Chinese.

Now he sat in the bomb bay himself. He'd learned which levers to pull to open the bomb-bay doors and to release the bombs and what to do—besides cussing—if the levers didn't work the way they were supposed to. No one expected Chinese fighters to come up, but you never could tell.

And—maybe most important—he'd been briefed on how and when to use the oxygen apparatus. "It may not kill you if you don't," the pilot had explained. "We don't usually fly that high. But if you forget you may be kind of stupid when we land, and you may stay that way. So remember, *neh? Wakarimasu-ka?*"

"*Hai. Wakarimasu*," Fujita had answered. Understand he did.

One thing he hadn't really understood was how flimsy and make-shift a warplane could seem when you scrambled up inside it. From the outside, the Ki-21 looked like an aerial shark: all deadly purpose. When you got in there and saw the ribs and realized that the fuselage was covered with aluminum skin almost thin enough for you to stick your hand through . . . Well, it gave you a different feel for things. True, the interior walls of many Japanese houses were no more than translucent paper— but Japanese houses didn't go where angry people were liable to shoot at them. The bomber did.

He also hadn't understood how noisy it would be in there. The roar and vibration from the twin engines made him wonder if the fillings in his back teeth would shake loose. It wasn't really an idle kind of wondering, either. He sat back there, shivering in spite of his fur-lined leather flying suit, sucking in oxygen that tasted of the rubber lines it came through, and hoping like anything he wouldn't have to visit an Army dentist when he got back to Burma.

If he got back to Burma. Yes, he'd known the Chinese shot at Japanese planes, but he hadn't really understood what that meant. He hadn't felt the bomber buck like a spooked stallion when an antiaircraft shell burst nearby. He hadn't watched a ragged-edged hole suddenly appear in the fuselage's skin when a fragment ripped through it. He hadn't thought about what would have happened had that fragment ripped through him instead of hitting thirty centimeters farther back.

"Dump the bombs!" the pilot shouted through the voice tube. "Dump 'em right now so we can get the demon out of here!"

"*Hai!*" Fujita shouted back. He worked the levers the way he'd been taught. The fragment hadn't damaged their mechanisms, anyhow. Down fell the porcelain casings, one after another.

The bomber banked steeply as it turned. The engines roared louder. Fujita took a deep breath of oxygenated air. He'd got the action he'd asked for, all right. Oh, had he ever!

# Chapter 15

Across the border lay Belgium. Aristide Demange had only contempt for the Belgians. Demange had plenty of that for the whole human race, but his reasons for scorning the Belgians were different. Like some Swiss and Canadians, they had the gall to speak French without being part of France.

And they were weak sisters. The Germans had overrun them in short order twice now in this century. They'd overrun them, and then they'd occupied them, and the Belgians had rolled over with their bellies in the air and accepted occupation. So it seemed to him, anyhow. And, this time around, the Belgian Fascists helped the Nazis every way they could.

Walloons—the Belgians who spoke French—blamed the collaboration on the Flemings, the ones who spoke Dutch and could play as if they were Aryans. But there were Walloon would-be Nazis, too. A character named Léon Degrelle had formed a Walloon Legion that fought for Hitler in Russia. Degrelle had got wounded and won himself a Knight's Cross. These days, the Walloon Legion was back here in the

West, ready to fight against "the forces of Jewish plutocrat capitalism"—France and England, in other words.

That really disgusted Demange. If the Belgians didn't want to be liberated, why spend money and men on the job? Because orders were orders, that was why. But he'd heard somewhere that Hitler had said that, if he'd had a son, he would have wanted him to be like Léon goddamn Degrelle. If that wouldn't gag a maggot . . .

As far as Demange knew, only authentic *Boches*, not homemade copies, crouched in the muddy trenches on the far side of the mined and wired border. For the Germans he had solid professional respect. For their Belgian imitators? If you came up against those *cons*, how many prisoners would you bother to take?

More and more planes—English with their red-white-and-blue roundels red at the center and blue on the outside, French with the same colors reversed—flew from west to east night after night to drop their loads of hate on Belgium, Holland, and Germany. The *Luftwaffe* returned the compliment, though not so often.

French guns started shelling German positions inside Belgium. Young François got all hot and bothered—it looked as if the big attack was on at last. Then the *Boches* fired back. He didn't like that so much. Who would have?

France had started the war with great swarms of quick-firing 75s left over from the go a generation earlier. Thanks to Versailles, the Germans had had to rebuild their artillery from scratch. Their 105s had outclassed the older French guns: bigger shells, longer range. Now France had enough 105s of her own to compete on even terms. *And it only took us four years. Isn't that grand?* Demange thought cheerfully.

Orders came for a probe into Belgium. The Germans had attacked with everything they had in the winter of 1938. Attacking with everything you had didn't seem to belong in the French vocabulary.

At the officers' assemblage where the orders were announced, Demange asked, "A probe? Isn't that what the doctors shove up your ass when your piles get impacted or whatever the hell piles do?" He didn't care what he said. What was the worst thing they could do to him? Bust him down to sergeant again? He'd kiss them on both cheeks. Bust him down to private? He wouldn't mind too much, unless he had some real *salaud* of a sergeant (one, say, like him) telling him what to do. Ship him to the front? He was already here.

His frankness made majors and lieutenant colonels and other such Important Personages wince. His own superior, a young captain named Marcel Gagné, was used to him by now—and stuck with him, too. "We're trying to shove it up the *Boches*' ass," he said mildly.

"If we're gonna shove, we oughta *shove*," Demange insisted. "You don't give it to your girlfriend halfway, do you?"

Eyeing the officers, he figured some of them gave it to their boyfriends instead. If he came out with that, though, they *would* find something worse than demotion to do to him. All too often, the exact truth was the worst thing you could use.

Instead, he found a different question to ask: "Will we have any armor support?" If the answer turned out to be no, he hoped he wouldn't get too badly damaged before the stretcher-bearers carried him to an aid station.

But the Most Important Personage—a brigadier general, no less—nodded. "We will," he said, beaming as much as a big shot was ever likely to. "Some American *chars* we have purchased, and some of our own as well."

"How about that?" Demange said in glad surprise. New French tanks had a gunner instead of making the commander fire the main armament. They all carried radios, too. The designers had swiped both notions from the Germans, but so what? They were good ones. The American tanks, though they carried radios, too, were like some of the older French models. They mounted a small gun in the turret and a bigger one in a hull sponson. But they were faster than the old French machines, and the Americans manufactured stuff in quantities other countries could only dream about.

Demange was actually optimistic when French guns hammered the Nazis' front lines. The sensation felt so strange, he had trouble recognizing it. Even the gloomy, drizzly weather didn't dampen his spirits. The last time he'd felt this way was in the autumn of 1918, when the Kaiser's boys realized they couldn't hold out any more. And they couldn't—but they'd gone and shot him before they folded up for good.

Whistles shrilled, up and down the French trenches. "Come on, you bastards!" Demange yelled to the men he led. "We'll get 'em!" For a few minutes, he even believed what he told them.

Then the German guns came back to life. No, the French barrage hadn't silenced them—that would have been too much to hope for. Shells started falling amidst the advancing men in khaki. One came down right on some poor *cochon*. When the smoke and flame cleared, nothing was left of him but one boot. Machine guns spat death and mutilation. Concrete firing positions weren't easy for artillery to take out. Tanks could do it, though.

The tanks did take out some of the machine-gun nests. And German 88s posted a bit farther back took out some of the tanks. Neither the American *chars* nor the French ones could stand up against those massive AP rounds. As far as Demange knew, no tanks could, not even the monsters the Russians built.

Here and there, Germans surrendered when French troops overran their positions. "*Kamerad!*" they would shout, or, if they spoke some French, "*Ami!*" And sometimes they got the chance to go back into a POW camp, and sometimes they didn't: Monte Carlo, only played with human lives.

Those tanks that survived smashed lanes through the iron bramble fields of wire. French soldiers who had to dive when gunfire opened up nearby often clambered to their feet swearing and bleeding. Demange did himself. Much of the wire was old and rusty. He tried to remember the last time he'd got tetanus antitoxin.

He couldn't. He didn't waste time worrying about it. Of all the things he expected to die from, lockjaw came low on the list.

One of the American-built tanks hit a mine not far in front of him. The beast stopped short with a thrown track. The tank crew bailed out and hotfooted it to the rear, using their machine's carcass to help cover them from enemy fire. No more than half a minute after they escaped, an 88 hit the *char* and set it ablaze. A tank that wouldn't go was a tank waiting to die. Most of the time, it didn't have long to wait, either.

Here came Marcel and Jean. The tall Red and the short one looked as filthy and as scared as any other soldiers where things got hot. "Here's your Riviera, dearies!" Demange called to them. "See, there's Stalin over on the next beach towel. Why don't you wave?"

They gave him identical horrible looks. Sometimes what you'd asked for was the worst thing you could get.

Little by little, the French attack bogged down. Demange hadn't looked for anything else, not after those rose-colored first few minutes. In fact, they'd pushed farther than he'd thought they could. Some of them settled down in German trenches. The *Boches* built finer field fortifications than anybody. He'd seen that in the last war. It remained true this time. The Russians used better camouflage, but they cared nothing for their soldiers' comfort. The Germans did.

They also cared about pushing the French back to the border. Their artillery banged away all through the long night. Of course they had the range to their own former front line. A burst not far from Demange killed two of his men and sent three more off to the butchers in masks. One of the *poilus* was in bad shape. If they slapped an ether cone over his face and let him die, they might be doing him a favor.

But the advance went on the next morning. That surprised Demange— astonished him, in fact. Maybe the fat old fools in Paris meant it after all. Who would have thought so? Demange still wasn't sure he did.


THIS WASN'T THE first time Alistair Walsh had found himself in Calais. It wasn't the second time, either. That had been back in late 1938, when the British Expeditionary Force crossed to the Continent in alleged support of Czechoslovakia. Czechoslovakia went down the drain several hundred miles away. The BEF fired not a shot till long after Prague was occupied and Slovakia had detached itself from the Czecho part and declared its Nazi-sponsored independence.

If you had to be somewhere not fighting, there were worse places than Calais. It wasn't England, but you could—literally—see Blighty from there. Most of the shopkeepers and waiters and barmaids spoke English. The bars weren't pubs, but they came close. The beer and cider were both good, and Calvados . . . There was a hell of a lot to be said for Calvados.

To his regret, Walsh didn't get to linger in Calais this time, not the way he had four years earlier. He got off the ferry that hauled him across the Channel, walked down the dock, and climbed into the back of an enormous lorry from out of Detroit. Almost before he knew it, he was bouncing down a narrow, badly paved road heading east.

The lorry—*truck* was the Yankee word, but he had no truck with it—had a canvas canopy of brownish green. That kept him from peering anxiously up at the sky. If Stukas screamed down on this column of lorries . . . He'd been through that when the Fritzes made their big push into France. He didn't care to repeat the experience.

He knew too well the Germans didn't care about what he cared to do. He couldn't hear much over the bang and rattle of tires on potholed asphalt, the engine's steady grunting, and the chatter of the other soldiers who filled the big passenger compartment.

Most of them were young enough to be his children. They shared fags and pipe tobacco. A couple had flasks full of one kind of distilled lightning or another. None of it was as good as Calvados, but Walsh didn't fuss. A knock of anything strong made him worry a bit less about whatever might be flying overhead.

"If they're Stukas, you'll hear the Jericho Trumpets—the sirens they've got fixed to their landing gear," he said. "Whoever thought those up, I'd like to wring his neck like a pullet, bugger me blind if I wouldn't. The Fritzes want to scare you so much that you piss yourself, and the bastards know how to get what they want, too."

"Blimey, don't they 'arf!" said a younger man, a lance-corporal. "I went and did it first time they screamed down and bombed me, and I'm not ashamed to say so." He wore the ribbon for the Military Medal; no one was likely to call him yellow.

"Anybody who's seen combat and says he hasn't had to change his drawers once or twice—well, maybe he's telling the truth, but he's got himself one tight arsehole if he is," Walsh said.

None of the others commented on that. More than one, though, looked up at the canvas stretched over steel hoops as if thinking rather loudly. Walsh had been through enough to let him come out with things others knew but would sooner not have said.

In due course, the unstrafed string of lorries stopped. The soldiers piled out. Walsh already had a round chambered in his Sten gun. That involved a certain amount of risk: the safety on the nasty little sub-machine gun was no more reliable than any other piece of the botched-together weapon. If the Sten wasn't the ugliest piece of armament in the world, Walsh had no idea what would be. But it did the job—if the job was something like house-to-house fighting. For longer ranges, a rifle beat it all hollow. But it fired much faster than a rifle could.

They were closer to the sea than Walsh had been in 1938. Gulls wheeled and screeched overhead. They were worse scroungers than sol-diers, if such a thing was possible. The breeze came off the water, and smelled of salt and sand. Pretty soon, if the guns pounding up ahead were any indication, the breeze would start stinking of blood and shit and death. Walsh savored the clean smell while he could.

Before he went forward and won the chance to pick up one more wound (or worse, but no one ever wanted to think about worse) for King and country, regimental HQ had to find a slot for him. A bespec-tacled subaltern in a tent diplomatically distant from the gun pits—as safe a slot as a man in a front-line regiment could find—clicked his tongue between his teeth.

The fellow was about to post him somewhere when a runner came in and set a scrap of paper on the folding table he was using for a desk. The young second lieutenant glanced at the paper and said, "Bloody hell!" He looked up to Walsh. "Can you handle a company for a few days, Staff Sergeant? I realize it's a deal to ask, but Lieutenant Ormesby just copped one. He was a friend of mine: a year ahead of me at Sand-hurst." He touched the bit of paper. "Doesn't sound good."

"Sorry to hear it, sir," Walsh said. "Always hard when a mate gets hurt." He knew that too well himself. "I'll have a go at the company if you want me to, but aren't there any other officers besides Lieutenant, uh, Ormesby?"

"Not in that company," the subaltern said. "If you can handle person-nel matters, I'll take that Sten off your hands and go forward myself."

Walsh liked him better after that. He wasn't back here only because he didn't want to get any closer to the action, then. Truthfully, the ser-geant answered, "I'd do more good up there. You wouldn't care to see the balls-up I'd make of your work."

"Right. Well, off you go, then." The junior officer explained to Walsh how to find his new post, adding, "Mind how you move up from the apple orchard. The Fritzes throw mortar bombs at you if they see you."

"Thanks for the heads-up." Walsh ducked out of the tent and waved to the men serving the 105s. Even in this chilly weather, they worked stripped to the waist. Up he went. Teams of aid men with Red Cross armbands brought back a steady stream of wounded. One of them might have been the unfortunate Lieutenant Ormesby, but Walsh didn't pause to inquire.

The subaltern's apple orchard had been pretty well torn up. Walsh might not have recognized it if he hadn't been looking for it. He stuck some twigs into the strip of inner tube he'd put on his tin hat just above the brim. That might help break up his outline. Or nothing might help. The craters in the field ahead argued that the Germans were much too alert.

Well, all he could do was his best. He dashed forward, dodging like a rugby half who smelled a try. He'd got almost all the way to the battered village past the field before the boys in *Feldgrau* lobbed a couple of mortar rounds his way. Both fell a good hundred yards behind him.

" 'Oo the 'ell are you?" asked a grimy, unshaven Tommy in a uniform he hadn't changed for a long time. The way he curled his lip made Walsh ashamed of his smooth chin and clean clothes.

He gave his name and rank regardless, finishing, "They sent me up to take charge of things till they can find an officer for the company."

" 'Appy bleedin' dye." The Tommy curbed his enthusiasm very well. Suspiciously, he asked, "You ever smell smokeless powder before?"

"You weren't even a gleam in your pa's eye the first time I got shot," Walsh answered. "The last time was this past summer. I'm just back to duty after the wound healed."

"Hrm." A grunt. The soldier rubbed his bristly chin. "Well, you *may* do, then." He still sounded anything but sure.

"You can tell me where to head in later, if you still want to," Walsh said. "In the meanwhile, don't you think we'd better dig these holes deeper?" He grabbed his own entrenching tool so the other man could see that *we* was no figure of speech.

"Bugger me blind! You *do* know what you're about." Now the Tommy spoke in tones of deep and genuine astonishment. In minutes, dirt was flying from shovels all over what was left of the village.

AS HANS-ULRICH RUDEL scrambled out of his Stuka and the ground-crew men covered the revetment with camouflage netting, he breathed out a long, weary sigh. His breath smoked. Sergeant Dieselhorst lit a cigarette. "Another one down," Dieselhorst said, his cheeks hollowing.

"That's about the size of it," Hans-Ulrich agreed. He hurried out of the revetment. He usually relished the smells of gasoline and motor oil and hot metal that clung to his Ju-87. Not today, for some reason. He needed fresh air—and Dieselhorst's nasty cigarette sure didn't help.

It was cool and cloudy, but it wasn't raining and it wasn't freezing. Not all the fields around the airstrip had gone yellow and lifeless, the way they would have in Russia with winter nearly here. Some still showed green. Half a kilometer away, past the barbed wire, a Belgian farmer in overalls puttered around in one of them.

Sergeant Dieselhorst came up beside Rudel. The pilot smelled the cigarette smoke even before he noticed the other man's footfalls. Nodding out toward the Belgian, Hans-Ulrich remarked, "I wonder what that clown's doing—know what I mean?"

"You mean you wonder if he's keeping an eye on us," Dieselhorst said.

Hans-Ulrich nodded. "Right the first time."

The sergeant chuckled harshly. "Well, in Russia you wouldn't've needed to wonder. He damn well would have been." Another chuckle, even dryer than the first. "Of course, in Russia we would've shot any Ivan who got that close to one of our bases."

"Belgium's a more crowded place," Hans-Ulrich said, which was putting it mildly. After a moment, he added a wistful coda: "And some of the Belgians like us, too."

"There is that." Sergeant Dieselhorst softened the concurrence with a coda of his own: "Some of the Russians liked us, too. Of course, their other choice was Stalin. He could make damn near anybody look good by comparison."

"Naughty." Hans-Ulrich wagged a finger at him. "Are you trying to get me to report you to the *Sicherheitsdienst*?"

"Nah." Dieselhorst shook his head as he ground out the cigarette under his boot. "If you were gonna do it, you would've done it by now."

One more thing the veteran was right about. Some of what Dieselhorst said about National Socialism and about what it did to the *Reich*'s foreign policy went far beyond what was safe. But how many times had the rear gunner and radioman saved Hans-Ulrich's one and only neck? More than he cared to remember. He hoped he understood what gratitude was. The sergeant might not care for the people who ran Germany. He'd served the country well for a long time, though. Didn't that matter more?

The SD and the *Gestapo* would have said no. Sometimes, you needed not to listen to what certain other people were saying, no matter how loudly they happened to be saying it.

Instead, Hans-Ulrich listened to the distant rumble of artillery. It was so easy to listen to, he wished it were more distant still. Recognizing the German guns was easy. The others . . . He'd been away from this front too long. "Are those French cannon or English?" he asked.

Albert Dieselhorst cocked his head to one side, considering. "French, sir, I think," he said at last. "The 75s are, for sure. I don't know about the 105s. They sound like a new mark to me, so I can't tell who made them. Any which way, 105s are bad news."

In the last war, foot soldiers had hung all kinds of nicknames on the shells their guns fired and on the ones the enemy aimed at them. Boys playing at war after the shooting ended naturally used the names they got from their fathers and uncles and older brothers. Hans-Ulrich knew them as well as any *Frontschwein* in the Kaiser's army. The kids shooting at one another with toy guns in 1950 would probably need some new names for their imaginary shellbursts.

When Rudel spoke that conceit aloud, he startled a laugh out of Dieselhorst. "I never would have wondered about that in a million years, sir," the older man said. "Must be a reason you're an *Oberleutnant* and I'm just a dumb *Feldwebel*."

"I'll tell you what you are," Hans-Ulrich said. Sergeant Dieselhorst gave forth with a questioning grunt. Rudel told him: "You're a sandbagger, that's what."

The sergeant laughed some more. He wagged a still-gloved finger in Hans-Ulrich's face. "And where did the likes of you learn about card players' wicked habits . . . sir?"

Rudel's ears heated. If there was one thing he hated, it was getting ragged for being a minister's son. He hated it all the more because he was one. "Playing cards isn't against my religion," he said stiffly.

"Then how come you don't do it more?" Dieselhorst probed.

"Because I'm lousy, and losing money's against my religion." Hans-Ulrich jabbed at himself before his crewmate could do it: "And hey, I'm not even a Jew."

"I bet that's not what you told your girl in Bialystok." Sergeant Dieselhorst did his own revising this time: "No, it wouldn't've mattered, would it? Unless you got yourself a clip job I don't know about, she'd have worked that out—or worked it in—for herself."

"Give it a rest, why don't you?" Hans-Ulrich answered, not rising to the lewd suggestion. He missed Sofia more than he'd thought he would when the squadron came back to the West. She wasn't just an amusement for when he got some leave. She'd lodged in the crevices of his mind the way a piece of gristle could lodge between the teeth. His thoughts worried at her as his tongue would have worried at the gristle. He needed some mental floss to get her out of there, but didn't know where to find it.

"That's what she said, right?" Sergeant Dieselhorst's grin was perfectly filthy. It was also perfectly friendly. If it hadn't been, Hans-Ulrich might have tried to deck him. He also might have got a rude surprise for his trouble—a thought that had crossed his mind before. He had size and youth and speed on his radioman/rear gunner. When it came to experience . . .

So it didn't turn into a fight or anything close to a fight, especially when Dieselhorst's smile *was* friendly. Instead, Hans-Ulrich said, as much to himself as to his crewmate, "Maybe I'll write her a letter. Find out how she's doing, y'know? Find out if she misses me even a little bit." If she didn't, maybe he could stop missing her.

But the sergeant's grin disappeared. "You sure that's a good idea, sir?" he asked, in tones that couldn't mean anything but *You out of your expurgated mind, sir?*

You could screw a woman who was a *Mischling* first class. You could have a fine old time doing it, too, as Hans-Ulrich had reason to know. If she was a Polish national, and so not subject to the laws against German Jews and half-breeds, so much the better. But if you showed signs that you'd been rash enough to fall in love with her, well, that would give the SD something to think about, sure as the devil it would. Not even the most loyal, most naïve fighting man (and Rudel won top marks on both counts) looked forward to that.

"Mm, well, maybe not," Hans-Ulrich allowed.

"There you go." Now Dieselhorst's features showed nothing but relief. "When you find yourself a Belgian honey, you can forget all about the other one."

"Sure." Hans-Ulrich didn't want to make the older man worry about him. He didn't argue or quarrel or make a fuss. He just said, "Let's go get debriefed, *ja*? We've wasted enough time gabbing."

Off they went, to report on what they'd seen and done over the border in northeastern France. And if Hans-Ulrich wrote a letter in his tent that night, Sergeant Dieselhorst didn't need to know about it. Chances were Sofia wouldn't answer anyhow. She hadn't answered any of the letters he'd sent her from Russia. *She* knew it wasn't a good idea. Hans-Ulrich, on the other hand . . .

IVAN KUCHKOV SPRAWLED in the mud, eyeing the woods ahead. "Is that a motherfucking white flag?" he called to Sasha Davidov. "Or do my cocksucking eyes need rifling so they'll carry farther?"

"It's a white flag, Comrade Sergeant," the point man answered.

"*Da*. It fucking is. Now—next question. Can we trust the *khokhol* cunts showing it?" Kuchkov generally trusted Ukrainians as far as he could throw them. He trusted Ukrainian nationalist fighters even less. Some of them were out-and-out Nazis. Some of them hated the Red Army a lot worse than the Nazis did. (That they might have good reason to hate it bothered him not a bit. Nobody had good reason to want to kill him, not as far as he was concerned.)

"I can't answer that one, Comrade Sergeant," Davidov said. "You've got to make up your own mind."

"Fuck," Kuchkov muttered. He knew he wasn't the brightest candle on the altar (not a good Soviet comparison, but a good Russian one).

But his choices here seemed stark. He could get into a bigger fight than he really wanted or he could treat with the guys who used a stupid-looking blue-and-yellow flag and an even dumber-looking trident to show they weren't Soviets or even Russians. Swearing some more under his breath, he got to his feet and waved a dirty snotrag: the biggest piece of white cloth he had.

"Don't shoot, you whores!" he yelled toward the woods. "We'll parley!"

If they had a machine gun in there, they could cut him in half. A drunken rifleman could have blown out his kidneys. Standing here waving that stupid hanky, he knew it much too well. He felt naked, with a bull's-eye painted on his chest.

"Well, come on," someone in amongst the trees shouted back. The bastard's Russian had a Ukrainian accent thick enough to slice, but it *was* Russian of a sort. Sensibly, the nationalist didn't show himself. He went on, "We won't shoot you till after we talk."

"Hot shit," Ivan muttered, but not loud enough to let the Ukrainians hear him. As he started for the woods, he told Davidov, "Give me a fucking hour. If those bitches haven't turned me loose, yell once. After that, get your cocks in gear and clean 'em out. You hear?"

"*Da*, Comrade Sergeant," the Jew answered. He had to understand as well as Kuchkov did that that would be unfortunate for the sergeant.

"Put down your piece," a Ukrainian with a PPD of his own said when Ivan got to the edge of the wood. Kuchkov set the submachine gun on the ground. He still had a pistol in an inside pocket of his padded jacket. He said nothing about it, or about the knife sheathed at the small of his back. He didn't plan on using either one, but he had them.

The nationalists wore a motley mix of peasant clothes and bits of uniform pilfered from Red Army men and Nazis who didn't need them any more. One fellow had a tobacco-brown tunic he must have got off a Romanian. A khaki patch kept a bullet hole from letting in cold air.

Kuchkov was going to ask who the Ukrainians' boss was, but realized he didn't have to. A guy with a cloth cap, a gingery beard, and wire-framed glasses—damned if he didn't look like Trotsky's kid brother—ran their show. "Say your say," he told Ivan. "If we don't like it, we'll make you sorry."

"I'm already fucking sorry," Kuchkov said. Baby Trotsky's smile didn't get to his eyes. A good thing, too, because the Red Army sergeant went on, "But you pricks'll be a lot sorrier if you don't listen up."

They growled. Some of them hefted their weapons: like their clothes, a crazy mix of Soviet and Fascist designs. They didn't have the mindless discipline both Germany and the USSR thumped into their troops. If one of them felt like killing Ivan, he was liable to go ahead and do it.

Their leader gestured. That calmed them—a little. He nodded to Kuchkov: not a friendly nod, but one that did allow the Russian to exist a while longer, anyhow. "Go on. We're listening."

"I'm here to tell you you should all get lost," Ivan said. "The Nazi cunts, they're falling back in the Ukraine. You fuckers aren't too dumb to see that for yourselves. And fuck all your mothers if you can't work out what it means. Pretty soon, the Red Army won't have to worry about those Fascist turds any more. Oh, no—they'll worry about you shits instead. And they'll land on you with both feet if you're still around to be landed on."

"We aren't afraid of the Red Army," Baby Trotsky said. His followers' heads bobbed up and down.

"You scared of the NKVD pricks? You scared of the fucking camps?" Ivan demanded. "You assholes're out here playing soldier in the woods. You scared of your wives and your sisters getting gangbanged back in the villages?"

"Fuck you in the mouth, Russian pig," one of the nationalists said. That was a woman's voice. Her German tunic was enough too big to mask her boobs. And she was as rough-skinned and dirty as any of her comrades, if less hairy. She was also as ugly as any of them.

Even Kuchkov could tell saying that wasn't smart. "Get lost," he repeated. "We need these fucking woods. The whole corps is moving up. We're damn well gonna give it to the Hitlerites, and we'll give it to any other cocksuckers who get in our way, too. But if you, like, go and disappear, I don't know who the fuck you are. I don't give a shit, either."

"Then what?" their leader asked bitterly. "Chekists? Commissars? How many have they already murdered down here?"

*You pricks had it coming.* Ivan didn't say that, either. "You fight my guys, you'll fucking lose," he did say. "You can't whip us without the Nazi pricks, and they can't whip us even with you assholes."

That drew more growls from the Ukrainian nationalists. "We ought to kill you just for coming out with such shit," Baby Trotsky told him.

"Chance I took when I came over here," Ivan answered with a shrug. "But if you do, my thieves are coming after me, and they won't put down their machine pistols when you tell 'em to. They'll fuck you all in the mouth with them, fuck your mothers if they won't. I left a smart kike in charge of them. He'll take care of all that shit—you bet he will."

The nationalists' leader spat on the muddy ground. "Kikes! They're Christ-killers *and* they're Reds. Say what you want about Hitler, but he's got the right idea on them."

"I don't wag my dick at any of that political bullshit," Kuchkov said, more or less truthfully. "So listen up, fuckers. You can shoot me, and then you can fight my guys. Or you can clear out and give somebody else shit later. What's it gonna be?"

Baby Trotsky couldn't just issue orders like a proper officer. No, the Ukrainians had to put their heads together and hash things out. When they did, they used their own language. Ivan could follow maybe one word in four. Some of them wanted to do for him; he was pretty sure of that.

But their leader didn't. At last, his view prevailed, even if some of the other bandits looked disgusted. Returning to Russian, Baby Trotsky said, "All right, you can have these goddamn woods. Give us two hours to withdraw."

"That's what you told her, too, I bet," Ivan said. The ginger-bearded guy snorted. Kuchkov went on, "You got a fucking deal."

"That's just the kind of deal I think we have," the nationalist said bleakly. He pointed in the direction from which Kuchkov had come. "Go on. Get lost. Two hours, remember. Move sooner and we'll shoot at you."

"You don't need to stick your cock in my ear. I heard you." Ivan headed back to his own men. The Ukrainians hadn't swiped his PPD, as he'd at least half expected.

"Good to see you in one piece," Sasha Davidov said. "Time was getting low. What's the deal. Is there one?"

"Two hours for them to fuck off. Then the woods are ours," Kuchkov said. To his amazement, the Red Army men raised a cheer for him. He couldn't remember the last time anything—well, anything but pussy—made him feel so good.

# Chapter 16

**W**ehrmacht quartermasters doled out winter clothing as if they'd had to pay for it themselves. Wearing chevrons on his left sleeve helped Willi Dernen acquire some for himself. The padded jacket he got reversed from white to blotchy camouflage. So did his quilted trousers. And his felt-and-leather overboots were almost as good as Russian *valenki*.

He whitewashed his helmet, too. "Could be worse," he allowed. "Our first winter in Russia, we had to make do with ordinary uniforms and whatever we could steal from the Ivans."

"I remember," Adam Pfaff said. "Snow smocks made from bed sheets—that kind of crap."

"Oh, yeah." Willi rolled his eyes. "And the nails in the regular marching boots that sucked cold right up into your feet."

"Jesus Christ! Don't you jokers ever do anything but piss and moan?" Arno Baatz said. "We've got this good stuff now. Why do you want to keep bitching about the old days? We made it through, didn't we?"

"Some of us did, anyway," Willi said darkly. "Some of us froze to death."

Awful Arno glared at him. "Quit pissing and moaning, I told you!"

"No, you didn't, *Herr Unteroffizier*. You asked me if we ever did anything else. We do: we kill Ivans."

Baatz opened his mouth. Then he shut it again without saying anything. He stomped off, his own winter gear slung over his left arm. "He'll make you pay for that," Adam Pfaff predicted.

"I've been paying since I put on the goddamn uniform," Willi said. "Some units have good corporals and sergeants. Just by the law of averages and dumb luck, they're bound to. But me, I've been dealing with Awful Arno Baatz since 1938. Where's the justice in that?"

"Justice? Ha!" Pfaff sad. "Count your blessings he hasn't screwed you over worse than he has."

"If those are blessings, the anti-sin cannon"—*Landser* slang for chaplains—"shoot more shit than the quartermasters do," Willi replied.

"That's how it looks to me, sure as hell. Most of what the chaplains come out with is pure shit." Pfaff looked back over his shoulder to make sure he hadn't said that loud enough for Awful Arno to overhear. Baatz had all the usual small-town, small-soul pieties, and expected everyone else to come equipped with them, too.

Something off in the distance, almost too faint and too low to hear . . . Willi's head swung that way, as a dog's would have. "Those are panzers," he said—not quite the worst thing he could think of (the worst thing he could think of would have been a volley of the Russians' screaming rockets—Stalin's Organ, soldiers called them), but close enough.

Adam Pfaff brought it closer yet: "Those are Russian panzers."

Willi nodded glumly. For one thing, they were coming out of the east, where the *Wehrmacht* had no panzers. For another, the Ivans' diesels sounded different from the gasoline engines his own country used. To Willi, they sounded more sinister, more evil, but he would have admitted he was prejudiced.

Awful Arno's face was a study. He wanted to deny that there were panzers in the neighborhood. If he couldn't do that, he wanted to deny that they belonged to the Red Army. If he couldn't even do *that* . . . Well, no wonder his ugly, overfed mug was a study.

He yelled for the radioman. That worthy couldn't come quickly, not with his set and the batteries that powered it in a heavy pack on his back. Awful Arno wasn't just yelling by the time he did arrive. The underofficer was screaming: "Get us an 88! *Schnell!* Call the regiment! Call the division! Call your granny if you want to—I don't care who you call! It doesn't matter if you pull that 88 out of your asshole! Just get it here! On the double!"

Pfaff giggled helplessly. Willi found himself doing the same thing. He was much too likely to get killed in the next few minutes, but here he was, laughing like a fool. If you had to go, he supposed there were worse ways. He didn't want to go, but he was unpleasantly aware he might not get a choice.

Well, there was always a choice. You could run away. But it wasn't much of a choice, not here, not now. No guarantee the T-34s wouldn't catch up with you anyway. No guarantee the guys on your own side wouldn't shoot you in the back for bolting. And the certain sour knowledge that you'd be letting your buddies down. That carried more weight than either of the others.

The radioman gabbled into his microphone or telephone or whatever the hell you called it. He fiddled with the set—switching frequencies? Then he talked some more, louder and more urgently.

Willi didn't hang around to find out how that particular story wound up. He ran for his foxhole. The Ivans had learned better than to send panzers forward without infantry support (so had the *Wehrmacht*). He couldn't do much against thirty tonnes of steel with a scope-sighted Mauser. But he could make the luckless ground-pounders who slogged along with the Russian panzers good and miserable.

Horizons and landscapes in Russia seemed ridiculously wide. They did if you'd grown up in the more confined spaces of Western Europe, anyhow. There were the T-34s: tiny as mice at the moment, but getting bigger all the time as they clattered forward. And those little bugs scuttling along between them and behind them, those bugs were the Red Army foot soldiers from the slings and arrows and grenades and Molotov cocktails of outrageous *Landsers*.

They didn't look like bugs through his scope's crosshairs. They were men then, by God—men in the almost-Swiss-pattern helmets the Russians stamped out, men carrying rifles that might not be quite so good as his but that were plenty good enough for most murderous purposes. If he didn't do for them, they would damn well do for him. Even if he did do for some of them, the rest—or those panzers—might finish him all the same.

He fired. One of the Ivans spun and toppled. He was proud of himself. Even with a sniper rifle, he couldn't hit out past a kilometer every time. Nope, not even close, especially on a moving target. But there was one Red Army man who wouldn't come any farther forward.

Not far away, a mortar team opened up with their 81mm stovepipe. The Germans had started the war with a smaller, shorter-ranged mortar. Seeing how useful this caliber was to the Red Army made *Wehrmacht* designers imitate it. *Why don't they do that with the goddamn T-34?* Willi wondered.

The mortar team got lucky. One of their bombs came down right on top of an advancing Russian panzer. The big machine went up in a spectacular display of fireworks. The crew couldn't have had any idea of what hit them. There were plenty of worse ways to go. Willi'd seen too many of them, and hoped not to meet any of them in person.

He also hoped the explosion would make the other panzer crews think the 88 was here. It could kill them from farther away than they could reach it. No such luck, though. The Ivans came on. Pretty soon, they stopped, but only so they could shell the Germans in front of them. They didn't shoot especially well, not by German standards. Splinters whistled past Willi. They shot too well to suit him.

Hauled by a half-track, an 88 arrived in the nick of time, like the cavalry in an American Western. The comparison fit, not least because the Germans called their foes Indians. The Ivans fought like savages, that was for sure. Willi didn't even know the gun was behind him till it blasted two T-34s in quick succession.

The surviving enemy panzers turned their fire on the 88. If they could smash it or kill its crew before it got done murdering them . . . In that case, this movie wouldn't have the happy ending the director and the screenwriters should have come up with.

Willi popped up out of his hole like a jack-in-the-box, squeezing off shots at the oncoming Russian foot soldiers. As with his first round, some he was sure he hit. Some who went down might have been diving for cover after bullets cracked close to them. You might not want to miss, but you did when you were short on time to aim.

Up he popped again. He got an Ivan in his sights. And another Ivan got him. A *Stahlhelm* stopped splinters. A rifle round? Not a chance. He knew an instant's surprise, nothing more. Yes, there were worse ways to go, not that he knew anything about that any more, either.

SARAH HAD GONE to a lot of trouble remembering to sign her married name. She'd written *Goldman* only a couple of times after Isidor put the ring on her finger. *Bruck* flowed from her pen, at first with a mental discipline her father would have admired and then, as she got used to it, more naturally.

Officially, Bruck she remained. Without Isidor beside her, though, without his parents, without the bakery (and, thanks to the Nazis, without whatever the bakery had been worth), she didn't feel like a Bruck any more. She was back with her own parents, having nowhere else to go. Didn't that turn her into a Goldman again?

"If you want to think so, then it does—for you," her father said when she asked him about it.

"You'll always be our baby, no matter what you call yourself," Mother added, which helped and didn't help at the same time.

Samuel Goldman went on, "Even if you're Sarah Goldman in your head, you'd better stay Sarah Bruck on paper. If you turn into somebody else, what will happen? Some Party functionary at the *Rathaus* who can't count to eleven without taking off his shoes will wonder what's going on. Is a dirty Jew trying to pull a fast one? You don't need that kind of *tsuris*."

He dropped the Yiddish word into his professorial German the way he might have used a Greek or Latin *terminus technicus* into a lecture when he was still allowed to teach at the university. He used it for the same reasons he would have trotted out the classical languages, too: because it said something with no precise German equivalent, and to show the world he knew such things.

"More *tsuris* I need like a hole in the head. I've got plenty already," Sarah agreed. Father rarely used Yiddish. He looked down on it—it was the jargon *Ostjuden* spoke. Jews from Eastern Europe, with their beards and caftans and long dresses, had seemed as alien to him on German soil as they did to his Aryan neighbors. He'd hoped their odd look and habits were what fueled the Nazis' anti-Semitism. He'd hoped . . . in vain. The Nazis hated Jews because they were Jews, and that was the long and short of it.

He sighed now, and made a small production out of rolling a cigarette from dog-end tobacco and a scrap of newspaper. It was a big, fat cigarette; his butt-scrounging must have gone well on his shift in the labor gang. The match he scraped alight filled the kitchen with a nasty reek. A moment later, the smoldering newspaper and tobacco filled it with another one. He smiled as he inhaled all the same.

"We're still here," he said. "That puts us ahead of a lot of people."

"Samuel!" Reproach filled Hanna Goldman's voice.

"What?" Father said. Then he got it. He grimaced. "I'm sorry, Sarah. Sorry for what happened, and sorry for reminding you of it like a *shlemiel*." There was another bit of Yiddish with no exact German equivalent.

"It's all right," Sarah answered, which was at least approximately true. "Sometimes it hurts like you wouldn't believe. Sometimes . . . Sometimes it hardly feels like I was married at all. I know that's a terrible thing to say, but it's true. It's one of the reasons I feel like a Goldman again."

"You weren't married very long, poor thing," Mother said gently.

"And wartime marriages can be crazy things," Father added. "I saw that the last time around. Some of the girls the men I fought with married . . . Well, the ones who lived fixed things afterwards. Or, a couple of times, they made it work when I didn't think they had a prayer. You never can tell." He blew smoke toward the ceiling and left things there.

How *had* he felt about her marrying a baker's son? However he'd felt, he hadn't said much. He must have realized he couldn't do anything to change what she'd decided to do. When you couldn't change something, keeping your mouth shut about it wasn't the worst idea in the world.

She thought she and Isidor would have been able to work through the rough spots life threw at them. They'd done pretty well in the little while they were together. But life threw more rough spots at Jews in Germany than ordinary married couples faced all over the rest of the world.

Come to that, life threw more rough spots at everyone in Germany than people in most of the world had to worry about: the RAF, for instance. Sarah had hoped the RAF would blow every Nazi in the *Reich* to the moon. When it killed her husband and in-laws instead . . . What was she supposed to think about it then?

She'd asked herself the same question ever since British bombs fell on the bakery. Now she asked it out loud.

Her father and mother looked at each other. Neither said anything for a little while. At last, Mother said, "They weren't trying to kill the Brucks. They were trying to kill the Germans who were trying to kill them."

"I know *that*," Sarah replied with a touch of impatience. "If I didn't, I *would* hate them."

"During the last war, sometimes our guns would tear up the French farms and the like when we were going after their soldiers," Father said slowly. "It wasn't anybody's fault, not after the war got rolling. The farmers . . . just got in the way."

"Like the Brucks?"

"Like the Brucks," he agreed. "If you want to blame somebody, blame the people who started the war, not the ones who got stuck in the middle."

He didn't say who he thought had started the war. They still weren't sure their house wasn't wired for sound, even if the *Gestapo* had never given any sign it was listening. Sarah could draw her own conclusions. Yes, that Czech, that Jaroslaw Stribny, had assassinated Konrad Henlein. But it wasn't as if Henlein, the Sudeten German leader, hadn't been doing his best to tear Czechoslovakia to pieces.

Henlein wouldn't have done that if it weren't for Hitler and the German Nazis. He would have gone right on teaching gymnastics in his little provincial town. He probably still would have been a German nationalist. But, before 1933, nationalists had been a minority among Sudeten Germans. And, before 1933, they were a peaceful political movement, one of many peaceful political movements in a democratic country made up of a crazy quilt of different national groups.

After Hitler brought the Nazis to power, all that changed. Hitler heated the fire. Hitler stirred the pot and set it seething. Konrad Henlein paid with his life. Jaroslaw Stribny paid with his, too. The whole world paid with . . . how many millions of lives?

"*Heil* Hitler!" Sarah whispered.

Her parents looked at each other again. She wanted to clap her hands over her mouth. Neither of them had ever said that, not that she remembered, not even ironically or sarcastically. No, that wasn't quite true. Father had, in jokes he told. But that felt different from this.

As if reading her mind, Father said, "Don't worry about it, sweetheart. We know what you mean."

Mother nodded. "Oh, yes."

Sarah started to cry. She'd done that all the time right after Isidor and his parents got killed, but she hadn't for a while. Now all the pain flooded back at once. She felt ambushed; she hadn't believed that could happen to her. Getting taken by surprise only made it worse.

When Mother put an arm around her, Sarah pushed her away and cried harder than ever. "Let her be," Father said. "She'll feel better once she gets it out of her system. Sometimes things come to a head, that's all, and you have to lance them like a big old boil."

While Sarah wept, she didn't believe she'd ever feel better. Once she'd cried herself out, she found she did. This was an ordinary rough spot. The next night, the RAF bombed Münster again. Sarah hoped nothing fell on anyone who didn't deserve it. Too much to hope for, she knew, but she did it anyway.

"YOU KNOW SOMETHING?" Vaclav Jezek said.

"I know all kinds of things," Benjamin Halévy answered, which was certainly true enough. "Whether one of them is your something, though"—he shrugged—"that, I don't know."

"Right," Vaclav said. "Y'know, sometimes you're too fucking cute for your own good."

"*Jdi do prdele*," the Jew answered sweetly. "There. Is that plain enough for you?"

It meant something like *Up your ass*. It could be an invitation to fight, but not the way Halévy said it. "Same to you," Jezek said. "Now where was I going before you derailed my train of thought? I can't remember."

"Why am I not surprised?" Halévy said.

This time, Vaclav came out with, "*Jdi do prdele*." He snapped his fingers. "Oh, yeah. I've got it. Going on leave sucks—sucks hard."

"We're in the army," Halévy pointed out, "or as much of an army as the Republic's got—and that didn't go to France. Everything sucks. That's how armies are supposed to work."

He almost always said interesting things. That one might keep Vaclav thinking for days. But it wasn't what the Czech sniper wanted to talk about. "Going on leave sucks," he repeated stubbornly. "When we get back to Madrid, all we can do is drink like pigs and screw whores."

"What else would you want to do when you're on leave?" Halévy asked reasonably. "What else is there?"

But Vaclav had an answer for him: "I want to go back to Prague, God damn it to hell. I want to see my family. Christ, I want to see if I've still got a family. I want to talk Czech with somebody besides this bunch of jerks."

He waited. If Halévy laughed at him, he really might feel like brawling. But the corners of the Jew's mouth turned down. "Oh, you poor bastard. You poor, sorry bastard," he said, more sympathetically than Jezek would have imagined he could. "I don't know what to tell you. You sound like you've got it bad."

"'Fraid so," Vaclav admitted. "I've been away too goddamn long. I've almost got my cock shot off too goddamn many times. And for years now the Nazis have been fucking the shit out of my country."

It wasn't Halévy's country, or not exactly: not so much because Halévy's parents were Jews, but because he'd been born in Paris. He spoke perfect Czech. He'd stayed with the government-in-exile's forces when he could have bailed out of the war altogether. He might even have had better reasons to hate the Nazis than Vaclav did, and that wasn't easy. But Czechoslovakia itself didn't have the same hold on him as it did for the other men in this muddy stretch of entrenchments.

He sighed now. His breath smoked. Winter could get very respectably cold on the plateaus of central Spain. "I don't know what to tell you. You can't buy a ticket at the train station and just go," he said.

"Don't I know it!" Vaclav exclaimed. "I can't even write to anybody back there. It's like all of Central Europe is a hole in the map."

"Have you tried writing through the Red Cross in Switzerland?" Halévy asked. "I don't know for sure, but they might be able to get letters back and forth. Censored and all, sure, but still."

"Huh!" Jezek said in surprise. "You know, I never thought of that."

"Like I said, I don't know—I haven't had to worry about it," Benjamin Halévy said. "But if you try and you don't get an answer back, how are you worse off?"

There was another good question. Vaclav had to scrounge paper and a pencil off the Jew. He scribbled a note to his father. None of the Czechs had an envelope, let alone a Republican stamp. He got those from Chaim Weinberg, the American International whose Yiddish he could more or less follow.

"I write to my folks every now and then, so I've got that kind of shit," Weinberg explained. "My old man thinks I'm *meshiggeh* for being here, but so what? We're still family, y'know?"

"He thinks you're what?" Vaclav's German wasn't perfect, and he didn't know that word, or even if it *was* German.

"Some people say *meshuggeh*." Weinberg tried to be helpful, but didn't succeed. Then he spun his right forefinger by his right ear.

"Oh." Vaclav got that, all right. He sometimes thought the Americans was nuts, too, though for reasons no doubt different from the ones Weinberg's father had.

He addressed the envelope in care of the International Red Cross in Geneva and sent it off. He had no idea whether the Red Cross would answer him or his folks would or nobody would. He was inclined to bet on the last. But, as Halévy said, how was he worse off if that happened?

He did get a card from the Red Cross—the first mail he'd had since he couldn't remember when. It was printed in German (which he could read) and French and English (which he couldn't). The German said *We are attempting delivery of your letter. We cannot guarantee acceptance.* Presumably, the message in the other languages was the same.

In the meantime, the fighting ground on. The war in Spain was going on seven years old now. By all the signs, it might last forever. The Republicans advanced bit by bit. They'd gain a couple of kilometers. A Fascist counterattack three days later would throw them back one and a half. They'd regroup and push another thousand meters north and west. Sanjurjo's men would recapture half of that.

Almost every morning before dawn, Vaclav would sling his antitank rifle, crawl out into no-man's-land, find somewhere to hide, and wait to see what kind of bastards in yellowish khaki he could pot. His work was so regular, he felt as if he ought to punch a time clock when he went out and came back.

He felt proud of himself when he blew the head off another German officer trying to teach the Nationalists how to fight more like the *Wehrmacht*: shoveling shit against the tide, in other words. He almost pitied the German as he pulled the trigger. That didn't stop him from killing the man, but did leave him thoughtful.

Spaniards were brave. No way around that. Both Spanish Republican troops and their Nationalist foes attacked and defended with a ferocity Vaclav admired and didn't want to imitate. But attacks went in late. They didn't always go in where they were supposed to. Artillery support was haphazard at best, and sometimes didn't come at all.

Vaclav had fought the *Wehrmacht*. Czechoslovakia had built its armed forces on the German model, of which it had far more experience than people here did. Men in *Feldgrau* didn't fuck up the way the Spaniards did. They were human, sure. They goofed. But their besetting sins were different, and didn't include sloppiness. If that bastard from the *Legion Kondor* hadn't gone out and got smashed every night . . . Well, he'd never have the chance now.

Whenever Vaclav punctuated someone more than usually prominent, he threw Marshal Sanjurjo's side into a tizzy. The Nationalists started shooting off machine guns and letting fly with mortars and banging away with their 77mm guns and 105s. None of the Fascist hate came anywhere near him. No one in the enemy trenches must have spied his muzzle flash. That was nice. He might even get another shot from this hiding place.

And he did, toward afternoon, at a fat Spaniard who had to be at least a colonel. To his vast disgust, he missed. The Spaniard dove for the deck; he didn't topple bonelessly, the way he would have if that muscular bullet had pulled the plug on his drain. You couldn't win them all. Jezek got pissed off whenever he didn't, though.

This time, the enemy machine guns probed more accurately. He flattened himself against the dirt as the rounds cracked past not far enough overhead. It would get dark pretty soon, but not nearly soon enough to suit him.

After the sun went down, a Czech picket almost shot him when he didn't come out with the day's word fast enough. Factory workers sometimes went through tough days, too. They had shorter hours and better pay, though, and most of them weren't lousy. Vaclav dropped down into the trenches and lit a cigarette.

WHEN ANASTAS MOURADIAN exhaled, his breath puffed out in a big white cloud. He'd been in colder places. In Siberia, this would have been a mild winter's day. In Siberia, it could get cold enough that the water in your breath instantly turned to ice crystals when you let it out. It made a noise when it did: the whispers of stars, they called it there.

Stas had never heard the whisper of stars. He'd heard enough different people talk about it to believe it was real, though. This wasn't anywhere near that cold. But it was cold enough to freeze the ground so planes could fly again. The fall *rasputitsa* was over.

Lieutenant Colonel Tomashevsky explained the mission in the simplest possible terms: "We're going to knock the Fascist hyenas' cocks off. If they want to fuck around with the *Rodina*, we'll make the cunts pay." Even Mouradian, for whom Russian was a second language, knew a mixed metaphor when he heard one regardless of whether it was laced with *mat*. A composition teacher would have left angry red scrawls all over the squadron commander's paper.

Real life didn't grade things the same way. The assembled flyers—most of them Russians—laughed and whooped. One or two of them pumped their fists in the air. *Mat* had started out as the slang of hoodlums and lowlifes. The camps and the war were like wicks through which it soaked into the wider Russian world.

"Seriously, though," Tomashevsky went on, "the Hitlerites are getting new tanks that are giving our boys grief. If we blast the stuffing out of the railroad lines and the train stations, the tanks'll have a tougher time coming forward. So that's what we'll do."

He stabbed at a map on a folding stand with a pointer. "Bobruisk today," he said. One corner of his mouth twisted upwards. "A different bombardment unit has been given the honor of heroically attacking the railroad yards at Minsk."

Stas didn't let out a big sigh of relief, but several flyers did. Minsk lay farther west than Bobruisk, which meant a longer flight over German-occupied territory. Minsk was a bigger, more important place, too. The flak above it would be fiercer. The Pe-2s would be more likely to meet up with Messerschmitts over Minsk.

*Let someone else sweat out the tough mission today*, Mouradian thought. *I've had my share of those and then some.* If he could help defeat the Hitlerites by flying a milk run for a change, he'd gladly do that.

The squadron commander whacked the map with the pointer. "We'll make our approach from the southeast and escape in the same direction," he said. "Word is that the Nazis have emplaced some new batteries north of the yards."

Some Party member or Jew had probably risked his life to bring that word to the Soviet authorities. Or maybe it was some Russian peasant whose sister had been raped by a squad of Germans. Hitler's men hadn't gone out of their way to endear themselves to the population on the land they'd seized. Just the opposite, in fact. The frightening thing was how many Soviet citizens collaborated with them anyhow. What that said about the glorious wisdom of General Secretary Stalin . . .

What that said about the glorious wisdom of General Secretary Stalin was not for the likes of Anastas Mouradian to judge. All he had to do was bomb the stuffing out of Bobruisk and try to get back in one piece so he could go bomb some other Fascist-held town tomorrow or the day after.

Sergeant Mechnikov, who would actually yank the levers that let the bombs fall from the plane, had had his own briefing—or maybe, like a lot of sergeants, he knew things without needing to be told. "Bobruisk," he announced when Stas and Isa Mogamedov met him by the Pe-2.

"That's right," Stas said.

"Beats the snot out of Minsk," the bombardier declared. He'd been plucked off a *kolkhoz* for the military and stuck in the fuselage of a bomber because he had the muscles to do the job. He didn't care what he said. He came right out with what Stas only thought. Maybe he'd end up in a camp on account of that. Or maybe he was NKVD, and trying to pull something unpatriotic out of the officers he flew with. You never could tell in the USSR. No wonder so many people didn't see the Hitlerites as worse than what they already knew. . . .

*He won't pull that out of me*, Stas thought as armorers trundled bombs across the frozen airstrip toward the Pe-2 on four-wheeled carts. Having such thoughts to begin with was dangerous. Letting anyone else know you had them was suicidal.

Stas ran through the mechanical checks on the Pe-2 with his usual care. Young Lieutenant Mogamedov had leaned toward sloppiness on such details till he found Stas wouldn't stand for it. More often than not polite as a cat, Stas didn't go around saying things like *you stupid, thumb-fingered Azeri*. Mogamedov, to his credit, didn't want Stas even thinking things like that.

So many things in war you couldn't control. If something you could watch out for upped and bit you because you got careless . . . You'd curse yourself as you hit the silk—if you got the chance to hit the silk.

It all looked good today. The Pe-2 picked up speed as it jounced along the strip. It climbed into the air when Mouradian pulled back on the stick. He spiraled up into the sky and found his place in the formation. The other bombers' guns would help cover his machine. He would do the same for his comrades. It might even help, a little.

A few scattered tracers rose up at them as they crossed the fighting front. German? Soviet? Both? *Both* was the best bet. The slim, graceful Pe-2s looked more like *Luftwaffe* aircraft than most in the Red Air Force's inventory. Red Army men commonly tried to shoot down anything they had doubts about. None of the flak troubled the squadron.

"Do you think the Fascists will let their air defenses farther west know we're on the way?" Mogamedov asked.

"Of course they will," Mouradian answered. In the Soviet Union, such attention to detail was anything but guaranteed. The Germans made most of their mistakes by being too precise, too complicated—and, fairly often, by taking it for granted that their foes would show the same kind of automatic competence they did themselves.

Lieutenant Colonel Tomashevsky led the squadron by a zigzag path, dodging in and out of clouds whenever he could. Stas approved of not making life easy for anyone trying to track them. Somebody would be, sure as the devil's auntie.

A railroad line, straight as a stretched string across snow-dappled ground, guided them to Bobruisk over the last few kilometers. Something in the town was burning, obscuring the railroad yards. No, Stas realized: more likely, the Fritzes had got word the bombers were on the way and had sent up smoke screens to make things hard on them. Hitler's minions were much too good at that.

Their flak was heavy and accurate, too. The 88s that tank crews hated so much could also fling destruction kilometers into the sky. Tracer rounds and black bursts with fiery hearts told the gunners where to send their following volleys. Stas was into his bombing run, and had to fly straight for the yards. The Pe-2 bucked in the air from near misses like a horse ridden for the first time.

The plane just ahead of him in the formation took a hit that tore off half its right wing. Burning terribly, it tumbled toward the ground. Stas hoped the crew could bail out. He had to fly his own machine, and couldn't look down to see. Sometimes distraction was a blessing: not a Marxist-Leninist thought, but a true one.

"Drop the bombs!" Mogamedov shouted into the voice tube. Away they went. Mouradian swung the Pe-2 around, hard, and jammed down the throttles as he streaked away to the southeast. Another bomber fell out of formation with one engine smoking badly and the prop feathered.

The wounded plane lasted no longer than a lame elk would have among wolves. Messerschmitts tore into it. Down it went, and the German fighters roared after its brethren. But the Pe-2 did have a good turn of speed. The Germans caught only one. Stas thanked the God in Whom he officially didn't believe that it wasn't his.

# Chapter 17

**C**arlos Federico Weinberg stared gravely at his father. "Papa," he said.

"Yes, I'm your papa," Chaim agreed. He thought the toddler's voice held a note of doubt. Maybe he was too sensitive, and imagining things. Then again, maybe he wasn't. The only times he got to see the kid were when he came into Madrid on leave.

He supposed he ought to be glad La Martellita let him see Carlos Federico at all. It wasn't as if she'd wanted to have a baby, or to stay married to him one second longer than she needed to give Junior a last name.

Seeing the kid also meant seeing the mother. La Martellita looked tired. Well, anybody bringing up a child by herself had a right to look tired. Chaim knew he looked tired, too. Soldiering was one of the few things on God's green (at the moment, hereabouts, God's brown) earth that could make a man as tired as a woman with a baby.

Tired or not, La Martellita also looked gorgeous. Chaim didn't, never had, and never would. He eyed Carlos Federico again, this time with a new perspective. "He's lucky," he remarked to La Martellita.

"How's that?" she asked.

"He looks like you," Chaim said. "When he grows up, the girls will all fall at his feet. He won't be a tough, homely scoundrel like his old man."

"If you think you can sweet-talk your way back into bed with me, forget it," La Martellita said. Chaim hadn't really thought so, even if he had had certain hopes along those lines. She went on, "By the time he grows up, we will enjoy full social equality in the Republic. Looks won't matter as much as they do in bourgeois society."

"*Puede ser*," Chaim replied. But why did he say *maybe* to La Martellita instead of *bullshit*, which is what he would have told anyone else? Why? Because she was beautiful, that was why.

People who looked good had things greased for them. Chaim guessed they always would, come the revolution or not. People like him always had to jump and scramble to get anywhere. A lot of the time, people like La Martellita and Mike Carroll (who would be getting back to the front soon—the docs had done a better job on his leg than Chaim had dreamt they could) didn't even need to reach out and grab. Things fell into their laps whether they reached or not.

La Martellita's black eyes sparked. She was about to demonstrate dialectically why looks wouldn't matter when true Communism arrived. Chaim didn't feel like getting into a screaming row with her, which was what would happen if he presumed to doubt. Sometimes forearmed was forestalled. Instead of doubting, he said, "How about I take you somewhere for something to eat?"

He still spoke Spanish with the syntax of a New York Jew. Well, he damn well *was* a New York Jew. The locals could follow him, which was all that mattered when you were a damn furriner. La Martellita decided not to give him an ideological flaying after all. With a nod, she said, "We can do that."

Soldiers didn't make much. Neither did Party functionaries. But, unlike her, he gambled with what he did make. What else was he supposed to do with it? Sometimes the dice and cards ran your way for a while. He carried a good-sized wad of banknotes in a front pocket. Only a fool asking to meet a pickpocket carried his cash on his hip.

He pushed the buggy that held his son. He was proud to push it. He beamed when people looked inside and cooed at Carlos Federico. They did that more often here than they would have back in New York City. Whatever prosperity this poor, miserable world had left was concentrated in the place where he'd been born. Maybe that was why, like misers, so many New Yorkers hoarded friendliness as if it were gold.

Some of the Madrileños gave him odd looks as they went by. He was used to that, and didn't resent it . . . too much. It rarely happened when he walked through the city by himself. But when he was a homely guy with a gorgeous woman pushing a baby buggy that proved he'd got the gorgeous woman's knickers down—oh, yes, he got the odd looks then.

And he would have bet dollars to dog-ends that he'd go right on getting them once true Communism came, assuming it ever did.

He sighed. He wished like anything he were still getting La Martellita's knickers down. *Wish for the moon, too*, he thought mournfully.

She wasn't married to him any more, which didn't mean she'd given up on trying to improve him. "Don't get into any brawls, all right?" she said as they walked into a café and wine shop not far from her block of flats.

"Who, me? *¿El narigón loco?*" He brought out the nickname with pride.

"Try," La Martellita urged. Chaim gave forth with a resigned nod. Spaniards were allowed, even expected, to have a fiery temper. In a foreigner, it seemed an exotic affectation. In a foreigner who also chanced to be a Jew . . . Well, that was how he'd got the nickname.

He'd been in this joint before. La Martellita had been here a lot more often than he had. The waiter who showed them to their table—a guy with a limp and a gray mustache, which explained why he wasn't at the front—bowed and scraped over her. You weren't supposed to do that in the Republic, which was about radical egalitarianism if it was about anything. Maybe it was force of habit, more likely a tribute to La Martellita's looks. She didn't ream him out about it, but accepted it as no less than her due. Gorgeous people took such attentions for granted. They might, but Chaim sure didn't.

He ordered paella for both of them. They drank white wine while they waited for the guy in the kitchen to work his magic. Carlos Federico started to fuss. La Martellita nursed him. Chaim gallantly looked away. He remembered those breasts too well. The little boy fell asleep. La Martellita gently set him back in the buggy.

"Pan is very hot," the waiter warned as he set it down. Several crayfish sat atop the yellow rice. They were *treyf* on the hoof, of course, as if he cared. He sucked the meat and the juices out of their shells with as much gusto as if he'd been born in Madrid.

La Martellita sighed when she tasted the rice. "Turmeric," she said, "not saffron."

"What do you expect? There's a war on, you know." Chaim wasn't inclined to fuss. Compared to the slop and the monkey meat he ate in the trenches, the paella was terrific, ersatz spices or not.

She gave him a severe look. "Things should be done properly. Rules are there for a reason."

"If you say so." He really was trying hard not to fight. He was a Marxist, even a Marxist-Leninist. She was a Marxist-Leninist-Stalinist. It made a difference, all right. She liked telling other people what to do more than he did. He told her what to do anyhow: "Here. Have some more *vino*."

She let him pour for her, but she said, "You won't get me drunk enough to go to bed with you, either."

"Who, me?" he replied, as if that were the farthest thing from his mind. He never would have got to sleep with her the first time if she hadn't been gassed to the gills.

They scraped off the rice that had stuck to the iron pan. A lot of Spaniards thought that was the best part of the paella. Chaim didn't, but it was miles from bad. He set money on the table. Bills over here were a lot fancier than boring American greenbacks. Greenbacks spent better than pesetas, though, even if they weren't so pretty.

Was that also true of homely people. He thought about it while they walked back to La Martellita's apartment. He'd had enough wine to make it seem important on the cosmic scale of things.

La Martellita had had enough to let him kiss her in the blackout darkness outside her building. But she slapped his hand away when he tried to slip it into her blouse and cup one of those perfect breasts. "No, I told you."

A no from her meant *no*, not *maybe* or *try again later*. Swearing in several languages, Chaim mooched dejectedly back to the café and got very drunk.

ADI STOSS POURED oil into the Panzer III. "This is better shit than they gave us when we first came to Russia," he allowed, praising the lubricant with a very faint damn. "I don't *think* it'll turn to mucilage when the weather gets really cold."

"The new and improved—again!—antifreeze won't freeze up, either . . . I hope," Hermann Witt more or less agreed.

"I hope so, too, Auntie Freeze," Adi said sweetly.

Theo Hossbach bent down and scooped up enough snow for a snowball in his mittened hands. He delivered the editorial to the back of Adi's neck, so that a lot of it slithered down inside the driver's coveralls. Adi did an excellent impression of a man with ants in his pants.

A snowball fight was more fun than servicing the engine any old day. The whole crew joined in. They pelted one another with snow till their black panzer outfits might have been winter camouflage smocks. Theo also got a snowball smack in the snoot. Fortunately, whoever threw it hadn't squeezed it down real tight. Otherwise, he might have needed to see the medics on account of some stupid horseplay. They wouldn't have liked that, and neither would he.

Of course, the work didn't go away just because you ignored it for a while. Theo greased the bow machine gun with lubricant that also promised not to turn to sludge when the mercury in thermometers froze solid (which, to any German's horror, was known to happen during Russian winters). What the manufacturers' promises were worth . . . Well, they'd all find out.

If Sergeant Witt was an optimist, he concealed it very well. "The bosses of the companies that make this junk, they're back in the *Reich*, drinking champagne and stuffing their faces with roast goose and pinching the chambermaid's ass."

"They can kiss *my* ass," Adi declared. "And the crap they sent us that first winter almost cooked our goose when it didn't do what they promised."

The panzer commander nodded. "They should come up to the front for a while. That would be an education for them, by Jesus!"

"Our field marshals should come up to the front for a while, too," Kurt Poske put in. "The orders they give, it's plain enough they don't know what the hell it's like up here."

Adi favored the loader with a crooked grin. "Look out, world! Another one's going Bolshevik on us!"

He pitched his voice so no one outside the tight-knit crew could possibly hear him. That word made Theo nervous all the same. Did joking Red Army men call their buddies Nazis and give forth with salutes Hitler would have loved? If they did, they had to be as careful as Adi was. Some ways of tweaking authority could prove more dangerous than they were worth.

Stolidly, Kurt answered, "I'm no fucking Bolshie. I just don't want some numbnuts with gold braid all over his collar tabs getting my dick blown off on account of he thinks we can work miracles."

"It's the season for miracles, all right." Adi launched into "Silent Night." His baritone came close to professional quality.

Hermann Witt looked up from the radiator. "Where the devil did *you* learn that song?" The same question had occurred to Theo, but he wouldn't have asked it.

But nothing seemed to faze Adi today. "Why, in the convent, Auntie Freeze. The nuns taught me all kinds of fascinating things." The drama critic in Theo said Adi's leer was overdone.

Sergeant Witt snorted. "Did they teach you how to bolt the carburetor back on?"

"*Aber natürlich,*" Adi replied. "Where'd the eight-millimeter wrench go?"

After they slammed down the armored engine cover, Adi climbed into the driver's seat and started the engine. It fired up right away, which said the new lubricants were indeed better than the old—and also said Russian winter hadn't yet clamped down with full authority. The rest of the crew came aboard. Before long, the heater made Theo as uncomfortably warm as he had been chilly. The happy medium was as extinct for him as it was in the world generally.

Witt's panzer and the other two runners from the platoon went out to patrol the German lines. Every white lump left Theo worried. Was

that a whitewashed T-34, sitting there in ambush waiting for some un-
wary German crew—this one, for instance—to trundle by?

Half an hour into the patrol, a signal came in from battalion HQ:
"Return to your base at once."

"Acknowledged," Theo said; his voice sounded rusty in his own
ears. He wanted to ask what was up, but figured the guy back there
somewhere safer wouldn't tell him. Instead, he relayed the order to Sergeant Witt. Doing that wasn't so bad. He was just a phonograph record,
passing on someone else's words. He wasn't doing anything dangerous,
like initiating speech on his own.

Witt swore. "Why are we supposed to do that? We've still got a pretty
fair stretch of ground to cover."

"Don't know." When Theo did have to speak for himself, he tried to
get the maximum from the minimum.

This time, Sergeant Witt swore some more. "Why didn't you ask
them, for Christ's sake?" He answered his own question before Theo
could: "Because you're you, that's why. . . . The other panzers are heading back. We'd better follow them—sure don't want to stay out here by
my lonesome. Go with 'em, Adi."

"I'm doing it, Sergeant." Adi Stoss turned the Panzer III toward the west.

When they got back to the battered village that housed their company, it was boiling like a pot forgotten over a big fire. "What the hell is
going on?" Sergeant Witt shouted from the panzer's cupola: or perhaps
something rather more pungent than that.

The engine was still growling. Buttoned up inside the iron shell,
with earphones on his head, Theo couldn't make out whatever answer
the sergeant got. He did hear Witt come out with some more fancy profanity. He looked a question across the radio set to Adi. Maybe the driver
knew what was going on.

Sure enough, Stoss said, "We're pulling back to make a shorter de-
fensive line."

"Oh, yeah?" Amazement jerked the words out of Theo. The *Wehrmacht* had gone toe-to-toe with the Red Army ever since the Germans
came to Poland's rescue. *Landsers* never gave back any territory unless
the Ivans drove them off it. Retreat without orders was a capital crime.
And orders like that didn't come.

Only now they did. What was different? Theo realized he didn't have to wear the crimson stripes of a General Staff colonel on his trousers to figure it out. When the *Reich* started its Russian adventure, Hitler had managed to arrange a cease-fire in the West. For a while, English and French contingents even fought side by side with the *Wehrmacht*.

Now the West was waking up again. Quite a few German units had already left the Soviet Union to make sure the *poilus* and Tommies didn't swarm into the Rhineland and the Ruhr. And the Ivans had turned out to be tougher than the *Führer* ever dreamt they would be. The Nazis like to say the *Führer* was always right. Well, so he was . . . except when he wasn't.

One thing you had to give him: he didn't make small mistakes. Nobody could say that about Russia. Other things, yes—plenty of them. But not that. And if the *Reich* didn't have enough soldiers and panzers and planes hereabouts to hold the line, pulling back to a shorter one did make a certain amount of sense—provided there were enough to hold that shorter one.

*We'll find out, won't we?* Theo thought. Hitler might have done better to patch up some kind of peace with Stalin till he'd whipped France and England for good. Then he could have turned east without worrying about his other flank. But what were the odds of Nazis and Communists ever making any kind of pact? Theo shook his head. No, that just couldn't happen. Not a chance.

JULIUS LEMP ALWAYS went up before boards of his superiors as if he were going to the dentist. He hoped things wouldn't hurt too much, and that the senior officers would numb him up a little before starting in on the really painful stuff.

So here he was in Wilhelmshaven. His uniform jacket reeked of mothballs, but he couldn't do anything about that. He hardly ever wore the goddamn thing. Except for that chemical smell, he was as spruced-up as he could get. Well, almost. Not even for a board of his superiors would he put the stiffening wire back into his white-crowned cap. A floppy hat was part of a U-boat skipper's idea of himself.

He came to stiff attention before all those gold-ringed sleeves and regulation uniform caps. Saluting, he said, "Reporting as ordered!" His voice might have come from the throat of a machine.

But then the highest-ranking big cheese on the board—a rear admiral, no less—replied, "At ease, Lieutenant Commander Lemp."

At ease? All the starch oozed out of Lemp's backbone when he heard and understood that. "Lieutenant . . . Commander?" he whispered. He hadn't been promoted since the war started. He'd long since assumed he would never see any rank higher than lieutenant, save perhaps posthumously. Discovering he'd been wrong took the wind from his sails, even in a navy of diesels and batteries and steam.

"Yes, yes," the rear admiral said with a gruff nod. "You've lived down your sordid past, shall we say?" He nodded again, more gruffly yet. "Christ on His cross, Lemp, you've *lived*, and too many others haven't. Might as well let your experience—and the *Ark Royal*—count for something, hey?"

Even the aircraft carrier had been no lock to win the next higher grade. "*Heil* Hitler!" Lemp—Lieutenant Commander Lemp—managed, and shot out his right arm. With politics as touchy as they were, showing your loyalty to the regime could never be wrong.

Unless, of course, it could. The *Kriegsmarine* had never warmed to the *Führer* and to the Nazis the way the Army had (to say nothing of the parvenu *Luftwaffe*, run as it was by one of Hitler's old henchmen). A couple of the men on the board gave Lemp unblinking stares, as if they were old tortoises watching a fox slink by.

No matter what your view of things political was, though, you couldn't afford to seem lukewarm about the powers that be, not in the Third *Reich* you couldn't. Five arms shot out in unison across the table from him, each with more gold at the cuff than he'd ever wear. Five throats chorused, "*Heil* Hitler!" No one was perceptibly behind anyone else.

The rear admiral produced two small, hinged imitation-leather boxes from his briefcase and shoved them across the table at Lemp. "Here are your new shoulder boards, with the appropriate pips, and here are the new stripes for your sleeves. Congratulations. Belated congratulations, maybe, but congratulations even so—Lieutenant Commander Lemp."

"*Danke schön, mein Herr.*" Dazedly, Lemp took the boxes. Each was stamped in gold leaf with the *Kriegsmarine*'s eagle—which, like the Army's and the *Luftwaffe*'s, clutched a swastika in its claws. He stowed them in the jacket's pockets: pockets he hardly ever used. When he put it on, he'd found a ticket stub in an inside pocket from a film he'd seen before the war started.

"Have we got anything we really need to know about U-30's latest patrol right this minute, gentlemen?" the rear admiral asked his colleagues. His tone warned that they'd damned well better not. And they didn't. He nodded once more, with an older man's dour satisfaction, and gave his attention back to Lemp. "*Sehr gut.* You are dismissed. I hope you enjoy your liberty while the repair and replenishment crews go over your boat."

"*Danke schön,*" Lemp repeated. Liberty! He hadn't even thought about that. He'd have to go out and get drunk. Not only that, he'd have to get the whole crew drunk, from his exec and the engineering officers down to the lowliest "lords": the junior seamen who bunked in the forward torpedo room.

How much would the carouse cost? More than the jump in pay from lieutenant to lieutenant commander brought in for a couple of months—Lemp was only too sure of that. Well, you couldn't make an omelette without chocolate and powdered sugar and whipped cream. And it wasn't as if a U-boat skipper who spent most of his time at sea got a lot of chances to throw his cash around. He could afford it. Whether he could afford it or not, he knew he had to do it.

He saluted the board again, this time with a proper military gesture rather than the one from the Party. Did the senior officers show a touch of relief when they gave back the same salute? If they did, Lemp didn't have to notice, not today he didn't.

His feet scarcely seemed to touch the ground as he walked back to his U-boat. Ratings and junior officers saluted him. He returned their gestures of respect and gave back his own to the handful of men he passed who outranked him. The journey from the board room to the boat was more than half a kilometer, but seemed to take no time at all.

That tall figure on the conning tower could only be Gerhart Beilharz. The *Schnorkel* expert greeted Lemp with an enormous grin, a salute—most unusual on a U-boat, where such surface-navy formalities went down the scupper—and the words, "Congratulations, Lieutenant Commander!"

Lemp gaped. "How the devil did you know, when I just now found out myself?"

Beilharz's grin got wider. Lemp hadn't thought it could. "Jungle telegraph, how else?" the younger man said.

And that was about the size of it. Lemp knew he'd never get anything that came closer to a straight answer. Nothing went faster than the speed of light . . . except gossip at a naval base. Maybe somebody from the repair crew had heard something and brought word to the boat. Or . . . Oh, who the hell cared?

The sailors who hadn't yet headed out for the taverns and brothels of Wilhelmshaven made a point of shaking their skipper's hand and thumping him on the back. "About time!" they said; several of them profanely embroidered on the theme.

*They like me. They really like me,* Lemp realized, more than a little surprised that they should. He knew himself well enough to know that he wasn't an enormously likable man. His focus was too inward; he had next to nothing of the hail-fellow-well-met in him. And he was the skipper, the great god of his small, stinking world. You could respect a god. You could admire one or fear one. Loving one, despite what the preachers claimed and proclaimed, was a lot harder. Gods and mortals didn't travel in the same social circles.

Except sometimes they did. Lemp gathered up the officers and ratings still aboard the U-30. "Come along with me, boys," he said. "We'll see how many crewmates we can gather up, too. I'm buying—till you head for the whorehouses, anyway."

"Three cheers for Lieutenant Commander Lemp!" Peter shouted, and the sailors lustily followed the helmsman's lead. Turning back to Lemp, Peter added, "You should get promoted more often, Skipper."

"Damn right I should," Lemp replied, which made his men laugh raucously. They hadn't started drinking yet, so it must have been a good line for real.

Despite flak guns on rooftops and in parks and little squares, Wilhelmshaven had taken bomb damage. Of course a German naval base near the Dutch border would make a juicy target for the RAF. But the air pirates wouldn't come over while brief winter day lit the landscape (not so brief here as it was up in the Baltic or, worse, the Barents Sea, where the sun stayed below the horizon for a long stretch around the solstice).

The men poured down beer and schnapps. Lemp bled banknotes. Well, he'd known he would. If he got plastered himself, he wouldn't care . . . so much. He drank till his head started spinning. When the men sought pleasures even more basic than beer, Beilharz guided him to an officers' *maison de tolérance*. Hearing that he was celebrating a promotion, the madam let him go upstairs with a pretty, round-faced young redhead for free.

"I'm a patriot, I am," the madam declared. "*Heil* Hitler!"

"*Heil!*" Lemp echoed. He patted his girl on the backside. Before long, he'd salute her in a way older and more enjoyable than any Party rituals.

THESE DAYS, LEATHERNECKS and swabbies aboard the *Ranger* walked soft around Pete McGill. It was a compliment of sorts, but one he could have done without. When you showed you could damn near kill a guy with your bare hands, naturally people on the carrier would notice. Just as naturally, they'd go out of their way to make sure you didn't want to do unto them as you'd done unto Barney Klinsmann.

Barney was out of sick bay at last, and back on light duty. He still insisted he'd fallen down stairs. Nobody believed him, but the polite fiction kept Pete out of the brig.

Two new carriers had steamed to Pearl from the West Coast. They were both makeshifts. Their official title was escort carrier. Everybody called them baby flattops or sometimes jeep carriers, though. They were freighters with flight decks, was what they were. They could hold only half as many planes as a fleet carrier like *Ranger*, and they couldn't make better than eighteen knots unless you dropped 'em off a cliff.

That was the bad news. The good news was, they were here now. New fleet carriers were supposed to be in the pipeline, but it hadn't spit them out yet. They were expensive and complicated and slow to build. You could make baby flattops in a hurry. Okay, they had their drawbacks. Drawbacks or not, they let Uncle Sam fly more planes in the Pacific. Pete was all for anything that did that.

Bob Cullum pointed out another flaw the escort carriers had: "Goddamn things are ugly as sin."

"Well, so are you, but the government still thinks you're good for something." Pete smiled when he said it—the other sergeant was senior to him. And he was just needling Cullum. He didn't want to get into another fight. No one would have accused him of being a peaceable man, but he aimed as much of his rage as he could at the Japs.

"Ah, your mama." Cullum also made a point of smiling. He might not be eager to tangle with Pete—after what happened to Klinsmann, nobody was—but he didn't want to back down to him, either. More to the point, he didn't want to be seen as backing down.

Pete understood that. He didn't have a lot of empathy. But he'd served long enough in Peking and Shanghai to understand the idea of face. He could see that making Bob Cullum lose face wouldn't be good for him. A senior noncom could always come up with ways to make a junior noncom's life miserable. So he didn't push things, and neither did Cullum, and they both stayed tolerably content.

Then the *Ranger* and the two baby flattops—they were the *Suwannee* and the *Chenango*—steamed out on patrol, and Pete was more than tolerably content. Hitting back at the Japs still roused a fierce, primal pleasure in him, better than anything this side of sex (and more closely related to it than he understood—he was anything but an introspective man).

Because the escort carriers couldn't get out of their own way—they cruised at fifteen knots—it also struck him as a patrol in slow motion. The *Ranger* and all the escorting cruisers and destroyers had to amble along at the same paltry pace. But Wildcats from the converted freighters joined the combat air patrol above the flotilla. If they ran into a

Japanese force, two more squadrons of dive-bombers and torpedo planes would tear into the enemy.

That did matter. It might end up mattering one hell of a lot. On the other hand . . . "We better not let the Japs catch us unawares, like," Peter remarked to Sergeant Cullum at gun drill one morning. "It ain't like the baby flattops can get away from 'em. They can't run, and they can't hide, neither." He beamed, pleased at his own wit.

If Cullum even noticed it, he didn't let on. He broke into an off-key rendition of "Way Down Upon the Suwannee River" and an equally atrocious soft-shoe routine by the dual-purpose five-incher.

Pete was not inclined to strafe him the way Brooks Atkinson or any other critic in his right mind would have. He was too busy being amazed for that even to occur to him. "Fuck me up the asshole!" he exclaimed, and pointed across the blue, blue Pacific at the slowpoke escort carrier. "She *is* named for that dumb river, isn't she?"

"Speaking of dumb . . ." Cullum said pointedly. "You just now noticed, Hercule Poirot?" He pronounced it *poi-rot*, as if the native Hawaiians' staple had gone bad.

"Who?" Pete wouldn't have known who Hercule Poirot was even with his name said the right way. Sherlock Holmes he could have handled. Anyone more obscure? He would have dropped the ball. Hell, he *had* dropped it. He went on, "I knew the fucking song. Jeez, who doesn't? But I never figured it was about a real place."

"Well, it is." Now Bob Cullum spoke with exaggerated patience.

"Well, ain't that nice?" Unconsciously, Pete used the line and the intonation of a performer in a Vitaphone Variety—an early stab at a talkie, well before *The Jazz Singer*—he'd watched when he was a kid. Japanese interrogators could have shoved burning bamboo slivers under his fingernails without getting him to remember the skit with the top part of his mind.

Floatplanes launched from the cruisers' catapults were the flotilla's long-range scouts. You had to hope they would spot Japanese ships before the Japs spotted them. And you had to hope that, if they did, they'd be able to relay a warning before some slanty-eyed son of a bitch in the cockpit of a Zero hacked them out of the sky.

Neither of those hopes struck Pete as especially good. American scouts had already missed Japanese naval units more than once in the Pacific. And one of those sedate floatplanes wouldn't last long against a Zero, much less against a swarm of Zeros. It'd last . . . about as long as the *Suwannee* would, say, in a gun duel with a Jap battlewagon.

Not that the *Ranger* would last one whole hell of a lot longer. But the *Ranger* could make twenty-nine knots. She might manage to flee from such an unfortunate encounter. The *Suwannee* and the *Chenango* couldn't even do that. A battleship would devour them at its leisure.

Something overhead that wasn't a Wildcat or a floatplane drew Pete's nervous glance. Then he relaxed . . . fractionally. "Gooney bird," he explained to Bob Cullum, who'd sent him a quizzical stare.

"Ah." The other leatherneck nodded. "Yeah, they're all over this stretch of the Pacific, aren't they?"

"Damn right they are," Pete said. "They're just about big enough to shoot down, too."

"Bad luck!" Cullum said. "No luck's worse'n that! Fuck, I'd sooner bust ten mirrors than shoot an albatross."

"Okay, okay. All right, already. Keep your hair on, man. I was just kidding around." Pete knew about how hurting an albatross was worse than breaking a mirror while walking under a ladder as a black cat sauntered across your path. Anybody who'd ever put to sea in the tropical Pacific did, even if—like Pete—he'd never heard of *The Rime of the Ancient Mariner*.

But Bob Cullum took the superstition to extremes. No matter how much Pete apologized, the other Marine muttered about curses and misfortunes for days. By the time he finally shut up, Pete was tempted to head for Midway with a machine gun and a flamethrower, to wipe the breeding colony of gooney birds off the face of the earth.

Only one thing stopped him: the Japs held the island. He wondered if they felt the same way about albatrosses as white men did. If not, they might be settling the great big birds' hash for him. He could hope, anyhow.

# Chapter 18

"**S**ir!" Sergeant Hideki Fujita stood at rigid—to say nothing of corpselike—attention. His salute was so perfect, even so extravagant, that the pickiest, the most worst-tempered, drillmaster could have found nothing wrong with it. "Reporting as ordered, sir!"

"At ease, Sergeant," Captain Ikejiri said. Fujita eased his stiff brace a little, but still felt anything but easy. What noncom would, when summoned out of the blue by an officer? The first thing that went through Fujita's mind was *What have I done now?* Sensing as much, Ikejiri went on, "You're not in trouble."

"Sir!" Fujita repeated, and went back to attention. When they were really after you, didn't they try to lull you into a false sense of security?

"At *ease*, Sergeant," the captain said again, more sharply this time. "How would you like to get away from Burma—about as far away from Burma as you can go and stay in the Japanese Empire?"

"Sir?" It was the same word for the third time in a row, but now Fujita meant it as a question.

"I'm asking you. I'm not telling you. You can say no. You won't get in trouble if you do say no, and no one will think less of you if you do,"

Captain Ikejiri said. "But you've been eager to see action, and here—or rather, there—is a chance for you to see more than you would if you stayed in Myitkyina."

"I don't understand, sir," Fujita said cautiously.

"I know you don't. That's why I called you in: to explain what your choices are." Ikejiri let his patience show. "You will know there was some talk of using our special techniques against the Englishmen in India."

He was a good officer, a conscientious officer. Even here, with nobody listening but Fujita, who was already in the know, he didn't talk openly about bacteriological warfare. He took security seriously, so seriously that he censored himself, perhaps without even noticing he was doing it.

"Oh, yes, sir!" Fujita nodded. He would have loved to give England a taste of Japan's medicine.

"Good. Then you will also know that it was decided not to proceed with this. The concern was that we were too likely to be found out, and that that would not be advantageous for the Empire," Ikejiri said.

"I had heard that, *hai*." Fujita nodded once more. Like most ordinary soldiers, he was all for giving the white men the plague or smallpox or cholera or whatever else Japan had in its bag of tricks now, and for worrying about consequences later. Eagerly, he asked, "Do we have permission to operate against England now, sir?"

"Against England? No," Captain Ikejiri said, and Fujita's chin went down onto his chest in disappointment. But the officer went on, "We do have permission to begin special warfare against the Americans in Hawaii. If they can't use those islands, they will have to try to fight the war from the coast of their continent. Obviously, that would be difficult and expensive for them, and most desirable for us."

"Yes, sir. I can see how it would be," Fujita replied, picturing a map. An extra three or four thousand kilometers of sea voyage each way? Oh, the Americans would love that!

"The special unit will be set up on the island called Midway," Captain Ikejiri said. "The Navy has long-range bombers that can reach the Hawaiian islands from Midway. I am being transferred to the new facility. I would like to have some men along I know I can rely on. So, Sergeant—will you come to this Midway place with me?"

"Yes, sir!" Hideki Fujita didn't hesitate. He knew nothing about Midway Island except that it wasn't Burma. What else did he need to know?

Nothing in Burma, nothing that had anything to do with Burma, happened right away. That would have annoyed Fujita more had it also surprised him more. He'd spent a long time in the Army now. He'd come to see how very little that had to do with soldiering happened right away—the main exception being the arrival of an unwelcome bullet or shell.

No, transfer requests had to snake up the chain of command. Approvals—assuming there were approvals—had to wind their way back down. Transportation orders needed to be cut. Planes had to get off the ground.

In due course, the unit threw a farewell party for Captain Ikejiri and the noncoms and private soldiers who would accompany him to Midway. It got kind of drunk out. In one skit, the men who were staying behind mimed his party falling off the edge of the world. They howled laughter. Fujita found himself less amused. Captain Ikejiri clutched the hilt of his officer's sword hard enough to whiten his knuckles.

"Take it easy, sir," Fujita whispered to him. "If you start taking heads, people will talk about you."

Ikejiri smiled thinly. "I know that, Sergeant. I really do. But I thank you for reminding me just the same. The temptation is there, believe me." With what looked like a deliberate effort of will, he moved his right hand away from the curved sword.

He and the men who accompanied him and their caged animals and infected fleas and bacteriological cultures crowded an Army transport plane that looked a lot like an American DC-3 (the resemblance was not a coincidence; Japan had been building the design under license since before the war). From Myitkyina, they flew to Bangkok—Siam was a Japanese ally.

They got stuck there for a couple of days. No one seemed to have heard they were coming, which meant no one wanted to allocate the transport fuel so it could go on. If Captain Ikejiri had been annoyed at the going-away party, he was furious now. When he stormed off the plane, Fujita wondered if Siamese—or Japanese—heads would roll.

But the telegram proved mightier than the sword. Once Ikejiri used his connections, what must have been a peremptory wire came back to Bangkok. Local officials fell all over themselves refueling the transport and getting it out of there. They might have feared that some of the unit's diseased fleas would get loose and touch off epidemics in their town. Watching Captain Ikejiri's smile of grim satisfaction as gasoline gurgled into the plane's tanks, Fujita suspected they might have had excellent reason for such fears.

The airstrip at Hanoi was heavily guarded. Japan had taken over French Indochina. The French had had troubles of their own with the Annamese and other native peoples. The locals didn't want to be occupied by Japan, either, even if the Japanese were Asians rather than white men. Whether they wanted that or not, they didn't have enough guns to stop it. But they did have enough to make nuisances of themselves: thus the barbed wire and machine-gun nests around the airstrip.

At least the Japanese in Hanoi didn't seem astonished that the transport had come down out of the sky. They gassed it up, did a little work on one engine, and sent it on its way. The natives didn't shoot at it as it gained altitude. If they knew what it carried, they wouldn't want that cargo raining down on their countryside. They weren't supposed to have any way of knowing, but how much did that prove?

From Hanoi, the transport droned across the South China Sea to Manila. Manila, seen from the air, was a surprisingly big city. It had taken a lot of damage when the Rising Sun replaced the Stars and Stripes, not much of which had been repaired. The jungle-covered islands of the Philippines gave way to more ocean as the transport flew on to Guam. By the time the wheels hit the landing strip, Fujita hoped he would never set foot in another airplane as long as he lived.

But he couldn't even escape the one he was on. And he still had a long way to go before he finally made it to Midway. He'd had no idea the Pacific was so vast. He'd also had no idea Midway was so small, so flat, and, except for its position, so utterly insignificant.

The really scary thing was that it was another two thousand kilometers from Midway to the Hawaiian islands, and four thousand from those islands to the U.S. mainland. Whatever else you said about this war, it had scale. He'd just come a quarter of the way around the world to position himself to strike a blow against the Americans. He'd have to do plenty more traveling before he could actually attack them.

**HERB DRUCE POURED** himself a bourbon on the rocks. He handed Peggy another one. They clinked glasses. "'Here's to Three Men well out of a Boat!'" Herb quoted.

Peggy drank. The bourbon flamed down her throat. "That old thing," she said with a chuckle. She didn't know how many times she'd read *Three Men in a Boat*. Whatever the number was, it was large. Victorian foolishness on the Thames made a perfect antidote to the harried modern world.

When she said so, her husband nodded. But then he said, "Jerome K. Jerome lasted long enough to watch that foolishness die—literally. He drove an ambulance in France during the last war."

"Did he?" Peggy exclaimed. "I didn't know that."

"It's the truth," Herb said. "You could look it up, if you felt like looking it up. Or you could just believe me if you wanted to live dangerously."

"I'll try that," Peggy said. "If I need more exercise later, I'll take a shot at jumping to conclusions."

"There you go." Herb nodded. "Plenty of people get plenty of practice at that one, though, so the competition's pretty stiff." Ice cubes clattered as he knocked back his drink. He stared down into the glass; he might have been wondering how it had emptied so fast. When he continued, it was on a slightly different note: "If I'd been in the right place at the right time, I could've met him when I was Over There."

"That would've been something," Peggy said.

"Sure would. Would've mattered more to me than anything I did do, even if I didn't see it that way twenty-five years ago." Herb started fixing himself a fresh drink. "Want another one, too?"

"You bet." Peggy drained her own glass, then handed it to him for the refill. After they clinked again, she asked, "So which Boat are you well out of?"

Her husband coughed in faint embarrassment. "Remember that business in Tennessee?"

"The one you couldn't talk about 'cause J. Edgar Hoover would shoot you through the window with a Tommy gun if you even started to open your mouth?"

Herb coughed again. This time, his embarrassment wasn't nearly so faint. "Yeah, that," he admitted.

"Well, what about it?" Peggy asked.

"I don't have to go back there any more, on account of they've closed down the project. Turned out to be a bust, a boondoggle. No, let's call a spade a stinking shovel. It was a rathole, was what it was. And God only knows how many millions of dollars they poured down it, too. If I were a Republican, I'd take it to the *Chicago Tribune.*"

"Oh, puh-leeze!" Peggy sounded as disgusted as she felt. "Westbrook Pegler and company? All they want to do is hold FDR's feet to the fire."

"Eleanor's, too," Herb corrected with lawyerly precision. "I'll tell you, though, Roosevelt deserves a hotfoot for this one, swear he does." He stopped—reluctantly, but he did.

"This isn't the serial before the feature," Peggy snapped. "You can't leave me with a cliffhanger like that. C'mon—give. You know I don't go yakking all over the place."

"I'm not supposed to," Herb said, more to himself than to her. She kept quiet, hoping he would talk himself into it. Which he did: "Well, nuts to that. The project's dead as King Tut. And you're right. You don't blab. So . . . These scientists had some kind of scheme—I think it was based on something that leaked out of Germany in some kind of way, but don't hold me to that—anyway, a scheme for making a super-duper bomb, one that could blow up a whole city."

"You mean like in the pulps with the green men with the eyestalks and the built blondes in the brass bathing suits on the cover?" Peggy said. You saw them on the newsstands all the time. She'd bought a few—who didn't? The stories were usually better than those wretched covers, even if that wasn't saying much. You didn't want to be seen reading them: they were almost as bad as Tijuana Bibles.

"Uh-huh, just like those." Herb nodded once more. "But there were some people who you'd think had their heads on straight pushing this thing. Einstein, for instance."

If you knew about one nuclear physicist, it had to be Einstein, with his mustache and his flyaway hair. He was a Jew. He'd got out of Germany not too long before the Nazis would have made escape impossible. "Even with him, it was no go?" Peggy asked.

"You got it," Herb said. "Oh, maybe the thing would've worked in the end. Maybe. But it would've taken years and years to figure out how, and it would've cost billions in the end."

"Billions?" Peggy wasn't sure she'd heard right. "With a B?"

"With a B," her husband agreed solemnly.

"Wow." She had trouble even imagining that much money. She remembered that, when the astronomers discovered Pluto (and when Walt Disney named Mickey's mutt after the new planet), they said it was so-and-so many billion miles from the sun. How many *so-and-so many* was, she couldn't recall. Any many billion miles was still a hell of a lot. "They didn't really blow that much, did they?"

"Nah." Now Herb shook his head. "Just millions. I don't even think they blew tens of millions. The accountants'll have a field day working it out to the last dime—you bet they will. But the government threw up the stop sign before the guys with the glasses and the slide rules and the funny foreign accents could get rolling in style."

"Thanks to you." Peggy was proud of him, and wanted him to know it.

"Well, not just thanks to me." Herb was too modest to claim the entire success for himself. But he was also proud that part of it belonged to him. He went on, "One of these years, we may need something like that, if it turns out to be possible after all. We sure don't need it right away, though. We've got more important things to worry about now."

"Like licking the Japs?" Peggy suggested.

"Yeah, like that. Like making sure they don't land in San Francisco is more like it." Herb rolled his eyes at the way the war in the Pacific was going for the United States.

Peggy asked, "How come Einstein and the other scientists were pushing this super-duper, super-expensive bomb so hard?"

"Well, I don't know all the details. I'm no slide-rule twiddler myself." Herb sounded glad that he wasn't, and who could blame him? "But like I said, there was some kind of experiment in Germany right after the war started. It didn't get published—the Nazis quashed that.

But the physicists gossip amongst themselves, war or no war, just like lawyers or doctors or ladies playing bridge or anybody else. Einstein got wind of it some kind of way, and he sweet-talked FDR into throwing money at it. For a while, anyhow." He grinned, glad he'd helped put the kibosh on such foolishness.

If it was foolishness . . . Unease trickled through Peggy. "Did the Nazis try to keep quiet about this experiment or whatever it was because their big brains are working on the super-duper bomb, too?" It wouldn't be so good if they got one, which was putting things mildly.

"If they are, they'd do better to set their Reichsmarks on fire and throw them away," Herb declared. "They'd get rid of 'em quicker if they did, but that's the only way they would. Believe me, babe—nobody's gonna figure out how to pull off this stunt any time soon, if it's possible at all."

"Okay." Peggy sure wanted to believe him. She made herself one more bourbon on the rocks. That helped.


EVERY SO OFTEN, Mitsubishi G4Ms on Midway took off for night raids on the Hawaiian islands. Hideki Fujita admired the Navy bombers. They were fast and sleek and had enormous range.

After a while, though, he got to talking—and he got to drinking—with the ratings who dropped bombs on the Americans and who manned the 20mm cannon the G4Ms carried as a sting in the tail. Their opinion of the plane they flew was much lower than his.

To begin with, they called the G4M the Flying Cigarette Lighter. "You know why it's got such range?" one of the rear gunners demanded in the tent that served as a noncoms' club. He was pouring down sake as if he feared they'd outlaw it tomorrow; his face had gone red as the rising sun.

"So it can do things like fly from Midway to Hawaii and back?" Fujita suggested—reasonably, he thought. He didn't like to hear the plane maligned, not when he'd be heading from Midway to Oahu or one of the other islands in a G4M himself before too long.

"*Iye!*" The rear gunner vigorously shook his head. "No!" he repeated, even louder than before. "It's got that range on account of it's a lightweight. And it's a lightweight 'cause the engineers who designed it were full of shit." He gulped more sake.

"Huh?" Fujita wasn't sure he'd heard right.

"Full of shit," the Navy man said again, so he had. "No self-sealing gas tanks. No armor for the crew. No wonder it starts to burn if an American shoots a dirty look at it. The dumbass engineers wanted it to be fast. *Zakennayo!* No bomber's gonna be fast enough to outrun fighters. You go up in that damn thing, it's almost like you're cutting your belly open." He mimed commiting *seppuku*. Then he upended his cup again and poured more from the pottery pitcher.

"Thanks a lot," Fujita mumbled. His own first flight was only a few days away.

"Huh?" the rear gunner said. Then he nodded, more to himself than to Fujita. "That's right. You're going up in one of those sorry bastards yourself, aren't you? Almost forgot about that. Gonna give the Yankees a little present, right?"

"That's the idea, anyhow," Fujita agreed.

"Something better than ordinary bombs, they say," the Navy guy persisted.

"That's the idea," Fujita said once more.

"So what is it?" the rear gunner asked. "Poison gas? Something like that? Everybody on Midway's going bugshit trying to figure out what's up with you people. You all keep your mouths shut as tight as a whore's legs before you pay her."

"We aren't supposed to talk about it," Fujita answered primly.

"Yeah, yeah. Who am I gonna tell? What am I gonna do? Hop into a G4M, fly it down to Honolulu, land there and start singing to the Americans? Give me a break, pal!"

Fujita saw he'd have to make himself clearer: "We have orders not to talk about it."

"No kidding, you do! I still think that's a bunch of crap." The Navy man downed another cup of sake. "And you know what else? Just before you clowns got out here, the docs lined up the whole garrison and gave us shots like you wouldn't believe. My arm swelled up like a dead cow. I couldn't hardly do anything with it for the next three days."

"I didn't have anything to do with that. Like you say, I wasn't even on

Midway yet." No matter what the rear gunner thought, no matter how sore his arm had been, the doctors here had known exactly what they were doing. The germs Captain Ikejiri had brought along weren't fussy about whether they infected Americans or Japanese.

The Navy man wasn't done complaining, either. "And how come they're delousing us all the time now? You'd think we were filthy or something. They didn't do that before you guys came. It's fucking weird, you ask me."

"I haven't got anything to do with that, either." Fujita told the technical truth there, but no more than the technical truth. Delousing treatments also killed fleas, or had a better chance of killing them than anything else on Midway was likely to do. And, when fleas were liable to carry the plague, killing them looked like an even better idea than usual.

"Weird," the rear gunner repeated. He could say what he wanted. Fujita couldn't say anything at all, not about what the rear gunner wanted to know. Even drunk, he knew he couldn't. If that left the other fellow unhappy, it was his hard luck.

Fujita's own hard luck came when he climbed up into a G4M's bomb bay. The groundcrew men loaded the bay with the pottery-bomb casings that held rats loaded with fleas and other disease-dispersal agents. Night was falling. They were in subtropical latitudes—not so far south as Burma, but subtropical even so. There wasn't a lot of difference between summer and winter nights. But there was some, and they would take advantage of the extra darkness at this season of the year.

The G4M rolled down the rough runway and climbed into the air. The engines' drone seemed to come from somewhere inside Fujita. He put on his oxygen gear and also ran oxygen lines into the casings. That wasn't guaranteed to keep the rats alive—but then, keeping them alive wasn't completely necessary. The fleas were tougher. *They'd* make it to Hawaii, all right. Having the rats able to run around might spread sickness faster, though.

Even if night soon fell, navigating was easy. Midway lay at the northwest end of a chain of little islands that ended with the bigger ones of Hawaii. Peering out through a machine-gun blister, Fujita watched one low islet after another pass beneath the bomber. It was as if whichever fire *kami* spat out the main Hawaiian islands got more and more tired as it also spat out the ones that lay north and west of them. Or maybe those northwestern islands were the old ones, and the bigger islands, the ones where people actually lived, just hadn't worn down yet.

It was interesting to think about. Fujita doubted whether anyone would ever actually know. When Kauai came into sight, the G4M took a long loop around it. The Americans had airstrips there. Night fighters found targets more by luck than any other way, but why find out whether this was some round-eyed pilot's lucky night?

On to Oahu. This was only one plane. With any luck at all, the Americans wouldn't pay any attention to it. If they did notice it, wouldn't they just think it was one of theirs, doing whatever a plane flying over Oahu in the middle of the night did?

Right up until they started shooting at him, Fujita hoped they would. After that, he just hoped he would live. He watched tracer rounds climb up toward the G4M. They were beautiful. He hadn't had such a good view in China. He felt as if he were on top of a fireworks display, looking down at it from above. Then the shells started bursting. The bomber bounced in the air. Fujita wished that Navy guy had never told him what a flimsy piece of construction a G4M was.

"Open the bomb bay! Drop the bombs!" The pilot flying the plane sounded scared enough to wet his flight suit. That did nothing for Fujita's own confidence.

He yanked at the levers that opened the bomb-bay doors. They weren't in the same place as they were in a Ki-21, but he knew where to grab and how to pull. Opening them, though, gave him a much better view of the antiaircraft fire that was trying to knock him down. More levers—again, positioned differently from those in the Army bomber he'd flown before—let the casings full of germs and diseased animals fall free. Along with them went a few incendiaries and ordinary high-explosive bombs, to give the enemy something else to think about and to distract him from the ones that were the main point of the mission.

"Bombs away!" he reported, as if the pilot hadn't already put the G4M into a tight turn and headed back toward Midway at full throttle. He closed the bomb-bay doors again to improve streamlining. They gave Kauai an even wider berth on the way home: the Americans there would be alerted now. But they never saw a single enemy fighter. And, better yet, not a single enemy fighter saw them.

SHIRTLESS LIKE THE rest of the Marines and sailors in line with him, Pete McGill stood under the warm Hawaiian sun. Back on the mainland, there were plenty of places where the snow was still as high as an elephant's eye. If you didn't already have a good tan here, even the winter sun stood plenty high enough in the sky to fry your hide.

"This is a pain in the ass, you know?" Bob Cullum groused.

"Is that where they're gonna shoot us?" Pete said. "I thought they were gonna get us in the arm. That's why we're like this, right?" He thumped his bare chest. Thanks to the shoulder that had got smashed up in the Shanghai movie-house bombing, he wore some impressive scars. Men from other ships, who weren't used to seeing him with his shirt off, eyed his torso with respect.

"I dunno," Cullum answered. "It ain't like they tell anybody what's going on, for Chrissake."

"And this surprises you because . . . ?" Pete said. Cullum threw a slow-motion punch at him. Just as slowly, Pete blocked it. They both grinned.

A balding guy with a big, hairy beer belly that yelled *Petty officer!* growled, "Knock off the horseplay, you two!"

"That's 'Knock off the horseplay, you two sergeants,'" Pete said. Cullum nodded. The petty-officer type looked disgusted. He couldn't beat them over the head with his rank, because they had about as much as he did.

The line snaked forward. It looked to Pete as if every enlisted man at Pearl Harbor was in it. Officers had their own queue, which would be a lot shorter. Civilian employees at the base would get their turn tomorrow. Pete wouldn't have minded letting them go first.

A pretty blond secretary in a thin cotton blouse and a silk skirt that showed off shapely legs walked by. She carried half a dozen manila folders. Eyeballs clicked as leathernecks and swabbies gave her the once-over. A few wolf whistles rang out. She ignored them with the air of someone who had a lot of practice ignoring such things.

"I'd like to stick her," Cullum said, "and not in the arm, neither."

"Amen," Pete agreed reverently. "That's table-quality pussy, all right."

In due course, he and Cullum advanced into the mess hall. Instead of cooks slinging powdered eggs and vulcanized bacon, doctors stood there with needles gleaming in the electric light. The single line divided into several. Each doc stood by a little cloth-draped privacy area. "Ahh, shit," Cullum said. "We are gonna get it in the ass."

"Looks that way." Pete agreed again, this time with a mournful nod.

As a matter of fact, he got a shot in each arm and one in his left lower cheek. "You may be kinda sore the next few days," said the doc who injected him. "Don't worry about that, or about some swelling. It's all normal."

"Happy day . . . sir," Pete said. Doctors were officers; some of them got pissy if you didn't give them formal respect. "What the devil's going on, anyway, if you're stabbing everybody like this?"

"I'm afraid I'm not authorized to release that information," the medico said with a sniff.

"Well, what happens if I swell up like a poisoned pup and die?" Pete hoped that was a waddayacallit—a hypothetical question. He'd got the hypo part, in triplicate.

Whatever you called it, it didn't faze the doctor one damn bit. "What happens then? I'll tell you what, Sergeant. Your next of kin sue Uncle Sam for every nickel he's got, that's what. And Uncle Sam throws his lawyers at their lawyers, and it all grinds through the courts till, oh, 1953. Then they settle for five dollars and sixty-nine cents, which is about what you're actually worth. Only your folks have to split it with the shysters, so they end up screwed after all. Oh, and you're still dead, in case you were wondering."

Pete shuffled away, defeated. The middle-aged man in the white coat was armored in a cynicism that made his own seem made of Kleenex. And his folks wouldn't even sue the government. They were too busy trying to make ends meet with their lousy little Bronx candy store.

"I bet I know how come we got punctured like that," Cullum said when they got together under the warm sun again.

"I'm all ears," Pete said. "Looks crazy as shit, but I hear real good."

"Funny guy—funny like a chancre," the other sergeant said with a snort. "My guess is, they're sticking us for everything this side of house-maid's knee on account of they're gonna ship us to some crappy tropi-cal island crawling with mosquitoes and leeches and Japs."

That made more sense than Pete wished it did. "How come they can't vaccinate you for machine-gun bullets? I wouldn't bitch about that shot . . . not too much, anyhow."

"Amen!" Cullum said. "Amen like the spooks sing it in Father Divine's church. Machine guns are no fun at all, not unless you're on the trigger end."

"You got that right. 'Course, even a stopped clock's right twice a day," Pete said. Cullum gave him the finger. Pete rubbed his arm. Damned if it wasn't starting to swell. And, by the way his rear end felt, he'd sit with a list for the next few days.

He needed a little while to realize that Bob Cullum's idea, no matter how reasonable it sounded at first, didn't explain why civilian workers at Pearl were getting their shots, too. So were the sailors on the *Ranger* and the other ships in the harbor. *They* wouldn't be splashing ashore on some steaming beach, looking to blow the head off the first Jap they saw before he could do the same to them. Neither would the Army flyboys at Hickam, but they were meeting the needle, too.

And then Honolulu radio ordered civilians to report to hospitals or clinics or their private doctors for inoculations. "These are purely pre-cautionary measures," the announcer said. Then he made a liar out of himself: "No shirking will be tolerated, however. Individuals must dis-play valid immunization certificates to acquire rationed goods of any sort. If physicians run short of vaccine, be sure more is coming from the mainland at top priority. But there is no cause for alarm. If symptoms develop, do not delay—report to a physician immediately."

"Run that past me again?" Pete said when he heard the announce-ment. Several of the *Ranger*'s other Marine noncoms nodded.

"Symptoms of what?" Cullum asked. The radio man with the unctu-ous voice didn't explain. Pete didn't know about Cullum, but *he* hadn't really expected that the fellow would.

Fifteen minutes later, the man behind the microphone repeated the order. As far as Pete could tell, he used the identical words this time. Of *course* there was no cause for alarm. Everything was just a precaution.

But if symptoms developed, you had to drag your sorry ass to a doctor right away. If you didn't get your shots like a good little sheep, you wouldn't eat or drive.

Over the next couple of days, Pete heard the announcement often enough to get really sick of it—and to be able to repeat it in his sleep. None of the people who read it spelled out what the ominous symptoms were. If you came down with them, evidently you'd know.

Then Bob Cullum asked him, "When you were in China, did you ever see the plague?"

"See it? No." Pete shook his head. "I heard about it, sure—it happens over there. But you don't want to see it. If you're close enough to see it, you're close enough to catch it. Trust me, you don't wanna do that." He paused. Slower than it might have, a light bulb went on above his head. "How come? Is *that* what the radio's jabbering about?"

"That's what I hear," Cullum answered.

"Fuck," Pete said. "I never heard of the plague in Hawaii."

"Skinny is, the Japs done it some kind of way. That and three or four other kinds of shit. That's how come they turned us all into pincushions, like."

"Fuck," Pete repeated. "This ain't the kind of war I signed up for, y'know?" Which, as he understood all too well, didn't mean it wasn't the kind of war he had.

# Chapter 19

M otor noises coming out of the east meant trouble. Theo Hossbach knew that as well as any man alive—as well as any German soldier alive in Russia, the only kind of men he cared about. Motor noises coming out of the west, like these right now, weren't so bad. They were most likely German panzers moving up to the front . . . unless the Ivans had broken through somewhere else and were swinging around to stick it up this part of the line's ass.

Theo made as if to swivel his ears toward the sounds, as if he were a cat. He knew guys who could wiggle their ears, but he wasn't one of them, no matter how he tried. He did listen as hard as he could. After half a minute or so, he relaxed fractionally. Beside him, Adi Stoss blew out a stream of cigarette smoke and nodded. He seemed easier, too.

"Gasoline engines," he said.

"*Ja*," Theo agreed. The diesels that powered T-34s sounded different. He would have had a hard time explaining the difference to someone who didn't already hear it, but it was there, all right.

Adi kept listening. So did Theo. What else was there to do, standing here in the middle of Russian nowhere—which had to be the most expansive nowhere in the world—next to a Panzer III that wasn't running right this minute? And, even if those were gasoline engines . . .

"They sound funny," Adi said. A moment later, he amended that: "They sound *big*."

"*Ja*," Theo repeated. He was less annoyed saying the same thing twice than he would have been if he'd had to come up with something new. He was also suspicious, as any cat or veteran would be at meeting something new. An unfamiliar gasoline engine was liable to belong to a Soviet machine, not one that sprang from the *Reich*'s factories.

The same unpleasant thought must have crossed Adi's mind. He jerked a thumb toward the driver's position. "Think I ought to hop in?" Crewmen on other panzers were asking one another the same question. Some of them weren't asking—they were jumping in and firing up their chariots.

But Theo shook his head. He grudged another word: "Wait."

Adi laughed harshly. "I may as well. Anything that sounds as nasty as that'd squash a Panzer III like a bug." Now Theo nodded; again, they'd thought along with each other. Adi pointed down the rutted dirt track that led west: eventually, to something resembling civilization. "Here they come!"

Theo squinted, trying to make out the lines of the approaching machines. They advanced in line. He took that as a good sign. Ivans would have spread out so they weren't firing right past—or maybe into—one another.

"They look like ours . . . I think," Adi said slowly. "But sweet jumping Jesus! They're fucking enormous!"

"*Ja*," Theo said once more, concurring with both judgments at the same time. The panzers—there were half a dozen of them—did have a slab-sided, Germanic look. Russian machines used sloped armor much more: it helped deflect or defeat enemy fire. The Russian scheme was better; anyone who faced a T-34 would say the same thing, assuming he survived the encounter. But you didn't need to be an engineer to tell the two design philosophies apart at a glance.

As for enormous . . . At first, Theo thought he was looking at some of the new Panzer IVs, the ones with the long-barreled 75s. He needed only that glance, though, and his ears, to be sure he was wrong. These beasts dwarfed Panzer IVs. They dwarfed every German panzer he'd ever seen up till now. About the only panzer they didn't dwarf was the monstrous Russian KV-1.

Closer and closer they came. They had the black German cross on their turrets, not the Ivans' red star. Of course, if the Russians were pulling some kind of stunt, they wouldn't forget a detail like that. But Theo didn't believe it. These *were* German panzers. They just weren't German panzers he recognized. *Details, details*, he thought giddily.

Adi let out a low, awe-filled whistle. "Fry me for a pork chop if they don't have 88s in their turrets. I told you they ought to do that!"

Theo whistled, too, on a nearly identical note. The 88 was the only German gun that could certainly make a T-34 say uncle. But a big, clumsy towed antipanzer cannon had trouble getting to the right place at the right time. When Russian roads were bad—which was to say, almost always—they had trouble getting anywhere.

"That guy in the long-snouted Panzer IV said something big was in the works," Adi went on. "Boy, he wasn't kidding. These critters are *huge!*"

Panzer crewmen from Theo's company ran toward the new machines. They might have run toward a troupe of strippers with more eagerness. But then again, they might not have. Women were wonderful fun, no doubt about it. They reminded you why you were alive. But these panzers would help keep you that way. Which counted for more?

Theo found himself running, too. Adi loped along beside him. The driver could have outrun him—Adi could outrun just about anybody—but didn't bother. "What do you call these babies?" he shouted to the man standing head and shoulders out of the cupola on the closest panzer's tremendous turret.

"*Panzerkampfwagen* Mark V," replied the fellow in the big machine. Theo wanted to throw a clod of dirt at him. What a bloodless answer! Mark I, Mark II, Mark III, Mark IV—yes, of course, Mark V. But something better was surely called for, wasn't it? Grinning, the newcomer went on, "The other name is Tiger."

"All right!" Adi pumped a fist in the air. Theo didn't; that wasn't his style. But he came closer than he usually did. Tiger! There was a name to conjure with! When a Tiger bit you, you stayed bit.

Someone else asked, "How far out can you hit with that gun?"

"Past two kilometers," the panzer crewman—probably the commander, since he used the cupola—answered confidently. "And what we can hit, we can kill."

There, Theo believed him. Jealousy stabbed the radioman: pure sea-green envy. He wasn't sure his Panzer III's 37mm gun could even reach out 2,000 meters. If it could, he wasn't sure it would knock over a man, much less an enemy panzer. Life wasn't fair.

Adi found a new question: "How many more of those beauties are coming after you?"

"More?" The Tiger crewman sounded offended. "What do you want, egg in your beer? We're here. We'll do for the Ivans. You think a T-34 can beat a panzer like this?"

"Um, the Ivans have a lot of 'em," Adi said. The guy in the Tiger waved that aside. Theo wondered whether he'd ever fought Russians before. If he hadn't, he was about to get an education. Yes, half a dozen of these brutes could turn a lot of T-34s to scrap metal. But the Red Army *had* a lot of T-34s. It had a hell of a lot of them, as a matter of fact. Sooner or later, they'd get lucky against the Tigers. They were bound to. Then what?

Theo found out the next day. They went hunting Russians: the Tigers, with a few Panzer IIIs along as guides. Theo's was one of them. That left him less than thrilled. The Tigers were also splotchily white-washed, which in spring made sure T-34s would find them.

Finding the Tigers, the Russian panzers roared to the attack. Smoky diesel exhaust spewed from their tailpipes. Maybe they thought the German machines were long-gunned Panzer IVs, against which they still stood an excellent chance. They discovered their mistake in a hurry. The Tigers could hit from as far out as that crewman claimed. And sloped armor didn't keep out rounds from an 88. One T-34's turret flew through the air and landed, upside down and blazing, by the chassis.

"The T-34 tips its hat to the Tiger!" someone from another panzer yelled in Theo's earphones. He would have liked the joke better if he hadn't heard it before.

Pretty soon, the surviving Russians decided they wanted to go on surviving. They fled. The Tigers raced after them, as well as anything that heavy could race. One of the Panzer III commanders shouted a radio warning to them. Arrogant in their land dreadnoughts, the Tiger crews went right on racing. One of them raced over a mine and threw a track. It slewed sideways and stopped. The others quit charging ahead at top speed, anyhow.

"Fucking told you so, you asslicks," the Panzer III commander said. There in his small, old-fashioned machine, Theo smiled. He couldn't have put it better himself.

FRANCE AND ENGLAND might be back in the war against Hitler, but Alistair Walsh still wasn't sure how serious about it they were. He hoped it was just the same attitude he'd seen in the trenches the last time around: a sensible reluctance to get shot without the prospect of a decent reward.

Back then, the Germans had shown the same spirit. Not now. Now the Fritzes in Belgium were angry and embittered that they had a war on their hands. A wounded prisoner who spoke some English scowled at Walsh. "Your folk are traitors to Aryanhood. You are traitors to Western civilization."

"Too bloody bad, mate," Walsh said cheerily. "Want a fag?" He held out a packet of Navy Cuts.

"*Danke.*" The *Landser* took one. Walsh gave him a light. After a deep drag, he went on, "Wait until you see our *geheime* weapons. Then you sing a not so happy song."

"What's *geheime*?" asked Walsh, whose German didn't run much further than *Hände hoch!*

"It is secret," the German answered after a little thought of his own.

"What d'you mean, it's secret? You'll sing like a canary if we want you to," Walsh growled. Neither of them had enough of the other's language to clear up the confusion in a hurry. Light did dawn at last. Walsh went on, "Well, what kind of secret weapons have you got?"

"If I knew, they would not secret be," the Fritz said. "But the *Führer* has them promised, and the *Führer* is always right."

"My left one," Walsh jeered. That meant nothing to the German, and the sergeant didn't bother explaining. He sent the prisoner off to the

287

rear to let someone who could really talk to him ask him questions. He even told the men taking him back not to do for him unless he tried to run for it. With one arm all bandaged up, that didn't seem likely, but you never could tell.

The Tommies pushed toward Chimay, one more place that had seen a boatload of hard fighting a generation earlier. The Germans pushed back every chance they got. Whenever they had to abandon a farmhouse or a village, they booby-trapped it to a fare-thee-well. One luckless Englishman incautiously lifted a toilet seat and never got the chance to flush.

"Could have buried him in a jam tin, the bloody twit," a pioneer told Walsh. He chuckled nastily. "He was bloody afterwards—I'll tell you that."

"Pity the Belgians didn't warn him," Walsh remarked.

"Those buggers?" The military engineer spat. "Likely tell! Odds are better they would've warned a German."

Walsh spat, too. He knew what the other man was talking about. "You ever run up against the Walloon Legion?"

"The Rexists' collabos?" The pioneer shook his head. "Haven't had that pleasure yet. Nice to think I've missed something, any road."

"They're worse than the Germans, to hell with me if they're not," Walsh said. "Your Fritz, now, chances are he's a conscript. He's a good enough soldier—the Fritzes always seem to be, damn them. But he won't always have that fire in his belly, if you take my meaning."

"Oh, yes." The pioneer nodded.

Thus encouraged, Walsh warmed to his theme: "The Walloon Legion, though, they're all volunteers. They have to convince the Nazis they're mean enough to deserve to carry a Mauser. And once they get to, they don't dare let the side down. The next Rexist bastard who surrenders will be the first. They were Nazis before the shooting even started, and they likely expect we'll shoot them out of hand."

"And do we?" the other man asked in interested tones.

"I never have." Walsh left it there. Quite a few English soldiers reckoned the Walloon Legion traitors and did give them short shrift. War was a nasty business any way you looked at it. He wondered whether it really had been glorious back before machine guns and poison gas. Maybe . . . as long as a poet was writing from a safe distance.

More English tanks accompanied the infantry than had been true the last time Walsh was on the Continent during the Germans' winter rush toward Paris. These machines were faster and better armed than the early models, too. All the same, the high command didn't have the panache with them that the chaps on the other team did. But Walsh was glad to have them around even so. They made him feel safer, whether he truly was or not.

For a little while, he hoped the Allies could do unto Germany as Hitler's minions had done unto them a few years earlier. The English and French were pushing forward, after all. A reversed blitzkrieg would be sweet. His side had finally learned not to spread their armor all along the line in penny packets, but to mass it so it might actually accomplish something. The Fritzes were hard schoolmasters, but their lessons stuck.

He soon discovered they had more of those lessons than they'd taught in 1938 and 1939. That wounded POW who bragged of secret weapons might have known what he was talking about after all. British tanks rattled across the field between Chimay and another small town called Marienbourg. Walsh and his men loped along between them to discourage *Landsers* from sneaking up and chucking grenades through the tanks' hatches.

*Something* moved in amongst the bare-branched trees of an orchard ahead. "That's a tank," a Tommy called.

"Well, what if it is?" one of his buddies replied. "We've got a few o' them buggers our own selves."

Walsh felt very much the same way. He wasn't scared to death of Panzer IIIs or IVs any more, not when he had armor of his own at hand. Odds were his side would have more machines than the Nazis did, so sooner or later Fritz would have to pull back.

This tank came out of the orchard into the open when the Tommies were still more than a mile away. At first, Walsh thought it was a Panzer IV with a long gun: a formidable opponent, but one who had to be suicidal to show himself like that. It did seem large for a Panzer IV. Even so . . .

As soon as it opened fire, he realized it was no Panzer IV. Two shots smashed two English Valentines. The other English tanks started shooting back. Their AP rounds bounced off the German monster's armor. Almost contemptuously, it knocked out another Valentine, and then a Matilda II.

The English crews were brave. They tried to get closer, to give their plainly outclassed guns some kind of chance against this . . . whatever it was. That only made them easier targets. Methodically, as if it had all day, the German tank murdered them. One pillar of greasy black smoke after another marked their pyres.

"They put an 88 in the dirty bastard!" Alistair Walsh heard the horror in his own voice. With an 88 and the thick armor they obviously also had, that German crew could kill every single tank bearing down on them. If they got enough ammo, chances were they could kill every tank England had on the Continent.

His countrymen inside the Matildas and Valentines needed only a couple of minutes more to come to the same conclusion. They broke off their attack and scurried back toward Chimay as fast as they could go. That wasn't fast enough for two of them. The German behemoth didn't disdain knocking them out as they retreated.

Then its coaxial machine gun also started chattering, as if to warn the English foot soldiers: *All right, I know you're there, and that's close enough.* By then, Walsh required no more convincing. He wouldn't find out this afternoon what Marienbourg looked like. If he was very lucky, he'd get another glimpse of the ruins of Chimay.

THE VERY IDEA of flying against enemy panzers inside Belgium affronted Hans-Ulrich Rudel. "They've got no business messing about here!" he fumed to his radioman and rear gunner. "They agreed this was part of the *Reich*'s sphere of influence when they made peace with us."

Sergeant Dieselhorst was considerate enough to blow his stream of cigarette smoke away from Hans-Ulrich. "And then they unagreed when they broke the truce . . . sir," he said, plainly giving his pilot the benefit of the doubt by using the honorific.

"But they aren't supposed to do that," Rudel complained.

"Well, the only way to stop them is to blow them up," Dieselhorst answered. "If we don't do that in Belgium, chances are we'll have to do it inside of Germany. Then we'd be blowing up our own people, too."

"Mm. You've got something there, I suppose." Rudel's nod was reluctant, but a nod nonetheless. "Much better that we should blow up Belgians. Especially these miserable Walloons. They're nothing but a bunch of Frenchmen flying the wrong flag."

This time, Albert Dieselhorst pointed to the medal Hans-Ulrich wore around his neck every waking moment when he wasn't bathing or entertaining someone of the female persuasion. "I saw in one of the service papers that they gave a *Ritterkreuz* to a Walloon."

"You're joking!" Hans-Ulrich said.

"So help me." Dieselhorst raised his right hand, first and second fingers slightly crooked above it, as if he were swearing an oath. "For conspicuous bravery against the Ivans. The *Führer* presented it to him personally."

All that detail convinced Hans-Ulrich the noncom wasn't making up the story to annoy him. He smelled politics just the same. "Must be to keep the Rexists happy—and to keep them in line."

"Stranger things have happened." Sergeant Dieselhorst chuckled raspily. "Even if that sounds more like something I'd come out with than what I'd expect from you. I'm surprised you didn't notice the piece, though. From what it said, Hitler really liked that guy."

"He's lucky, whoever he is," Hans-Ulrich said.

"I guess so," Sergeant Dieselhorst replied, in tones ambiguous enough that Rudel had trouble telling whether he was agreeing or showing doubt. The sergeant went on, "Any which way, if we find Tommies or real French fries in amongst the Walloons, we've got to do for them."

"*Ja*," Hans-Ulrich said, still with no marked enthusiasm. It wasn't that he didn't want to kill Englishmen and Frenchmen. He did, with all his heart. He hated them far more fiercely than he had when the war was new. If only they'd stayed on the *Reich*'s side against the godless Reds, the filthy doctrine of Communism might have been wiped off the face of the earth by now.

As things were, Russia not only remained in the fight, the Ivans were gaining ground in the East. And, like so many rooks and carrion crows,

England and France were doing their best to peck bits off Germany even before she was dead.

That she might die was what infuriated and depressed Hans-Ulrich at the same time. He could see that the *Führer*'s foreign policy had failed, and might have failed disastrously. He could see it, yes, but he had no idea what to do about it or even what to think. It was an eventuality for which nothing in his life or training prepared him.

Right now, the only thing he saw worth doing—and the only thing that would keep him out of the stockade—was to fly against the foe whenever he got the chance . . . and whenever the *Luftwaffe* decided he could do it. With two fronts to cover, German fighters were spread thin. With none of them in the neighborhood, anything the RAF and the *Armée de l'Air* flew shot Stukas down without breaking a sweat.

These days, he couldn't do as he'd done against the Russians: smash a panzer, rise into the sky to dive again, smash another, and then repeat several more times. Unlike the Reds, the Western Allies had almost as many radio sets as the Germans. Their planes would be on you by the time you were swooping down on your second panzer. So you blasted one, got out of there as fast as you could, and then tried to find another one to kill somewhere else.

It was inefficient. When Hans-Ulrich complained about it, Sergeant Dieselhorst returned him to reality with a single pungent line: "Getting a shell through the motor and going down in flames is pretty fucking inefficient, too . . . sir." After that, Hans-Ulrich found other things to complain about.

An order from the *Führer* came to all men fighting on the ground and in the air. No one was to retreat any more, Hitler declared. German forces were to die where they stood if they couldn't advance. *Thus we best protect the sacred soil of the* Reich *against enemy desecration*, the directive thundered.

No one in the squadron said anything after Colonel Steinbrenner read the order aloud. The CO's voice showed nothing of what he thought about the typewritten words on the sheet of paper he held. He might have been reading out the *Führer*'s laundry list.

He might have been, but he wasn't. Nobody said anything while the squadron was assembled in a mass, no. But after Colonel Steinbrenner turned away, small knots of friends formed and started hashing it out. They were knots whose members trusted one another not to betray them to the *Gestapo*.

Hans-Ulrich didn't have any friends like that. Most of the time, he didn't miss them. He was proud of being a white crow. Now, though, he really wanted to find out what his *Kameraden* thought.

He knew how he'd eventually learn, of course. Sergeant Dieselhorst would tell him. The other *Luftwaffe* men trusted the sergeant. And Dieselhorst trusted Rudel. You had better trust the man with whom you flew. If you didn't, you'd both end up dead.

That didn't necessarily make you friends, though. Hans-Ulrich knew the noncom thought he was a prig, and still wet behind the ears. He was stubbornly proud of his priggishness. In spite of being young— no, because of being young—he would have denied the other if Diesel- horst threw it in his face. Dieselhorst didn't; he had other things on his mind.

"It's stupid, you know," he said without preamble. "It's especially stupid if you're stuck on the ground like a rat and you can't go and fly away when you get in trouble. Sometimes the only choices you have are falling back and getting killed right where you are."

"It's a problem," Hans-Ulrich admitted.

"It's not a problem. It's goddamn dumb, sir." Sergeant Dieselhorst had the air of a man clinging to patience as if it were a cork life ring in the Atlantic. "The enemy will kill you if you hold your ground. Your own side will kill you if you retreat. What does that leave you?"

*Victory!* was the word that leaped into Hans-Ulrich's mouth. It didn't leap out again, and into the cool spring air alongside the landing strip. He was much too sure Sergeant Dieselhorst would laugh at him if he came out with it. Instead, cautiously, he answered, "Not much."

"Oh, yes, it does—on this front, anyhow," Dieselhorst said. "I wouldn't give up to the Russians for all the tea in China. Chances are they'd kill me for the fun of it, you know? And they'd have more fun before they let me die. Am I right or am I wrong?"

"Oh, you're right about that." Rudel had always figured he'd stick his pistol in his mouth if he looked like getting caught by the Ivans.

Dieselhorst's grunt was oddly warming; it said something like

*Well, you know a little bit, anyhow.* But he went on, "Here, though . . . You surrender to the Tommies or even the French, you've got a chance to see the end of the play. They may shoot you—that kind of shit just happens—but they won't torture you. And if they'll kill you for sure if you keep fighting but only maybe if you give up, what are you supposed to do?"

Surrender was treason to the *Vaterland*. Hitler's decree left no doubts on that score. But Hans-Ulrich wanted to come back from the war alive, too. He didn't say anything at all. Albert Dieselhorst grunted again, and the pilot felt as if he'd passed some obscure test.


FRENCH 75S AND 105S boomed behind Aristide Demange. He sneered at the popguns, as he sneered at so much in life. He wished they were all 105s, as most of the Germans' cannon were. Then they could give the *Boches* just as much hell as they'd had inflicted on them in this war. But no. Too much to hope for. The enormous stocks of 75s left over from 1918 would soldier on till the Nazis blew up the last of them—and the last of the artillerists who served them, too.

Shells from the guns of both calibers burst somewhere on the German side of the line. Smoke and dirt rose into the air. The show looked impressive. Demange knew too well that it looked more impressive than it was. The 75s fired with a flat trajectory. That gave them good range for a piece of their caliber. But, unless they caught you out in the open, they probably wouldn't hurt you. Their shells couldn't drop down into trenches and holes the way rounds fired from howitzers could. Along with their bigger ammo, that was what made howitzers so dangerous.

"Are we going to advance now?" François asked Demange. Was he still eager in spite of having watched his friends get gunned down in the last brilliant assault? If so, then he really was a few pins short of a cushion, or more than a few.

"Wait a bit," Demange said. "Unless you feel like killing yourself now, I mean. In that case, be my guest." He waved invitingly toward the barbed wire ahead. However inviting the wave was, though, no motion showed above the parapet in front of the hole where they crouched. He didn't know a German sniper was peering this way through a scope, but he didn't know one wasn't, either.

François, whether dumb as rocks or with altogether too much in his trousers, looked at him as if he'd started speaking Albanian or something. "Don't you want to beat the *Boches*?"

"Sure I do," Demange answered. "I want to live through beating them, too. I want to gloat about it. I want to make them die for their fucking country. I don't give a fart about dying for mine."

"But—" François started. Demange wondered if he would come out with that *Dulce et decorum est* bullshit. It had been outdated centuries before the last war, but some provincials never got the news.

Before François got the chance to make an outdated jackass of himself, the Germans woke up and started shooting back. They never needed long. Their guns went after the French cannon that had annoyed them, and they started dropping mortar bombs near the trenches to discourage French foot soldiers like François from getting frisky.

"Down!" Demange yelled. He was already doing it. So were the *poilus* who'd been in the front lines for a while. The new fish took longer, the way they always did. They didn't realize they were in trouble till they got hurt. That, of course, was just exactly too late.

Demange hated mortars even more than he hated a lot of other things. You couldn't hear the bombs leaving the tubes. You mostly couldn't hear them till they whistled down. Then you had to hope—you had to pray, if you happened to be a praying man, which he wasn't— they didn't whistle down right on top of you.

The shrieks that rose from the French positions all seemed to come from at least a hundred meters away. Fragments snarled through the air over Demange's head. Dirt and perhaps some of those fragments pattered off his helmet.

He glanced over toward François. "Still got that hard-on to charge the *Boches*?"

"Maybe not so much, Lieutenant," the new kid allowed.

"Well, then, maybe—just maybe, and I wouldn't bet more than a sou on it—you aren't as stupid as you look," Demange said. François had started to smile at him. The expression congealed on his face like cooling fat.

Sometimes, of course, the *cons* with the white mustaches and the gold and silver leaves on their kepis were stupider than even a guy fresh out of basic ever dreamt of being. Or rather, those *cons* had the chance to be stupid on a scale a raw private couldn't begin to imagine. When François wanted to advance against the Germans, a word from Demange sufficed to quash him. When the fools with the fancy hats ordered an army corps to advance, nobody could quash them . . . except the bastards in *Feldgrau*, of course.

The Germans had some new toys that the *cons* in the expensive kepis didn't seem to know about. By now, even jerks like François knew the Tiger tank by name and had acquired a healthy respect—make that fear—for it. The generals ordered French armor forward as if the Tiger were no more than a gleam in some Nazi engineer's eye. French tankmen, however, like the frogs in the saying, died in earnest. When they came up against Tigers, they—and their machines—also died in large numbers.

And the Germans pulled a new machine gun out from under their coal-scuttle helmets. Demange didn't know what French generals thought of the German MG-34. He hated it himself. It fired much faster than any French machine gun, spraying murder out for a thousand meters from wherever it happened to lurk. And it could lurk anywhere. It was aircooled and light, and could be fired from a tripod, a bipod, or even, in an emergency, from the hip.

Prisoners said the new Nazi machine gun was called the MG-42. Demange supposed that stood for the year in which it went into production, the year now vanished with all the others that had gone before. Whatever the name stood for, the gun stood for trouble.

It made the MG-34 seem retarded, which Demange wouldn't have believed possible till he saw—and heard—it for himself. Once you heard an MG-42 in action, you'd never mistake it for anything else. It fired so fast, shots blurred together into a continuous sheet of noise.

Naturally, firing that fast heated the barrel red-hot in short order. The efficient *Boches* issued an asbestos mitt to their machine-gun crews. In a pinch, some cloth would also let you take off the hot barrel so you could replace it with a cool one. The whole business needed only a few seconds. Then you went right back to slaughtering whatever you could see.

With French tanks smashed like dropped eggs, with French infantry falling as if to a harvester of death, the corps' attack didn't get far. Demange ordered his company to entrench even before word came down from On High that the generals had decided that they weren't going to sweep triumphantly into Berlin after all. He took a certain sour pride in suffering fewer casualties than the other companies in the regiment. *Fewer,* unfortunately, didn't mean *few*; they'd got badly mauled. But they could—he hoped they could—fight back if the Fritzes decided to counterattack.

The Germans would be taking a chance if they did. Demange deliberately placed his new line at the western edge of one of their minefields. If they wanted to hoist themselves on their own petards trying to come to grips with his *poilus*, they were welcome to, as far as he was concerned.

His men would also have trouble advancing from their position, of course. He didn't worry about that. If Corps HQ wanted him to go forward, they could damn well send some sappers to help clear the way. He didn't think they'd do that any time soon. Their last rush of blood to the head—or, more likely, to the cock—had proved too expensive.

He couldn't complain about the zeal with which his men dug in. Dirt flew from their entrenching tools as if their mothers' sides of the family were all moles. They'd been out in the open a couple of times now, exposed to shellfire and to those horrifying machine guns. The farther away from that they got, the happier they were.

There was François, doing his best to burrow all the way to New Zealand. "So how do you like advancing now, kid?" Demange inquired.

François had a cigarette in the corner of his mouth, much the way Demange did (even if it was a Gauloise). It twitched as he answered, "Fuck that shit . . . sir."

Demange grunted laughter and thumped him on the back. "There you go. It sounds better than it is, just like everything else. Well, everything except fucking." François laughed, too. He sounded jaded, like a veteran. Hell, he'd lived through two attacks. He was a veteran now.

# Chapter 20

**S**pring rain turned the trenches northwest of Madrid into mudholes. It might not have been as bad as the Russian spring *rasputitsa*, when a winter's worth of snow melted all at once and turned everything into a quagmire, but it wasn't fun, either. Instead of warthogs and hippos, Nationalist and Republican soldiers clumped through these mudholes. Neither side's officers were enthusiastic about ordering attacks in such weather; they would only bog down. The brass relied on machine guns, and on snipers like Vaclav Jezek, to remind their foes the war was still on.

After night fell, Vaclav crawled back to the line from the shell-pocked horror of no-man's-land. He was filthy from head to foot. He'd wriggled through puddles and muck he couldn't see to avoid. When he pissed and moaned about it, Benjamin Halévy said, "Don't get your bowels in an uproar. You aren't a whole lot dirtier than anybody else."

A shout rang out from the rear: "Chow's coming!"

Halévy added, "And you're just in time for supper. Could be worse."

"I suppose," Vaclav said dolefully.

Supper did only so much to lift his spirits. The stew was red with paprika and fiery with chilies. The cooks were Spaniards. They liked it that way. Vaclav didn't. He ate it anyhow. The gravy held turnips and potatoes and God knew what all else. If he was lucky, the meat he spooned up was goat. If he wasn't so lucky, it was donkey—or possibly Nationalist, though it didn't seem tough or stringy enough for that.

Whether he liked the chow or not, he emptied his mess tin. Hunger made the best sauce. He was washing out the tin in a galvanized pail when another visitor from behind the lines arrived: "Mail call!"

Vaclav went right on washing the tin. The rest of the Czechs went on with whatever they were doing, too. Who was likely to write to them in the island of exile? The fellow with the waxed-canvas sack called out a few names. He made a hash of them: he was an International, but not a Czech. Then he said, "Jezek! Vaclav Jezek!" He pronounced the sniper's first name *Vaklav*, not *Vatslav*, but foreigners did that more often than not.

Taken by surprise, Vaclav dropped the mess tin in the mud and had to rinse it again. "I'm here!" he said, first in Czech and then in German, which a non-Czech had a better chance of following.

The International replied in the same language: "Letter for you."

"I'll be damned." Vaclav said that in Czech. He shoved through his countrymen to get to the guy with the mail. Several of the Czechs murmured jealously. It wasn't as if he hadn't done the same thing as other soldiers who got mail and he didn't.

"*Hier, Freund*," the International said, and handed him an envelope.

"*Danke. Danke schön.*" Vaclav took it over to a fire. He shielded it from the rain with his hand. When he got close enough to the flickering light to read, his heart did a pole vault. That was his father's handwriting! His letter had got through to Prague, and he'd got an answer.

The stamp in the upper corner of the envelope didn't look familiar to him. He swore under his breath: the damned thing had Hitler's face on it, complete with ugly mustache. Printed over the *Führer* were the words *Böhmen u. Mähren*—the German for *Bohemia and Moravia*. The Nazis had even taken away the name of his country!

He tore the envelope open. If only the real Hitler were so easy to mutilate! The letter inside was short. He had a little trouble reading it; some German censor's rubber stamp blurred and covered up a few words. But he managed.

*My dear son,* his father wrote, *so good to hear from you after so long! Your mother and I and your two sisters are all well. I am sorry to have to tell you that Grandpa Stamic*—that was his mother's father—*passed on a year ago. It was a liver disease, and had nothing to do with the war. Work is hard, but there is work. We eat well enough. Be safe. We will pray for you. With love, Papa.*

"What's the word?" another Czech asked.

"My dad says there's food in Prague. He's working hard. One of my grandfathers died." It all sounded so flat when you came out with it. But to have heard! To have heard for the first time since the fight in the Sudetenland went to hell!

"So the Nazis really do let letters through if the Red Cross handles them?" The other Czech soldier sounded as if he had trouble believing the German occupiers showed even that tiny bit of mercy and of adherence to international law.

"It's my old man's handwriting, sure as I'm standing here, so I guess the assholes do." Vaclav sounded the same way, because he was amazed. Expecting anything good or even decent from Germans—especially from Germans in uniforms with swastikas on them—wasn't easy for Czech exiles.

"I'll send my folks a letter, too," the other soldier declared. "Up till now, I just figured I was wasting my time."

Vaclav nodded. "Well, sure. Same here. Christ, this is the first time I've heard anything from anybody back in Prague since I went over the border and let the Poles intern me."

"Give the Red Cross some credit," Benjamin Halévy said. "Even Hitler thinks twice before he lets them see him acting like a dickhead. Sometimes he does it anyway, mind you, but he does think twice."

That got the Czechs suggesting where Hitler could stick his second thoughts. Vaclav doubted whether even a man considerably more limber than the *Führer* was likely to be would have been able to stick them in some of those places, let alone twist them once he'd done it. The soldiers had played such games before. It was one more way to coax a few laughs out of misery and to make fifteen minutes or a half hour go by faster than they would have otherwise.

Then somebody noticed Hitler's face on the stamp. The guy wanted to use it for toilet paper. "Forget that, pal," Jezek said. "Anybody gets his shit in the *Führer*'s mustache, it'll be me. I just wish I could do it for real."

"Don't we all?" Halévy said. "The queue for that would stretch all the way from here to Berlin—and you'd better believe plenty of Germans would line up along with everybody else."

"Yeah, well, they can wait way at the back. They don't get to crap on him till all the others have had their turns," Vaclav said.

"Sounds fair to me." The Jew nodded. "If it wasn't for them, none of the rest of us would've had to worry about him."

They embellished that idea for a while, too. Then the Nationalists lobbed a few mortar bombs their way. Mortars and the finned shells they hurled were cheap, easy to make, and didn't have tight tolerances. They were well suited to manufacture in Spain, in other words. The way things were right now, Hitler and Mussolini had trouble shipping goodies to Marshal Sanjurjo. Spaniards—even Fascist Spaniards—were stubborn people. Sanjurjo went right on fighting, doing all he could with what he had left and what he could figure out how to build for himself.

Huddled in the mud, Vaclav said, "I wish England and France would send the Republic a couple of hundred tanks. New tanks, I mean, not the worn-out junk they don't want for themselves any more. We'd have the Nationalists howling for mercy and on the run in about a week."

"Wouldn't even take that long," Halévy said, his voice muffled because his mouth wasn't more than a centimeter out of the muck. "But don't hold your breath, not unless you want to turn bluer than a French uniform from the last war."

"Don't they care whether they win?" Vaclav demanded.

"Good question. I wish I had a good answer for you," Halévy replied. "Remember, they both sent armies into Russia to fight on Hitler's side. They don't want Germany to conquer them, but they aren't dead keen on knocking the Fascists flat, either."

Jezek wished he could have called the Jew a liar. But if England and

France had been serious about taking on the Nazis, they would have hit Germany hard from the west as soon as Hitler attacked Czechoslovakia. It hadn't happened then. All this time had passed since. Everyone had spent oceans of blood and snowdrifts of money. And the Western democracies still weren't more than half serious about the war.

The Spaniards were, on both sides. Mortar bombs kept falling on the Czechs' trenches. The foreign tanks that might have turned the war around were nowhere to be seen.

IVAN KUCHKOV HAD watched Soviet forces retreat for years. Now the Red Army was moving forward in the Ukraine, even though it wasn't winter. The Germans still fought hard in every village and on every north-south water line, no matter how small, but they were distracted in a way they hadn't been before. Now they had to worry about the West, too, and they'd taken a lot of men out of the Soviet Union to fight back there. The ones who were left could slow down the Russians, but couldn't stop them.

Right this minute, Kuchkov's company wasn't even facing Fritzes. The bastards in front of them were Romanians. Some of the swarthy men in the dark brown uniforms were brave enough. More surrendered on any excuse or none. They didn't want to be here. They didn't have artillery and tanks to put some weight on their side, the way the Hitlerites did.

So they came up to the Russians with their hands held high, hopeful smiles on their faces. "*Kamerad!*" they shouted, just as the Germans did.

They were miserably poor. Hardly anyone, even the officers, had anything worth stealing. Their field ration was cornmeal mush—*mamaliga*, they called it. They were willing—eager, in fact—to share it with their captors. Kuchkov wasn't so eager to take it. Most of the time, he could do better scrounging off the countryside.

"Friends?" asked the Romanians who'd picked up bits and pieces of Russian. "Friends now?"

"You're fucked now, is what you are," Kuchkov would tell them. "You're totally fucked, as a matter of fact."

Most of the time, they couldn't understand him. Or maybe they didn't want to understand. They'd managed to surrender. They hadn't got killed trying. The hard part was over. Now they could sit in POW camps till the war was over. Then they'd go home. The worst thing they had to worry about was whether their girlfriends were blowing the guy next door while they were stuck behind barbed wire.

That's what they thought, anyhow. They were only Romanians. Germans knew better, and often saved a last bullet for themselves so they wouldn't have to give up to Red Army men.

Yeah, the prisoners would end up in camps. Maybe they'd even be called POWs. But maybe, having got their hands on the enemy soldiers, Soviet authorities wouldn't bother with games any more. That was how Ivan would have bet. The poor damned Romanians would probably go straight into the gulags, and odds were they'd never come out again.

Chopping down trees in Siberia's endless forests? Building roads? Digging canals? Mining gold, up north of the Arctic Circle? The possibilities were endless. All of them used up men at hideous rates. You might die a few centimeters at a time, but you'd die, all right. At least the last bullet finished things in a hurry, and you didn't hurt any more after that.

None of the Russians said a word about such things to the Romanians. It wasn't that the prisoners wouldn't have followed, though most of them wouldn't have. It was more the front-line soldiers' impulse to cause themselves as little trouble as they possibly could. Pretty soon, the Romanians would realize they might have been smarter to fight it out. Some of them would have had a chance to get away. By the time they did figure that out, though, the NKVD would have taken charge of them. And that would be too late.

Kuchkov watched them trudge off into captivity. They were laughing and singing and cracking jokes in their incomprehensible language. That wouldn't last long.

"Pretty soon, the poor, sorry shitheads'll see the fucking joke's on them," Kuchkov said. He wasn't used to feeling sorry for an enemy. Neither the Germans nor the Ukrainian nationalists invited sympathy. But the Romanians were pathetic beyond belief. The big bosses in their country had grabbed them, poured them into uniforms, handed them rifles, and sent them off to war with a pat on the back and a good, loud *Lots of luck, suckers!*

They might as well have been Russians, in other words.

That, Ivan Kuchkov kept to himself. No one would ever have accused him of being bright. He knew too well that he wasn't, and that he never would be. But he was not without his own measure of animal cunning. And anyone who'd lived through the Great Terror of the 1930s knew what you could say and what you had to swallow. Anyone who'd lived through the Great Terror knew you'd goddamn well better not mumble in your sleep, either.

The Romanians hadn't been gone for long when artillery—German artillery—started pounding the Soviet positions. The Nazis were cocksuckers, but they weren't dumbshit cocksuckers. They understood that they had to give their allies some spine, because the Romanians sure didn't come equipped with any on their own. And the Nazis understood that the dark-skinned men in the tobacco-brown uniforms with the funny helmets were liable to try to bail out on them any which way. If the Romanians tried it, the Germans who gave them spine would also do their best to give them grief.

Sitting where the Nazis sat, Communist Party bosses would have done exactly the same thing. They might wear different uniforms and spout different slogans, but they thought the same way.

No matter how clearly Ivan Kuchkov saw that, he saw even more clearly that it was one more thing to shut up about. His own country's rulers would ruin him if they knew they reminded him of the Nazis. And the Nazis would kill him on general principles, sure, but they'd make a special point of killing him if they somehow learned they reminded him of Communist apparatchiks.

Which said . . . what? Probably that you couldn't win any which way. Ivan had learned that lesson when he was very small. You couldn't get out of the game, either. Grabbing a barmaid and jumping on a freighter to somewhere like Peru or Mozambique wasn't just physically impossible. It lay far, far beyond his mental horizon.

Staying in the game as long as he could didn't. The first German 105 was still a rising shriek in the air when he jumped into a foxhole he'd dug. Fragments whined over the hole, but none bit him. Dirt rained down on him. A clod thumped off his helmet. It scared him for a moment, till he realized it was only a clod. Smaller bits fell into the narrow space between the back of his neck and his tunic's collar band. It made his back itch. He hated that. He wiggled in the foxhole, trying to make the dirt go down. Considering what the bombardment could have done to him, the annoyance was tiny, but it was real.

More shells came down. In between the thunderous bursts, Kuchkov heard somebody shrieking. "Poor prick," he muttered, and pulled himself deeper into his foxhole. He understood noises like that. Anybody who'd been at the front for even a little while did. One of the soldiers had a bad one.

If the man was lucky, they'd drag him back to a sawbones who'd stick an ether-soaked rag under his nose and then patch him up as best he could. Lucky? Very lucky. More likely, he'd keep screaming till he passed out or till he died.

Another shell came down. Something wet splashed the back of Ivan's hand. It wasn't just wet—it was hot and red. "Fuck!" he said, and rubbed off the blood against the hole's dirt wall. Absently, he noticed that the wounded man's screams had stopped. That burst had probably finished his story once and for all. After a hit like that, there wouldn't be enough left of him to bury.

*Could've been me,* Ivan thought. It could have been, but it hadn't. Not yet. Not this time. All the same, he found himself envying those Romanians shuffling back to the prison camps, and who would have imagined that?

CORPORAL ARNO BAATZ worried about his own men almost as much as he worried about the Russians. The way he looked at things, that was what a good underofficer was supposed to do. How could the *Reich* hope to win a war with the undisciplined louts who filled the *Wehrmacht*'s ranks unless somebody rode herd on them and kept them in line? It couldn't be done, or so things seemed to him.

The men didn't appreciate his efforts. They thought that, just because they were up at the front, they could get away with anything.

Maybe some corporals would have let them do it. But *Unteroffizier* Arno Baatz wasn't one of those soft, yielding souls.

Did they thank him for his care about regulations? It was to laugh. They were as insubordinate as they could get away with, and a little more besides. They swore at him when his back was turned, or sometimes to his face. When they thought he couldn't hear them, they called him Awful Arno.

He knew he'd worn the nickname for a long time. That just meant he'd hated it for a long time. There were plenty of times when he preferred fighting the Ivans to keeping track of the ruffians in his squad. The Russians were honest. He knew they wanted to kill him. His own men . . .

"Pfaff!" Arno snapped.

Adam Pfaff was cleaning his Mauser. He'd painted the piece a nonregulation gray. The company CO didn't want to make a fuss about it, but it distressed Baatz's orderly, order-craving soul. Pfaff was an *Obergefreiter*, a senior private, so Arno couldn't even stick him with the fatigue duties that would have brought him back to the straight and narrow. Pfaff thought the lousy chevron on his sleeve meant his shit didn't stink.

He was also selectively deaf. Right this minute, he pretended to be altogether focused on getting some oiled rag down the rifle's barrel with the pull-through of his cleaning kit. Well, Arno wasn't about to let him get away with that nonsense. *"Pfaff!"* He shouted it this time.

"Oh, hullo, Corporal." Adam Pfaff looked up from what he was doing, his face the very image of stubbly innocence. "Did you want something?"

"Damn right I do." Arno didn't bother to hide his irritation. He rarely did. "Go take over for Dirk at the forward sentry station."

Pfaff gave him a dirty look, which warmed the cockles of his heart. The *Obergefreiter* was a born barracks lawyer. Baatz waited for him to claim that was one of the duties from which his pipsqueak rank exempted him. If Pfaff tried it, Arno intended to shoot him down in flames. *Do it anyhow, 'cause I told you to* was always reason enough—if you were giving the orders, anyhow.

But Pfaff just sighed and reassembled his rifle with a few quick, practiced motions. Even Arno Baatz had to admit he made a decent combat soldier when he wasn't whining. Pfaff lit a cigarette as he got to his feet. "You *will* remember to send somebody to take over for me?" he said, his tone implying he thought Arno would do no such thing.

"Not me. Far as I'm concerned, you can stay in that hole till 1951." Baatz laughed to show he was joking. And so he was . . . up to a point. The laugh sounded nasty even to him.

Well, he wanted to get a rise out of Pfaff. To *his* annoyance, the *Obergefreiter* just ambled out of the ruined Russian village without giving any sign that he was irked.

A few minutes later, Dirk came back. "What's going on up there?" Baatz asked him.

"Not much, Corporal. Ivans seem pretty quiet right now," the soldier answered. Then he asked a question of his own: "Any of that stew left? My belly's growling like a mean dog."

"Might be a little." Arno made a face. "It's not what you'd call a treat." Buckwheat groats and turnips and onions and mystery meat, all of it boiled together till you could hardly tell where one ingredient stopped and the next started . . . No, it wasn't what he would have ordered if he were stepping out with a pretty girl back in Breslau.

But Dirk said, "Beats the hell out of empty." And that was also true. War in Russia had taught Arno more about empty than he'd ever wanted to learn. Dirk headed toward the hut that housed the field kitchen.

Off in the distance, artillery rumbled. Baatz gauged the far-off thunder. Well to the south, he judged, German and Russian guns thumping each other. It was something he needed to notice. Unless it picked up, it was nothing he or his superiors needed to worry about.

A *babushka* scurried to the well, a big saucepan in her hand to carry the water she drew up. She dipped her hand to Baatz and murmured, "*Gospodin*," as she slipped past. He ignored her. The way the Russians lived . . . It was pathetic and disgusting at the same time. No running water or electricity outside the big cities. No paved roads outside the big cities, either, which had come as a nasty surprise to the motorized *Wehrmacht*.

Arno Baatz curled his lip. *We need to clean out this whole country and start over again from scratch*, he thought. He imagined a German farming village, full of handsome German farmers and their good-looking

German wives and happy children taking the place of this screwed-up dump. In his imagination, even the cows and pigs were plump and contented.

No cows and pigs at all were left here. If the Russians hadn't slaughtered them, the Germans had. Only a couple of old men and a few more ugly old women still lived in this place. The younger men probably wore Red Army khaki and carried machine pistols. Maybe some of the younger women wound up in German military brothels, servicing a couple of dozen soldiers every shift. Arno hoped so. What else did they deserve?

A *Kettenrad* chugged into the village. Captain Fellmann, the company's latest CO, hopped out and waved to Baatz.

The corporal came to attention and saluted. "What's up, sir?" he asked. He might be hell on wheels to the men below him in rank, but he always showed his superiors perfect military formality.

"We're pulling back. Gather your men together and head west," Hans-Joachim Fellmann said. "We're shortening the line so we don't need so many troops to hold it." He made a sour face. *Shortening the line* was what radio newsreaders said to explain away a retreat. It might be true this time, with the *Reich*'s manpower stretched so thin. Even if it was, that made it no more palatable.

Baatz saluted again. *"Zu Befehl, mein Herr!"*

"All right. I'll see you back at regimental HQ in three or four hours. We'll all move out then." Captain Fellmann jumped back into the *Kettenrad*. The driver gunned the engine. The funny-looking little machine putt-putted off to the next German outpost.

Arno Baatz let out a long, mournful sigh. So much for his vision of replacing this rotten little settlement and the lousy Ivans who infested it with a proper German farm town full of proper Germans. It would stay in its native squalor. The *Führer*'s much larger and more grandiose vision for shoving the Slavs out of Europe and back past the Urals was also going a-glimmering with the German retreat, but Baatz lacked the imagination to see all that in his mind's eye.

He chuckled nastily. Tempting to take the rest of the squad out of the line and leave Adam Pfaff in his forward foxhole with an eye peeled for Russians. Would he find them—would they find him—before or after he started wondering why nobody'd come up to relieve him?

However tempting it was, Baatz didn't do it. No German on the Eastern Front would leave even his worst enemy to the Ivans' tender mercies. And Adam Pfaff wasn't Arno's worst enemy.

Or, now that Dernen had copped one, maybe he was.

Whether he was or not, the corporal sent Dirk back up to retrieve him. No point giving the *Landsers* anything new to gossip about. They found plenty on their own. The squad trudged away from the village. The Russians could have it. The Russians, as far as Arno Baatz was concerned, were damn well welcome to it.

THEY SAID U-BOATS could roll in a bucket. They said all kinds of stupid things, but they were dead right about that one. And the North Sea was no bucket—not unless you compared it to the North Atlantic, anyhow. Roll the U-30 did. The boat pitched when a wave caught it bow-on, too.

Up on the conning tower, Gerhart Beilharz turned to Julius Lemp and said, "Skipper, you need to get promoted again, is what you need. Another party would be a hell of a lot more fun than this."

"Work before pleasure," Lemp answered. "Work after pleasure, too, unfortunately."

"I know." The tall engineering officer nodded. "They haven't figured out how to make you work *during* pleasure, but I bet some bald old *Herr Doktor Professor* at the University of Tübingen or somewhere has a research grant to see what he can do about that."

"Wouldn't surprise me one goddamn bit," Lemp agreed. "I'd like another promotion party—but I'm not holding my breath. I didn't think I'd ever get the last one."

"You deserved it," Beilharz said loyally.

"Glad you think so." Lemp never would have made Beilharz's acquaintance to begin with if he hadn't been an officer with a screwed-up career. They'd given his boat a *Schnorkel*—and the accompanying *Schnorkel* expert—because they didn't much care what happened to it (or to him) after he sank an American liner under the mistaken belief it was an English troopship. They didn't cashier him for the mistake (which German propaganda loudly and stridently denied), but he'd spent a devil of a long time as a lieutenant.

He raised the field glasses to his eyes once more and went back to scanning a quadrant of the sky and the horizon. Ratings in foul-weather gear covered the other three quadrants. You'd never find a target if you didn't look for it. You'd never spot the plane that was looking for you, either, not till machine-gun bullets slammed into your hull or bombs fell from the belly of the flying beast.

Beilharz went on talking: "Nice to get up here every once in a while—not just for the fresh air, but so I don't have to worry about banging my stupid head."

"You're not tall enough to bump it on the sky," Lemp agreed. He went on swinging his binoculars through their automatic arc. He had no trouble carrying on a conversation at the same time without getting distracted. A U-boat skipper who couldn't do several things at once would quickly discover he wasn't up to filling the role.

"Everywhere else, though," Beilharz said. *Everywhere* certainly included the U-30's pressure hull. The inside of the steel cigar seemed cramped even to men below average height. The passageway was barely wide enough for two sailors to squeeze past each other. Getting through the four circular pressure doors inside the boat's hull was an exercise in gymnastics. And all sorts of pipes and fittings, many of them with points or sharp edges, hung down from the top of the cylinder.

You could easily gash your scalp even if you weren't tall. All you had to do was hurry or just be careless for a moment. Every patrol, the pharmacist's mate sewed up several cuts like that.

Even barefoot, there were two meters of Gerhart Beilharz. He was too big a sardine to fit well into his tin. He had to fold up like a carpenter's ruler to sleep in an officer's bunk. (As captain of the U-30, Julius Lemp boasted a cabin—a tiny cabin—to himself, complete with a cot. He was the only man aboard who did. Anywhere else, the space would have seemed claustrophobic: it was, for instance, much smaller than a jail cell. It remained the height of luxury on the U-boat.)

Beilharz couldn't hurt himself while he was asleep, not unless he fell out of the bunk. Awake and on the move, though . . . Hurrying forward and aft in an apelike stoop wasn't enough to save his noggin from the slings and arrows of outrageous ironmongery. Whenever he went below, he wore a *Stahlhelm*. That protected his cranium, at the cost of occasional repairs to ceiling fixtures when he forgot to duck.

One of the ratings on watch with Lemp tapped him on the arm. "Skipper, I think there's something off to the northwest—bearing about 295."

*"Ach, so?"* Lemp came to a hunter's alertness. "Here's hoping you're right, Rolf. Been a quiet cruise so far." He swung his own field glasses a little north of west. He frowned as he studied the horizon. "Something . . . maybe." Mounted on an iron post on the conning tower was a pair of larger, stronger binoculars. He peered through them. The frown lines got deeper. "Looks like a diesel plume, I think—one a lot like ours."

"Another U-boat?" Rolf and Lieutenant Beilharz asked the same thing at the same time. You didn't need to solve crossword puzzles or read detective stories to jump to that conclusion.

Lemp nodded. "That's my guess. First thing we have to do is make sure it's not one of ours. Nobody else is supposed to be in the neighborhood, but you can never count on that stuff. If it's not, we'll sink the steel turd."

"I couldn't see the hull—only the exhaust," Rolf said.

"Same here, even with the big glasses." Lemp nodded again. "Let's go below. We'll take her down to *Schnorkel* depth and get in closer to find out what we've got. It'll be a lot easier for us to see them than for them to spot us."

Bootsoles clattered on the steel rungs of the ladder down to the pressure chamber. Lemp was the last man off the tower. He closed the hatch behind him and dogged it tight. Water gurgled into the ballast tanks. Beilharz raised the *Schnorkel* tube as Lemp raised the periscope.

"Snort behaving?" Lemp asked.

"Sure is, Skipper," the engineering officer answered.

They chugged toward the other U-boat at seven knots. Lemp peered through the periscope. He had to be sure before he loosed an eel or two. No career would survive sinking a *Kriegsmarine* U-boat.

Whatever the other boat was, no one aboard it had any idea he was stalking it. He soon became sure it wasn't a Type VII like his own or one of the large Type IXs. They didn't have that smooth bump at the bow. As he recognized it, excitement tingled through him.

"It's an English U-boat, a Type S or maybe a Type T," he said. They were bigger than his boat, about the size of a Type IX—and that bow bump let them carry ten forward torpedo tubes, which made them very bad news if they found you first. But they hadn't, not this time. Lemp went on, "I can see . . . *Ja*, I can see the White Ensign flying from the conning tower. And they don't know we're around."

He began setting up the problem, juggling speeds and courses and angles. It was almost like a training exercise—except that in a training exercise the quarry wouldn't dive and start stalking him if it realized it was being hunted. Leopards didn't usually hunt other leopards through the jungle. If one took another by surprise, though . . .

His heart thudded with tension as they slid up to firing range. An alert seaman on the Royal Navy submarine was bound to spot the snort and the periscope . . . wasn't he? Lemp ordered the *Schnorkel* taken down. They'd do the rest on the batteries.

He launched two torpedoes. Away they whooshed on charges of compressed air. They had about a kilometer to run. They'd gone a little more than half that distance when the enemy U-boat began a sudden, frantic turn. One eel missed the target, but Lemp watched the other strike it in the stern—square in the engine room, in other words.

The English boat went down in a twinkling. The German U-boat men didn't celebrate the way they usually did when they sank an enemy vessel. They seemed uncommonly subdued.

Lemp wasn't surprised. He felt the same way. A tiny swing of luck, and the English boat might have sunk them. They'd done what they had to do, but they weren't proud of it.

# Chapter 21

Sarah Bruck was peeling turnips when the air-raid sirens began to shrill. She looked at her mother. "Are they crazy?" she said. "It's one in the afternoon." The RAF never came over Münster in broad daylight.

Hanna Goldman shrugged. "Maybe it's a drill."

"Then the people who run the drills are crazy," Sarah said. When she started thinking about it, that didn't seem at all unlikely to her. They were Nazis, so they might well be *meshuggeh*.

But, through the sirens' warble, she soon heard the drone of aircraft engines overhead. She and her mother lay down under the dining-room table: not much protection, but the best they could do.

Bombs whistled down on their city. After a couple of minutes, flak guns all over Münster thundered to irate life. Sarah thought she understood the reason for the delay. The gun crews wouldn't have been standing by their weapons in broad daylight, the way they did at night. They would no more have expected a daylight raid than Sarah had.

Whether they'd expected one or not, they'd got one. She thought some of the engines roaring up there high in the sky belonged to *Luftwaffe* fighters, not bombers from England. She didn't know what to feel about that. Like the gunners, they supported the regime that tormented her and the rest of Germany's Jews. But they were trying to drive away the English pilots dropping bombs on her head. One of the young Englishmen up there right now might have dropped the bomb that had killed her husband and his family.

So shouldn't she hope a German pilot in a Messerschmitt shot down that Englishman? An eye for an eye and a tooth for a tooth? The way things were going, a blind world would gum its food from now until eternity.

A great crashing roar shook the house and rattled the windows. That wasn't a bomb going off; that was a plane's whole bomb load blowing up at once as it smashed to earth. At least one fighter pilot or flak-gun crew had scored a success. No more than a minute later, another bomber crashed down a little farther away.

"They're paying for this," Sarah's mother shouted into her ear.

"They are, yes," Sarah agreed. Was that a good thing or a bad? She still couldn't make up her mind. *Both at once* was what she wanted to say, but she didn't think her father would reckon that an acceptable choice.

Thinking of Father made fresh fear stab through her. None of the bombs had fallen close to the house. But he was out in the city somewhere, patching up some of the damage from the RAF's night raids. She was pretty sure she and Mother would come through this attack all right. But she had no way of knowing where Father was or what sort of shelter from the falling death he'd be able to find. Would he walk through the front door tonight? Would someone from the labor gang knock on the door to let her and Mother know he'd never come home any more? Or would he just be . . . gone?

Sarah kept her fears to herself. No doubt her mother had them, too, and stayed quiet about them so as not to worry her. Misery didn't always love company. Sometimes things got worse when you shared them, not better.

Bombing raids always seemed to last forever. When you got the chance to look at a clock afterwards, you were astonished at the small interval during which the RAF planes were actually overhead.

This time, they left after just more than twenty minutes. The sirens went on warbling a while longer. The flak guns went on firing, too. A few chunks of shrapnel clattered down on the roof slates. Nothing sounded heavy, not this time. Once, a big chunk of falling brass had smashed a slate. Father'd gone up there and fixed things before the next time it rained.

He'd been proud of himself for days afterwards, too. He'd done something useful, and he'd done it well. It wasn't the kind of thing a professor of classics and ancient history would have known how to do. As far as he was concerned, it made his forced departure from the university and his conscription into the labor gang at least partway worthwhile.

As the all-clear finally sounded and as the antiaircraft-gun crews at last decided the bombers were really gone, Sarah had to hope memories like that weren't all she had left of her father. He might be a decorated and wounded veteran of the last war, but as far as the Nazis were concerned he was still a damn Jew.

She and her mother crawled out from under the table. "Well," Hanna Goldman said, hands fluffing at her hair, "supper's going to be later than I thought."

"It's a nuisance, but what can you do?" Sarah wasn't about to let anyone, even her mother, win a dryer-than-thou competition.

But, even after the sorry stew—turnips and potatoes and cabbage and a parsnip or two for a hint of sweetness—started bubbling on the stove, any little noise out in the street made her head whip around. Was that Father coming in? Or was *that*? Or *that*? Each time, the answer turned out to be no.

Mother's head might have been on the same swivel. Neither of them said a word about it.

But those *were* footsteps coming up the walk. And they were Samuel Goldman's irregular footsteps. He'd limped ever since he caught one for the Kaiser, even if the *Reich*'s current lords and masters gave him precious little credit for it.

His key turned in the lock. The door opened. To Sarah's amazement, her father's face bore an enormous grin. He wore a shabby tweed jacket.

He'd lost a lot of weight on bad food and hard labor, so it hung loose on him. It did most of the time, anyhow. It was tight today, and he held one hand under his belly to support whatever was under there.

"What have you got?" Mother exclaimed, beating Sarah to the punch by a split second.

Instead of answering directly, Father said, "The Englishmen and the Americans did us a favor today. They were trying to murder us, of course, but they did us a favor anyhow."

"The Americans?" Sarah said. "What have the Americans got to do with it?"

"They sold the RAF these planes—Flying Fortresses, they're called." Father said it in English and then in German. *Fliegende Festungen*: it sounded impressively martial. He went on, "They're day bombers, all right. They're stuffed full of armor and machine guns so they can fight their way to where they're going—except when they get shot down. Some of them did. I watched it happen. But they plastered the rich part of town. We went there to help fight fires and fix water mains and the like. And so . . ."

He carefully undid his coat. A small ham and several fat sausages fell on the sofa. So did several tins of meat and a small, squat bottle of cherry brandy.

Sarah squealed. Her mother just stared at the sudden bounty, her eyes open wider than eyes had any business opening. Samuel Goldman looked proud and sheepish at the same time. "Yes, I'm a looter. Yes, I'm a thief," he said. "But everybody was doing it, and I'm sick of going hungry all the time. I've got four packs of cigarettes—American cigarettes!—in my inside pockets, too. I don't know how the Party *Bonz* whose house we went through got hold of them, and I don't care, either. He's smoking down below right now, is my best guess. He was nothing but raw meat in a uniform when we found him."

An untimely demise like that should have saddened Sarah. But she heard herself saying, "I hope he was the pigdog who gave Isidor and me so much trouble when we wanted to get married, that's all."

"There you go." Father nodded.

Mother said, "Now I'm glad the stew isn't done yet. I'll chop up one of those sausages and throw it in."

"That sounds wonderful," Sarah said. Pretty soon, it smelled wonderful, too. It tasted as good as it smelled. They drank little glasses of brandy to celebrate the feast. Father lovingly smoked a Pall Mall. It smelled different from the dog-ends he usually had to use. By his blissful expression, it also tasted different.

Father scrounged all kinds of wonderful things when the RAF hit Münster. But he got to do that because the English wrecked homes and shops and killed people. You couldn't win. You couldn't even come close.

CHAIM WEINBERG KNEW all the stupid things people said about war. One of them was that you never heard the one that got you. The Nationalists were throwing mortar bombs at the Internationals' trenches. That had to be their second favorite sport, right after what they and most of the rest of the world outside the USA called football.

Nothing had come down especially close to Chaim. Sanjurjo's men were missing by so much, in fact, that he was joking about it with Mike Carroll. "See?" he said to his buddy, who hadn't been back in action long. "The front line is the safest place you can come."

"Maybe you're right," Mike said. "I—"

There was a brief whining hiss in the air, an understated bang . . . and all the lights went out for Chaim. When they came on again—he didn't think it was more than a few seconds later, but he never knew for sure—he saw everything red and his left hand was on fire. He didn't need long to figure out why his vision had that crimson film. He'd caught a nasty scalp wound, and it poured blood into his eyes. And his hand . . . It might have looked worse if he'd set it on an anvil and let someone smash it with a sledge hammer, but it also might not have.

And he was the lucky one. Mike was down and groaning and clutching his belly. Blood poured out between his fingers. A butcher couldn't have gutted a lamb more neatly—or more thoroughly.

"Fuck!" Chaim said. "Oh, fuck!" He pulled a hanky out of his pocket. He tried to wipe some of the blood off his own face, then stuck the cotton square on top of his head to slow down the flow there. Scalp wounds always bled like mad bastards and looked worse than they were. He knew that. If this one hadn't also cracked his skull, he'd get over it. If it had, he was screwed and he couldn't do anything about it any which way.

His ruined hand . . . He had wound dressings in a pouch on his belt. Trying to open one one-handed was something no wounded, half-addled man should have done—except he had no choice. He did a shitty job—there was no other word for it—of wrapping gauze around the wreckage. Then he had to do what he could for his friend.

All that time safe. All that time lucky. Both of them. He hadn't caught any real wound at all, and Mike only the one in his leg. Well, that streak got smashed to hell in a split second. Mike had wound dressings, too, but he had more wound than they could hope to dress. He also had a couple of morphine syrettes. Chaim injected him with both of them. Even that was plainly sending a very small boy to do a man's job, but it was the last favor Chaim could give his buddy.

He'd thrown away the second empty syrette when he wished he'd given himself some of it. Too late. He didn't have one of his own, even if he had reminded himself to get hold of one. His hand was screaming louder every second. He wanted to scream himself. He wanted to, and a moment later he did. It wasn't as if he hadn't earned the right.

Mike's groans quieted. Either the morphine was easing his pain or he was dying. Maybe both those things were true at once. Chaim didn't know. Even if he had, he couldn't have done anything about it.

"*Señor* . . . ," someone behind him said: one of the Spaniards who'd joined the Abe Lincolns. Chaim turned to face him. The kid blanched and crossed himself. "*¡Madre de Dios!*" he gabbled. As Chaim had seen with La Martellita, Catholicism stuck to even the Spaniards who reckoned themselves most aggressively modern and secular.

"I seem worse than I am," Chaim said, hoping like hell he was telling the truth. "See to Mike first, *por favor*. I gave him morphine, but. . . ." He started to spread his hands, but arrested the gesture before it was well begun. Moving the left one, even a little, made it hurt more than it already did.

"You have not had morphine yourself?" the Spaniard asked. Chaim shook his head. That hurt, too. The kid took a syrette out of his own belt pouch and stuck him. Then he bent down beside Mike Carroll. He crossed himself again—a quick, convulsive motion. He looked up at Chaim. "I do not believe he can live, *Señor*."

"Do what you can for him." Chaim sounded eerily calm. The drug was hitting almost as hard as the mortar bomb had. He still hurt, but it was as if his body were several kilometers from his brain.

The Spaniard yelled for stretcher-bearers for Carroll. Then he said, "And I will take you back to an aid station. Can you walk?"

"I don't know. We'll both find out, won't we?" Chaim said. What would they do with his left hand? No—what would they do *to* it? Would he keep it? If he didn't, how would he, how could he, get along without it? The morphine made all the questions seem much less urgent than they would have without it. He got to his feet. "I'm sorry, Mike. I'm sorry as hell." He draped his good arm over the Spaniard's shoulder. "Let's go. We'll see how far I get."

He made it all the way to the aid station. That surprised him, and seemed to surprise his helper more. By the time he got there, though, the shot was wearing off. But a doctor took one look at the blood all over his face and at the dripping bandage on his hand and stuck him once more. The pain receded again.

Morphine or no morphine, he whimpered when the man peeled off the bandage and examined the ruin of his hand. "Can you save it?" Chaim asked.

"*No sé, Señor*," the man replied. "It does not looked good, but . . . Well, perhaps."

By the way he spoke, Chaim realized he hadn't even intended to try till he heard the question. "Do what you can, please," Chaim said. "I don't think I can use a rifle one-handed, and I want to get even with Sanjurjo's *putos*."

The ghost of a smile briefly bent the doctor's lips. "Let me do what I can here. Then I will send you back to Madrid. Dr. Alvarez there has done some things that surprised more than a few people."

"*Gracias. De la corazón de mi corazón, gracias*." Chaim did the best he could with his clumsy Spanish. *From the heart of my heart?* He wouldn't have said it that way in English.

He got the message across. "*De nada, Señor*," the doctor said. This time, his smile lingered long enough to let Chaim be sure he really saw it. The man went on, "Now I will give you ether and make some preliminary repairs. Then—Madrid."

"Madrid," Chaim echoed. The ether rag came down on his face.

He thought he would go back to Madrid in an ambulance. He rode in the back of a beat-up Citroën truck with three other wounded men. He was groggy and dopey and hurt a lot in spite of the dope. His hand was swaddled in thick white bandages that got redder and redder as the truck rattled along. His scalp, he discovered, was also properly bandaged. He'd had his hair clipped or shaved off, too. No doubt he looked stupid as hell.

When they got to the hospital, a male nurse asked, "Which is Dr. Alvarez's patient?"

"*Aquí estoy*," Chaim answered. *Here I am.*

Dr. Alvarez proved to speak English with an accent much more elegant than Chaim's. He'd studied medicine in London. He cut off the bandages and examined the wound and what the sawbones at the aid station—a man whose name Chaim had never learned—had done to it. Thoughtfully, the English-trained Spaniard rubbed his thin, dark mustache with a forefinger.

"What do you think, Doc? Can it stay on?" Chaim asked. Speaking English was a relief. Half addled by pain and morphine, he suspected he would have made an even worse hash of Spanish than usual.

"Oh, yes. I am certain of it—as long as we can avoid an infection in the wound, anyway," Dr. Alvarez said. "And I hope . . . No, I believe . . . I believe that, once the surgical repairs are complete, you will have some function in it. Not full function, perhaps, but you will be able to use your thumb and some of your fingers."

"Surgical repairs?" Chaim repeated. "You're gonna carve on me some more?"

"It is necessary," Alvarez replied. Maybe he thought Chaim didn't want more surgery and he had to talk him into it.

If he did, he was dead wrong. "Let's get on with it, then," Chaim said. The operating room was spotless and had the antiseptic smell of carbolic acid. As long as Nationalist planes didn't bomb the hospital, Chaim figured he'd come through fine. He smiled at the nurse who put the ether cone over his nose and mouth, and she had gray hair and a face like a horse. Oblivion swallowed him.

ANASTAS MOURADIAN PLAYED indifferent chess. Even if it wasn't the microcosm of war people who didn't know much about war (or, sometimes, about chess) often claimed, it was a way to make time go by when you weren't flying. It was less popular than swilling vodka, but easier on the liver.

He found himself playing more now that he was flying with Isa Mogamedov. The Azeri not only didn't drink like a Russian, he didn't even drink like an Armenian. He hardly drank at all, in fact. Stas wondered if he was a pious enough Muslim to find alcohol sinful.

Mogamedov didn't say he was, not even when Russian pilots and bomb-aimers teased him for his abstemiousness. Stas didn't tease him and did play chess with him. Isa would have been an idiot to admit he was a serious believer. The war had put a damper on the Soviet Union's aggressive atheism, but hadn't stifled it altogether. Mogamedov just smiled and shrugged and said things like, "If I drink a lot, I get sick, so I don't drink a lot."

He played better than Stas did, but not so much better that Stas had no hope of beating him. He managed a victory about one game in five, which encouraged him to keep playing even though he got trounced most of the time. He sometimes wondered whether Isa threw a game every now and then to keep him interested, but asking about that might have been even less polite than inquiring about religion, so he didn't.

Naturally, all the flyers who played fancied themselves as reincarnations of Botvinnik or Tal. Mogamedov beat most of them as easily as he handled Stas. Pretty soon, instead of asking for games, they contented themselves with kibitzing when he and Mouradian sat on opposite sides of the board.

As far as Stas was concerned, kibitzers were only slightly more welcome than German flak. Most of their advice and criticism came his way, because even the dullest of them could see that Isa didn't need much help—if that was what it was—from them.

Stas managed to get into a complicated, crowded midgame position while only a pawn down. He felt moderately pleased; as often as not, the writing was already on the wall by this time. He scratched behind one ear while pondering what to try next. After some thought, he moved a knight.

"Oh, you wood-pusher!" exclaimed one of the vultures hovering over the board.

"When I want your opinion, Arkady, I'll beat it out of you," Stas said with his sweetest smile.

Isa sat corpse-still while he was studying a game. His face might have been carved from limestone for all it gave away. When he'd made up his mind, he reached out and took hold of a bishop. It slid across the board and assassinated Stas' king's rook's pawn.

"See?" Arkady said. "What did I tell you?"

"Noisy in here, isn't it?" Stas said to nobody in particular. Expecting the Russian to take a hint was like expecting the Second Coming day after tomorrow. You could do it, but you'd soon end up disappointed. Braining Arkady with a vodka bottle might have won his attention. It would have made people talk about Stas, though.

He moved the knight again. This time, the move served some obvious purpose: it threatened the bishop that hadn't gone pawn-killing. Isa pulled it back one square. Stas' knight advanced again, this time to threaten a rook. Isa slid the rook along the rear rank till it protected the bishop from behind. Of itself, Stas' hand moved the knight yet again. This time, it forked Isa's rook and his queen.

Mogamedov smiled, something he hardly ever did during a game. "You saw all that from the beginning, didn't you?" He didn't sound angry or accusing: more like a father who'd just watched a boy do something important on his own, and do it well.

"I did." Stas, by contrast, sounded amazed, because he was. "It was like . . . like . . . the sky opening up in front of me, or something."

Isa nodded. "It feels that way, yes, when you get the long sight of the board. You should try for it more often."

"I didn't try this time," Stas said. "It just happened, that's all." He felt like an innocent bystander, the way he might have if he were suddenly to witness a highway smashup.

"You *planned* all that?" Not so innocent bystander Arkady, by contrast, sounded like someone who didn't believe it for a minute.

"*Da*. I did," Mouradian answered. He'd seen something like ten moves ahead. He'd never done anything like that before. No matter what Isa said, he doubted he ever would again, either. His head wasn't geared that way—only it had been, this glorious once.

Isa Mogamedov raised an eyebrow in Arkady's direction. "Just because you can't do something yourself, Comrade, that doesn't necessarily mean other people aren't able to."

The other, less obnoxious, kibitzers whooped. One of them whistled softly, which might have stung Arkady more. The Russian's face and ears went hot and red. He stormed away. Without any fuss, Isa moved his queen. Stas took the rook. The game went on. He managed to hang on to the advantage the knight's tour had given him and to win.

Afterwards, though, when the board was put away and the kibitzers had disappeared, he spoke in a low voice: "You made an enemy there, I'm afraid."

"Who? Arkaday?" Mogamedov snapped his fingers. "That's how worried about it I am."

"He's a Russian. He'll know more Russians." Stas spoke with the resigned annoyance of a nominally equal citizen in a Soviet state where Russians still dominated by weight of numbers and weight of history.

Mogamedov shrugged. "If they stick me in a gulag, I'll probably die pretty soon. If I keep flying against the Nazis, I'll probably die pretty soon, too. So what difference does it make? Chances are it won't be any fun either way."

Stas opened his mouth. Then, realizing he had nothing much to say to that, he closed it again. After a moment, he managed, "Well, you've got me there."

"We're fucked, is what we are," Isa said.

"Can't argue with that, either," Stas said. "But if that's the way you feel, you ought to drink more."

"I don't enjoy it," the Azeri answered. "I feel like an idiot while I'm drunk. I act like an idiot while I'm drunk, too. And the next morning I feel like dogshit. So what's the point?"

He didn't say anything about how sinful alcohol was, or about how the Prophet had forbidden it. No, his reasons were rational, the kind of reasons a Russian teetotaler (assuming such a furry fish existed) might advance. His reasons were also the kind a Muslim might bring forth when he was talking with a Christian he didn't fully trust.

They'd flown together. They'd relied on each other for their lives. They'd had to, or the NKVD would have disposed of them if German fighter pilots or flak gunners didn't beat the Chekists to the punch. But Mogamedov didn't think Stas wouldn't grab the chance to feed him to the men who ran the camps.

That saddened Stas. It made him mad. It didn't surprise him one bit. He wasn't sure he could count on Isa Mogamedov that way, either. The fewer chances a Soviet citizen took, the less he revealed himself to the wider world, the better off he was likely to stay. If he made fewer friends than he might have otherwise, what was that but one more part of the price he paid for survival?

PEGGY DRUCE WONDERED whom the Republicans would run against Franklin Delano Roosevelt when the leaves turned in 1944. She assumed FDR would run again if the war was still on, and the war didn't look like stopping any time soon.

She shrugged, there alone in the front room of her comfortable Main Line house. The question seemed important and unreal at the same time. With the election at the tail end of next year, there wasn't a GOP field to start betting on yet. Even if there had been, somebody was still liable to pop out of nowhere, the way Willkie had in 1940. Almost a year and a half away? That was a couple of eternities in politics.

She wished Herb were at home. They could hash things out together. He was bound to have an opinion about what kind of candidate the Republicans would field, and about what the fellow's chances might be. Whatever Herb's opinion was, he would have some good, solid reasons to give it weight. He always did.

But Herb was in . . . where was Herb this time? Texas, Peggy thought. Or was it Alabama? Wherever he was, he was slashing red tape and saving Uncle Sam money. Uncle Sam ought to be grateful, but Peggy didn't labor under the illusion that he would be. Chances were the government would be so amazed anyone could save it money that it wouldn't believe such a thing was really happening.

Peggy still wondered what all the ivory-tower chemists or physicists or whatever they'd been were doing now that their gravy train was derailed. Billions of dollars? Billions of dollars on a super-duper bomb that might not work and would take years and years to build even if it did?

You had to be practical. Herb understood that, understood it down to the ground. You couldn't expect people like Einstein to. He lived in the ivory tower, not just in it but on the very top floor. Okay, he was good at throwing equations around. Fine. Wonderful. Equations cost nothing but paper and ink, or maybe a blackboard and chalk. When you started dealing with the real world, you needed people like Herb Druce.

No, the government would never give him the credit he deserved for slaying the vicious boondoggle. Peggy did. Some money was bound to get wasted. Wasting money was one of the things governments were for. That only got worse during wartime. But you had to do what you could to keep from wasting more than you could help.

She smiled as she lit a cigarette. Feeling good for Herb, feeling good about him, was good. She needed that; she could feel herself needing it. They still weren't where she wished they would be.

Blowing a stream of smoke up at the ceiling, she wondered if they'd ever get there again. No way to know. There might be a scab over the wound in their trust, but the wound remained. One of these days, it might heal up and turn into a scar. She kept hoping it would.

She smoked the cigarette down to a very short butt, then stubbed it out in the brass baseball-glove ashtray that Herb liked. Then she turned on the radio. The dials lighted up right away. She knew she would have to wait for the tubes inside the big wooden cabinet to warm up before sound came out.

When it did, she changed the station as fast as she could turn the dial. That fast, bouncy jazz might be fine for jitterbugging soldiers on leave, and for the girls they'd sling over their shoulders or between their legs. Peggy wanted something with a real tune to it, though, not that pounding backbeat powered by bass fiddle and drums.

What she wanted was one thing. What she could find was liable to be a different kettle of crabs. A comic with a raspy voice and a Brooklyn accent—he seemed to want you to think he was Jimmy Durante's cousin—made stupid jokes about how crowded trains were these days.

Trains *were* crowded. With gas rationing so tight, you couldn't drive to Grandpa's if the old man lived two states away. You had to take the train. And soldiers and sailors on leave or on official business had priority for seats. Okay, you could crack jokes about that. But comparing yourself to the cheese in a sandwich was just, well, cheesy. That was a joke Peggy made for herself, and it was a lot funnier than the ones Mr. would-be Durante was coming out with.

She didn't waste more than a minute listening to him. On the next station she found, an earnest woman was explaining how to can vegetables. "Your victory garden will turn into a defeat unless you get the greatest possible use from it," she declared.

That was bound to be true, but it wasn't interesting, at least not to Peggy. She found some classical music. Stations were cautious about putting Wagner and other Nazi favorites on the air. If Germany and the USA did go to war, they'd probably disappear from broadcasts. But this was Vivaldi's *The Four Seasons*. Yes, Mussolini was on Hitler's side and Vivaldi was Italian, but he'd been dead so long it hardly mattered any more.

The Vivaldi was pleasant; as with Bach, you could listen very closely and admire how everything worked and how it all fit together—or you could just listen. Peggy just listened for a while. Then she decided she'd rather hear something else, so she looked for another station.

She found a detergent drama. Mama had just found out her daughter was falling for a guy with black-market connections. Music that had nothing to do with Vivaldi swelled dramatically as Mama tried to figure out whether to turn him in or to start rolling in lamb chops and other goodies she couldn't hope to get honestly.

Peggy was sure Mama would rat on Rocky. That was the Right Thing to Do, so it was what people in soap operas did. Everything would come out fine in the end anyway, but that was how things worked in soap operas, too. A real Mama probably would have run out and got some mint jelly to go with the lamb chops, but people in Radioland didn't do stuff like that.

She didn't care enough to keep listening. Another twist of the dial captured a quiz show. Herb liked those. He was good at them, too—often better than the contestants. The capital of South Dakota? The King of Prussia during the Seven Years' War? The American League batting champion in 1921? He'd come out with the answer before a contestant could ring a bell. And he'd be right, too. Herb knew all kinds of weird things. That probably made him better as a government examiner.

Peggy also knew a lot of weird things. The difference between her and Herb was that she didn't passionately care about the capital of South Dakota, while he did. She supposed it was the same kind of difference as the one between people who played cards for the fun of it and the ones who wanted to serve up their opponents on a platter with an apple in their mouth. She nodded to herself. She played a decent game of bridge, and she enjoyed it. Herb fought for every point as if he were crawling under barbed wire to make a trench raid on the Hun.

So she could take quiz shows or leave them alone. She soon left this one alone. She finally found some news. The Navy said its submarines had sunk a Japanese destroyer and two freighters. That sounded good, but not good enough. She didn't think the war in the Pacific could have been much more mishandled if she were running it herself.

Then the newsman said, "The RAF used American-built Flying Fortresses to conduct daylight raids against German manufacturing centers. The bombers, also known as B-17s, performed well and inflicted heavy damage. They have also been used by our Army Air Force to strike Japanese-held Pacific islands."

Hitler had made Spain a proving ground for his planes and tanks. Now the *Führer* was on the receiving end as FDR did the same thing. What went around came around. Peggy would have bet dollars to doughnuts that old Adolf thought it was better to give than to receive.

# Chapter 22

A couple of miles behind Alistair Walsh, the English artillery had lined up as many guns as the artillerists could get their hands on, all of them hub to hub. They'd piled up as many shells for them as they could, too. And now they were shooting them at the Fritzes in western Belgium.

They'd started two days earlier, and they showed no signs of stopping. The staff sergeant hadn't been at the Battle of the Somme; he hadn't been old enough to join the Army in 1916. The bombardment before the Tommies went over the top must have been a lot like this, though.

The Battle of the Somme, of course, had been a bloody disaster, in both the slang and the literal senses of the word. A week's worth of shelling hadn't been enough to knock out German cannon and, more important, German machine guns. Something like 50,000 got killed trying to advance the first day of the attack, and the numbers didn't shrink much in the days that followed. And all they acquired were a very few square miles of muck and corpses pulverized as thoroughly as modern science knew how.

He hoped—Christ, he prayed, and he wasn't a man in the habit of praying—things would go better this time when the order to advance came. The tank was supposed to have consigned trench warfare and days-long bombardments to the same dustbin of history that held cavalry charges and infantry squares and catapults. Tanks made warfare mobile again. So all the big brains insisted, anyhow.

Then the Germans brought their Tigers into Belgium. Tigers smashed English tanks and French *chars* as if their armor were tinfoil. Not a single Allied fighting vehicle had a gun that could punch through a Tiger's frontal plates.

Tigers were slow. They weren't very maneuverable. They were so wide and heavy, they strained bridges and sometimes even broke them. Going forward, they left a lot to be desired. But God help you if you were in a Crusader or a Matilda and you had to try to shift them.

God hadn't helped enough. Thanks to the Tigers and their own good soldiering and general stubbornness, the Germans had kept England and France from taking back most of Belgium.

Thus the reversion to the last war's tactics. *If we kill them all and smash the whole countryside to rubble*, the thinking seemed to be, *we'll be able to walk through them and then get on with the war.*

It might work. Stranger things had happened . . . hadn't they? The generals seemed confident. Of course, from everything Walsh had heard, they'd seemed confident at the Somme, too. Even if this did work, would England and France have to repeat it ten miles farther east, and then another ten miles later after that? If they did, would any Belgians not in exile be left alive to reclaim their country? Would any country be left for them to reclaim?

Fascinating questions, all of them, but not questions even the most senior NCO was in any position to answer. Walsh mainly worried about what would happen once the shelling stopped and the officers' whistles ordered the advance. Most of the Tigers, he assumed, would survive. A few would take direct hits on the turret or engine decking and go up, but most would remain.

What about the ordinary *Landsers* in their holes? Whether the guns could do for them would determine whether this was a replay of the Somme or something with a happier ending from the English point of view.

At the Somme, even English troops in sectors where the Fritzes got smashed had trouble going forward because the ground was so torn up. When they did advance, the ground complicated resupply or made it impossible. Now there were tanks and Bren-gun carriers and other tracked vehicles that could cope with the worst terrain. That would help.

Not all the shells here flew from west to east. The Germans shot back whenever they saw the chance—and, no doubt, whenever they managed to get shells to their big guns. Some of it was counterbattery fire. That didn't bother Walsh. When the buggers in *Feldgrau* took their whacks at the English front line, though . . .

All he could do was hunker down and hope nothing landed close enough to murder him. He'd picked up a Blighty wound in each fight so far. If he got hit again, he couldn't count on being so lucky three times in a row.

RAF bombers pounded the Germans, too, the usual planes by night and a few squadrons of American Fortresses by day. Spitfires escorted the day bombers, but the *Luftwaffe* savaged them anyhow. Watching one fall out of the sky in a flat spin with two engines on fire made Walsh think there might be more rugged ways to make a living than the one he'd found for himself.

Little by little, the English bombardment lifted. It didn't die out altogether, but went after more distant targets. Ever so cautiously, Walsh looked out over the forward lip of the hole in which he crouched. If people ever sent a rocket to the Moon, whoever peered out from the cabin might see a landscape that looked a lot like this one. Oh, he wouldn't spot shattered tree stumps on the Moon—or Walsh didn't think so, anyhow. And all those battered coils of barbed wire also struck him as unlikely . . . unless the Lunarians were fighting a particularly vicious war amongst themselves. And if there were Lunarians, they might be.

Tanks rumbled and clanked forward. Infantrymen trotted along with them to protect them from determined Fritzes with grenades and Molotov cocktails or other handheld unpleasantnesses. Walsh wasn't sorry his company hadn't been told off for that little job. They'd done it before. Whenever you took the lead, you wanted to make sure you had all your policies paid up.

*Blam! . . . Clang! . . . Boom!* Walsh didn't see the enemy tank or anti-tank gun that opened up on the English armor. He recognized the flat, harsh bark of an 88, but wasn't sure whether the dreaded German beast was mounted on a Tiger or in an emplacement all that gunnery hadn't taken out. Either way, the *clang!* was a round penetrating a tank's vitals, while the *boom!* was all the ammo inside the iron coffin going up at once. The turret flew off the stricken tank. It came down fifteen or twenty feet away, and squashed a luckless Tommy. The poor beggar was doubtless dead before he knew it, not that that would be much consolation for him and his mates.

*Blam! . . . Clang! . . . Boom!* Another English tank turned into a burning hulk. The surviving tanks started shooting, but at what? Walsh still couldn't see the cannon that was murdering them. Then German MG-34s and the newer, still more vicious MG-42s opened up on the foot soldiers stumbling across the broken ground.

Walsh had hated MG-34s since he first made their acquaintance in the war's early days. They were as portable as Bren guns—you could even pick one up and fire it like a rifle if you had to—but put three or four times as much lead in the air. MG-42s were even worse. They fired so fast, you couldn't really hear the separate rounds. An MG-42 sounded like a buzz saw, and cut men down like a buzz saw, too.

Officers' whistles shrilled. "Follow me, men!" a captain shouted. "Our armor will lead us into the Germans' rear!" He clambered up out of his hole and dogtrotted after the tanks and the men who'd advanced with them.

*Follow me!* almost always produced the desired effect. So did a calculated show of bravery like the one the captain gave. "Come on, lads!" Walsh called to the Tommies within earshot. "No help for it—let's be at 'em!" He got out of his own lovely foxhole and went after that captain.

He'd already seen more than enough to make him sure the attack wouldn't do what the generals hoped it would. The bombardment hadn't smashed the Nazis' tanks or wiped out their machine-gun nests. Which meant neither foot soldiers nor armor would be seeing the Germans' rear any time soon.

To show that to the brass hats, though, the Army had to pay the butcher's bill. Walsh slipped in some mud and sprawled on his belly. A couple of rounds from a German machine gun cracked through the air where he probably would have been if he hadn't taken a header.

Another man was down not far away, wailing and clutching at his thigh. Walsh crawled over to him. He did what he could to dress the wound. He gave the Tommy morphine. He stayed with the poor fellow as long as he could, or a little longer. It let him do something useful that didn't put him in too much danger of getting killed. At last, reluctantly, he had to return to the attack. He could already see it wasn't going anywhere. Eventually, the blokes who gave the orders would realize the same thing. His job now was to stay alive till they did. If their orders in the meantime would let him.

**A SOFT BED.** Clean sheets. A shower ever day. Regular meals with enough food in them. Except for a scalp laceration and a mangled hand, Chaim Weinberg would have said he hadn't had it so good since he got to Spain.

Once the scalp wound got cleaned up and stitched, it healed on its own. X-rays showed that that mortar fragment might have dented his hard head, but hadn't cracked it.

His hand was a more complicated, more painful business. Dr. Alvarez kept doing things to it, waiting till it got halfway better, then doing more things. When Chaim complained about operations every couple of weeks, Alvarez said, "I will stop if you like. You will have a claw with a usable thumb. Is that what you desire?"

"What I want is for the goddamn mortar bomb to've come down somewhere else," Chaim answered. "I'd still be in one piece, and they wouldn't've had to plant poor Mike." Carroll had died on the way back to the aid station. Word took a while getting to Chaim in Madrid, but he knew now.

"I cannot do anything about that now, nor can you," Dr. Alvarez said patiently. "I *can* do something about your hand—if you wish me to proceed, of course."

"Yeah, go ahead," Chaim said. "I'm sick of getting carved on, but go ahead. You give me something I can use well enough to help me handle a rifle, that's what I want."

More ether. More pain. More morphine. He wondered if he'd end up a junkie by the time this was all over with. That was one more thing he'd just have to worry about later.

He was pretty doped up after the latest surgery, his hand elevated and wrapped in enough bandages to make a suit of clothes with two pairs of pants, when La Martellita walked into his room. "Wow," he said. "*Hola*, beautiful! I hope like hell you're real, not something I'm imagining on account of the drugs."

"Of course I am part of objective reality. There is nothing else." La Martellita sounded absolutely certain—but then, when didn't she?

Chaim started to giggle. "Yeah, you're you, all right." No matter how luscious she looked, that uncompromising tone couldn't belong to anyone else.

She sent him a severe look. "I came to see you because you were wounded in the service of the Republic."

If she came to see everybody who got hurt on the Republican side, Internationals and Spaniards alike would jump out of their trenches and charge Marshal Sanjurjo's machine guns. Even woozy from morphine, Chaim knew he'd only piss her off if he said so. Male horniness was a part of objective reality she didn't much care for.

Instead, he asked, "How's your Russian boyfriend? Will he get mad if he finds out you came to see me?"

Her sculpted nostrils flared. "I am not his property. I am every bit as much a free citizen as he is."

"It's okay by me, sweetie," Chaim assured her. "How about the kid?"

"He is well. He is happy," La Martellita said. *And he doesn't miss you one bit*. Blunt though she was, she didn't say that, but it hung in the air anyhow.

"Good. That's good," Chaim said. "If you come again, I'd like to get the chance to see him."

"Again?" Now La Martellita sounded surprised, as if he should have known he was damn lucky she'd come once. *I guess I should have*, he thought. But she grudged him a nod. "*Pues, puede ser*," she said. *Well, maybe*. He knew he had to be content with that. It was more than he'd expected to get.

He tried a different question: "And what's going on with the Party these days?"

That got him more than he'd expected, too. La Martellita gave forth with a blow-by-blow account of all the Marxist-Leninist-Stalinist wrangling she knew about in Madrid, in Barcelona, and in Moscow over the past couple of months. By the verve she used to narrate, she might have been broadcasting the Joe Louis-Max Schmeling heavyweight championship fight. She was just as sure about who was the good guy and who was the crook as any of the clowns screaming into their microphones had been then.

Chaim didn't have to listen very hard. He could just watch her and admire her. He even seemed to be doing that from a distance considerably greater than the one between him in bed and her at the bedside. He knew why, too. Morphine was a wonderful drug in all kinds of ways. It blunted pain that laughed at medications like aspirin.

Most of the time, though, seeing and hearing La Martellita would have made Chaim want to drag her down and jump on her. Not now. Now his admiration, while still there, felt far more abstract, almost as if he were approving of the way a perfect statue had been carved. With morphine sliding through his veins, he just wasn't horny.

Anything that could make a guy not horny while he was around La Martellita was heap big medicine indeed. Chaim admired the drug in much the same way as he admired the woman.

In due course, she said, "You're probably lucky you're laid up. If you weren't, your big mouth would only get you into trouble."

"I wouldn't be surprised," Chaim answered, not without pride. "I never did think Party doctrine was like going to Mass, and that only the priests were sure to have it right." One other thing morphine could do, as he'd already discovered, was to make you say (or let you say, depending on how you looked at things) what you were thinking.

In a land where the Party called the shots, that was beyond merely dangerous. La Martellita's kissable mouth narrowed to a thin, red line. "I am going to do you a large favor," she said. "I am going to remember you are my son's father. Because I am going to remember that, I am not going to ask you what you mean when you make such counterrevolutionary cracks."

"*Gracias.*" Chaim meant it, which saddened him. She really *was* doing him a favor. He'd heard of men in the Soviet Union who ended up on trial because of stuff they mumbled when coming out of anesthesia after surgery. He didn't know for sure that such stories were true, but he believed them. Some stuff, you couldn't make up. It was too unlikely.

"*De nada*," La Martellita said, in such a way as to remind him that, if it was nothing, it was a large nothing. "And now I had better go."

Away she went. Her behind would have drawn a backfield-in-motion penalty on any gridiron in the USA (Canada, too). No doubt she was reminding Chaim of what he couldn't get his hands on any more. She couldn't know that the morphine made him stop worrying about whether he got his hands on it or not.

After her exit, Dr. Alvarez came up and asked Chaim, "You know that woman?"

"Nah," he said blandly. "Who was she, anyhow? Kinda cute."

His deadpan was good enough to make Alvarez start to answer him. The sawbones stopped with his mouth hanging open and sent Chaim an exasperated stare. "You are being difficult on purpose."

"Darn right I am," Chaim agreed. "It's one of the things I do best. You don't believe me, ask La Martellita."

"You do know her, then," Alvarez said in now-we're-getting-somewhere tones.

"Doc, I knocked her up. I was married to her for a little while," Chaim replied. "What about it?"

For the first time, he impressed Alvarez for something other than the sorry state of his smashed left hand. One of the surgeon's eyebrows twitched a few millimeters. "Oh," he said. "You're *that* fellow."

"That's me." Chaim nodded. "Uh, can I have another shot, please? Damn thing's starting to bite me again."


AT WILHELMSHAVEN, JULIUS LEMP accepted his superiors' congratulations for sinking the Royal Navy submarine. He shaved off the scraggly beard he'd grown on the U-30's latest cruise. And he talked shop with the maintenance crews who brought the U-boat up to fighting trim again.

One of the men working on the engines was Gustav the diesel mechanic. Lemp passed the time of day with him as if he'd never got called on the carpet for asking the mechanic a few questions he still thought harmless. He never let on that he knew talking with Gustav had landed him in the soup before. That was how you played the game. The less innocent you really were, the more you pretended.

He got his trouser snake tended to at the officers' brothel. He made damn sure he stuck to the business of pleasure there, and that he said nothing even remotely political. Like Gustav, and like the veteran petty officer behind the bar at the officers' club, the girls were bound to report to somebody. He judged that particular somebody was much more likely to be a *Gestapo* or SD operative than the base commandant.

In due course, he found himself back at the bar. He'd known he would. You could drink longer than you could screw. Plenty of officers, from ensigns for whom that might almost not have been true to a commodore for whom it certainly was, filled the tables.

That gray petty officer was tending bar when Lemp walked in. "I hear you had good luck, sir," he said. "First one's on the house."

"Thanks," Lemp said. "Now that makes me want to go out and sink things, by God." He waited for the barkeep's chuckle, then went on, "Let me have a schnapps, in that case."

"Here you go, sir."

Lemp knocked back the drink. It tasted more like something that ought to go into a cigarette lighter than proper booze. It went down his throat as if someone had already lit it. If it hadn't been free, he would have complained about it—or, if he'd already had a few, he might have thrown it in the petty officer's face.

As things were, he set coins on the bar and said, "That hit the spot. Let me have a refill—and pour yourself one, too."

"That's nice of you, sir," the petty officer said. "I don't usually—if I did, I'd get too smashed to do my job. But I will this time." He fixed two fresh drinks. They both came from the same bottle he'd used to give Lemp the one on the house. The man behind the bar clinked glasses with him. They drank together.

"Strong stuff," Lemp remarked, in lieu of saying *rotgut*.

"*Ja.*" The barkeep nodded and shrugged at the same time, which made him look like something out of a bad movie. "What can I do, though? This is as good as we're able to get."

"Well, that's a shame," Lemp said. Anything more, anything like *The Reich is in deep water if* Kriegsmarine *men have to guzzle paint thinner like this*, would have made the petty officer write a note as soon as he stepped away from the bar.

With a nod, Lemp ambled over to the tables and sat down at one. Nobody else was using that little pocket of space. He wouldn't have minded company, but he got the feeling most of the officers in the club didn't want his just then. They were pouring down booze with the dedication of men who intended to be swallowing aspirin tablets in the morning.

Here and there, they talked with one another in groups of two or three. They kept their voices down. Lemp made a point of not seeming to listen. He had the feeling that he might have an accident when he went outside if any of those little groups of officers decided he was trying to eavesdrop. Would it be a fatal accident or only an instructive one? That came from the large group of questions more interesting to ask than to answer.

A commander got up from one of those tables. He raised his arm in the Party salute. *"Heil Hitler!"* he said in normal tones that seemed abnormally loud, and made for the door.

*"Heil!"* echoed his comrades in . . . well, in whatever. They also raised their voices to come out with the Party greeting and farewell. Then they lowered them again and went back to talking about something that didn't need so much noise. Whatever it was, Lemp couldn't make it out. He could, and did, make a point of not seeming to try.

Whenever men got up to leave or joined groups of friends, they went on exchanging *"Heil!"*'s. A cynical man might have said they were making a point of doing it so no one with a suspicious, cynical mind would suspect whatever they talked about in those near-whispers.

Lemp didn't suspect them. Of course not. He didn't have anything in the least resembling a cynical, suspicious mind. Again, of course not.

While ostentatiously not listening, he got to the bottom of his next schnapps. Foul though the stuff was, it called for reinforcements. He heard it calling more clearly than he heard anything that was going on at those other tables. He raised an index finger and waited for the petty officer behind the bar to notice him.

It didn't take long—the fellow was back there for a reason. A very young sailor, so young he hardly needed to shave, carried Lemp's drink over to him on a tray. "Here you go, sir," he said.

"*Danke schön*," Lemp answered, trying not to laugh in the kid's face. That broad dialect said the youngster was just off a Bavarian farm, a place about as far from the ocean as any in Germany could be. Well, plenty of Bavarians had turned into tolerable sailors—better than tolerable, even—once the *Kriegsmarine* knocked them into shape. Chances were this fresh-faced lad would, too. But, in the meantime, he still sounded like somebody just off a farm from the back of beyond. A casting director in a comedy couldn't have found anybody who talked less like a sailor.

More of that wicked schnapps snarled down Lemp's throat. The cynical, suspicious mind—the one he didn't have at all, of course—wondered whether the kid worked here *because* he talked like that. If such an obvious bumpkin fetched you drinks, wouldn't you go on talking about whatever you'd been talking about? Wouldn't you assume he wouldn't pay your words any mind and couldn't understand them even if he did?

Sure you would. And wouldn't you be surprised when the *Sicherheitsdienst* started whacking you with pipes and rubber hoses and pulling out your toenails a few days from now? Wouldn't you wonder how Himmler's hounds had got their teeth into you? Sure you would. And would you even remember the hick with the thick South German accent who'd brought you a fresh drink in the officers' club? Sure you wouldn't.

*Maybe I'm all wet. Maybe I'm full of it. Maybe I'm seeing shadows where nothing's casting them*, Lemp thought. But he didn't believe it, not for a minute. Things didn't happen by accident, not in the National Socialist *Grossdeutsches Reich* they didn't.

And if all the little gaggles of officers talking to one another and anxious not to be overheard meant anything . . . If they did mean anything, they most likely meant the people who ran the National Socialist *Grossdeutsches Reich* had reason to try to find out what they were saying.

As part of one of those little gaggles, Lemp might have had a thing or two to say himself. Whether the other officers would have taken him seriously was a different question. They might have figured him for an *agent provocateur*. For that matter, some of the gaggles would already have an *agent provocateur* or two in them. If you made the mistake of joining the plots he spun, you were a dead man—a stupid dead man—talking.

Lemp decided he wasn't so bad off sitting here by himself. All he had to worry about was this lousy schnapps. He gulped his glass dry, then raised a finger to show the bartender he wanted to worry about some more of it.

THE SUN ROSE off to Vaclav Jezek's right. The Republican and Nationalist lines here ran almost due east and west. He could see farther and farther: not just the inside of the shell hole where he lay, but also the pocked landscape that stretched out to and beyond Marshal Sanjurjo's barbed wire and entrenchments. If he turned to peer back over his shoulder, he could see his own countrymen's entrenchments and barbed wire, too. They looked the same as the enemy's.

What he had to remember was, the farther he could see, the farther from which he could be seen. He'd done what he could to make that harder. The antitank rifle had bits of branches wired to the barrel to break up its outline (the wire was carefully rusted so the sun wouldn't flash off it). His helmet had more foliage stuck to it. Strips of burlap and still more greenery fixed to his tunic meant that, from any distance, he didn't look like a man at all. He'd rubbed his face and hands with dirt. A sniper who wasn't careful wouldn't have a long career.

But even a sniper who was careful could have something go wrong. Or the enemy could have somebody uncommonly good hunting him. The first thing he knew of that would be the last thing he knew of the world.

He pressed his eye up to the telescopic sight. There were Sanjurjo's men, all right. The ones at any distance behind the forward trenches went about their business without a care in the world. Artillery or mortars might hurt them, but they couldn't do anything about those. They didn't worry about riflemen, who could hit them only by accident.

Jezek could hit them on purpose. They had to have family in the provinces, the way he had family in Prague. If their kin lived on this side of the line, they might not have heard from them for as long as he'd gone without a letter from home.

But so what? They were still Fascist shitheads, followers of their fat almost-*Führer*. Vaclav smiled, remembering all the honors with which the Republic had showered him for exterminating General Franco. He'd get even more if he could blow Marshal Sanjurjo's head off. *And if ifs and buts were candied nuts, we'd all have a wonderful Christmas*, he thought.

He scanned the area behind the Nationalists' lines, trolling for targets. No overweight marshal in a gaudy uniform presented himself to be shot. Since the Czech hadn't expected to spot Sanjurjo, he wasn't disappointed when he didn't. He kept searching for other officers who might deserve to catch an antitank round in the teeth.

German soldiers wore medals even into combat. But the Nazi officers, and even the sergeants, often turned their shoulder straps upside down so enemy snipers couldn't single them out by their rank badges. It wasn't cowardice. You could say whatever you pleased about Hitler. The men who fought his war for him were as brave as any. No, their desire not to show off their rank came from simple military pragmatism. A practical fellow himself, Jezek got that.

The Spaniards, now, the Spaniards were different. Maybe they hadn't got the Middle Ages out of their system. Or it might have been an overdose of *machismo*, assuming that wasn't the same as the other. Whatever it was, when a Spaniard—especially a Fascist Spaniard; they had the disease worse than the Republicans—got to be a colonel or a general, he wanted not just his subordinates but the whole goddamn world to know he'd arrived.

And so his uniform glittered with brass buttons—or perhaps they were gilded. His cap was a production an Austro-Hungarian officer from the turn of the century would have envied, which was really saying something. You could recognize him for what he was from a couple of kilometers away.

If you lugged an antitank rifle into place and waited patiently, you could kill him from a couple of kilometers away, too.

A loudspeaker came to life. Someone who sounded indecently cheerful for this hour of the morning started yelling in Spanish. Vaclav ignored the propaganda. He didn't speak enough of the language to follow it, anyhow. Benjamin Halévy, who did, said the guy usually went on about how wonderful the Nationalists' rations were. Typical horseshit, in other words.

What the bastard sounded like was somebody trying to seduce a deaf girl. He sounded sweet and smarmy and much too loud. Did he ever draw anybody across no-man's-land for a big plate full of Sanjurjo's slumgullion? Whether he did or not, he kept trying.

All he managed to do with Vaclav was remind him he was hungry. The Czech poured some olive oil that wasn't quite past it on a roll that pretty much was and gnawed away. Olive oil at its best tasted medicinal to him; in Prague, you were more likely to find it at a drugstore than in a grocery. Why would you want the stuff when you could have butter instead?

Why? Olives didn't thrive in Czechoslovakia. In Spain, they grew like weeds: the short, pale-barked trees with the gray-green leaves were everywhere you looked. Butter didn't want to keep in the Spanish heat, either; that the Spaniards were casual about cleanliness couldn't help. And so . . . olive oil.

A dust cloud on a road leading up to the front said something motorized was heading this way. "Well, well," Vaclav muttered, there in his hole. "What have we here?" He swung the elephant gun so the sight would bear on the approaching vehicles.

What they had were three Italian CV33 tankettes—the English would have called them Bren-gun carriers, and they were based on the English design. Two mounted a pair of 8mm machine guns in their little turrets, while the one in the lead carried a 20mm cannon. They bore the Nationalist emblem—a white circle with a black X through it—so Vaclav supposed they had Spanish crews.

They'd been obsolete for years. At its thickest, their armor was only

15mm. They were just the kind of vehicles his equally obsolete antitank rifle was designed to fight.

Obsolete didn't always mean useless. Real tanks would have smashed them in short order. Vaclav doubted the Republic had any real tanks within twenty-five kilometers. Armor was hard to come by in a backwater like Spain. Against soldiers with nothing better than rifle-caliber weapons, the tankettes could prove as deadly as they had in Abyssinia and other backwaters.

Vaclav waited. He didn't want to open up on the CV33s at extreme range. Even his fat bullets would need plenty of oomph to punch through their steel, thin though it was.

As soon as the Czechs and Internationals in the trenches saw the tankettes, they started shooting at them with machine guns. The rounds sparked off their armor. The CV33s kept coming. The machine-gun fire did discourage most of the Nationalist foot soldiers from coming with them. Vaclav liked that. Even if he could stop the tankettes, foot soldiers might hunt him down and get their revenge.

The CV33s' machine guns and toy cannon—it wasn't too different from what a Panzer II carried—spat death at the Republican line. Vaclav fired at the cannon-carrying tankette. Swearing at the elephant gun's vicious kick, he worked the bolt and fired again. The tankette slewed sideways and stopped.

He swung the massive French rifle toward one of the others. A shot through the front hull to discourage the driver, another through the turret to make the gunner unhappy. A hatch popped open in the turret as the tankette nosed down into a crater and didn't come out again. Vaclav fired once more. The would-be escapee's chest exploded into red mist. What was left of him slid back into the CV33.

Now . . . What would the last one do? If it knew where he'd been shooting from and plastered his hole with machine-gun bullets, he might not get the chance to return fire. But the no doubt badly trained crew hadn't seen him and had seen enough. The tankette turned around and tried to get away.

He put two rounds into—probably through—the engine. The armor was thinner there. Gasoline and motor oil hit hot metal in places they weren't supposed to. Smoke and fire roared up through the cooling vents. The smoke let the tankette's crew get out and get away.

As if the antitank rifle were a lover, Jezek patted it. He'd stopped an armored assault in its tracks. As long as he was up against something as outdated as the piece he carried, he could still do just fine.

# Chapter 23

**P**ete McGill was glad to be out on patrol aboard the *Ranger*. Yeah, bad shit could still happen to him. A Jap sub might sink the carrier. Three Jap carriers might show up, heading straight for Pearl. Their Zeros would make short work of the combat air patrol, and then their dive-bombers and torpedo planes would make short work of the *Ranger*.

But he was a Marine. They paid him—not much, not even with three stripes on his sleeve, but they did—to go where bad shit could happen to him. He did his stolid best not to worry about it.

Besides, he could have been worse off. "You know what?" he said to Bob Cullum.

"You'd sooner be in Philadelphia?" the other leatherneck suggested, proving his taste in flicks ran to W.C. Fields.

"I'll tell you, man, right this minute I'd sooner by anywhere but Honolulu," Pete answered. "I'd sooner be out here, and I shit you not. God damn the Japs. God damn the rats."

"Who would've imagined we'd see anthrax in Honolulu in this day and age?" Cullum said. "I never even heard of anthrax till they started giving shots. And the plague, too."

"Plague was one of the things we always worried about on duty at the legation in Peking," Pete said. "We had lots of traps and lots of cats to keep the rats away. Never saw it while I was there—told you that before—but some of the guys who were old hands when I first came, they said they'd lost buddies from it back in the day."

"I hear you," Cullum said. "But I bet there's been plague in China as long as there've been Chinamen. Not like that in Hawaii. There wasn't any till the Japs went and brought it to us. None of that anthrax shit, neither."

"I wouldn't put anything past the Japs, not anything at all. Stinking slanty-eyed assholes." Pete hardly even noticed he was cursing them, he did it so automatically.

"Boy oh man, I bet all the bars and the cathouses on Hotel Street are going broke." By the way Bob Cullum said it, that was the worst consequence of the outbreak of disease in Honolulu. Mournful still, he went on, "I mean, you lay a broad and you don't use your pro kit, maybe she gives you the clap. Nobody dies from the fuckin' clap. It just hurts like hell for a while when you piss."

"Uh-huh." Pete nodded. "Come down with the clap and you worry about trouble with the brass. Come down with anthrax or the plague and you worry about trouble with Saint Peter."

Sergeant Cullum laughed. "Good one! Now we just hope like hell we don't have any rats on the ship."

"I've never seen one," Pete said. Sure, the *Ranger*'s mooring lines always wore the usual outward-facing hollow copper cones designed to keep the rodents from boarding. The carrier also boasted a ship's cat. They'd got a big red tabby out of the Honolulu pound and named him Rusty. How much hunting he did, though, was open to question. He spent a lot of time in the galley, where the cooks fed him and fed him. He was already noticeably plumper than he had been when he came aboard.

Even if he'd spent all his time going after rats, whether he could have murdered every last one of them was also open to question. Pete remembered a photo he'd seen of a couple of dozen dead rats and mice found aboard a freighter after the ship was fumigated. Also in the photo was the ship's cat, which hadn't got off before they turned loose the gas.

An albatross soared past the carrier. It didn't really have a wingspan as wide as a fighter's, but it sure seemed to.

"Goddamn Japs don't just break international law. They kick it while it's down and then they shit on it." Cullum returned to the business at hand.

"You got that right." Pete nodded again. "They fight us the same way they fight the Chinamen—dirty. You believe what you read in the papers, they started this germ-warfare crap on them years ago."

"I believe that. The fuckers have it down to a science," Cullum said. "But if you believe everything you read in the papers, you're a sucker and a sap, is what you are."

"Oh, sure." Pete knew that. Not knowing it, he supposed, was the mark of a sucker and a sap. He absentmindedly scratched an itch. Then, noticing what he'd done, he rolled his eyes. "Every time I itch, I wonder if I'm gonna squash a flea when I scratch."

If you did kill a flea when you scratched, you had standing orders to report to sick bay on the double. The docs down there couldn't do anything much for you if the glands under your arms and in your groin started swelling up, but they had an isolation ward so maybe you wouldn't infect your shipmates.

"And when you gotta shower with seawater and saltwater soap, bet your ass you're gonna have itches," Cullum said. "If they let us take Hollywood showers all the time, I almost wouldn't mind the plague, y'know? It'd be doing me some good, anyhow."

"Then you wake up," Pete said. "Not enough fresh water on the ship to use for washing."

"Tell your granny how to suck eggs," Cullum retorted. "And clean the wax outa your ears while you're at it. I said *if*."

The *Ranger*'s Wildcats buzzed in circles above the ship and its escorts, ready to do what they could if the Japanese attacked with airplanes instead of germs. From everything Pete had seen and heard, a Wildcat stood a chance against a Zero, but not a great chance. The American fighters had to slash and run and slash again. If you tried to dogfight a Zero, the first thing you'd wonder was how he'd managed to turn inside you and get on your tail. That was also much too likely to be the last thing you'd ever wonder.

A radar antenna spun round and round, round and round, on top of the carrier's island. It could warn of approaching planes long before you saw them or heard them. They were talking about using radar to direct gunfire, too. Pretty soon, it would all be one side's machines squaring off against the other side's machines. Men wouldn't have to study war any more, because they wouldn't be good enough at it to have a prayer of winning.

When Pete brought out that conceit, Sergeant Cullum gave him a funny look. "So what'll lugs like you and me do then?" he asked.

"Play football. Drink. Brawl in bars," Pete answered. "Same kind of shit we do now, only without the uniforms."

"But the uniforms are what makes it matter." Cullum had been a Marine even longer than Pete. He might have been reciting the Athanasian Creed. By the conviction with which he spoke, he more than half thought he was.

So did Pete. "I won't argue with you, man." Since he'd cut closer to the bone than he'd meant to, he changed the subject: "I wonder how much in the way of supplies will have got to Hawaii by the time we're back at Pearl."

"There's an interesting question!" Cullum exclaimed.

Interesting it was, as in the Chinese curse. The USA had to hang on to Hawaii. Without it, fighting a war against Japan was impossible. But Hawaii couldn't feed or fuel itself. Without shiploads of stuff from the mainland, it would starve. The last thing merchant sailors wanted to do was come down with some horrible disease themselves or bring it back to the West Coast. People on the West Coast were screaming bloody murder and having hysterics. Los Angeles and Oakland had held Kill-a-Rat Days, and proudly displayed piles of long-tailed little corpses. They were kidding themselves if they thought they'd got them all, of course.

"It's a mess, all right," Pete said.

"Everything we do in this lousy war is a mess," Cullum said. "You think we'll ever get one right from the start?"

"Don't hold your breath, is all I've got to tell you. You'll turn bluer than a Billie Holiday song if you do," Pete answered.

He scratched again. No flea crunched under his fingernail. He worried every time he did it anyhow. You couldn't *not* worry, even when you were fine. That might have been the scariest thing of all about germ warfare. Whether or not the germs got under your skin, the fear did.

THE JAPANESE NAVAL base—the former American naval base—on Midway made Myitkyina, Burma, seem like Tokyo by comparison. You could walk around on the little islet. None of it reached higher than a few meters above the sea from which it halfheartedly rose. After Burma's extravagant greenery, the few scrubby grasses that struggled to grow on sand and rocks seemed all the more pathetic.

You could go down to the sea and fish. That was more than just a way to make time pass by. Whatever you pulled out of the water, you could eat. For Japan, Midway was at the very end of a long, long supply line. It was also close to the American naval and air bases farther south and east. Not a lot of freighters made the journey to try to supply the imperial sailors and soldiers there. Not all the ships that tried succeeded.

So fresh-caught fish became an important part of what everyone there ate. Fujita gobbled as much sushi and sashimi in a month as he would have in a year in the Home Islands. You couldn't get sashimi any fresher than what you'd just caught yourself and cut to pieces with a bayonet or a utility knife.

Or you could hang around the barracks that had formerly housed American Marines and Navy men. Bombardment from the air and sea had battered the barracks as the Japanese took Midway. Repairs to the buildings were haphazard at best. Even so, the quarters—if not the food—seemed luxurious by the standards Fujita was used to.

He needed a while to learn to ignore the chug of the generators that powered the desalination plant. They ran night and day. Fresh water was in short supply on Midway. Cisterns captured what rainwater they could. Water would have been scarcer still if not for the plant, which was taken over from the Americans.

A noncom who'd been there longer than Fujita said, "When we attacked, we were careful not to shell the water-making factory, and our planes didn't bomb anywhere close to it. We were afraid the Yankees would blow it up themselves when they saw they were going to lose the island, but they didn't."

"That's good luck," Fujita said.

"*Hai.*" The other sergeant nodded. He was a stocky fellow a few years older than Fujita. His name was Ichiro Yanai. He went on, "It was like they never expected us to get here, and they didn't know what to do when we did."

"Russians can be like that, too," Fujita said. "White men are hard to figure out. Half the time, I don't think they know what they're going to do before they do it."

"Wouldn't surprise me one bit," Yanai answered. "But I don't care how inscrutable they are."

"There's a ten-yen word for you!" exclaimed Fujita, who hoped he understood what it meant.

Sergeant Yanai chuckled self-consciously. "It is, isn't it? . . . Where was I going with this? . . . Ah, *hai.* They were stupid here, is what they were. They could have given us all kinds of misery if they'd wrecked the waterworks so bad, we couldn't have fixed it. I don't even know if we make installations like this one. If we do, shipping one all the way out here sure wouldn't have been easy. And I'm not sure you can keep any kind of garrison here on nothing but rainwater."

Fujita looked around. Sand. Rock. Scrub. Sea—endless sea in every direction. Airstrips, with bombers and fighters near them in revetments covered with nets designed to make them look like more sand and scrub from the air.

Gliding in for a landing on one of the strips was not a G4M Navy bomber but an albatross. "Oh, this should be good!" Fujita said.

"*Hai!*" Yanai's eyes glowed in anticipation.

An airborne albatross was a miracle of flight. Fujita had never imagined that anything so enormous could also be so graceful. The birds spent almost their whole lives on the wing, and it showed.

An albatross coming in for a landing was a disaster waiting to happen. This disaster didn't have long to wait. The bird put down its weak little legs as if they were landing gear. If only it could have grown a wheeled undercarriage instead! It was going much too fast for its feet to have a prayer of stopping it or even slowing it down.

It somersaulted—tumbled, really—along the sandy tarmac, head over tail. Its wings stuck out at ridiculous angles. Why they didn't break—or break off—Fujita had no idea.

The albatross finally came to rest on its back. The first time Fujita watched one land like that, he was sure it must have killed itself. A G4M that flipped over would have burst into flames and incinerated its crew. But that first albatross had just wiggled up onto its legs and walked away. So did this one now. They were made to crash. The birds already on the sand ignored the spectacle that fascinated the two sergeants. Why shouldn't they? They'd all come back to earth the same way. Unlike the Japanese, they took it for granted.

"After we captured Midway, a newsreel crew came out here to photograph us so people back home could see what we'd done," Yanai said. "That was what they came for, but they ended up using a lot of their film on the albatrosses. They couldn't get over them."

"I believe it," Fujita said. "You never get tired of watching them. They don't come in the same twice in a row, not ever. They always find some new way to smash themselves."

"It's never one you expect, either," Yanai said.

"Has anyone found out what they taste like?" Fujita asked. They weren't like chickens, that was for sure—you wouldn't eat both wings and still be hungry for more.

"Oh, yes. They're pretty fishy—not what you'd call good," the other sergeant said. "You can eat them if you have to, but they're more fun to watch than they are to shoot."

"They're more fun than anything else you can do on this island," Fujita said, a certain edge in his voice. The base here wasn't big enough for the authorities to have bothered bringing in any comfort women to keep the troops happy. Extra mouths to feed, the old men reasoned coldbloodedly. The people in charge of things here had to be too old to get it up very often. Had Fujita known Midway suffered from that kind of shortage, he wouldn't have come a quarter of the way around the world to drop germ bombs on the Yankees' heads.

"Nothing I can do about that." Yanai had no trouble following him. "Nothing you can, either."

A few days later, American four-engined bombers hit the island. Zeros zoomed up to try to fight them off. The U.S. planes fought back. Unlike G4Ms, they could take a lot of bullets and keep flying. They also spat out a lot of bullets. They bristled with heavy machine guns. The Zeros shot down at least one of them, but a pair of Japanese Navy fighters tumbled into the Pacific.

Bombs whistled down on the island. They seemed to fall at random; the Zeros did at least joggle the Americans' elbows. Lying in a shallow trench, Fujita heard explosions far and near. He hoped the albatrosses weren't getting blown up. They hadn't done anything to deserve to be bombed.

He knew he had. War was like that. You hurt the people on the other side every chance you got, as hard as you could. If they didn't give up, they paid you back with all the strength they had. Eventually, one side or the other decided it had had enough and gave up.

It seemed a stupid way to settle the world's disagreements. No doubt it *was* a stupid way, only nobody had come up with a better one. People had been fighting wars, some smaller, some larger, for as long as there'd been people. Chances were they'd go right on fighting them, too.

*And Japan always wins in the end. Always,* Fujita thought. That made him feel a little better as the American bombs kept falling on Midway, but not so much as he'd hoped.

BULLETS CRACKED PAST, a meter or two above Aristide Demange's head. The Germans were spraying the French lines with machine-gun fire again. They wanted to keep Demange's countrymen from getting frisky.

Most of the rounds you never saw. Some were tracers, so the assholes serving the MG-34 or MG-42 could see what their stream of bullets was doing. When one of those flew by, you thought you could light your cigarette on the red streak it left in the air.

Demange lit a Gitane—with a match. He spat the tiny butt of the last one he'd smoked into the mud. A couple of good, hard puffs started reducing the new smoke as well.

*How many packs have I gone through since the war started?* he wondered. He didn't know the answer in numbers, but sometimes numbers didn't matter. He'd gone through as many packs as he could, and he had the cough to prove it. The only times he hadn't chain-smoked were when the tobacco ration didn't get through to wherever he happened to be.

He'd felt weird then: light-headed, dizzy, shaky. Probably too much oxygen getting through to his brain. He couldn't imagine what else might cause it.

Down the trench from him, the Communist private named Marcel groused, "Don't those *cochons* ever run low on ammo?" He was the tall one of the pair, not the short—Demange finally had them straight.

"Hold up the red flag with the hammer and sickle on it," the lieutenant said, Gitane bobbing in his mouth as he spoke. "That'll make the Nazis fold up and run away. Sure it will."

Marcel sent him a reproachful look. "The Fascist swine are in retreat in the Soviet Union, sir." Several more bullets cracked over them as the enemy murder mill traversed. Marcel grimaced. "They sure aren't in retreat here in Belgium."

"You *stupid* piece of shit." Demange enjoyed it when he could focus his boundless scorn for all mankind on one luckless individual. "The dumb *Boches* bit off more than even they could chew over there. They're fighting on a front a couple of thousand kilometers across. When they have to fight here, too, of *course* they're gonna get stretched too thin and have to fall back from the Ivans. It's not 'cause Stalin is the second goddamn coming of Jesus Christ, you dumb prick. It's because he has a fucking huge country."

"He runs it with power to the proletariat, too," Marcel said. "If we would only do that—"

He got no further. Demange cut him off. "My ass," the veteran growled. "I was there, kid. I saw the Russian proletariat. Hell, I shot some of the Russian proletariat. A bunch of those guys, when they found out we were Frenchmen instead of Germans, they went over to us faster than those machine-gun bullets are going over us now. Some of them went over to the Nazis, too, but most of 'em figured Hitler was an even bigger *salaud* than Stalin. That's the figuring you've got to do—which one of 'em makes the worst *con*."

"Hitler does," Marcel said confidently.

"Well, for now the big shots back in Paris think you're right,"

Demange said. "But that doesn't turn Stalin into a bargain. The only thing that could ever turn Stalin into a bargain is, mm, Hitler."

He was lighting another fresh Gitane when the Germans started lobbing mortar bombs at the *poilus* in the trenches. If you had a good, thick parapet in front of you and you kept your head down, machine-gun bullets were just an annoyance. As long as you stayed in your hole, you had to be mighty unlucky to get hurt.

Mortars whispered up and whined down. If one landed beside you, it would slice you into dogmeat even if you stayed behind your parapet. Demange despised mortars. So did every foot soldier who'd ever been on the receiving end of an attack. You couldn't hide from them, and the bastards on your own side wouldn't let you run away from them, either.

Screams rose from the next job over in the trench. Somebody over there had caught it, all right—caught it pretty bad, by the horrible noises he was making. Rolled into a ball in the bottom of the trench, Demange wished the bearers would cart off the luckless bugger. His shrieks were plenty to demoralize a whole regiment.

At last, they fell silent. Maybe he'd passed out. Maybe he'd died. Whatever had happened, he couldn't feel his tormented body any more. That was a mercy, and not such a small one. People could be so dreadfully wounded, they begged you to kill them and thanked you if you had the nerve to do it.

War movies didn't show stuff like that. A wound in a war movie meant a clean, white bandage—where were the blood and the mud?—and a nurse with big tits to bat her eyelashes at you while you recovered. If only life worked out so neatly . . . especially for that sorry fool over there.

The next interesting question was whether the Germans were going to follow up all this ironmongery with an attack of their own. They hadn't been doing that very often in Belgium. They were content to let the Tommies and *poilus* come at them, and to slaughter the Allies when they tried.

You never could be sure, though. Whenever you thought you knew what the *Boches* were up to, they'd let you figure you were right for a little while and then, when you were good and set up, they'd shove it right up your ass.

Regretfully, Demange unfolded from the fetal position. Even more regretfully, he got up on the firing step and peered over the top of the parapet. That brought the machine-gun bullets terrifyingly close to the top of the crest on his helmet. Why that stupid crest was there he'd never known, in the last war or this one. To give style? It didn't seem reason enough. The Tommies and the Ivans got along fine without crests. So did the Germans, whose helmets were hands down the best in both wars.

"Up! Up, you shitheads!" Demange yelled. "They're moving!" He unslung his rifle—no pissy officer's automatic for him—and started banging away at the oncoming *Boches*.

He felt better when French machine guns began gnawing at the enemy. The German attack soon ran out of steam. The Fritzes didn't have any tanks supporting their foot soldiers. The infantrymen sensibly decided there was no point to getting killed when they hadn't a prayer of making any real advance. They trotted back to their start line or at most hung on in shell holes between the lines.

After a while, a German officer stood up waving a white flag: a bedsheet nailed to a pole. Firing on both sides slowly died away. The officer strode forward, still carrying the flag of truce.

As soon as the German got within shouting distance, Demange yelled, "Far enough, pal!"

The *Boche* obediently stopped. "An hour's cease-fire?" he shouted back in guttural French. "So we can pick up our wounded?"

"Send your guys hiding in the craters back to your start line and you can have it," Demange answered.

"*D'accord*," the German agreed after a short pause for thought. "We gain little advantage from them anyhow."

Demange saw it the same way—for now. But the Germans might try to reinforce them under cover of darkness. Then they could make more trouble here tomorrow or further down the line. "An hour's cease-fire, starting—now!" he called to his own men. "Don't shoot at their stretcher-bearers, and let their troops go back out of no-man's-land." The German officer turned and bellowed *auf Deutsch*.

Out came the *Boches* with Red Cross vests and with Red Crosses painted inside white circles on their helmets. The effect, to Demange, was that of a wolf dyed pink. It still looked dangerous, but now it looked peculiar, too. The bearers hauled wounded men back toward German aid stations. Unwounded Germans scuttled away to their entrenchments. Demange guessed not all of them would abandon the ground they'd so painfully won, no matter what their officer promised. Nobody ever kept promises all the way. Demange wouldn't have, in the German's shoes. A night patrol would root out the ones who'd stayed behind, and then this stretch of front could get back to normal.

NO MORE FLYING Fortresses had raided Münster, for which Sarah Bruck thanked the God in Whom she had ever more trouble believing. Maybe the daylight raid cost the RAF more than it wanted to pay. Other English bombers still hit the town by night, though.

Samuel Goldman seemed absurdly cheerful about it. "Well, I don't lack for work, anyhow," he said one evening over supper. "For a while there, when England and France were at peace with the government, I was afraid they'd want me as much as a laborer as they did when I was a professor."

"Supper's good," Hanna Goldman said, which both wasn't and was an answer. The Nazis hadn't let Sarah's father go on teaching at the university. Expelling him from the faculty had been a disaster. If they threw him out of the labor gang, that would be a catastrophe.

He nodded to Mother now. "Not too bad, if I say so myself." He preened just a little. The spaetzle and the tinned fish that went with them had come from his inspired scrounging.

It wasn't impossible for Jews to survive in the wartime *Reich* without such help, not quite. Life might be lived, yes, but it wasn't worth living. Barely enough food, and almost all of it dreadful . . . They wanted you to know what they thought of you, all right.

When Father couldn't steal better edibles than German Jews were legally entitled to, he stole clothes. Sarah had no idea how he'd managed to stuff a cashmere sweater into one of his inside jacket pockets, but he had. Even the yellow Stars of David she'd sewn onto it, front and back, didn't seem to deface it too badly.

She supposed that was her vanity talking. After so long in the altered old clothes she'd got from the rabbi, anything nice seemed extra wonderful. With the wretched clothing ration Jews got, she might have been able to buy a sweater like that around the turn of the twenty-first century—provided she didn't need anything else in the meantime.

The only reason she had that sweater was that some Aryan woman had got blown to gory smithereens. Father and the other laborers in his gang, Jews and petty criminals alike, robbed the dead whenever they saw the chance. The people the RAF killed didn't need their things any more. The laborers who cleaned up the mess the bombers left behind did, desperately.

Sometimes Sarah salved her conscience by thinking that the woman who had owned her sweater was a raging anti-Semite, and that it served her right for the sweater to pass to a Jew. But she had no way of knowing that. The Nazi big shots who ran Münster did everything they could to make life miserable for Jews, sure. So did some ordinary folk. Most people in the town, though, were just trying to get by from one day to the next and hoping their relatives in the *Wehrmacht* were all right. They didn't have the time or the energy to run around screaming "The Jews are our misfortune!"

Sarah hoped her brother in the *Wehrmacht* was all right, too. That was all she could do. If anything did happen to Saul, she wouldn't find out about it. He had—she hoped he still had—his assumed name and identity. Whatever happened to him, wherever he was, he was bound to be better off than he would have been had the authorities grabbed him after he smashed in that gang boss's head when the vicious man hit him once too often for no reason.

Saul hardly ever got mentioned in the Goldman house. When he did, it was always in the past tense. Sarah and her mother and father never said a word about his hiding in plain sight of the National Socialist authorities.

Father didn't always scavenge goodies when the RAF hit Münster. Sometimes nothing was left to scavenge: houses and shops and blocks of flats often went up in flames. Sometimes younger, sprier men beat him to the goodies. And sometimes the firemen and police who were also on duty kept laborers from grabbing the way they wanted to.

"I'd mind that less if they didn't steal for themselves," he said after being thwarted by a fireman. "But they do. I've watched them."

"Not fair!" Sarah said in angry sympathy.

He smiled crookedly. "Yes? And so?" She had no comeback for that.

When his scrounging was bad, the luck she had shopping mattered more. That luck would never be good, of course. Jews were allowed in stores only just before closing time, after Aryan customers had picked over whatever happened to be available. But sometimes what she could get was truly awful, while sometimes it was only wretched. Like everything else, misery had its degrees.

Since the trams were also denied to those who wore the yellow star, she walked all over Münster trying to find this, that, or the other thing. She often thought she used as much energy getting food as she took in when she finally ate it. She didn't know what she could do about that, either. She and her parents were all much thinner than they had been before the Nazis took over. She doubted there were any German Jews who weren't.

Late one afternoon, she was coming home with a kilo and a half of flour she'd got across town. Despite the long trip, she was pleased with herself. For what you could get hold of these days, the flour looked pretty good. It had some peas and beans and dried potatoes ground into it, but everybody's flour these days was like that. People old enough to remember did say the bread in the last war had been even worse, stretched with sawdust and maybe even clay. Sarah could hardly believe it, but there you were.

And here she was, coming up to the square that fronted on Münster's Catholic cathedral. The square was about half full of people: women, boys, old men. Most of the men of military age were either wearing one uniform or another or working long hours in factories to give the *Reich*'s soldiers and flyers and sailors the murderous tools of their trade.

Some men wore police uniforms, not military ones. Some of them were in the square, too, between the crowd and the cathedral. They clutched truncheons. Two or three of them carried Schmeissers instead. They all looked nervous.

Sarah felt nervous. A crowd not organized by the state was astonishing in Hitler's Germany. Sarah scuttled along the walls of the buildings on the far side of the square, as far from the crowd and the police as she could get. She felt like a mouse who'd walked into a gathering of cats by mistake. Maybe they wouldn't notice her—or the yellow stars she wore.

The crowd began to move toward the cathedral, and toward the thin line of police in front of it. Voices rose: "Give us back the archbishop! Give us back the archbishop!"

Archbishop von Galen had presumed to protest the way the *Reich* disposed of mental defectives (though he'd never said a word about the way the *Reich* treated its Jews). The *Gestapo* had grabbed him and hustled him off to prison or a concentration camp. And Münster's Catholics had rioted. The authorities put them down and made more arrests. But that they'd risen once was a prodigy.

That they'd been put down and were rising again was whatever went two steps past a prodigy. *And that I'm here right now is whatever's two steps past a calamity*, Sarah thought. She hurried along as fast as she could without running and drawing notice to herself.

"Give us back the archbishop! Give us back the archbishop!" The crowd's chant swelled ever louder.

A police official with a megaphone shouted through the chorus: "Disperse this criminal assembly, in the name of the *Grossdeutsches Reich*!"

"Give us back the archbishop, in the name of God!" The chant changed.

When Sarah heard the harsh crack of gunfire then, she could scarcely believe it. Some people in the crowd screamed and ran away. Some fell, injured or killed. And some roared and charged the police. They roared louder when they got their hands on a few of the uniformed men. Sarah made her escape. For once, no one paid any attention to a Jew.

# Chapter 24

rno Baatz had always wished the soldiers who served under him would like him better. But he'd always assumed it was their fault they didn't. And, working from that assumption, he'd always wound up disappointed.

He'd always wished his superiors liked him better, too. Before the war started, he'd gone through the six-week training course that lifted him out of the teeming swarm of private soldiers and into the more glorious ranks of those with the authority to tell that teeming swarm what to do.

Even a corporal enjoyed such authority, and Arno enjoyed it as much as any *Unteroffizier* ever minted. He was official and officious. He knew the rules and regulations. He lived by them, and he made the men in his charge live by them as well.

He was a good soldier himself. He wore the ribbon for the Iron Cross Second Class on his tunic. He wore his wound badge, too—wore it with pride. He'd been an *Unteroffizier* a devil of a long time. Since before the shooting started, in fact. None of the men set over him had shown the slightest inclination to promote him to sergeant so he could use his talents on a bigger group.

*So I can give orders to more people*, he thought. Yes, he knew what he wanted to do, all right.

That he didn't get the chance he was sure he deserved only left him even more sour than he would have been otherwise. Combine that with the *Wehrmacht*'s failure to knock the Red Army out of the war, and Arno Baatz was a less happy man than he might have been.

These days, the Russians were in the driving seat on the Eastern Front. Germany had to respond to one Soviet thrust after another. Smolensk wouldn't fall this campaigning season, either. Moscow? Moscow wasn't even a pipe dream any more. As long as the *Reich* could hold on to Byelorussia and a chunk of the Ukraine, things . . . weren't too bad.

He had no idea what the name of the collective farm his section was defending might have been. He didn't even know whether it had ever enjoyed a name. Maybe the damn Jews who ran the Bolshevik state just tagged it with a number so they could more efficiently keep tabs on it.

He set up the new section MG-34 where it could rake the fields to the east with fire. If the Russians wanted to charge across those fields in the drunken mass attacks they loved so much, they were welcome to try.

"As long as we have enough cartridge belts, we can kill off a couple of divisions' worth of Ivans," he declared proudly, once the men had brought the machine-gun position up to his exacting standards.

"If they don't throw any panzers at us, anyway," Adam Pfaff put in.

Baatz scowled at the unruly senior private. "When I want to know what you think—"

"You'll kick it out of me," Pfaff broke in. "I know."

"Tend to your business," Baatz snapped. "Keep the Russians off the gun crew and we'll do fine."

"*Zu Befehl*," Pfaff said, which was a reply not even Baatz could fault. The *Obergefreiter* strolled over to his foxhole, slid in, and pointed his rifle in the direction from which the Russians were most likely to come. Baatz wanted to grind his teeth every time he set eyes on the Mauser's gray-painted woodwork. You weren't supposed to do that to a rifle. It was as far outside of regulations as it could get. But Major Schmitz, the battalion CO, let Pfaff get away with it. You couldn't win.

Pretty soon, Baatz had other things to worry about (though the gray Mauser, like a broken tooth, seldom escaped his mind for long). A volley of Katyusha rockets screamed down on the collective farm. Luckily, the Russians aimed a little long. Most of the horrible things smashed down behind the section's position. The buildings on the *kolkhoz* had been tumbledown wrecks before the rockets hit. Now they were burning wrecks. The wind blew the smoke away from the *Landsers*. Baatz wished it would have screened them. At least they would be able to see the Ivans from a long way off now.

"Any chance we can get reinforcements, Corporal?" Adam Pfaff asked. "Mighty lonely out here."

"We are ordered to hold this collective farm. *We* are," Baatz said importantly. "We'll do it."

"Harder if we all get killed," Pfaff remarked.

"Is that defeatism?" Arno asked. Pfaff didn't answer. Baatz hadn't thought he would. Defeatism in the field was a capital crime. A drumhead court martial would pass sentence after a complaint.

Of course, getting overrun by the Russians was also a capital crime, and probably one with a punishment less merciful than a firing squad or an officer with a pistol would show. Stirrings off toward the eastern horizon warned that the Ivans were going to make their push soon.

Flares from little German strongpoints to the north and south said the men holding those stretches of the front were also awake to the building threat. Baatz fired a green flare of his own to show that he was, too. He remembered scaring off some Soviet panzers with red flares. That had been quick thinking from Dernen, no two ways about it, even if he was a troublemaker most of the time. Well, Dernen wouldn't be doing any quick thinking now, not after he'd stopped one with his noggin.

"*Urra! Urra!*" That deep roar, right now just at the edge of hearing, made the short hair at Arno's nape prickle up. The Russians were nerving themselves for the charge. They were all liquored up when they started yelling like that, sure as hell they were, almost past the point of feeling pain or caring whether they lived or died. And they had no choice but to go forward. NKVD men would shoot them down from behind if they faltered.

"*Urra! Urra!*" Here they came, still out of range but terrifying all the same. They'd linked arms as they dogtrotted forward in row after row. The skirts of their greatcoats flapped between them. "*Urra! Urra!*"

Most of them would have machine pistols, not rifles. They'd need to get in close before they could use them. "*Urra! Urra!*" They were ready to get in close, too. They seemed as determined, as unstoppable, as storm waves rolling up a beach and sweeping aside whatever lay in their path.

Then German mortar bombs started dropping among them. Dirt fountained up at every burst. Men close to the explosions fell or flew through the air. The Ivans who didn't get hit closed ranks and kept coming.

When the lead wave of men in dun-colored uniforms got within about a thousand meters, Baatz yelled to the men at the MG-34: "Let 'em have it!" The man at the trigger tapped the machine gun's rear end after every burst, spraying bullets back and forth in short bursts. Other German machine guns, MG-34s and MG-42s, were hammering the enemy along with this one. Russians toppled, one after another. The commissars spent lives the way a drunken sailor spent money on popsies.

Indifferent in the face of destruction, the Russian survivors kept closing up and coming on. "*Urra! Urra!*" The roar was loud now, and getting louder every second.

Baatz brought his own rifle up to his shoulder and started shooting. He wasn't sure he hit anyone, not with so many other weapons knocking Ivans down, but hitting had to be easier than missing. He worked the bolt again and again, slapping in clip after clip.

A few bullets came back from the Russians, but only a few. If they didn't break pretty soon, though, they'd open up with all those goddamn submachine guns, and then there'd be hell to pay. Baatz carried several potato-masher grenades on his belt. He hadn't actually thrown one in a long time. You were in trouble if you needed them. He shifted in his hole so he could grab them in a hurry. He was liable to be in trouble now.

But then, quite suddenly, the waves of Ivans streamed back, not forward. Flesh and blood, even Russian flesh and blood, could take just so much, and the Germans here had enough firepower to dish it out. Dead and wounded men littered the battlefield. The machine guns went on firing, turning the wounded men into dead ones and making sure the ones who didn't move wouldn't. You could bet some of the bastards out there were trying to play possum.

"Fuck me," Adam Pfaff said, as if from very far away—Baatz's ears still rang. "We lived through it again, I think." For once, Arno couldn't argue with him at all.

THE SQUADRON HAD a new airstrip. They'd flown off runways in front of Smolensk. Then, as the Germans advanced, they'd flown from a base in back of the fortress city. Now they were at another strip in front of Smolensk. It wasn't the one they'd used before, but Stas Mouradian didn't think it was far away.

Naturally, he wasn't the only one who noticed the change and what it meant. "We're pushing the Hitlerites back," Isa Mogamedov said as they settled in for their first supper at the new strip.

Stas nodded. He gnawed the meat off a boiled pork rib. Mogamedov was eating ribs, too. He might not drink much, but he didn't strictly keep the Muslim dietary rules. At a base where the cooks were pork-loving Russians, he might have starved to death if he had.

After Stas swallowed, he said, "They *are* falling back, the bastards." He didn't want merely to be seen agreeing with his copilot and bomb-aimer. He wanted to be heard, too. Mogamedov might well have had similar motives in speaking up to begin with. You couldn't just be loyal to the Soviet Union. You had to let everybody know how very loyal you were.

You especially had to do that if you weren't a Russian. If you came from the Caucasus like Mouradian and Mogamedov, or from one of the Central Asian republics, you might be a member of the club by affiliation, but you weren't—you couldn't be—a member by birth. And so you had to work all the harder to show you deserved to belong.

One of the other flyers turned on the radio that sat on a crate in a corner of the mess tent. Inside the crate was the truck battery powering the set. When the radio had warmed up, the tail end of something new and martial from Shostakovich came out of it. Mouradian nodded again. That had to be better than the sugary pap they played so often.

The Shostakovich ended with a thunder of kettle drums. Not quite *The 1812 Overture* with a real cannon, but it did suggest pounding artillery. Then the announcer said, "Moscow speaking." Everyone leaned toward the radio—it was time for the news.

"More of the Ukraine has been liberated by the ever-glorious Red Army of the workers and peasants of the Soviet Union," the announcer declared in proud tones. "The Fascist sharks and the Romanian sucker fish that cling to them continue to retreat."

"Sucker fish!" Stas exclaimed in genuine admiration. Some Party writer had probably won himself a bonus for that. The Romanians and Hungarians were usually jackals in Soviet news broadcasts, sometimes vultures, sometimes Hitler's lackeys. But that was a new one. Stas wondered if it would stick or be forgotten tomorrow. He hoped it would last. He liked it.

Then he laughed out loud, because Isa Mogamedov bugged out his eyes and opened and closed his mouth several times. Stas hadn't dreamt the Azeri could turn into such a convincing fish.

He'd missed a little of what the newsreader was saying. Well, no great loss. He knew things were going well here in Russia. That he was eating supper at this new air base and not at the old one told that story far better than the announcer could.

"In Egypt," the man said, "the English government has confirmed that the transport carrying the theater commander, General Montgomery, was shot down by a Nazi fighter. General Auchinleck has been named to replace Montgomery."

That the Germans could shoot down an English theater commander was not good news. The generals involved were no more than foreign names to Stas.

"On the Continent, English and French troops have made only the most minimal gains against the Hitlerites in Belgium," the newsreader continued scornfully. "Fighting of a scale and seriousness to match that which the *Rodina* has suffered since the German invasion has yet to be seen there."

"Right!" a flyer near Stas said. "Just right!" He pounded the table with his fist to show how right it was. Several other pilots and bomb-aimers nodded.

Stas wondered whether he was the only fellow in the whole squadron who'd been issued a working memory. Germany and the USSR didn't border each other. Hitler never would have had the chance to invade the Soviet Union if Stalin hadn't got greedy. Stalin had assumed that, with the Nazis bogged down in the West, they wouldn't be able to do anything about it if he helped himself to a chunk of northeastern Poland.

Which only went to show that, unless you were doing geometry, you shouldn't run around assuming things. Marshal Smigly-Ridz yelled for help from the *Führer,* and he got it. And the Western democracies hadn't minded a bit when the Nazis took on the Soviet Union. In fact, they'd even pitched in themselves for a while.

But saying something like that on Radio Moscow would be the same as saying that General Secretary Stalin, the wisest and most beloved of all men, the great leader of the people's revolutionary vanguard, had screwed the pooch when he tried to steal Vilno or Wilno or Vilnius or however you wanted to spell the worthless place. Since General Secretary Stalin obviously hadn't, obviously couldn't have, screwed the pooch, the newsreader came out with this bilge instead.

And he expected his audience to believe him. Stas paused thoughtfully. No, that might not be quite true. The newsreader expected his audience to behave as if it believed him.

He would get what he expected, too. Stas imagined himself standing up here and announcing to his comrades what had really led up to the German invasion of the USSR. He also imagined what would happen right after that. If someone had a pistol handy, he might not even live long enough to get arrested. Whoever plugged him would win a commendation, and probably a promotion to go with it.

If nobody here happened to be armed, his comrades would grab him, wrestle him to the ground, and hold him till the NKVD could take charge of him. His troubles would be just starting then, not ending. All things considered, getting shot would be better. At least then everything would be over with at once.

People from Leningrad and from the Ukraine to Siberia (but not to Vladivostok, lost to Japan thanks to some more of the great General Secretary's brilliance) would be listening to Radio Moscow right now. The ones who did still remember the way things had actually worked would be making the same automatic calculation Stas had just made.

They would come to the same answer he had. How could anyone who didn't aspire to martyrdom possibly come to any other answer? You had to live, as much as the war and the Chekists would let you.

No one would ask any inconvenient questions, not out loud. That was the point of this exercise, of the terror that had ruled this broad land since the Revolution.

Stas wished for some vodka—not something he was used to doing. Even thinking this way was dangerous. The more you did it, the more likely you were to slip. And if you slipped, they would catch you. Hell, sometimes they would catch you even if you didn't slip. They'd catch you on general principles, or because they needed to fill a quota and one of the guys they were really after had gone fishing that day before they could clap the handcuffs on him.

The newsreader went on to brag about the marvels of Soviet productivity. Stakhanovite aluminum smelters from a Magnitogorsk plant had set a new record—*another* new record!—in outproducing norms by 350 percent. A shock campaign in a coal mine near the Don River produced similar stunning results. Of course it did. All you had to do was believe what Radio Moscow told you.

**HERB DRUCE KISSED** Peggy's cheek on the platform at the Broad Street Station. "Off I go again," he said. "Nevada this time—can you believe it?"

"Just barely," Peggy answered, which wasn't far from true. To someone from Philadelphia, Nevada was nothing but alkali desert, jackrabbits, and Hoover Dam. She had trouble seeing how anything out there could be big enough or important enough to require the services of an ace troubleshooter like her husband.

She didn't say so. They never talked much about what Herb was up to where other people could hear. Herb didn't talk about a lot of it even with her.

"All aboard!" The shout rose from the conductors. The PA system announced the train's imminent departure.

"See you," Herb said, and climbed onto the train, attaché case in hand.

"Love you!" Peggy blew him a kiss. He was already finding his seat; she didn't think he saw her do it.

She let out a long sigh as she left the platform, left the station, and headed for the family Packard, which was parked not far away. You couldn't do much driving on the crappy gasoline ration the government doled out, but today Herb didn't feel like coming down here on the streetcar with his attaché case and a couple of big old suitcases. This trip would be longer than usual, so she'd splurged and driven him.

Peggy sighed again when she slid behind the wheel to go home. She didn't know all the details of what Herb would be doing out there in the Great American Desert. From what little he'd said, she didn't think he knew all the details yet, either. He'd find out more about what was going on when he actually got there. But it looked as if he'd be gone for weeks, not days.

She put the car in gear and swung out into traffic. There wasn't much. Everyone else had to worry about the crappy gas ration, too. She zipped along on the way home, as she and Herb had zipped along coming down to the station. That was the one good thing you could say about rationing. Traffic jams were a thing of the past.

You could get a little bit of gas. Peggy didn't know what she'd do if one of the tires went, though. Hardly any rubber goods were available to civilians. An article in the paper had talked about a burning tool mechanics could use to cut new and deeper treads into tires that had gone bald. That didn't sound safe to her. Then again, riding around on bald tires wasn't exactly safe, either.

She pulled into the driveway. A wartime accessory she *was* thinking of getting was a gas cap with a lock and key. Since rationing clamped down, some people liberated gasoline with a siphon and a bucket. They either burned it themselves or sold it on the black market.

"Bastards," she muttered, then quickly looked around. No, no neighbors out to be scandalized by her unladylike language. Well, good. If she was going to scandalize people, she wanted to do a first-class job.

She walked into the house. One more big sigh in the foyer. She'd spend more time rattling around here like a pea in an oversized pod. Things with Herb weren't everything they had been or everything they might have been, but she still liked having him around.

A robin hopped on the front lawn, cocking its head to one side as it searched for bugs and worms. Every so often, it caught something. Peggy watched as one fat earthworm wrapped itself all the way around the robin's yellow beak, struggling for all it was worth against getting eaten. The worm wasn't worth enough. The robin bit it in half and swallowed the writhing pieces one after the other.

Unexpected tears stung Peggy's eyes. Wasn't that poor damned earthworm doing the same thing as all the sorry little people who got caught in the war's iron jaws? Sure it was. It only wanted to live, the same as they did. But the robin didn't let it, any more than the war spared those people.

The robin, at least, had the excuse of being hungry. If it didn't eat bugs and worms, it would starve. What was Hitler's excuse, though, or Tojo's? They already headed great nations. What more could they possibly need? Would they be fatter and healthier and happier if they devoured other nations' small stores of happiness?

They evidently thought so.

Before Peggy quite realized what she was doing, she walked into the kitchen and opened the cabinet where the liquor bottles lived. After a bourbon on the rocks—or, say, two bourbons on the rocks—she might be able to look at the world through a less jaundiced eyed.

Or two bourbons on the rocks might turn into a good many more than two, and she'd wake up tomorrow morning with a head like a drop-forging plant and a mouth like a latrine trench. Then she'd have one to take the edge off . . . and then everything would start all over again.

It wasn't as if she didn't know some quiet lushes, and a few more who weren't so quiet. But she also knew what she thought of them. Nothing wrong with a drink every so often. Nothing wrong with a drink or three, even, every so often . . . as long as you were holding the bottle. When the bottle got hold of you, you turned into one of the people other people thought about that way.

So the bourbon on the rocks could damn well wait till after dinner. In the meantime, she lit a Chesterfield. Nothing wrong with cigarettes, by God! Not even if her granny would have got the vapors seeing her smoke one like a loose woman. Nothing wrong with coffee, either. She turned on the stove to heat up what was in the pot sitting there.

When Herb was out of town, time crawled by. A postcard from Reno—which, by the gaudy picture on the front, billed itself as the biggest little city in the West—was no substitute for the man himself. *I won fifty bucks at a slot machine the night I got here*, he wrote, *and I've been putting it back a dime at a time ever since.* He didn't say anything about what he was doing way the hell out there, but she wouldn't have expected him to.

She made one of her own patriotic forays into the Lehigh Valley, which kept her hopping for a few days. A speech at an Odd Fellows hall near the Civil War monument in what they called the Circle in Easton had the crowd eating out of her hand. The next morning, a Sunday, the Easton Democrats who'd sponsored her told her they'd never seen anybody else sell war bonds like that.

"All in the wrist," she answered, not without pride.

A young man who looked like a black Irishman—the town seemed about a third Irish, a third German, and a third everything else—gave her a lift back to the train station. "I bought a bond myself," he said. "Paying my own salary, like. I'm going into the Marines next week."

"Good luck to you," Peggy said from the bottom of her heart.

"Thanks," he answered. "I'll take whatever I can get." That struck her as a sensible attitude. But if he was so sensible, why was he joining the Marines?

Because he was a man, so he could. Peggy made speeches and did volunteer work and used all the other substitutes for fighting a middle-aged woman could find. And if she sometimes had a drink or three to blunt the edge of loneliness, she did keep hold of the bottle, not the other way around.

She coped. It was with some astonishment that she realized Herb had been gone almost two months. Even by his standards and those of the government that ran him around, it was a long time to be away.

A couple of days after that thought crossed her mind, a fat manila envelope plastered with stamps was stuck in the mailbox. The postmarks on the stamps were from Reno. The return-address label was from a law firm there. "What the hell?" Peggy said, and carried the envelope and the rest of the mail inside.

The envelope held a sheaf of typed and printed legal papers. Paper-clipped to the front was a note in Herb's familiar scrawl. *I'm sorry, Peggy,* it said, *but honest to God I think this is for the best. I still like you more than anybody, but I just don't love you any more. As you'll see, the house is yours, free and clear. So is a big chunk of the bank account, and so is the car. I've got myself an apartment not far from the office. Not great, but it'll do. Take care. When I get home, I'll explain it all some more—or you can spit in my eye if you'd rather. Herb.*

She numbly flipped through the papers. He'd established legal residence in Nevada. He'd petitioned for and been granted an interlocutory decree. Terms were . . . pretty much what he'd outlined in the note. They were fair: more than fair, in fact.

It all felt like a boot in the stomach just the same. "Jesus Christ in the foothills!" Peggy yipped. "I've been Reno-vated!" Then she started to cry.

**RAF FIGHTER-BOMBERS STREAKED** low above the *Luftwaffe* strip near Philippeville. Machine guns and cannon blazing, they shot up anything they saw. Then, their engines roaring flat out, they pulled tight turns and streaked off to the west no more than a hundred meters off the ground.

Hans-Ulrich Rudel and Albert Dieselhorst huddled in a zigzagging trench alongside the runway. A bullet thumped into the back wall of the trench, half a meter above Hans-Ulrich's head. He dug his nose even deeper into the dirt than it already was.

When the enemy planes disappeared, Sergeant Dieselhorst said, "You know, I'd rather go to the dentist and get a tooth pulled." His voice sounded muffled. He hadn't pulled his face out of the dirt yet, either.

"Without novocaine," Hans-Ulrich agreed. Cautiously, he did stick up his head. He felt like a turtle coming out of its shell to see if the hawks were gone.

They were, but they'd left something to remember them by. One of the squadron's Stukas burned in its revetment. Earthen walls and camouflage netting hadn't saved it. The netting was on fire now, too. A column of greasy black smoke mounted from the dead Ju-87 and blew off toward the *Reich* on the breeze.

Dieselhorst looked out, too. His forehead and chin had mud on them. *So do mine, I bet*, Hans-Ulrich thought. He rubbed his nose, which was also bound to be muddy. Dieselhorst gave forth with what good news he could: "It's not our plane, anyway."

"No, it isn't," Hans-Ulrich agreed. "And the *Jabos* weren't carrying bombs—or else they'd already dropped them somewhere else. They didn't crater the runways. We can fly off them."

"You're right. We can." Dieselhorst sounded less than delighted at the prospect. "But are you sure you still want to? It's a different world out there these days."

He wasn't wrong. Rudel wished he were. The Stuka was designed to fly where the *Luftwaffe* dominated the air, where Bf-109s kept enemy fighters away from it. The dive-bomber wasn't quite a sitting duck in flight, but it sure was a waddling duck, especially when weighted down by panzer-busting cannon pods.

"What else can we do?" Hans-Ulrich said. "If they order us up, we'll go. And we'll do the best we can while we're up, too."

"Of course we will," Sergeant Dieselhorst answered. They'd flown all those missions together. Even if they didn't always like each other, that bound them together more tightly than some husbands and wives. Each of them would have been dead a dozen times if not for the other. Then the sergeant went on, "Have to hope we come down in one piece, though."

"Hope? Yes," Rudel said. "But sometimes you do what you have to do because other people depend on you to do it right."

*And you've got to do it no matter what happens to you.* He didn't come out with that. Sergeant Dieselhorst understood it perfectly well. The difference between them was that Dieselhorst hated it, while to Hans-

Ulrich it was just a price that might have to be paid as part of the cost of doing the *Führer*'s business. He wasn't eager to pay the price, but he was ready.

They flew again, against batteries of English heavy guns that German artillery hadn't been able to take out. The Stuka had been invented as an extension of artillery. It was the ideal kind of mission for the dive-bombers—as long as German fighters could keep enemy planes off them.

Somebody had to think the mission was important: both Bf-109s and FW-190s flew top cover for the Stukas. Some Focke-Wulf fighters were also being used as ground-attack planes, beginning to take on the role the Ju-87 had held for so long. FW-190s were much faster and more maneuverable than Stukas—no doubt about that. But they couldn't put their bombs down right on the center of a fifty-pfennig coin. They couldn't terrorize enemy soldiers with Jericho Trumpets, either. They were too modern. They had retractable landing gear, not the Stuka's fixed installations.

Hans-Ulrich liked the kind of plane he flew. He'd been in the Stuka since the war started. He didn't want anything new. The Ju-87 might look obsolete, but it was still up for jobs no other aircraft could match. The squadron wouldn't have been attacking this English artillery unit if that weren't so.

The front near the Belgian border seemed pretty quiet as the Stukas flew over it. Both the French and the English had made some spasmodic lunges against the *Wehrmacht*'s defenses. They'd got bloodied for their trouble, and hadn't seemed so eager since.

A little flak came up at the Ju-87s, but only a little. Some machine guns winked petulantly upward, too, even if they had not the slightest chance of reaching high enough to hurt the planes.

Back behind the lines were gun pits by the dozen, by the score, by the hundred. Seeing so many down there gave Hans-Ulrich pause. The Western democracies might not be thrilled about the war, but they weren't giving up on it, either. They were just fighting it on the cheap, with shells rather than with soldiers.

They had more flak guns protecting the artillery. Unlike the ones up by the trenches, these were in earnest. Puffs of fire and smoke shaped like armless men sprang into being not far from the Stukas. Hans-Ulrich's plane bucked in the air after a near miss.

"I see the target," Colonel Steinbrenner said into Rudel's earphones. The squadron CO tipped his plane into a dive. "Follow me down."

One after another, the Stukas did. As Hans-Ulrich started his dive, Sergeant Dieselhorst reported, "Our fighters are mixing it up with the Indians."

"Let's hope they can hold them off till we drop our bombs," Rudel answered. He didn't know what else he could say. They would certainly be faster and more maneuverable once they'd shed a tonne of explosives and sheet metal. Not fast. Not maneuverable. Not enough to escape enemy fighters. But more of each.

Down below, the heavy English guns swelled from little plasticine toys to scale models to the real things in seconds. The real things, damn them, had still more flak guns interspersed among them. The Stuka right in front of Rudel's took a direct hit and fell out of the sky. The pilot and the man in the rear seat never had a prayer.

Rudel yanked on the bomb-release lever. The big bomb under the Ju-87's midline fell free. He pulled the stick back, hard, fighting to bring up the nose. Everything went black for a split second as the blood drained from his head. Then Sergeant Dieselhorst's exultant shout brought him back to himself: "You knocked that baby ass over teakettle!"

"Good," Hans-Ulrich said. "Now we have to get out of here in one piece." He gunned the Stuka for all it was worth—which, unfortunately, wasn't much. If a Hurricane or a Spitfire broke through the fighter screen higher up and dove on him, he'd go down like the luckless fellows in the Ju-87 right below his.

What made one man die while another lived? It was and wasn't an odd question to wonder about while racing along just above the tree-tops. His father wouldn't have wondered. The stern minister would have said it was God's will, and that would have settled that—for him, anyhow.

*Well, of course it's God's will. Everything is God's will,* Hans-Ulrich thought. But that only shifted the question. Why was God so arbitrary?

Why did He decide one fellow's time was up and let another, worse, chap live to a ripe old age and father eight children? Where was the justice in that?

Because He was God, and He could. It was an answer of sorts, but not one that brought Hans-Ulrich any comfort.

What brought him comfort was *not* seeing any RAF fighters boring in on his lumbering plane, *not* hearing Dieselhorst's machine gun go off in what would probably be a futile gesture of defiance as an enemy swooped down on them. Yes, it was amazing how comforting negative information could be.

# Chapter 25

"C'mon, you whore. Let's clean your cunt." Ivan Kuchkov shoved the pull-through into the barrel of his PPD submachine gun.

Sasha Davidov was tending to his PPD, too. He raised a dark eyebrow. "You know, Comrade Sergeant, anybody listening to you would think you were talking about something else."

"Fuck your mother, *Zhid*! Like I give a shit," Kuchkov told the skinny little point man. His voice held no particular malice. That was just the way he talked, to his weapon and to the people around him. He listened to the phonograph record in his mind of what he had said a moment before and started to laugh. "All right, fuck me, too. That is pretty cocksucking funny."

Along with the men in his section, he crouched in a clearing in some bushes near a stream. Artillery muttered in the distance. There were Germans within a couple of kilometers, but not far within that distance. Ukrainian nationalist bandits were liable to be prowling around, too. They might be closer than the Fritzes; they were commonly better at sneaking up on things.

They were also dumber than the Fritzes. Couldn't they see that, regardless of whether Hitler or Stalin won the war, they were going to get it in the neck? Did it really matter to them whether they got it from the *Gestapo* or the NKVD?

For now, without orders to move against the Hitlerites, Kuchkov didn't intend to do one single goddamn thing but sit here and play with his dick. He fought when he had to. He didn't mind killing Germans, not even a little bit. But they could kill him, too. Why give them unnecessary chances?

Somebody off in the distance made a noise. Bushes were good for all kinds of things. They kept people on the other side from seeing you, and they warned you when trouble was on the way. Kuchkov quickly reassembled his PPD and slammed the big snail drum of a magazine into place under the weapon. If that noise meant trouble, he could throw a lot of rounds at it before he had to worry about reloading.

His men were all grabbing for their weapons and making sure they had a round chambered. Everybody here had been through several fights—no blushing virgins at this dance.

One of the sentries Ivan had posted around the encampment called out a challenge. Ivan heard some kind of answer, but couldn't make out what it was. He didn't have long to think about it, because a split second later a rifle shot rang out.

"C'mon!" Ivan said to Sasha Davidov. As quietly as they could, they scrambled through the bushes toward the gunshot. Kuchkov picked the Jew because his quiet was likely to be quieter than anybody else's.

And so it proved. Sasha and the sentry coming back to the encampment nearly ran into each other. "*Bozhemoi*, Vitya!" Davidov barked. "I almost scragged you there."

"I halfway wish you did." Vitya Ryakhovsky's face was white as newfallen snow, his eyes wide and filled with horror. "At least it'd be over quick then. I just shot the *politruk*."

"Fuck me in the mouth!" Ivan said. He had to bite down hard to keep from adding *You stinking bitch! I wish I'd done that!* However much he wished it, it wasn't one of the things you came out with, not unless you wanted to hand your buddies your balls forever. Instead, he stuck to business: "What the piss happened?"

"I was there, where I was supposed to be," Vitya answered. "I'd dug a good foxhole, and stuck branches and stuff in the dirt to hide it. I heard a noise—somebody pushing through the bushes."

"We all heard it," Sasha broke in. "I wouldn't be surprised if they heard it back in Kiev."

"Uh-huh." Still pale as death, the sentry went on, "So I challenged. But this guy told me to tie my cock in a knot. That's not the word, so I fired. I figured he was a Ukrainian bandit or something. And I hit him. Only—"

"It was the political officer," Ivan finished for him. That stupid, arrogant answer sounded like a *politruk*, all right.

Vitya nodded shakily. "It was. Christ have mercy, I didn't know!"

"Is he dead?" Sasha Davidov asked.

"He's dead, all right—dead as *makhorka*." Ryakhovsky nodded again, grimly this time. "I got him right in the bull's-eye, just above his nose."

"Let's make fucking sure," Kuchkov said. "Take us to him." Wounding a *politruk* might be even worse than killing one, if such a thing were possible. A wounded political officer would testify against you, and of course they'd listen to him first and to you not at all. That was how things worked.

But the soldiers wouldn't have to worry about that here. Maxim Zabelin lay crumpled on his side, his own machine pistol next to him. He still looked pissed off; his features hadn't relaxed into blankness yet. The hole above his nose was small and neat. Going out, the round from the Mosin-Nagant had blown off most of the back of his head.

"What are we going to do?" Sasha Davidov whispered.

Kuchkov had been worrying at that himself. Reluctantly, he said, "Vitya, we've got to take it to the lieutenant. All the bastards at the camp heard your dick shoot off, y'know? We can't fucking cover it over in hay. Some cocksucker'll get toasted and blab, and then you'll catch it ten times as bad."

"Couldn't I just run off?" Ryakhovsky asked miserably. He didn't like the odds, and Ivan didn't blame him.

But Sasha said, "No, you can't do that, Vitya. Not this time. They'd think you murdered Lieutenant Zabelin on purpose and then did a bunk. If they grabbed you after that . . ." He didn't go on, or need to. Vitya could paint those gruesome pictures inside his own head.

"Listen to him. He's a goddamn smart sheeny," Ivan said. "You better come. You got a chance, I think. The lieutenant, he's a halfway decent prick." *For an officer*, he thought, but he didn't say that. Vitya had plenty to worry about without it.

The luckless (or lucky, depending on how you looked at things) sentry came along almost apathetically, as if he knew he couldn't do anything about whatever was going to happen to him. No, not *as if*. He couldn't, and that was the long and short of it.

Lieutenant Obolensky and the men with him had camped several hundred meters east of the stream in a ruined farmhouse whose surviving walls would shield his fire from the Germans' eyes. "What's up, Sergeant?" he asked when Kuchkov and Ryakhovsky and Davidov came back to him.

"Comrade Lieutenant, we've got us one cunt of a problem," Kuchkov answered. He elbowed Vitya in the ribs. "Tell the lieutenant what the fuck happened."

Stammering, Vitya did. "I wouldn't've fired if he'd given me the word. Honest to God, Comrade Lieutenant, sir, I wouldn't've!" he wailed at the end.

Lieutenant Obolensky didn't say anything at all for more than a minute. By his face, he was thinking hard, though. "I believe you," he replied at last. "But I'm not sure how much good that does you. I'm going to have to report this, too. I'm sorry, but I am. *My* dick gets cut off if don't."

"Yes, sir," Ryakhovsky said in doom-filled tones.

"Don't give up yet," the company commander told him. "Zabelin may have been a *politruk*, but he was a jerk, too. The higher-ups in the regiment know it. He'd be plenty dumb enough to try something like that, and of course he paid for it."

"The higher-ups in the regiment may know it." Vitya didn't sound any happier. He had his reasons, too: "But do the Party higher-ups?"

They might not. Ivan knew it, and so did Vitya. Party higher-ups had too good a chance to be jerks themselves. That often seemed part of how you got ahead in the Party.

Lieutenant Obolensky couldn't say any such thing, of course. He did say, "I'll do what I can for you. Fuck your mother if I don't." With that,

Ryakhovsky—and Ivan—had to content themselves. Fighting the Germans was straightforward enough. When you had to deal with your own side, though . . .

HERMANN WITT BEAMED at the new panzer. "Isn't that the prettiest thing you ever saw?" he said. "The prettiest thing without a pussy, anyhow?"

"Sorry, Sergeant." Adi Stoss shook his head. "A Tiger is the prettiest thing I ever saw that didn't have a pussy. But this is next best."

Theo Hossbach found himself nodding. That didn't count against his daily word ration. A Panzer IV with a long-barreled 75 couldn't match a Tiger, no. But it pretty much could match a T-34. After the Panzer III with its doorknocker of a gun, that was definitely within shouting distance of heaven on earth.

Lothar Eckhardt, who'd had to try to keep the whole crew alive firing that doorknocker, nodded along with him. "It'll be nice not to see our shells' drive bands sticking out of a Russian panzer's armor for a change."

"We're going to have to practice like mad bastards on the sights and fire-control system, though," Witt said. "They're a lot fancier than what we've been using. They've got to be, 'cause we can hit from so much farther away."

"We'll do what we need to do," the gunner told the commander. "We don't want to get any closer to T-34s than we have to, even in this baby. If we can hit them when they're likely to miss us, that's how I like it."

"You guys back in the turret have all the hard studying to do," Adi said, a certain gloating note in his voice. "My controls and my instruments are almost the same as the ones in the old III, and Theo's got the same radio set and the same machine gun as he did before."

"My coaxial machine gun hasn't changed any." But Eckhardt couldn't help adding, "The cannon sure has, though."

Theo thought Adi shouldn't have bragged that way. The same notion must have crossed Sergeant Witt's mind, because he said, "The suspension and the engine aren't the same. You guys can take the lead on dealing with the differences."

"Thanks a bunch," Adi said. Theo sent him a look that meant something like *I'll get you later*. Anything that had to do with the suspension—working a thrown track back onto the drive sprocket, for instance—involved backbreaking heavy labor.

"You're welcome. My pleasure," Witt said. His grin meant it would indeed be his pleasure to watch somebody else busting his hump over heavy labor like that. But the smile also promised he would get in there and help when the labor did get heavy. He was a good commander, and good panzer commanders did things like that.

"Best way we can practice with the new fire-control system is to go hunting Russians," Kurt Poske said.

"The whole company will be doing that," Witt said.

"I bet you're right," the loader answered. His own smile slipped. "I bet we find the fuckers, too."

No one said anything after that for a little while. Poske was much too likely to be right. Even though it was spring, the Red Army still held the initiative in these parts. Too many German soldiers and panzers and planes had headed west to keep England and France from breaking into the *Reich* to let the *Wehrmacht* mount any major strikes against the Russians. Rolling with the punches seemed to be the order of the day.

*If we can roll with them*, Theo thought. Of all the *Landsers* on the Eastern Front, he might have been the least likely to come out with that thought where a National Socialist Loyalty Officer could hear him. Of course, he might have been the *Landser* on the Eastern Front least likely to come out with any thought where anyone else could hear him.

His position in the right front corner of the Panzer IV's hull *was* very much like the one he'd had in the older panzer, though the mounting brackets for his Schmeisser were in a different place. He'd have to practice reaching for it till he didn't need to think about that. The leather on the radioman's seat still smelled like leather, not like old sweat. Russian panzer crews sat on cast-iron seats. When the Ivans plundered wrecked German panzers, they cut off the leather and fashioned it into boots and belts. They were chronically short of everything—except soldiers and munitions and hate.

The Panzer IV's engine sounded as if it was working harder than the Panzer III's had. It wasn't much bigger, and it had more weight to haul around. The Panzer IV with the big cannon had been uparmored as well as upgunned. Unlike a Tiger's, even a new Panzer IV's armor probably wouldn't keep out a hit from a T-34. But the panzer's long-barreled 75 could also pierce a T-34's steel shell.

Adi Stoss thought along with Theo, as he did so often. "We can kill them, and they can kill us," the driver observed. "Maybe both sides ought to be careful for a change."

German panzer crews had been careful ever since they first met the T-34. If you weren't careful around the Russian monsters, your folks got to decide whether your death notice should read *Died for* Führer *and* Vaterland or just *Died for the* Vaterland. Neither choice struck Theo as inspired.

Witt rode head and shoulders out of the cupola, the way he had in the Panzer III (and, for that matter, in the Panzer II before it). You could see so much more than you could through the periscopes in the cupola. Of course, you were also more likely to end up a casualty. Good panzer commanders from every army took the chance.

"Steer a little farther to the left, Adi," Witt ordered. "Might be something behind that little swell of ground."

"I'm doing it, Sergeant." Stoss used his steering levers to slow one track and speed up the other. He was still learning how much force he needed with this new machine to get the amount of turn he wanted.

Then Witt barked, "Panzer halt!"

"Halting, Sergeant." Adi stood on the brake.

The turret traversed with the smooth near-silence of hydraulics. Through his vision slit, Theo watched the long gun barrel stop at around ten o'clock. The barrel rose slightly. Theo couldn't make out what it was aiming at, but he had only the slit, not the magnifying scope that was fitted into the precise new sights.

A shell clanged into the breech. The gun moved again, microscopically. Then it roared. God knew it sounded more authoritative than the old 37mm. Impressive flame belched from the muzzle—and out to either side through the openings in the muzzle brake. Theo wouldn't have wanted to be standing to either side of the Panzer IV when the main armament went off. With all that fire and hot gas spat sideways by the muzzle brake, getting too close might prove a fatal blunder.

"Hit!" Witt and Eckhardt yelled the same jubilant word at the same time. They were the ones who could see it best. A moment later, a cloud of black smoke in the distance and a fireworks show of ammo cooking off left Theo sure they were right.

"We're out more than a kilometer," Adi said. "Can you imagine killing a T-34 at that range with the old beast?"

"No," Theo answered, startled into using a word.

"Me, neither," Adi said. "A good gun, good shooting—a kill. I wish we'd had these a year ago, or two. We would've done better, that's for sure. The Ivans had T-34s two years ago, damn them."

"*Ja*," Theo agreed. That was one of the nastiest surprises the *Wehrmacht* had got during its Russian adventure. Too many good people had died of surprise then.

"Wonder what'll happen to our old III," Adi mused. "What do you want to bet we sell it to the Hungarians or Romanians so some of their guys can get killed in it instead of us?"

"No bet," Theo answered. He wouldn't touch that one. It struck him as much too likely, and as just the sort of thing the *Reich* would do. The really scary thing was, even that beat-up old Panzer III would be better than what Germany's allies were using now.

WHEN THE SENTRY brought the two officers into the encampment, he looked scared. When Ivan Kuchkov saw the blue arm-of-service color on the officers' caps and collar tabs, he felt scared, too. He was damned if he'd show it, though. That wouldn't do him any good, and might screw him.

One of the NKVD men was a major, the other a captain. "Ivan Ivanovich Kuchkov!" the captain said. "Vitaly Alexandrovich Ryakhovsky!"

"I serve the Soviet Union, Comrade Captain!" Vitya Ryakhovsky gulped.

"I serve the Soviet Union!" Ivan echoed. You couldn't mess around with the Chekists. They got paid to give people grief. They commonly enjoyed it, too.

He was tempted to pick up his PPD and empty it into them. But if he did that he *would* have to run to the Nazis or to the Ukrainian nationalists. The nationalists were losers; he could see that. He thought the Nazis were also losers, at least in the Soviet Union. Besides, even if they weren't, what was the *Gestapo* but the NKVD in a different uniform?

"We are here to investigate the death of Lieutenant Maxim Svyatoslavovich Zabelin, the company political officer," the captain declared.

*No shit*, Kuchkov thought. *And all the time I figured you'd come to the front to see if we had enough fucking belt buckles.*

"You killed the company political officer, Ryakhovsky?" the major asked ominously.

Gulping again, Vitya said, "I did, Comrade Major, after he would not give me the password. I had no way to know he was not a Ukrainian bandit trying to infiltrate our position."

"So you say." The major's sneer announced he didn't believe such nonsense for a minute. He rounded on Ivan. "You, Kuchkov, you were with him when he shot the political officer?" He used the full phrase every time. He might never even have heard the word *politruk.*

"Not me." Ivan shook his head. "I was back by the campfire when the fucking shot went off." He talked the way he talked. Even when he made a stab at standard Russian, *mat* crept in.

"What did you do then?" the major asked.

"I went to see what the fuck Vitya was shooting at," Ivan answered. "When I got to where the political officer was at, he was one dead whore." He did remember not to give forth with *politruk* himself.

"What did you do then?" the major asked. Hadn't the dumb prick looked at Lieutenant Obolensky's report? What was being able to read for, if not for seeing shit like that?

"I thought, *This poor cunt's in trouble, and I bet I'm in trouble, too*," Ivan answered.

"Why did you think that?" the captain asked. "Did you have a guilty conscience? Had you been undercutting the company political officer's authority, as is much too common in underdisciplined front-line units?"

"Not me, Comrade Captain. You can ask the company commander. You can ask any of these assholes here, too. I don't do shit like that," Ivan said. *I'm not that motherfucking stupid*, was what he was thinking. You started badmouthing the *politruk*, somebody was bound to squeal on you. Then you were dogmeat waiting for a dog—or a pack.

What was interesting was that some front-line sergeants—maybe even officers—evidently did go around telling their men that *politruks* were dumb fucking blowhards. As if the men couldn't see that for themselves! But what you could see mostly had nothing to do with what you could say.

"We have spoken to your company commander," the major said.

"And?" Ivan pressed. He didn't *think* Lieutenant Obolensky would sell him down the river, but you never could be sure what somebody would do when he was afraid his own nuts might wind up on the chopping block.

"His story largely matches yours," the major said in grudging tones. "What this proves, however, is questionable at best. Front-line officers have an unfortunate tendency to preserve fighting strength irregardless of the cost in ideological purity."

Ivan had trouble following that. He thought it meant *They'd rather stay alive than make good Communists*. He approved of staying alive. If you had to be dead to make a good Communist (for a while during the Great Terror, that seemed to be about what it took), wasn't the price too high?

No price was too high if you were a Chekist. Ivan understood that the way he understood he needed air to breathe. He said, "Comrade Major, it was a fuckup. That's all it was. Vitya's a pretty fair soldier. The political officer, maybe he was farting around and thought he was funny. Shit, I don't know. But he didn't say what he was fucking supposed to say, and he paid the price for that. If Vitya'd plugged a real Ukrainian bandit the same way, you'd be here to pin a big old whore of a medal on him right now. You wouldn't be knocking pears out of trees with your dicks on account of this crap."

The NKVD officers looked at each other. Did they even know the *mat* phrase for wasting time? Ivan decided they had to. They *were* Chekists. That meant they naturally had a lot to do with *zeks*. What were Chekists for but putting *zeks* into camps and dealing with them once they were in there? And all the good, juicy *mat*, the *mat* with some flavor to it, came from *zeks*.

"We have to make sure no anti-Soviet activity is involved, that this was a genuine accident and not crime or rebellion disguised as one," the captain said.

Ivan wanted to tell him to fuck his own cunt with his little pine needle of a dick. He swallowed that, too. Pissing off the NKVD men would make them discover anti-Soviet activity whether it was there or not. Kuchkov didn't have to be any kind of big brain to see that. He just had to know what Chekists were like.

They rounded on Ryakhovsky again, trying to get him to admit he'd fired at the *politruk* on purpose. Vitya blubbered like a four-year-old after a spanking, but he didn't admit anything of the kind. No matter how scared he was, he understood he'd get the shaft but good if they could pin that on him.

"Easiest way to solve the whole thing would be to toss them both in a penal battalion," the NKVD captain remarked to the major.

That made Kuchkov's eyes slide toward the PPD again. Going to a penal battalion was a death sentence without a quick, neat bullet to the nape of the neck to get things over with in a hurry. If they aimed to do that, he had nothing left to lose. Neither the Ukrainian nationalists nor the Nazis could do anything worse to him than that.

But the major said, "Their CO does strongly vouch for them."

"We could throw him in, too," the captain said.

"We *could*," the major allowed. "It's a little more complicated with officers, though." He talked about men's fates the way a butcher talked about bacon and ham and chitterlings. All part of the day's work to him. Would a butcher talk that way in front of swine who could understand him? Some might. They just wouldn't care. This Chekist sure didn't.

"I hate to leave these bastards alone," the captain said. "Other fools will think they can get away with murder, too."

"Could be worse. We're pushing forward here. Chances are these cunts will get expended any which way." Aside from the *mat*—which he wouldn't have wasted on them—the major might have been talking about mortar bombs or belts of machine-gun ammunition, not human beings. He went on, "Besides, we don't have to fill out as much paperwork this way as we would if we stuck them in one of those battalions."

"Well, you've got something there." The captain sighed. He couldn't push his superior too hard. "All right, Comrade Major. We'll do it like that."

The major didn't even waste time warning Ivan and Vitya to keep their noses clean from here on out. He just spat on the ground and walked away. The captain followed in his wake.

"Did I hear that right?" Vitya asked wonderingly. "They didn't bother sending us to a penal battalion because . . . because . . ."

"Because filling out all the shitass forms'd be too fucking much trouble," Ivan finished for him. He pulled his water bottle off his belt and drank. It was full of vodka, not water. Those lazy pricks! That was how Russia worked, all right. And it didn't change one goddamn bit if you went and called it the Soviet Union instead.

"MOVE ALONG, YOU stinking Jew!" shouted an angry-looking man in a black uniform with SS runes on his collar tabs.

Sarah Bruck ducked her head and scurried around a corner. Münster was full of men from the *Gestapo* and the SD and whatever other security agencies the *Reich* and the National Socialist German Workers' Party boasted. They'd descended on the city the way vultures would spiral down toward a dead cow in a field. Münster had publicly protested against the regime and its policies not once but twice. Obviously, the local authorities couldn't keep order—or keep the lid on, assuming there was a difference. So blackshirts from all over the country would take care of it for them.

Officially, nothing was going on. Not a word about the swarm of security men showed up in the papers or on the radio. Goebbels wasn't about to let the rest of Germany know Münster had been kicking up its heels. That showed better sense than Sarah usually credited the Nazis with. If people in Münster could do it, people in other places might try to get away with it, too.

Sarah didn't go into the square that fronted on the cathedral. Nobody could go into that square. It was indefinitely off-limits. To make sure the locals heeded the order, SS men had set up sandbagged machine-gun positions in front of the house of worship. They weren't just ordinary blackshirts, either. They were from the *Waffen*-SS. They'd been fighting in Belgium or in Russia before Hitler and Himmler decided they could be counted on to shoot at ordinary Germans, too.

An old man came up the side street carrying a stringbag with a few wizened little potatoes and a head of cabbage in it. He limped the same way Sarah's father did. She wouldn't have been surprised if he'd also got shot in the last war.

Behind horn-rimmed glasses, his eyes flicked to the yellow star she wore. As they passed each other, he spoke in a low voice: "The SS is our misfortune!" He stumped on. Sarah stared after him in astonishment, but he didn't look back. He just kept walking.

After a moment, so did she. What else could she do? But if he took the Nazis' favorite anti-Semitic slogan and aimed it at their enforcers . . . If he did that, he couldn't be the only one thinking such things. Nowhere close, in fact. And if he was nowhere close to the only one thinking such things, well, no wonder the Party needed to flood Münster with SS men and mount machine guns in front of the cathedral.

Could the *Reich* fight its foreign enemies and its own people at the same time? Wasn't that how, or part of how, Kaiser Wilhelm's government came to grief? Whether it was or not, Hitler seemed determined to try. The *Führer* always seemed determined. Right? If you believed Goebbels, he was. Of course, if you believed Goebbels you were bound to have other things wrong with you as well.

She hadn't got far past the old man who didn't like the regime when another blackshirt shouted at her: "Show me your papers, kike!"

"Yes, sir." Letting them see they'd got your goat meant they'd won a point. She meekly produced her identity card. He scowled at it, but even he didn't have the gall to claim it was out of order. Scowling still, he thrust it back at her and waved her on.

Clocks rang five throughout the city. The bells in the cathedral tower stayed silent. They'd been silent since the latest riot. The Nazis wouldn't let anyone in to ring them.

These were the hours when Jews could come out and shop. They couldn't get much, but they could shop. Not even Aryans could get much. As it had in the last war, the Royal Navy's blockade squeezed Germany like a python. The coils might not get stronger all the time, but they never got weaker.

Even the mangel-wurzels looked sad. She got some anyway. Mangel-wurzels were what you ate when things like turnips and rutabagas cost too much . . . or when they were the only vegetables left in the bins. Today, they were. Unless Father had had a good day scavenging, meals for the next little while would be even grimmer than usual.

Sarah managed to get home with only one more SS man swearing at her. The way things had been lately, that counted as a pretty good outing. Father came in not long after she got back. He hid no goodies under his jacket. Spreading his callused hands in apology, he said, "We were repairing a crater in the street today. No chance to go hunting."

"Too bad," Sarah said. "Nothing but rubbish in the stores."

"That is too bad," Father agreed. "But did you notice the moon's just about full?"

She shook her head. "I didn't pay any attention to it."

"It's a bombers' moon, all right." Father sounded pleased at the prospect. "We'll see if they come over tonight. We'll see what they hit if they do. And we'll see how brave all the heroes new in town are if the RAF does decide to pay us a call."

"Some of them will come from places like Dresden and Weimar, won't they?" Sarah said. "Places that don't get bombed much."

"That's what I'm looking at, too." Yes, Samuel Goldman seemed to be looking forward to the RAF's arrival. The bombs didn't care that he was a Jew. They'd kill him as readily as they'd blow up an Aryan—more readily, because Aryans had better shelters. All the same, he went on, "Let's see how they like it here in the northwest, where we know there's a war on all the time."

Sarah told him about the man who'd said what he thought of the SS. "I have no idea who he was, but he knew what I was, sure enough."

"It's that intriguing?" Father said. "I wonder how many more there are like him."

"I was thinking the same thing," she said. "If the bombers do show up, maybe something will come down in the cathedral square. Wouldn't it be terrible if that happened?"

"Dreadful," Father said. They winked at each other. He went on, "And I've got a story of my own to tell."

Before he could, Mother called, "Supper's ready!" from the kitchen.

She was a good cook. When you were fighting against miserable ingredients, that helped only so much. Cattle ate turnip greens. As with mangel-wurzels, so did people who couldn't get anything better. It didn't make them tasty. Sarah didn't see how anything could.

After a while, she asked her father, "So what's your story?"

"Story?" Mother said.

"The one I was going to tell before I got invited to this feast," Father said. Mother looked wounded. He backtracked in a hurry: "I'm sorry, Hanna. It was a joke, but I guess not a good one."

"No," she said tightly. "Not. I'm doing the best I can, and I wish someone would notice once in a while."

"We do," Father said. Sarah nodded. Mother still didn't look happy. Father sighed. "Well, I stuck my foot in that. Do you want to hear the story in spite of everything?"

"Please." Sarah grabbed at anything that might turn the subject.

"All right, then." Before Father started, he made a small production of rolling himself an after-dinner cigarette. Once he'd taken a puff or two, he said, "I was talking with another guy in the gang—Emil, his name is. He's a pickpocket—a good pickpocket, too."

"Not good enough to keep from getting caught," Sarah observed.

"Nobody's perfect," Father said. "Anyway, though, he's got a cousin who's a *Feldwebel* in Holland, and he says his cousin says the Nazis asked the *Wehrmacht* to sit on Münster because things were getting lively here, and the *Wehrmacht* flat-out said no. I have no idea whether it's true, but it makes you think, doesn't it?"

"How could his cousin know something like that?" Sarah asked.

"Maybe he works the phones at the HQ of a division that would have occupied us. Maybe he plays skat with a lieutenant who's a general's son. I can think of ways," Father said. "Or maybe Emil was making up the whole thing. That wouldn't surprise me too much, either. So take it for what you think it's worth."

Not knowing Emil, Sarah wasn't sure what it might be worth. But if there *was* a rift between Party and Army . . . Father was right. It did make you think.

# Chapter 26

Nothing in Spain ever happened in a hurry. Vaclav Jezek had had to get used to that, no matter how crazy it drove him. Yes, he was a proud Czech. Yes, he hated Germany and everything Germany stood for these days. But German attitudes had rubbed off on his country, and on him. When a Czech said something would happen today, he meant it would damn well happen today, and not Tuesday a fortnight.

Spain, even Republican Spain (which tried to be efficient but had no idea how), didn't work like that. The people in Madrid who ran things needed a while to hear that he'd smashed up the Spanish tankettes. They needed a while to decide how excited to get about that—they didn't have a bounty on tankettes, the way they had on the late, unlamented (on this side of the barbed wire, anyhow) General Franco. And, once they had decided, what they'd decided needed a while to get to Vaclav.

He'd been issued a commendation for a brave and selfless service to the Republic. The gaudy commendation was on paper too thick and too crisp to do duty as either a cigarette wrapper or an asswipe. It was written in a language he couldn't read; Benjamin Halévy had translated it for him. It was, in other words, almost extravagantly useless.

But it came with a medium-sized wad of pesetas—not nearly so many as he'd got for giving Franco what he deserved, but definitely better than no pesetas—and a week's leave in Madrid. All things considered, Vaclav wished Sanjurjo's men would throw tankettes at the Republican line more often.

Instead of staying in a barracks, he'd spent some of the pesetas for a room at a hotel that hadn't been bombed in a couple of years. He'd spent some more at a different kind of house around the corner. And he'd bought himself a bottle of what claimed to be cognac and was bound to be strong if not smooth.

Now he walked into yet another different kind of building. In spite of a wonderful hot shower, in spite of getting his uniform cleaned, he still felt grubby going up the stairs. A woman typed at a desk in the lobby. He walked over to her.

She looked up and rattled rapid-fire Spanish at him. His own remained rudimentary. "Chaim Weinberg? What room, *por favor?*" he asked.

She flipped through a card file. He felt like cheering—she'd understood him! She found the card she needed and answered him. The only trouble was, he couldn't understand her.

"*¿Qué?*" he said. She repeated herself. He still didn't get it. Her nostrils flared in exasperation. Then she had a brainstorm. She wrote the number down: *374*. He grinned and nodded. "*¡Gracias!*" he exclaimed. When you had only a few words, you'd better make them count.

"*De nada, Señor,*" she replied. He actually got that. She pointed him toward the stairway. There was also an elevator, but it didn't seem to be working. Whether that was war damage or Spanish fecklessness, he couldn't have said. He had no trouble ascending. Getting wounded men up there might not be so easy, though.

He found room 374. Weinberg had it to himself, which definitely made him a special case. He wore a white hospital gown. His left hand was decked out in as many bandages as a mummy. When Vaclav walked in, Chaim's engagingly ugly mug, which had looked bored, lit up like an electric sign.

"Hey! What are you doing here, man?" The American International's Yiddish was hard for Jezek to follow, but he got the drift.

And Weinberg would be able to make sense of his German, too: "I heard you got hurt. I have some leave, and I wanted to see how you were."

"Thanks, pal. That's nice—that's mighty nice," Weinberg said. His smile faded. "I'm lucky to be here at all. One of my oldest buddies was just back from another wound, and the same mortar bomb that wrecked my hand went and did him in."

"I'm sorry. That's very hard—I know." Vaclav pointed to the shrouded hand. "How bad is it?"

"I'm damn lucky to have it at all. They almost took it off at the aid station. But one of the docs here, all he does is fix up hands. He's putting it together one step at a time, like. When he gets done, he thinks it'll be pretty good. Not like it's fresh out of the box, but pretty good."

"Glad to hear it." Now Vaclav understood why Weinberg rated a private room. If he was a fancy sawbones' pet guinea pig, they'd treat him well—when they weren't cutting him open, anyhow. "So you have a little something to celebrate, anyhow."

"I would've celebrated a dud a hell of a lot more, but yeah," Weinberg said. "How come?"

Vaclav held up the bottle of alleged cognac. "I brought something to celebrate with."

"I'm single again. You want to marry me?" the American said.

Laughing, Vaclav shook his head. "I'm not that desperate, thanks." He pulled the cork out of the bottle and sniffed. Rotgut, sure as hell. Well, he hadn't expected anything else. He raised the bottle. "Here's to you!" He drank. It was strong, all right, strong enough to put hair on a nun's chest.

"Let me have some!" Weinberg said. His larynx worked as he swallowed. "Whoo!" He eyed the bottle with respect as he gave it back.

"I would have liked something better, but this is what I could get," Vaclav said.

"Hey, I'm not *kvetching*, believe me," Weinberg answered. Vaclav figured out the word he didn't know from context. The American went on, "This is the first booze I've had since I got hurt. It's not exactly on the hospital menu."

"I believe that," Jezek said. "How good will your hand be, and when does the doctor here get through with it?"

"Good enough to use some, I guess. Better than the mess it was when I got here, I'll tell you that. If I were a lefty, I really would've been *yentzed*," Weinberg said, and again the Czech worked out an unfamiliar word's likely meaning. Weinberg continued, "Not as strong as it used to be, not as—as cunning, either. 'If I forget thee, O Jerusalem, let my right hand forget her cunning.'"

"*You* come out with that?" Vaclav stared at him. "You're a Red, right?"

"Sure I'm a Red." Weinberg sounded proud of it, too—proud and faintly embarrassed at the same time. "I haven't thought about any of that shit since I got bar mitzvahed to shut my old man up and he let me quit going to *cheder*."

"To what?" Vaclav couldn't unravel that one.

"Hebrew lessons. Religious lessons," Weinberg said. "But some of it stuck after all. What are you gonna do? Everybody's mind is like a rubbish heap, and sometimes the crap at the bottom floats to the top some kind of way."

*Is my mind a rubbish heap?* Vaclav wondered. He didn't want to think so. When he considered some of the weird, useless stuff he remembered, though, while things he should have recalled slipped right out of his head, he couldn't very well claim the American International was wrong. He didn't even try. He took another slug of flamethrower fuel instead.

"Me?" Chaim Weinberg said plaintively. Vaclav gave him the bottle. He drank from it, coughed, thumped his chest with his good hand, and gave it back. "Thanks, friend. You're good in my book. Y'know, this here is far and away the longest I've been out of the line since I got to Spain in '36."

Not many people had been fighting longer than Vaclav. Some Chinese and Japanese, some Spaniards, and a handful of Internationals like Weinberg. "It seems like I've carried a rifle my whole life," Vaclav said. "If the fighting ever stops, I won't know what to do with myself."

"Me, neither," Weinberg agreed. "That's why I want to get patched up—so I can go on doing what I've been doing."

*¡Viva la muerte! Here's to death!* One of Marshal Sanjurjo's generals was supposed to have used that for a toast. Most people who heard it thought it was disgusting and barbarous. Vaclav did, too . . . after a fashion. But he also understood it in ways most people didn't, never would,

and never could. Plainly, so would Weinberg. Like that goddamn Fascist, by now they were both creatures of the war, shaped in its image.

Between them, the two creatures of the war ended up killing the bottle.


THE *GESTAPO* MAN reminded Julius Lemp of a wall lizard, even though he wasn't green. He blinked very slowly, and he kept licking his thin lips with a pointed tongue. He made more trouble than a wall lizard ever dreamt of doing, though.

Blink. "You have aboard your ship, the U-30, an electrician's mate named"—blink, lick—"Eberhard Nehring." Blink.

"That's right. What about it?" Lemp tried to hide his contempt. The wall lizard with the high-crowned cap didn't even know submarines were styled boats, not ships.

"I will tell you what about it," the *Gestapo* man answered coldly. Lick. Blink. "You are to leave him ashore here at Wilhelmshaven when your ship puts to sea on its next cruise."

"What? What the hell for?" Lemp yipped. "He's the best I've ever seen for squeezing extra time and extra juice from the batteries. I need him, dammit."

"You may not have him." Lick. "He is"—blink—"politically unreliable."

"Are you out of your mind?" Lemp said. "What's he going to do? Scuttle the boat?" *He* did it right, not that the blackshirt would notice. "Knock my radioman over the head with a spanner and signal the Royal Navy where we're at?"

The *Gestapo* man eyed him as if he were a fat, foolish grasshopper just about within snapping-up range. "I am not required to explain to you the details. The fact is sufficient." Blink.

"*Quatsch!*" Lemp retorted. "If I leave Nehring ashore, I'll have to put to sea with some half-assed *Dummkopf* on his first patrol. And that kind of numbskull is liable to get me sunk. So you can explain or you can go fuck yourself."

When the *Gestapo* man blinked this time, it was in amazement, and not nearly so mannered as usual. "I could kill you for that, and I would not even have to fill out a report," he said, in a voice even more frigid than usual.

He was trying to put Lemp in fear. He needed to try harder. Lemp laughed at him. "Listen to me, man. The ocean can kill me. My own lousy boat can kill me. The enemy can kill me. So why the devil should I worry about *you*? If you don't level with me, I'm damned if I'll pay any attention to you."

"Notes on this conversation will go into your promotion jacket." Lick.

Lemp laughed again, raucously. "Like I care!" He hadn't expected to make lieutenant commander. He knew he'd never see commander.

Blink. "You are being difficult."

"You should talk! If you don't give me some halfway decent reason for leaving Nehring ashore, I'm going to take him with me, and you can pound sand up your ass. He's that good."

Maybe the *Gestapo* man wasn't used to running into somebody who didn't turn to gelatin around him. He licked his lips once more, this time in what looked like real distress. "Oh, very well. He is engaged in correspondence of questionable loyalty with his family in Münster." By the way the blackshirt said it, Münster was worse than Sodom and Gomorrah as a den of iniquity, and Nehring a nastier deviant than someone who snatched little girls off the sidewalk and did horrible things to them.

"What's the big deal about Münster?" Lemp asked.

"In Münster, they have twice made insurrection against the *Reich*." Blink. "Twice!"

"Was Nehring involved in any of this?"

"No, but"—lick—"his letters clearly show his awareness. He cannot be relied upon to serve the *Führer* as he should."

"I've relied on him to serve Germany for two or three years now," Lemp said. "He's done it, too, and done it damn well."

"They are not the same thing." Blink. The *Gestapo* man sounded sure.

"Of course they are!" So did Lemp.

"If you allow this man aboard your ship, I can—I will—have you fired upon as you leave the harbor. *I* serve the *Führer*!" Blink.

"But not Germany?" Lemp suggested.

The wall lizard's pale cheeks gained a little color. "I serve the National Socialist *Grossdeutsches Reich*, the one and only legitimate German government. I have its authority behind me when I tell you you may not use this politically unreliable individual."

"But—" Lemp tried once more, but broke off before he was well begun. The *Gestapo* man was implacable. Lemp gave up: "Have it your way. You will anyhow, won't you?"

"*Reich* security demands it," the wall lizard said smugly. Lick.

"*Wunderbar.*" Lemp turned away in disgust. He did fire a Parthian shot: "If some jerk of an electrician's mate comes aboard instead of Nehring and we get sunk on account of that, do you think it does *Reich* security one hell of a lot of good?"

Blink. "If the *Kriegsmarine* allows incompetents to fill these important roles, then it is the entity impairing *Reich* security. In due course, perhaps we shall examine that more closely."

Defeated, despising himself for not having the balls to tell the wall lizard where to head in, Lemp stormed away. As the *Gestapo* man had warned, Nehring was not among the ratings who boarded the U-30. A newcomer was, an inoffensive little man whose name, Lemp saw when he examined the fellow's papers, turned out to be Martin Priller.

As soon as Lemp got the chance, he summoned Priller to his tiny cabin. The new electrician's mate saluted. "Reporting as ordered, Captain!"

"Oh, belay that spit-and-polish crap," Lemp said wearily. "Save it for the surface navy—don't waste my time with it. Did they tell you why you were supposed to report here?"

"They said your boat needed an electrician's mate." Priller visibly suppressed a *sir*. "I am one, so they sent me."

"Did they tell you why we needed one?" Lemp asked.

"*Nein.*" Another obvious swallowed *sir*. "I figured your fellow didn't come back from leave or came down sick or whatever the hell."

"*Whatever the hell* is about the size of it." Lemp grilled Martin Priller on what he knew about U-boat batteries. The new man wasn't a *Dummkopf*. He also wasn't afraid to admit he didn't know something. He wouldn't be so good as Nehring, not till he had a few patrols under his belt, but with a little luck he wouldn't be hopeless, either, which was what Lemp had feared most. Grudgingly, the U-boat skipper said, "All right, go on back to the engine room. Do the best you can, and yell if you need help."

"I'll do that." Bobbing his head in a little nod, Priller pulled aside the cabin's curtain so he could escape into the corridor. He closed the curtain behind him as he hurried aft.

"*Scheisse.*" Lemp said it very softly. He still wished he had Eberhard Nehring there in his familiar slot. No matter what the wall lizard said, Nehring was about as political as a halibut, and if Münster was up in arms about the way things were going, whose fault was that? Nehring's? Not likely! Wasn't it the government's, for screwing up the war and the economy to the point where even uncomplaining Germans started showing they could take only so much?

Lemp had never cared much for politics. He didn't think they were fitting for a *Kriegsmarine* officer. But he wasn't a blind man. If he wrote anyone a letter with those thoughts in it, would the *Gestapo* let *him* take the U-boat out on its next patrol?

No. They'd sit him in a black room, shine blinding lights in his face, and hurt him till he told them who all his treasonous friends were. If he had no treasonous friends, they'd keep hurting him till he named some names anyhow. Then they'd grab those people and start in on *them.*

Was that any way to run a war? Or a country? Even the apolitical Lemp couldn't make himself believe it. But that was the war and the country and the government he had.


PEGGY DRUCE WAITED nervously in the foyer. She stubbed out a cigarette and lit another one. She didn't chain-smoke very often, but she did now. Behind her, a clock in the living room started to chime six.

Where the devil was Herb? She blew an angry stream of smoke toward the ceiling. You could always set your watch by him. Or you could have, until . . .

He knocked on the front door as the living-room clock bonged for the fifth time. Peggy had all kinds of reasons for being mad at him. Try as she would, she couldn't fault him for being late.

She opened the door. There he stood, as solid and familiar as if things between them had never soured. "Hi," he said, and then, "I'm sorry."

"Yeah." Her voice might have come from Greenland. They'd talked on the phone since he'd come back from Nevada, but this was the first time they'd set eyes on each other. She'd made a point of not being home when he came by to retrieve clothes and books and golf clubs and fishing gear and whatever else he'd taken.

He grimaced. "You don't have to do this at all, you know."

"I am trying to be civilized, just like you," Peggy answered.

"Okay." He didn't sound as if things were okay. He sounded as if he'd been ordered to charge a German machine-gun nest in France in 1918. With the same kind of bleak courage he might have shown then, he nodded and said, "Well, come on, then." As he led her out to his car by the curb, he chuckled in faint—or not so faint—embarrassment. "Fine set of wheels, huh?"

"Catch me!" she said. It was a long, angular Hupmobile from the first years of the Depression. The whole company had gone belly-up not long before the USA got into the war.

Herb shrugged. "I couldn't find anything better in a hurry. Lord knows what I'll do if it breaks down and needs parts. But I won't be putting a whole bunch of miles on it, so maybe it'll last a while."

He held the passenger door open for her. She slid inside. He went around and got behind the wheel. The car rattled when he started it. It seemed all the noisier because she was used to the silky-smooth Packard. The Hupmobile wheezed and rattled when he drove off.

Donofrio's was their favorite Italian place. Herb ordered spaghetti and meatballs. Peggy chose the lasagna. "You have chianti, George?" Herb asked the waiter.

"Only from California," George answered regretfully—he was a Greek playing at being a dago. "Can't hardly get no gen-u-ine Eye-talian stuff."

"Well, bring us a bottle just the same," Herb said. Peggy nodded. Vino might blunt the edge of what she was feeling. She wasn't the kind of person who'd let out a war whoop and swing the bottle at her now ex-husband's head if she got loaded. She didn't think she was, anyhow.

The guy in the bow tie and the red apron set the bottle on the table. Herb poured for both of them. He raised his glass. "Good luck to you."

Peggy couldn't even not drink to that. The wine was . . . red. "Thursday vintage," she guessed.

"Oh, it's older than that. Tuesday, I bet," Herb said. They bantered as if they'd been married for years. And so they had. And so they weren't. Peggy drained the big glass in a hurry, but no faster than Herb. He filled them both up again.

They were halfway down their second glasses when the food came. Donofrio's lasagna was as familiar as . . . as being married to Herb. "Why didn't you tell me you were going to do that?" Peggy asked. "Jesus, why didn't you even tell me you wanted to do that?"

Herb was using fork and tablespoon to twirl a bite of spaghetti. He paused and looked down at the plate for a moment. Then he met Peggy's eyes again. Sighing, he answered, "On account of I didn't feel like a screaming row, and that's what we would've had. When I found out Uncle Samuel was sending me to Nevada anyhow, I figured I'd use the time I was stuck there two different ways."

That did sound like him; he was nothing if not organized. And it cleared up something she'd wondered about: "So you didn't make up the story about going to Nevada because the government sent you there?"

"No." He shook his head. "I didn't lie to you."

"You just kept your mouth shut about what you were up to," Peggy said. That sounded like Herb, too.

"It's not the same thing," he insisted, a touch of stiffness in his voice. That might have been the lawyer in him talking. Or maybe he really believed it. Who the hell knew? How much did it matter now either way?

Peggy sharpened her tongue on another question: "Seen anything of Gladys since you got back into town?"

She had the satisfaction of watching him turn almost as red as the tomato sauce on his plate. But he shook his head again. "Nah," he answered. "I told you before—that didn't mean anything."

"Yeah. You told me. And I told you. And we were both telling the truth. And here we are." Peggy looked at the little strip of fishbelly-white skin on the fourth finger of her left hand, where her ring had lived for so long. Was honesty really the best policy? If they'd both just kept quiet, would they still be married? Would they still be happy enough with each other? Again, who the hell knew? She had trouble believing things could have turned out worse, though.

Herb also finished his sort-of chianti. What was left in the bottle splashed into their glasses without going very far. He waved to the waiter for reinforcements. "Thanks, George," he said when the fresh bottle came.

"*Prego*," George replied. Hey, it was a job.

"We're not far from the house, but will you be able to drive back to your new place if you get crocked?" Peggy asked.

"I'll do fine. Not enough traffic to worry about," Herb said. That was true enough.

When he finished his spaghetti, he shoved the plate aside and lit a cigarette. Peggy wasn't quite done, but she looked forward to hers, too. The one after dinner was the best of the day—even better than the one after sex, usually.

But she hadn't fired it up when she said, "When I got all those papers, your note said you didn't love me any more. Have you found somebody else? Not Gladys, but somebody?"

"Nope." One more shake of the head. "Maybe I'll go looking. Or maybe I'll just decide I'm an old goat who's only fit for his own company. I haven't worked that one out yet."

"Okay." Peggy had no idea whether it was or not. She also had no idea what she'd do along those lines herself. She wasn't sure she wanted a man who wasn't Herb in her life. Even if she did, she wasn't sure she could find one. She was . . . not so young any more. Herb had a couple of years on her, but so what? It was different with guys. A woman in her thirties wouldn't see anything wrong with a man in his fifties. The other way around? She snorted quietly to herself. Good luck!

"I wish things didn't work out the way they did," Herb said.

*Then why did you go to Reno?* But Peggy's bitter question died unspoken. That wasn't what he meant. He was talking about the things that led up to his going there. "We got stuck in the goddamn war," she said. "It killed . . . us . . . the same way it killed all those soldiers."

"It sure did," Herb said. "We get to try and pick up the pieces, though. The poor guys they go and bury can't even do that."

Peggy wondered if they were the lucky ones. Everything was over for them, and they didn't have to worry any more. But that was just self-pity talking. Any one of those poor damned kids would have traded places with her or Herb in a split second. She sighed and made herself nod. "Well," she said, "you're right."

IN HIS SEAT on the far side of the radio set from Theo Hossbach, Adi Stoss hit the Panzer IV's starter button. The weather was warm. The panzer was new. The motor caught right away.

"I could get used to this!" Adi said. Before Theo could decide whether to chide him for that, he chided himself: "As soon as I do, the beast won't start up like this any more." Theo nodded; Adi had that straight.

"Let me know as soon as we're warm enough to go, Adi, or even a little before that," Hermann Witt said from the turret.

"Will do." Adi watched the engine temperature and the oil pressure and the rest of the gauges on the instrument panel. All around them, the other panzers in the company were starting up and moving out, too. "We're just about ready, Sergeant."

"Then get rolling," Witt said. "Sounds like we're going to earn our pay the next little while."

Adi put the Panzer IV in gear. Along with the others, it rolled north and east. The Russians had punched through the German line in front of Gorki, and an armored column was driving on the city. The panzer company was part of the southern jaw of the *Wehrmacht*'s counter-attack. If the Germans could bite off the column, they could chew it up afterwards at their leisure.

If. From everything Theo heard in his earphones over the radio net, the Ivans had shoved a lot of men and machines through there. They were trying to take their own bites out of the German holdings in the East, and they kept learning more and more about how to do such things.

The company hadn't been on the move more than ten minutes before flights of Katyushas rained down on the panzers and on the infantry coming forward with them. Theo thought the screaming rockets' roar was one of the most horrible things he'd ever heard, even through thick steel armor. Hermann Witt ducked down into the panzer and slammed the cupola lid shut. Blast shook the heavy machine. Fragments clanged off it.

"Fuck!" Adi Stoss' mouth silently shaped the word. Theo nodded again. He couldn't have put it better himself. Adi went on, "God help the poor *Frontschweine* out there."

"*Ja.*" He got a word out of Theo. Katyushas slaughtered foot soldiers, and often panicked the survivors. A direct hit on the turret from one could brew up a panzer, too. He wished that hadn't crossed his mind.

He peered out through his vision slit. They were coming to Indian country—land the Ivans held. If the Katyushas had scattered German infantry, he needed to be extra alert to keep anybody in a khaki uniform from getting close to the panzer.

Sure enough, the Indians soon came out of the bushes—or rather, fired out of the cover they gave. That big flash had to come from an antipanzer rifle. The damned things were useless against modern armor: the loud clang as the round ricocheted from the Panzer IV's front plate showed as much. The Russians kept issuing them anyway. They could punch holes in armored cars and halftracks, but anybody who thought he could knock out a real panzer with one was only fooling himself.

It was the last mistake this Red Army soldier was likely to make. Theo hosed down the bushes with several bursts from the bow machine gun. He thought he saw somebody thrashing in there. He might have shot a nice fellow, a guy who liked dogs and mushrooms and harmless hobbies like woodcarving. Give the nice guy an antipanzer rifle, though, and he turned into someone who was doing his best to make sure Theo didn't get home to Breslau. Theo wasn't about to let that happen. No second shot came as the panzer rattled on.

A much bigger shell burst fifty meters in front of the Panzer IV. Dirt and fragments banged off the German machine. "Panzer halt!" Hermann Witt yelled. Adi halted the beast. An AP round clanged into the breech. The big 75mm gun traversed a little to the right, then roared. The shell casing clattered down onto the steel floor of the fighting compartment.

Theo didn't see a T-34 going up in smoke. That meant they'd missed. So did the way Witt shouted for another round. Theo's balls tried to crawl up into his belly, as if that would do him any good. They were reloading and aiming again inside the Russian panzer, too. If they fired first, if they fired straight . . .

But they didn't. A T-34's commander also had to aim and fire the gun. The German crew, with a specialist gunner, was faster and more efficient. They got in the second shot, and they made it count. The distant T-34 began to burn. The enemy diesel didn't explode into flames the way a German gasoline engine would have, but panzers had plenty of things besides fuel to catch fire.

"Forward!" Witt called.

Forward they went. The *Wehrmacht* wasn't having everything its own way—it hardly ever did in Russia. The Panzer IV rumbled past the blazing carcass of an assault gun—a cannon mounted in a panzer chassis without a turret. The cannon had only a very limited traverse, so the assault gun had to swing itself toward a target. On the other hand, it boasted a low silhouette that made it hard to spot. And assault guns were cheaper and easier to manufacture than panzers.

Somebody had sure spotted this one. Theo hoped the guys in the gray coveralls were able to escape when their mount got hit, but he wouldn't have bet on it. In case they had, he fired some machine-gun rounds more or less at random to make the Russians in the neighborhood keep their heads down.

A couple of rifle rounds pinging off the panzer near the vision slit told him he hadn't made all the Ivans duck. Even a sniper wasn't likely to hit a vision slit on a moving panzer, but anyone who'd been in the field awhile knew unlikely didn't mean impossible.

"Panzer halt!" Witt ordered. Adi stamped on the brakes. The main armament thundered. Shouts from the turret told of another hit—and another kill. Yes, this machine could smash T-34s instead of just letting them know it was in the neighborhood.

But more and more Russian armor seemed to be in this neighborhood. The Ivans were guarding their flanks better than they often did. They must have realized what the *Wehrmacht*'s counterstroke against their thrust was likely to look like, and made their own plans to keep it from working.

The Panzer IV rolled past more burnt-out vehicles, some bearing the red star, others the white-edged black German cross. Some of the twisted bodies in the fields and meadows wore khaki; just about as many were in *Feldgrau*.

*Clang!* . . . *Boom!* That was a Panzer IV taking a hit and brewing up not far away. Adi's mouth twisted. "We just lost some guys we know," he said. Theo nodded once more.

"Panzer halt!" Hermann Witt shouted again. Again, Kurt Poske slammed an AP round into the 75. Theo braced himself for another boom from the gun.

But he got a different kind of boom. Something slammed into the panzer. He felt as if he'd been clubbed.

"Get us out of here, Adi!" Witt said.

Adi tried. "Can't, Sergeant," he reported. "That one knocked off the right track."

"*Scheisse!*" Witt said. "All right—everybody out! The next one hits us dead center. Good luck, friends!"

Theo remembered the first time he'd bailed out of a crippled panzer. He'd gained a wound badge and lost most of a finger on his left hand. Well, no help for it. The panzer commander was right. He'd end up with the next Russian shell in his lap.

He paused only to grab his Schmeisser—yes, he knew where it was. Then he opened his hatch and scrambled out of the Panzer IV as fast as he could. Bullets spanged off the armor plate. They struck sparks, but they didn't strike him. Adi got out in one piece, too. They both scurried to the rear of the panzer, to put its bulk between them and, well, everything. The guys from the turret escaped through a hatch in its back.

"Welcome to the infantry!" Adi said with a sour grin. Theo cared nothing for the infantry. He didn't feel like a foot soldier. He felt more like a snail suddenly torn from its nice, hard shell and transformed into a miserable, squishable slug. He also cared nothing for this attack, which was plainly bogging down. All he wanted was to live to see tomorrow.

# About the Author

Harry Turtledove is the award-winning author of the alternate-history works *The Man with the Iron Heart; The Guns of the South; How Few Remain* (winner of the Sidewise Award for Best Novel); the War That Came Early novels: *West and East, Hitler's War, The Big Switch,* and *Coup d'Etat;* the Worldwar Saga: *In the Balance, Tilting the Balance, Upsetting the Balance,* and *Striking the Balance;* the Colonization books: *Second Contact, Down to Earth,* and *Aftershocks;* the Great War epics: *American Front, Walk in Hell,* and *Breakthroughs;* the American Empire novels: *Blood & Iron, The Center Cannot Hold,* and *Victorious Opposition;* and the Settling Accounts series: *Return Engagement, Drive to the East, The Grapple,* and *In at the Death.* Turtledove is married to fellow novelist Laura Frankos. They have three daughters: Alison, Rachel, and Rebecca.

# About the Type

This book was set in Minion, a 1990 Adobe Originals typeface by Robert Slimbach. Minion is inspired by classical, old style typefaces of the late Renaissance, a period of elegant, beautiful, and highly readable type designs. Created primarily for text setting, Minion combines the aesthetic and functional qualities that make text type highly readable with the versatility of digital technology